Valebridge
Ramshire
Holden Sea
N

Content Warnings

Your mental health matters to me. I encourage you to read through the content warnings in their entirety before starting this book. As a reminder, this book is intended for readers 18 years and older.

Attempted sexual assault, suicidal ideation, suicide, anxiety and panic attacks, ptsd, grief, death of a parent (in a flashback), harm to an animal (non descript), consumption of alcohol and tobacco, profanity, violence, and on page explicit sex.

This book ends on a cliffhanger.

ENCHANTRESS
AWAKENS
BOOK ONE

THROUGH THE
WICKED
WOOD

KRISTEN R. MOORE

Kirsgard Mountains
The Wicked Woods
Wickersham
Davenport
Galdosa River
Copenspire
S. Trinity Forest

To anyone that has ever had to claw their way out of a dark place.
To anyone still there.
To anyone that has ever had to muffle their silent screams in the middle of the night.
To anyone that puts on a smile the next morning anyway.
This book is for you.
& for Nan.

Prologue

The pale light of the falling full moon spills through the carved, marble windows. The noises of the revelers below are faint in comparison to the clacking of my boots against the stone floor, as I make my way down the empty hallway.

The heavy wooden door of the study is slightly ajar, the soft orange glow of the fireplace creeps through the crack and two familiar voices talk in hushed whispers on the other side.

Pushing open the door, its oak frame moves silently as I glide into the room.

The study has become the only place inside the castle that I can tolerate. Dark blue velvet drapes block any natural light from the carved windows. The walls are plastered with books from ceiling to floor in thick wooden cases. Worn spines in varying colors; blues, reds, greens. Ancient tales of magick throughout our country of Teravie and Valebridge History.

The aroma of the wood burning fire greets me first as the two men I've arranged to meet sit stiffly in wingback chairs facing away from the door. The deep red fabric paints a picture of crimson that frames the flickering heat of the fireplace.

A handmaid dressed in deep blue and gold takes notice of me right away despite my silent entrance.

"Good evening–"

She's cut short by the larger man near the fire. His graying hair neatly swept back, matching gray stubble lines his soft jaw.

"It's about time you've made it, the moon has nearly fallen," he grumbles, not bothering to turn in my direction. I shoot the handmaid a smirk, skirting around her to take a seat in the third chair by the fire.

"What the hell took you so long?" the second man asks, leaning toward me in his chair before catching his movements and settling back into a more casual position. Crossing one leg over his knee to keep it from bouncing. He means to come across as demanding, but I know better. He's been worried. He pushes his curly, dark tresses out of his face; his green eyes, wide as a doe, watch me as I straighten my back against the upholstered chair.

"Usual business," I say as nonchalantly as possible. That's all they need to know.

"Pardon, Your Majesty." The handmaid approaches again, the swoosh of her jeweled, navy gown catches my attention. Unusual attire for a handmaid, but given it's the full moon, I'm certain she's been allowed an exception for the evening. "Can I get you or your guest anything?" The rest of her question goes unsaid, but the king picks up on it anyhow. She's desperate to join the rest of the partygoers before the sun dawns.

"No," King Silas says flatly. "You're dismissed, Alena." He doesn't so much as glance at her, gesturing toward the door. The light of his many rings glisten in the firelight. Her exit is as silent as my entrance, the only tell that she's left is the click from the door as it shuts completely this time.

A weighted silence hangs around us as the fire crackles, plumes of heat tickle my bare chin as thick tendrils of smoke waft up the stone chimney. "I think I'll have a drink after all," I say. Rising from my chair, I dip my head at the other two men and raise my brows. A silent question to which they both answer with a curt nod.

"Three drinks it is," I mumble to no one in particular. The bar sits to the right of the chairs. My back faces the men as I scan the various crystal bottles and decanters until I find the preferred amber liquid. Pulling three short but heavy glasses, I begin to pour.

"The people are becoming uneasy with the change of the moon," Prince Roman says, in a voice that matches his worried eyes. Pathetic. *Perfect.*

"Nonsense," King Silas scoffs. Turning, I catch him as he waves a hand through the air, dismissing his son entirely. "It happens with every new moon. Unrest and revelry often appear the same. The Enchantresses know their place in the Kingdom. They have for many years."

Returning my focus to the three drinks, I top them off. Taking note of which one is mine, before rejoining the men by the fire.

"You speak so confidently of the Enchantresses, but you forget the uprising," I say, handing the drinks over before settling into my chair. "It won't be long before another happens, and with it would be absolute devastation. With the new law allowing them to breed, we'll be outnumbered ten to one. Unless we keep them under tighter restraint their magick could—"

"And you forget *your* place," the king hisses, and I fight to conceal the smirk dancing along my mouth. I've gotten under his skin. *Excellent.*

"Apologies," I say, raising my glass. He watches me with questioning eyes, and I meet him with an equally passive gaze. I know my presence is merely tolerated and not entirely welcome, but I lean into my chair, nonetheless. Making it known that I will not be scared away so easily. Not even by the king.

"An uprising hasn't happened in decades," Roman says, taking a cautious sip of his drink. His dark hair is long, too long, and the curls fall wildly in his eyes. "Shouldn't we be concerned? If history repeats itself..." His eyes snap to his father, letting the rest of his concerns go unsaid. Planting the seed just as I've asked. *Good boy.*

"We have a long-standing relationship with the Enchantresses. Paranoia from the past will only raise unnecessary concern," King Silas says, swirling the liquid in his crystal glass. "My meeting with Elwyn earlier proved my point. The Enchantresses are content with their stations inside of Valebridge. They're free to use their magick so long as it remains here under my watch. Free to breed as you so *eloquently* put it." A snarl in my direction. A smile in his. "It's been this way since my father, Richard, was on the throne. It was his law that healed our country after the uprising and it is his law that will remain intact.

"If the Guilds do not seek change, then no change will be had. The Enchantresses are not our prisoners, they are our allies. We worship the same deity, after all," he pauses, staring into the fire. "And should we not forget it is Mother Gaia who holds our fate and the fruitfulness of our lands. I will not discuss this any further." At this, his eyes finally snap to mine. I make note of the concern growing in them, the deep wrinkles that settle around the outer edges and between his brows.

"The Head Enchantress has been my trusted Seer for over a decade," Silas continues, still swirling his drink, not yet taking a sip. "If she does not see a cause to worry, then there is none." The King's words are final as he tips his glass to his lips, taking a long, slow pull of the dark liquid. "Is this what you insisted we meet about?" King Silas asks, shaking his head between sips. "You waste my time again, boy," he says, pointing a ringed finger in my direction, "and I'll have your head."

"Understood," I say, raising my glass toward the two men,

casting the dark-haired prince a wink of approval for his work tonight. The flush to his cheeks and thick swallow tells me all I need to know about where he stands. "Long live the king," I sneer before tossing my drink into the flames.

Part one:
— The —
Enchantress

CHAPTER 1
SORIN

Five Years Later

TOBACCO LOOMS HEAVILY IN THE AIR, LAYERING A hazy fog of smoke to the already dimly lit pub. Drawing my final card, I peek at it through squinted eyes.

Nine of Spades.

Keeping my face neutral, I eye the guards over the tips of the cards. I reel in a grimace as I glance down at the hand I've been dealt. The Eight and Nine of Spades in my hand are the only useful two out of the five. Dragging my eyes, I peer down to the cards face up on the ale-stained table. The Ten of Spades stares back at me, and I bite the inside of my cheek to keep from grinning. The patrons around the card table chatter, their voices lowering, as I flick the tip of my cigar into the heavy glass ashtray.

My heart races, the poor guards have no idea what's about to hit them. Nonetheless, I spare no pity for them. Anyone who still serves King Roman after the uprising is just as much an enemy as the king himself.

Slowly, the cards I have slipped up the sleeve of my shirt

slide down against my skin. Under the table, I give my arm a quick shake. Loosening the cards, they fall into my hand with perfect grace. I lay my cards face down on the table to hide my hand, concealing my smirk and pushing all my shillings toward the middle.

Distracted by my large bet, no one takes notice of the swap of cards. A Three of Hearts and Two of Diamonds for a Jack and Queen of Spades. I seamlessly slip the discarded cards back up my sleeve, thankful to have my lucky Queen with me. Glad I remembered to swipe it from Jarek before I left on this trip. The fool won't even realize the card's gone missing. Sure, it's a childish game between the two of us—stealing this card from each other, hiding it, and using it to our own advantage when we play poker—but the Queen of Spades has never let me down, and today will be no different. The Jack of Spades I'd hidden there was pure luck.

With the swap, I've lined up a perfect straight flush.

"All in, boys," I say as I pick up my cigar and bite down on the end. Leaning on the back two legs of my chair, I lace my fingers, placing them behind my head. My grin is wide around the cigar tucked between my teeth, as I wait for them to make their move. The guards opposite me share a glance. The smugness they wore only moments ago has faded as they contemplate their next move with one another.

I know for a fact the guards stationed in Copenspire make far less than those in Valebridge or even Davenport. Less rations. Less respect. Though, with the famines recently, I'm not sure how many rations even the bigger ports receive.

With the amount of money I've bet, there's no doubt at least one of the guards here will take the bait. I tilt my head to the side, showing my impatience as I take another puff from my cheap cigar, nostrils flaring as the acrid scent fills the air. Can't even afford decent tobacco here.

"What'll it be, gentleman?" the dealer, who is also the bartender, who is also the local butcher, asks.

Small town.

The guards appear to weigh their options, their faces giving their tell far before their hands do. The first guard slams down his cards and grunts in apparent frustration.

"I fold," he says. Not one to risk his fortune. I respect that. My eyes linger on the second guard. His broken nose and missing teeth tells me he has more scrap than the other. I raise my eyebrows at him, pushing him to make a decision. He hesitates, chewing the butt of his cigar, eyes drifting between his hand and the cards on the table. His ego wins this battle as he pushes his shillings toward the middle of the table, matching mine. The pile gleams under the light of the oil lamps. A few "ooohs" and "aaahs" echo around us as the patrons shift on their feet.

"Show us what ye have," the shorter guard who folded his hand snarls. Curling his lip, he spits his loose tobacco into an empty, glass bottle. I crane my neck to either side, stretching my hands out before me, unlacing my fingers. Getting ready for what I'm sure will be a decent chase if it comes to it. Setting my cigar in the ashtray, I flip over my cards, revealing the straight flush that's about to take his fortune.

The patrons erupt in laughter, clapping their hands wildly as if they've just witnessed a miracle. The guard's face boils, reddening in embarrassment. Or anger. It's all the same, anyhow. He balls his fists and attempts to stand, but I gesture for him to stop, pointing toward his cards with a wink. Begrudgingly, he flips them, cursing in my direction as he discards a two-pair onto the table. Not a bad hand.

But not good enough.

I tsk, casting the guard a quick smirk before I begin piling the large sum of coins into my bag. The guard makes an attempt to stop me, standing abruptly from his chair and reaching for the remainder of the coin, so I point my attention toward the dealer.

"A win is a win, is it not?" I ask. He's a large man with a

thick coarse mustache lining his upper lip. Comically unbalancing his face as a sheen of sweat beads atop his bald head. He shrugs, uncrossing his large arms to run a rag across his forehead. Permission enough. I finish pulling the coin into my bag, making sure to grab the Queen of Spades and stick it in my pocket without anyone taking notice. As the last of the coin hits my bag, the guards across from me mutter various curses, and I take a moment to revel in it.

Steal from the rich, and even more from the richer.

My father's words echo in my mind. Granted, these guards are nowhere near rich. Bottom of the barrel so to speak. But they work for the man directly responsible for the imprisonment and murder of so many innocents. So many Enchantresses. Merely doing my civic duty by stripping their pockets. Not to mention the tax I evade on my regular routes through Copenspire and Wickersham. All in the name of fairness. Why should people in Valebridge and under Roman's direct payroll thrive while everyone else suffers through the famines? It's the least I can do to chip away at the corrupt king.

At least, it's what I tell myself.

"It's been a pleasure," I say, spinning out of my chair to head for the door. No need to stick around for small talk, I'm already running behind. The weight of the coin on my hip pushes my feet to move faster, and it's with my haste that I make a fatal mistake.

The Three of Hearts I swapped for the Queen slips out of my sleeve, landing upright on the sticky floor. A momentary silence plagues the pub as a dozen pairs of eyes burn into my back.

Shite.

Without a second thought, I take off through the double doors that lead outside in a sprint. The sun is blinding in comparison to the dark pub. I've forgotten it isn't dusk. Squinting against the abrasive light, I make my way through the courtyard.

"Son of bitch!" the guards yell behind me. It's not long before they plunder through the doors of the pub after me. My feet pound through the cobblestone square, past the dwindling buildings making up the sleepy seaside town. Past the docks and the crippling white building they call a church. I veer opposite of the Holden Sea, away from the path that will lead me home and straight for the Southern Trinity Forest.

Surely, they'd be ridiculous to follow me there. The myths alone deter most anyone. Wolves and nymphs. Sprites and murderous crows. Most who enter, rarely are seen again. But still, I take my chances. The forest has been a home to me for all my life. I'm more comfortable among the trees than I've ever been in a proper town.

Cobbled thuds turn to soft pads as my boots hit dirt. The breeze carries a faint whiff of freshly ripened blackberries as I step into the wooded forest. I keep my pace, but the familiar clopping of horse hooves makes my stomach dip. I risk a glance over my shoulder. The two idiots I've conned out of fifty shillings ride feverishly toward the woods. The grizzly snarling across their chests only fuels my fire. The royal crest. Sliding over a fallen log, I instinctively reach for my bow. Only to remember, it isn't there.

Damn repairs. Maybe the guards aren't the only idiots today. A smile tugs at my mouth, replaying their faces as I stole their shillings. Adrenaline courses through my veins, the thrill of the chase propelling my every step. *It's been too long*, I tell myself. Pushing away my mother's voice telling me I'm too old for this.

"You're almost thirty, Sorin. It's time to stop with these antics." I can hear her voice clear as day.

I think the fuck not.

The clinking of the coin on my hip soon fades as the rush of white rapids drowns out all other noise. I stumble to a halt at the edge of the Galdosa River. Clearly not thinking this through, I quickly sift through my options as the stomping of hooves approaches rapidly behind me. Scanning the riverbank on either side, neither way holds promise of escape. To the left leads back to Copenspire. To the right, the riverbank dissipates completely, melting into the raging rapids and will eventually wind back to the sea.

My eyes catch on a boulder several feet down to the right, in the middle of the river. If I jump...

"In the name of King Roman, we command you to halt!"

For fuck's sake. I let out an annoyed breath, pinching the bridge of my nose before turning to face them. Their horses dance along the tree line. The men's reddened faces only add to my amusement. I tip my head back and let out a laugh before I take a few steps backward, opening my arms wide, daring them to follow.

"Cease, thief!" the guard I've conned yells the moment my boots hit the water. He pulls his bow from his back, readying an arrow. I have seconds, maybe.

Think, Sorin.

I spin on my heel and face the Galdosa River, ignoring his demands. The water rages wildly, the whooshing near deafening and the rippling white makes my stomach churn. But I've faced worse than this. Hell, I'm sure I'll face worse once I'm on the other side. *The Ravine of No Mercy* awaits, a place I am certain the guards will not follow.

Then again, I've been wrong before.

My eyes wander from the water to the ravine across from it. I have seconds to make a decision. The sound of hooves crunching pulls my attention, speeding my thought process.

The trees across from the river are thick enough even the sun fails to break through. But in a flash, I swear I see two flickers of gold looming from between the dense pines. For a moment, my heart lurches, catching on the set of eyes hidden in the trees. It can't be what I think.

Could it?

I don't let myself linger much longer before I tighten the rope around my bag of coins and plunge into the water just as an arrow whizzes through the air.

CHAPTER 2
ELORA

MY OBLIVIOUSNESS EARNS ME A SUDDEN FALL backward as I fail to see the next strike coming. Wincing, I land gracelessly on the forest floor, various twigs and rocks biting into my palms.

"I hate sprites," I mumble before pulling myself up from the ground. Dusting off my breeches, I face the tiny beasts again. Their glowing blue bodies are no larger than my palm, and I'm embarrassed to admit this isn't the first encounter I've had with them where I've left defeated. Though delicate in size, their quick wit and ability to fly has outsmarted me more than once. The buzz of their wings grows more rapid as swarms of them begin to circle where I stand.

It's not the first time I've cursed myself for being the only Enchantress without magick, but it is the first time I start to despise Mother Gaia for it. My mind flashes to my Awakening Ceremony all those years ago, the night I was to be gifted my magick from the Mother. Our one and only deity in Teravie. She provides life to all. Fruitful forests. Plentiful and peaceful seas. And to Enchantresses, she provides pieces of herself, her magick, to ensure Teravie is taken care of in her absence. Disappointment and guilt settle in my gut, replacing the frustration I have with the sprites.

"Fine," I relent, tossing the meager sack of blackberries in the sprites direction. "You win."

Again.

Their victory is short lived as they begin fighting each other for the contents of the bag. Food isn't always so hard to come by in the Trinity Forest, but this late in the summer season has every occupant of the woods desperate to stock up for the colder months. My stomach growls, so I decide before I return to my cabin, I'll check my fishing trap in the ravine.

Mother above, I could really use a win right now.

My hands drift to my daggers strapped securely on either hip. Still there. The twin blades are my most prized possessions. The hilts are wrapped in a beautiful, rich brown leather, intricate inlays of various leaves and flowers swirl up from the hilt and dance around the blades. Their presence has brought me so much joy in the past and now it just brings pain.

"Cade, I...you've outdone yourself. These are magnificent! I couldn't possibly accept such a gift."

Shrugging off the sudden memory and the threat of tears that accompany it, I turn toward the direction of the ravine.

To my left the Galdosa River comes into view. The water moves in calculated rhythm, the soft trickle turning to a violent cascade of rapids as it opens up to the Holden Sea. The reflecting sunlight bounces off the rippling water and casts a beautiful glow on the lower canopy of trees, creating a golden hue to the air. Pausing, I take a deep inhale of the crisp forest air, resetting myself after an embarrassing loss.

I could stay in this moment forever, the early morning before most of the woodland animals awake. The peacefulness of dawn encompassed by the sound of tumbling water and the glow of the trees. The incessant caw of a crow interrupts my moment of solitude, dampening the otherwise peaceful walk to the ravine. The same caw which wakes me every morning.

Always a moment too early. A scowl spreads over my face as I search the sky and tree branches.

"Damn bird," I grumble as the black crow comes into view, perching itself on a low-lying branch. As if in response to my hostility, it lets out one last caw before flying off above the treetops, leaving me alone once more.

Usually, I don't mind being alone. Prefer it, actually. But lately my mind has wandered far too often. Daydreaming of the days before King Roman's rule. Of my life that once was. Or more so, the life that could've been. Even after we fled Valebridge, where all Enchantresses reside amongst the king, my life on the mountain was filled with love and comfort. Cade's warmth is a ghost upon my skin as his hazel eyes flash in my mind.

Then, there she is. Drifting into my memory strong and swift.

Very rarely do I allow myself to think of her. But whenever I let my guard slip, my mother's voice seeps into the depths of my mind, haunting me there.

"My little susi." As she so often called me. So many nights the memory of her voice has roused me from a feverish sleep, leaving me caught somewhere between a dream and a nightmare. I shudder, remembering how close I came to giving into the demons last night. Shaking my hands at my sides, I force myself to move forward.

THE WIDTH of the ravine is always a wonder to me, no matter how many times I've approached it. *The Ravine of No Mercy*, as the locals in Copenspire like to call it. The tales of the woodland spirits are no more ruthless than others I heard as a child, but for whatever reason the people of Copenspire fear the ravine. Swapping tales of sprites and nymphs who lure humans to their eventual demise. Seeking their youth, blood, first born children.

Whether the tales of the *Ravine of No Mercy* are true or not, I can't say. Even after three years here, the pesky sprites are the most nuisance of all. Perhaps it's the Enchantress blood running through my veins keeping the other occupants of the woods away, thinking I possess magick stronger than theirs.

Or it could be that evil spirits and nymphs don't exist here at all. Even the Jade Guild hasn't been a bother. The Lord who reigns in the forest has been rumored to have sealed up his keep shortly after King Roman took the throne. Not letting anyone in *or* out. Giving up completely on the humans he is supposed to lead. As sparse as hunting and fishing has become recently, I imagine those with more mouths to feed are suffering even worse.

As for the wolves, I know of their existence, having witnessed them myself. Their faint howls often plague the air around my cabin, but I've done my best to remain unseen. The only time I saw one of the giant beasts, it was my first summer in the woods, and I'd been collecting berries much like I had today. The wolf watched me from across the ravine, just as I had watched it, but it never approached me. It just sat and stared after every move until eventually disappearing into the forest.

The ravine stretches for miles in either direction, the trees creating a thick blanket so hardly any sunlight makes it through to the ground. The vibrancy of the evergreen trees glisten in the morning light. I stop to catch my breath before entering, willing the voices in my head to silence before they even start. Breathing deeply, I inhale the scent of the early morning dew. Freshly dropped upon the forest canopy, tiny orbs of water glisten from the flowers and pine needles.

Unsheathing my right dagger, I step silently on my toes as I enter the thick, deep green sea of saplings. Giant boulders and river rock scatter the grounds, fallen logs covered in spongy green moss make the way through a maze for the layman. But I have learned these routes and could find my way through even on the darkest of nights. Being in the ravine makes the tightness in my shoulders release slightly. There's a certain peacefulness in the mundane. Of the day to day routines that have kept me sane all these years. And memorizing and hunting in the ravine has been my favorite of them all.

Stopping just to the right of the opening, I reach down and ruffle some dried leaves to check the snare I set a few days prior. Hoping for a ground squirrel or better yet a rabbit. Anything to fill my stomach.

Empty.

Continuing toward the center of the grove, trying not to linger on yet another day with an empty trap, I crane my ear and follow the familiar sound of running water. Tip toeing and eyeing my left then my right, dagger still in hand, I make my way over a few fallen logs before arriving at the deep river basin nestled in the ravines center. Through the gully, the river mouth is wide and fast, the gurgling of rapids drowns out almost every other noise the forest has to offer. Once at the water's edge, I place my dagger back in its sheath at my side and sit down on what I've claimed as my fishing rock. Leaning forward I snatch the rope I'd used to attach my woven trap and give a forceful tug, causing it to spring up out of the water.

My lucky day. A singular fish flails inside of the basket, its breaths quickening as I pull it from the water completely. The fish is small, no larger than my hand, but will be the perfect meal to get me through the day.

Besides, any gift from the Mother, especially on a day like today, is one I don't take lightly.

Out of the water, the fish flops from side to side, its gills working tirelessly, as it silently begs to be returned to its home. Not wanting to prolong its fate, I reach in and grab it. The scales are smooth and slippery to the touch with varying shades of gray and green. I place it on the large rock as I whisper my thanks. Pulling my dagger from my hip, I swiftly cease its life with a deadly blow to the head, sending out a silent prayer to the Mother as I do so.

"All that has been given life, shall have an end. I wish you peace on your next journey."

The tedious task of cleaning the fish shouldn't take more than a few minutes; I move quickly to ensure no predators have the chance to catch the smell, cutting a straight line from the base of the tail up to the underside of the throat. Blood spills out either side, staining the gray rock a red so deep, I don't allow my eyes to linger on it for too long. The color teeming with memories sets my jaw on edge.

Halfway through, a sudden *snap* sounds through the forest.

"In the name of King Roman, we command you to halt!"

Whipping my head up from the fish, I suck in a sharp breath while the rest of my body remains frozen. Slowly, I rise from my kneeling position, tracing the surrounding woods with my eyes. Nothing but low hanging branches, drooping with the weight of pine needles, stare back. The menacing *caw* of the resident crow wafts through the air, interrupting the silence of the woods, and I fight against rolling my eyes at the sound. Landing on a branch nearby, the bird lets out another *caw* towards the river. A second voice crashes through the woods; this time accompanied by a familiar thunderous sound which vibrates off the ground below my feet.

Horses.

"Cease, thief!"

Realizing the voices are coming from behind me, I spin my body, unsheathing my second dagger, and am greeted by two horsemen galloping across the riverbank.

CHAPTER 3
ELORA

THROWING MYSELF BACK DOWN, MY BREATHS ARE short and quick as my palms slick with sweat. It's then I notice a third man, only he is without a horse and currently headed straight for the river. A flood of relief washes over me as I realize I've gone unnoticed by the men. The contented feeling is quickly replaced by unease. I've lived in these woods at the southern edge of the Trinity Forest for three years, and I've never encountered another soul. These men have entered the ravine, my only sanctuary, my *home.*

You don't have a home.

The voices in my head mock my thoughts, but with a quick shake of the head to silence them, I begin to move. Light on my feet with daggers in hand, I creep toward the river to a nearby pine tree, using its massive trunk to shield myself. My eyes snag on the man headed toward the river. For a moment, I think he sees me. For a moment, his dark eyes blaze through the pine needles. For a moment, my heart skips a beat, leaving me gasping for air. Then, in a blink, he plunges into the icy currents.

This part of the Galdosa River is a constant white rage of water and movement, the giant waves forming tidepools and sucking down anything who dares cross its path. Tracking the man with my eyes, the water rips him down stream until by some miracle, he reaches a boulder. Clinging to the large rock, he lies protruding about halfway out of the water a few feet from the shore. Was he attempting to make it to the other side of the river? An ambitious goal, or a very stupid one.

The horsemen, who I now notice wear the grizzly bear crest of King Roman on their chest plates, begin their way toward the river. Their horses pace and stamp uneasily as they eye the waters tumbling depths and swift currents.

"You're more than welcome to join me in here, the water's lovely this time of year," the man in the water yells. His confidence is jarring given his current circumstance, his grip on the boulder loosening by the second.

"You're just as daft as you are ugly," one of the horsemen shouts. His voice, booming, carries over the white rapids and makes me flinch. Keeping my stance low against the pine tree, I continue to observe the three men below me.

"We can wait here all day, thief. I'm not sure you can say the same," the same guard says with a grin revealing several missing teeth. These must be guards stationed in Copenspire.

My stomach churns. Anger boiling deep in my veins as the men who wear the crest of King Roman encroach the river. The guard, no matter how vile, is right, however. The man can't hold on much longer. In fact, I'm not sure how he is still holding on at all.

Dismounting their horses, the men make their way to the water's edge. Shifting on my feet, I place my daggers back in their sheaths before sliding down to a crouching position.

"Return the shillings, and we'll call it fair. Maybe even let you live to see another day of your miserable life," the second horseman says, his balding head reflecting off the sunlight. His frame is much shorter but larger than the first guard's. Could a few shillings really be worth this effort?

The portly guards' boots dip into the water, his eyes scanning the area for the easiest way to the boulder. With a plan in place, the guards link arms. The shorter one in the front draws his blade and makes his way into the river. Using the second guard as an anchor, he plants an entire boot into the water. The slim guard follows behind, holding the reins of his horse like a tether to the shore. Wading waist deep, the current whips around him, but still they press on until they've nearly reached the boulder.

The thief's face is turned away from me, but his laugh is deep and assured. With a halfhearted salute to the guards, he lets go of the boulder. A small gasp escapes my lips as the man floats down the river, his body tossing and turning with the raging current. Must be a blasted idiot to think he could survive these currents.

"Dammit!" the slim guard screeches. "Back to the horses, we'll catch him downstream." The galloping of hooves fades into the forest as they set off into the thick woods, away from the river's edge. Mind still reeling from what I just saw, it takes me a moment to shake back to reality. Without thinking much further, curiosity fully piqued, I begin the jaunt downstream.

Quickening my pace, I dart through the trees veering toward the downward slope of the riverbank to my right. The water slows its course around the banking river turning toward a rock wall. If the current didn't sweep him under or he managed to avoid hitting his head on another boulder, I'd imagine he'd be...

There.

On the curve of the narrowest part of the river, the man has washed ashore. Knowing the horsemen will be back any minute, I lower myself onto my backside and slide down the dirt hill to the riverbank. As I approach the man, he lies face down on the rocky shore. Head turned away from me and sopping wet, I can't tell if he's breathing, and panic begins to race through my veins. Horse hooves sound distantly as the guards get closer on the opposite side of the water. Once the guards reach the bank, the slower current will be easy for the horses to cross. I must move quickly.

Lowering myself, I place my hand on the man's back, hoping for any sign of movement.

It's faint, but the slow rise and fall of his chest gives me hope. Relief floods my system, an unwarranted and confusing feeling. Nonetheless, I've decided I have to move him.

Without letting myself think any further, I take the man's hands in my own and attempt to drag him to a nearby tree. They're hot to the touch, despite being submerged in the freezing waters. He barely budges, his body weight plus the weight of the water seeping into his clothes will take a lot more strength than what I'm able to give.

Leave him.

The hiss of the demons in my head sounds like a challenge, and I want nothing more than to spite them. *You can do this*, I think to myself. *You can do this.* Shaking off my inner conflict, I try again. This time, I link my arms around the man's and lower myself for more leverage. Digging the heel of my boots in the rocks, I heave in an upward motion and take a step back. A small budge, but movement, nonetheless. I repeat this motion again, and again, and again. Sweat beads on my forehead and down my temples, but I only need a few more steps until we'll be hidden behind a giant pine tree. The thundering of horse hoofs clambering against the rocky shore stops me in my tracks.

"Aye! Down here! I think I see something!" One of the guards calls out from just beyond the treeline.

The shorter guard comes into view on his horse, cresting out of the thick forest trees on the other side of the river, the slim guard following closely behind. Frozen, I remain hunched before the thief. *Breathe*, Elora. *Breathe.* Before they can get any closer, I close my eyes, masking their natural golden color to a soft brown.

They'll still know.

An arrow whizzes through the air and plants itself into the

giant pine tree directly behind me with a cracking *thunk*. The hiss of another arrow hauling through the air catches me off guard. I rip a dagger free from its sheath, but before I can make use of it, the second arrow collides into my shoulder sending me backwards, until I crash into the earth beneath me. My head cracks on the rock laden ground and a piercing, sharp pain floods behind my eyes. The fall backwards has caused my dagger to tumble out of my reach. Inhaling a sharp breath at the sudden pain in my head, I attempt to sit up but am pinned in place.

The second arrow has shot through the fabric of my cloak and buried itself into the shore, pinning me to the ground.

Too late.

"Would you look at this?" One of the guards says, slamming his boot atop my wrist, using his other foot to kick my dagger even farther away. "Looks like we caught ourselves a little rabbit."

The round guard snickers, "Oh, aye, Ruben. She'll look swell stuffed and mounted on the wall. If the boys back at camp are lucky, maybe we'll even share."

"Let me go!" I spit toward them. Writhing my body to inch away, my movements are unsuccessful. I'm freed from my cloak but am now pinned by the two guards by either wrist.

The men share a laugh, as I attempt to scurry backward through the rocks, but the grip on my wrists is too tight.

Hope diminishes in my chest. Trapped. How did I let this happen? My rage turns on me as I face the predicament I'm now in. Kicking my feet, I don't give up.

"Easy, there." My gaze darts between the two men as the second guard continues, "We just want to know if you feel as soft as you look."

This will not be my story, not after everything. Not after Cade, and my mother. The portly guard begins to climb on top of me, as the slim one releases my wrist and makes his way toward the river. The man's breath is hot on my face and reeks of stale ale and rancid meat. My eyes begin to glaze over with tears, but I refuse to let them fall. He has made damn sure my dagger is out of reach, but he doesn't know I possess a second.

Since the slim guard has released my hand, it takes all but a few seconds for me to find my blade and sink it into the guard's chest. Pushing hard until it cracks against bone, I leave it embedded as he slumps over me. Rolling him off, I sit up, chest heaving.

In.

Out.

"What are you—" The second guard spins on his heels. His eyes widen at my blood-stained hands as I yank my dagger free from the dead guard's chest. But before he can move another step, a low predatory growl vibrates through the dense trees behind me. Every hair on my neck and arms raises. Dread washes over me as the guard stops. Minutes feel like hours, neither of us daring to move. Something stirs in my peripheral. The unconscious man from the river begins to move slightly, his body twitching as if trying to wake himself up.

Another growl.

Closer.

Louder.

Something sinister creeps from the woods engulfing the air with a powerful energy, swallowing up the oxygen around us. Struggling to breathe, my throat constricts as my pulse hammers in my chest. I tighten my grip around the hilt of my blade. The warm breath of the animal tickles my skin as it approaches my neck. With caution, the guard takes several steps backward toward the river, his eyes locked on whatever beast stands behind me.

Swallowing down a large gulp of air, I silently count to three.

One, *breathe.*

Two, *breathe.*

Three, *breathe.*

On the third breath I take my time turning my head, raising my blade. The wolf's face is enormous in size, mere inches away from my own. The iron tang of blood from its last kill still lingers on its teeth and invades my senses. Inclining its head slightly, the wolf gives a few sniffs, the hot air from its nose lands on my cheeks. His amber eyes stare with such intensity I want to look away, but something beyond my control forces my gaze to hold.

My chest heaves so heavily it hurts, the movements so rapid I fear my heart might come barreling out of it, but still I keep my eyes locked on the wolf. Baring its teeth, the wolf lets out another low guttural growl from deep within its throat, sending a chill down to my core. The tears I held back from the guards are now a constant stream down my face. As the wolf tips his head in the air, whatever trance I was under is broken. With a shuddered breath, I close my eyes and drop my hands, blade and all.

All that has been given life, shall have an end.

As the wolf spits out a deep bark, I let out a sharp scream and press my palms to my eyes, not caring about the blood that still stains them. Every bone in my body quivers under the sound of the wolf. The scrambling of boots on rock tells me the guard has had enough waiting. With the horses long gone, I imagine he's headed straight back to the river, seeking refuge on the opposite shore. Stars dance behind my closed eyes as I press my palms further into them, the ground trembles as the wolf lurches forward, flinging loose pebbles into the air. In a whirl of surprise, the beast knocks into me with its massive shoulder, tossing my body to the ground as he sprints towards the river.

Snapping my eyes open, I remain on the ground as the wolf dashes over the rocky terrain with ease and unexpected grace. High pitched shrills echo off the water, and I can't force my eyes away as I watch the scene unfold. The wolf catches up to the guard and sinks its large teeth into his leg. The crunch of a bone snapping echoes through the woods, the guard's screams constant and strangled.

Blood drips from the wolf's massive canines, covering his jaw. His white and gray fur is now a mix of red and brown as the hair begins to matte around its neck from the guard's blood. Arching his back, he lets go of the man and throws his head up to the sky, letting out a deafening howl. Covering my ears, I force my eyes to remain open despite the brutality before me. I let out a few small yelps, and I'm not sure if it's because of the excruciating sound of the wolf's howl or knowing I'll be his next victim. My pathetic cries must've been heard by the wolf because he whips his head toward me briefly, before refocusing on his prey.

But with the wolf temporarily distracted, the guard has somehow made it across the river. Dropping to his knees he lets out what sounds like a prayer. Closing his eyes, he brings his palms together to give thanks to whatever deity he thinks might listen. So wrapped up in his premature thanks, he doesn't notice the second wolf approaching from his behind.

This wolf has a slightly smaller build than the one on my side of the river, and is the complete counterpart in color. Whereas the first wolf is a stunning mix of bright white and dark grays, this wolf is purely black. With eyes so green they appear to glow, it begins its silent stalk toward the still oblivious guard. Its eyes narrow in his direction and before he can realize what is happening, the wolf's teeth sink into the back of his neck. Turning my head away at the impact, I can't bear to watch anymore blood spill.

Frozen in fear, I will myself to move. To run. To lift my hands and find my blade and end this wolf's life before it ends mine.

But a wicked thought stops me.

Maybe this is what I've needed all along. In some ways, it would be an easy out. To let the notorious wolves of the woods end my life here and now, saving me from the task I've so often thought about doing myself.

The gray wolf retreats from the water's edge, stopping to sniff the unconscious man as he passes by. Seemingly unbothered, the wolf turns his attention to me. Its muscular legs take long strides across the shore, near silent on giant predatory paws. The creature stands directly in front of me now, and in his presence, panic creeps over my skin and lodges itself in my throat. Darting my eyes between the wolf and the man, the man and the wolf, I curse myself for not running.

Sniffing my hair, the air exhaled from the wolf's nose tickles my ears and around my head. Withdrawing back, he throws his head up to the sky once more and lets out another beautiful howl, leaving a ringing ache in my ears. When his head lowers, I take a deep swallow and finally meet the wolf's gaze. His amber eyes are fierce and unwavering. His gaze, unbroken. For a moment, something stirs deep within me. A small tug on my heart, as faint as a summer breeze. A whisper through the wind to not be afraid.

Do not be afraid, I tell myself. Baffled by the sudden sense of peace I feel in the wolf's presence, I finally whisper a soft, "Thank you." With caution, I reach my hand up toward his face, baring my wrist in a show of submission. But before I can reach him, he takes a few paces backward and disappears into the belly of the forest, leaving nothing but bloodshed in his wake.

CHAPTER 4
ELORA

COLLAPSING ONTO MY BACK, THE SOUND OF THE river soothes my senses as I allow myself to let out a deep sob. Choking on my tears, I wipe my eyes with my palms as small grunts redirect my attention toward the riverbank. Suddenly remembering I'm not alone, I shoot upward and dart my eyes to the unconscious man in front of me. Only now, he's no longer unconscious. Sitting up, he cups the back of his head, the gleam of blood coats his hand as he brings it against his chest.

"Are you all right?" I ask, hating how my voice waivers.

He glances towards me as he cups the back of his head again. His dark brown hair is sopping wet and stuck out in various places from being whipped through the water. His brows match his hair in color as they furrow in my direction, creating a deep crease between them.

"Well, considering I just got my arse handed to me by the Galdosa, I'd say I'm in decent shape." His voice is low and rough but there's a softness to it I can't quite explain. The thief's dark brown eyes remain focused in my direction, and it's only now I realize what I must look like. Hair disheveled, the blood of someone else staining my hands and face.

"The contusion on your head, do you want me to take a

look?" I ask, wiping the last bit of dampness from my cheeks, itching to head toward the river and wash myself. My instinct is to flee but my mother's voice snags in my mind.

"You are an Enchantress, Elora. No matter what magick the Mother gifts you, it's your duty to serve and protect the lives of those who reside in Teravie. That is the way it has always been. It is the way it will always be."

"Are *you* all right?" He avoids my question with a question of his own, startling me out of my memory. "I'd say it was a close call for the both of us. What are you doing this deep in the woods anyway? A damsel like yourself—"

"I can assure you, I'm no damsel." The words are a bite as they leave my lips, but I feel no remorse for my tone. I should be used to men questioning the strength of women by now, but my cheeks heat despite it. "And yes, I'm all right." I lie through my teeth and push myself off the ground, dusting off the sandy bits of rock from my breeches.

"I didn't mean to insult you, love," the man says. "I just meant I've never ran into anyone else out here, least of all a woman traveling alone." He peels off his jacket and balls it up, pressing it against the back of his head, wincing as he does. My gaze narrows. If he would just let me take a look at his wound, I could help ease his pain.

His jaw tenses before he throws his jacket to the ground and frantically searches the contents of the bag on his hip. He lets out a long breath as he pulls a single card from his bag, kissing it before placing it back and cinching the bag shut. I avert my eyes as he starts peeling off his shirt. Making my way to the water's edge to wash the blood from my hands and face, I bite down on the inside of my cheek, gnawing at the flesh to distract myself from the bloodied guard I must step around to get to the river. Grateful the wind has carried his quickly decaying scent downstream and away from us. Drops of water hit the pebbled shore behind me as the thief wrings his shirt.

"You're welcome, by the way," I mumble, quiet enough it's barely audible.

"And for what do I owe a thanks?" I bite my tongue at his response, trying desperately to hold back from snapping at the smugness in his tone. In his defense, he *was* unconscious for the events that just transpired, but my patience is running thin. Would Mother Gaia really care if I didn't help this fool?

"Forget it," I say, wiping my washed hands on the front of my breeches. "For whatever reason, the Mother decided to spare you your life this morning, you should really be thanking Her." Swinging to face him, I suddenly miss the familiar weight of my daggers. As to not draw attention to myself, I scan the ground for my weapons, hoping he won't notice my missing blades and take it upon himself to find them first.

With a puzzled look, he gives his shirt a final wring before sliding it back over his head.

"Have we met before?" he asks. Ignoring his question, my eyes spot my blades near the tree line where I encountered the wolf. I set forth in their direction without another word to the man.

"Wait!" he shouts from behind me, but I don't stop. "I don't even know your name." I'm too focused on my blades to turn and look. "I have to at least know the name of the woman who can ward off the wolves of the woods," he shouts again.

My boots make an unsavory chewing noise against the rocks as I slam to a stop. "You were awake?" I ask, keeping my back toward him.

"Yes," he says through a soft chuckle. "Woke up right as the giant beast landed its teeth in that poor bloke's leg." The rocks crunch under his boots as he moves toward me. "Decided it'd be better to play dead than try and take on a predator of his size, and yet, there you were," he continues, his body now parallel with mine, "unarmed and vulnerable, left completely unscathed. Fascinating."

Shifting my eyes, I meet his gaze, the cold from the river

pours off him in icy invisible waves, as he takes another step closer. He cups his head again and glances down at me. Squaring my shoulders, I turn to face him head on.

"I guess you're not the only one the Mother was looking after today," I reply, matching his arrogance with my tone. His dark eyes are just as skeptical as they are curious. His gaze lingers over every inch of me, and in a show of pride, I don't turn away despite the heavy scrutiny I'm beginning to feel. It's strange to have him look at me that way. Slowly, curiously. A way no one has looked at me in years.

The demons in my head resurface, reminding me that despite the penance I place on myself daily for my family's death, it will never be enough. My heart lurches as the ache grows throughout my chest. Blurred memories of that night assault my mind as darkness begins to cloud my vision. Inhaling a forced breath, I push past the images rising and rising, swallowing hard against the lump in my throat.

"There isn't anywhere within walking distance of here aside from Copenspire," I manage to say, clenching my fists at my sides. "And considering today's events, you're probably not welcome there." Grabbing my daggers from the ground, I return them to their sheaths at my hips. "The temperature drops drastically in the woods once the sun sets," I continue, "and that wound on your head..." My skin prickles with the feeling of being watched, glancing back at the thief, his hardened stare is relentless as our eyes meet.

"What?" I snap, placing my hands on the hilts of my daggers.

"Sorry." He shrugs, his mouth turning up at the sides. "I swear I've seen that scowl before."

Shaking my head, I continue, "Anyway, I thought you might need a place to stay until your garments are dry, and whether you think it's an issue or not, that wound on the back of your head isn't going to heal itself." My words are short, and to the point, but the inside of my cheek is becoming sore from the constant chewing. An anxious habit I can't break. Surely, the Mother will be pleased with my final attempt to help this... thief. The man says nothing, his gaze holds on mine, and I begin to regret the offer. I don't even know this man and having him come back to my cabin, the only place I've been able to stay safe, is reckless.

Nodding his head slowly, the worried look switches back to the smugness I imagine he wears often. "Okay, then," he says. "I'll take you up on your offer. It appears you'll be saving me yet again." With a wink, he extends his hand toward me. "I'm Sorin." Keeping his hand hanging in the air, my eyes catch on the swirling black ink that crawls up his forearm. I've never seen skin marked permanently before. Unusual.

I hesitate a moment longer before reaching my hand to meet his. His hand is freezing from the river, skin pruned from being submerged, yet despite his cold touch, a bolt of heat stings through my palm.

"Elora," I finally say as I catch my breath and release his hand. Dropping mine back to the hilt of my dagger, I grip it tightly, ignoring the way my skin has warmed from his touch. Breaking our gaze, I quickly scan the area. A swarm of flies already feasting on the bodies of the men makes my stomach lurch. If the man knows what I am—an Enchantress—he doesn't let on. Keeping my eyes masked, I reach down to grab my cloak before starting for the woods. With a final glance back, I smile, leaving nature to take its course on what's left of the guards.

CHAPTER 5
ELORA

The walk back to my cabin drags longer than the month-long journey it took to get here from Kirsgard Mountain. Not only am I making this trek with a complete stranger, but now with the wolves potentially lurking around every corner, my senses are heightened. I suppose I always knew they were there, but this is the first time I haven't been able to hide from them and it has me on edge. So, I take my time, leading Sorin through a winding route, over and under fallen logs, around the other side of the ravine and back, keeping my steps light and eyes alert.

He follows close behind, not offering any conversation or questions about our path, the occasional snap of twigs under his boots the only proof he's still there. Glancing over my shoulder, I nod toward the exit. Leading us to a small burrow of bushes on the farthest side of the gully, hoping the maze I've created will be dizzying enough that he won't recall the way back once he's gone.

Stepping outside of the ravine, the sun is bright and puffy white clouds scatter about the sky. I admire the whimsical shapes, remembering a time when my mother and I would lay out on the terrace of the castle in Valebridge, making a game of how many different animals we could interpret from them. Lifting my chin toward the sky, my eyes close as I take a deep breath through my nose. My shoulders unclench slightly as the warmth of the sun spreads over me and the events of today begin to wash away. As I'm about to give my thanks to the Mother, an unfamiliar presence invades my moment of serenity. Snapping my eyes back open, I don't turn my head; instead, I focus my gaze on the trees.

Sorin's proximity is closer than I would typically be comfortable with, but seeing as I'm too tired to speak, I close my eyes again and return my focus to the sun and the sky. Letting out a silent *thank you* to Mother Gaia, I breathe in the world around me and sense my nerves settling with every intake of fresh air.

"It's beautiful here." Sorin's voice breaks the silence between us, forcing my eyes open once more. Annoyed that I can't finish a thought without him interrupting, I give up the task altogether.

"It's just around the corner," I mumble, pushing past him. Rounding the dense group of evergreen trees, my tiny cabin finally comes into view. Seeing my home still intact as if nothing happened today is just the kind of assurance I need.

Finding the abandoned hunting cabin was a miracle all those years ago. Although the roof was mostly holes and the interior rotted and filthy, I took my time cleaning it up. Fixing what needed to be fixed. Rebuilding this cabin is the most proud I've ever been. Putting my hands and mind and nervous energy to good use.

Now, the small wood cabin is my only refuge. The wild-flower seeds I planted last summer have bloomed, leaving bursts of pinks and yellows around the wooden frame of my home. Their faint scent drifts through the breeze, lavender and hyacinth calming my nerves. Inside is minimal; a makeshift bed, a pitcher and bowl I found, and a few other odds and ends. It isn't much, but it is everything.

"You live here alone?" Sorin's question hangs in the air as I point him in the direction of a small rack I built that rests just to the side of the cabin. Ignoring his question, I change the subject.

"You can hang your jacket there, if you'd like," I say. "The sun will be at its full height in the next hour, and should be mostly dry by nightfall."

"I appreciate the hospitality." Sorin chuckles lightly. "But you didn't answer my question. I've been through Copenspire many times over the last few years, and I've never heard of you. A woman who lives in the woods. Curious is all." Hanging his jacket on the rack, he spreads the arms loosely so it will dry more evenly. Keeping myself busy, I gather bundles of sticks for a fire.

"I've been here...awhile. And though it isn't much, it's better than Kirs–" I stop myself short, biting my tongue for almost telling Sorin where I last lived, Kirsgard Mountain. "I like to keep *quiet*," I continue, shooting him a scowl. "I don't worry myself with the business of others."

He laughs again but this time, makes a dramatic bow. "Point taken, lady of the woods, my lips are sealed." If I wasn't so annoyed by his constant chatter, I may have even smiled at his show of enthusiasm. Kneeling down, he begins placing the wood in the circle of the fire pit, forcing me to bite down on my tongue to keep from scolding him. I don't need his help to build a simple fire. Before I can snap at him again, he interrupts my thoughts. "I'll be out of your hair at morning's first light," Sorin says, grabbing a few more handfuls of wood. "Unlike you, I often find myself reveling in the company of others."

THE REST of the day is filled with my usual tasks, only this time they're quicker with Sorin's help. I hate admitting it, but having an extra set of hands is quite the luxury I didn't realize I missed. Sorin spent most of the afternoon gathering more wood for the fire, while I checked a few snares down in the valley. Refilling my pitcher with the collected rainwater from last night's storm, I return it to my cabin and grab a small sewing kit that I stole from a waste bin in Copenspire. There's an almost ease about the day, despite having company and despite the events from earlier.

With a bit of leftover thread, I carefully stitched Sorin's wound together. The act took three times longer than necessary due to his complaining. A wince every few minutes had me stopping to roll my eyes. Men and their low pain threshold.

By the time the sun has set, my body drags and screams to be taken to bed. The mental exhaustion from today finally weighs me down, my eyelids drooping with the promise of sleep. When Sorin insists on cooking our dinner, I don't protest. All I want is to sit. Or sleep. None of my traps had been fruitful, but I was able to locate a group of edible mushrooms that will stew well with some herbs from my small garden.

Sitting around the fire, neither of us has the energy to speak as we eat our dinner from wooden bowls in contented silence. Rising from the ground, I down the rest of my broth before turning to head to bed. But Sorin's words cut through me like a freshly sharpened blade.

"To many outside Valebridge," he says, low and deep, "it's difficult to tell an Enchantress from a human. You have all the same features. All the same parts." I spin on my heels to face him. My narrowed eyes meet his as he smirks, a dimple deepening the left side of his cheek. "But," he continues, "your energy is different. Powerful." I say nothing as he continues. Locked in place by the words I've dreaded to hear. *Enchantress.* "But it's your eyes," he says. "No one can mistake those eyes. Beautiful. Dangerous, even masked." Leaning back on a fallen log he crosses his legs at the ankle, relaxed by the fire like he's been here for years. I blink a few times, letting the mask I've been wearing all day fall until my golden eyes glow in the darkness. "You said before that you came here from Kirsgard Mountain, correct?"

"And what business is it of yours?" My words are curt and blunt, a defense mechanism I've become accustomed to for some time.

A small chuckle rises in his throat. "Ah, none I suppose," he says. "It's all right, you're safe with me. I won't harm a hair on your head so long as you swear not to harm any on mine." He shoots me a glance before returning his attention to the fire. I bite down on my cheek, contemplating telling him that while I am an Enchantress, I have no magick to use in the first place. "There will be no running off to King Roman with you as my bounty," he continues, snapping his gaze back to me. "You're safe." He finishes with a yawn as he stretches his arms high above his head.

Safe.

"And why's that?" I ask, taking the bait. I know King Roman has magick hunters looking for Enchantresses all across the country of Teravie, so why would he not try *himself* to collect the reward? "Seems as though you make your living in a distasteful way, why would you keep my secret?" I make my way back to the fire, the thoughts of sleep long gone. I should have trusted my gut and left him by the river. Who's to say he won't do exactly that, take me to Valebridge for a handsome bounty?

It was a matter of time before you were found.

He eyes me through the fire, the flames reflecting in his dark eyes, casting shades of yellow and orange across his tanned skin. "What if I told you, not all was lost for your kind?" He murmurs as I retake my seat. Shooting him a puzzled look, I tilt my head to the side. "The Awakening Stones survive, my lady," he whispers. "Or so rumor has it." His tone is casual and collected, but his words leave me gutted.

"That's not possible, the Stones were taken when—" I stop myself, not wanting the memory of that night to be brought up again in front of this stranger. Redirecting my gaze to the flames, my heart thumps loudly in my chest.

Sorin's gaze burns through me for a moment too long before he lets out a long sigh. "Well, rumor up the coast is that the Stones remain lost after the uprising," he says. "Or they're unable to be retrieved."

Uprising.

The word burns a hole through me as rage engulfs my every nerve. The false uprising the king has used as an excuse to lock Enchantresses up. Visions of Enchantresses being ripped from their homes invade my mind, all for the king to steal our magick. I dig my fingers into my palms.

Sorin, oblivious to my sudden spark of anger, huffs a laugh as he continues,"Interestingly enough, the rumors say the Stone's last known location was on Kirsgard Mountain...odd, isn't it?" He runs his hands through his dark hair. "That's what the rumors are anyway." He shrugs as he gently cups the back of his head, patting lightly over the wound I stitched up earlier. The slight wince that shoots across his face makes my lips turn upward.

Stoking the fire with my stick, I push an ember around until it lets small flecks of bright orange light up into the night air. Is it possible the Stones remain embedded at Nevek Peak atop the mountain? That no one could remove them? Or that no one has discovered their sacred place once all the other Enchantresses were taken or killed?

And whose fault was that?

Biting my bottom lip, my mother's voice floods my head once again as a memory is drawn to the surface.

"The year of Awakening is sacred to an Enchantress, Elora. You must take this seriously."

"Sorry, mama," I whispered, placing my hands in my lap and clasping them tight. It wasn't as if I didn't like learning, I was just so dreadfully bored.

"Now, listen. On each Enchantress's twentieth birthday,

Mother Gaia harnesses our powers from within us and makes them accessible. The Awakening Stones are part of the ritual and vital to its success, the most precious Stones known to exist." Pulling the Stones from a sealed box, my eyes lit up as the crystals flickered and glowed in my mother's hands.

"Earth, Fire, Air, Water. A Stone for each element, and an Enchantress, you my susi, *as the fifth." She smiled, before securely placing the Stones back in their box. "The Awakening magick is unique to each of us as it's specially chosen by Mother Gaia herself. Without the Ceremony, and without the Stones, an Enchantress will possess no magick."*

"What if I don't have any magick in me?"

My mother smiled again, her eyes sparkled and her onyx hair glistened in the moonlight as it crept through our window. "You are the magick, susi."

The thought sends a shiver down my spine. Shame and anger intermix as I recall my own fruitless Awakening Ceremony three years ago. How the night ended in nothing but blood with no magick at my disposal. But if the Stones were still there…I shut my eyes as I take a deep breath.

A small glimmer of hope warms my chest as the voices in my mind quiet themselves. If I can find my way back to Kirsgard, unearth the Stones, I could…I could…I pick my nail beds until they sting. What would I do with the Stones? Attempt another Ceremony? Lose the last bit of sanity I have trying to figure out why Mother Gaia skipped me?

Coward.

As quickly as the spark of hope appears, it dissipates, nothing more than a whisper in the dark. Lost in my train of thought, it takes me a moment to notice Sorin staring at me through the flames. His eyes shift from the top of my head, trailing down to my lips, then settle on the scar on my neck that peers through the top of my tunic. His eyes narrow at the sight of it and a muscle tenses in his jaw.

Tugging my tunic up to cover the raised flesh, I break the

silence and stand, letting out an exaggerated yawn. "Whether the Awakening Stones still remain or not—" I toss another stick into the fire "—I have no use for them. If you desire the Stones, by all means, enjoy your quest. But there's no use in wearing our voices out over a myth."

Turning towards the cabin, I shut down all the remnants of purpose I felt only moments ago. No, I would not return to the place that broke me, that ripped out my heart in front of my eyes, that turned every dream since into a nightmare.

"I could help you, you know." Sorin's words are barely a whisper, and yet, they ring loud in my ears, forcing me to stop halfway from the fire and my cabin. "And there are many others that would benefit from the Stones not landing in King Roman's hands. The blight across Teravie, the famines, the storms raging in the Holden Sea. The people across Copenspire, Wickersham, even Davenport have their suspicions that it's the Mother herself who is causing such catastrophe to our lands," Sorin says and my heart races in my chest. "To the people. Punishing us for the mistreatment of Enchantresses. If there's a way to take back some of that power, perhaps it would appease Her enough for the blight to stop."

"Pardon?" I ask, turning to face him. How could he propose the Mother would do such a thing? Sorin smirks as he pours a few handfuls of dirt onto the remaining embers of the fire. The smoke rises from the smothered flames, accentuating his dark features. His deep brown hair falls slightly above his eyes as he stands and takes a few strides in my direction.

"You're saying you think the reason hunting has been sparse and the storms across the seas is all because of King Roman?" I ask, disbelief thick in my voice.

He stops just a few inches shy of where I stand, glancing down at me before he speaks. "Doesn't it make sense?" he asks. "Roman has been mistreating Enchantresses for years, and the longer he continues his search for the Stones, the worse things get. Enchantresses are directly linked to the Mother, are they not?" Nodding, I cross my arms, unsure if I want to hear the rest of what he has to say. It's too overwhelming. Too unbelievable.

"So, you mean to tell me, that if there's a chance to find the Stones and bring power back into the hands of an Enchantress, you wouldn't take it?" Sorin presses on. "To not only stop Roman but to stop all this famine, the killing of innocent people due to starvation and stormy seas."

I've been so secluded here, I had no idea just how horrible things have gotten throughout Teravie. It would be a lie to say finding the Stones doesn't sound appealing. Stopping the king. Seeking revenge. *Justice*. Even more, if what Sorin is proposing is true, about Mother Gaia lashing out against us for Roman's mistreatment of Enchantresses, isn't that enough of a reason to stop him? It could also mean redemption. Redemption for what *I've* done. Redemption in the means of stopping the man who has ripped apart an entire generation of Enchantresses. But I know better than most what it is to lose, and I can't stand the thought of losing again.

"With the Stones back in the hand of an Enchantress," Sorin contines, "we could prove to Mother Gaia where our loyalties lie. With Her."

"I am no one," I admit much too quickly. "I wouldn't be much help." No, I would not be much help indeed. I was given the opportunity to gain my power, to save my mother, and it was wasted. But he doesn't know that. Doesn't know I am magickless, and because I'm a coward, I decide not to tell him. I don't need for him to have the upper hand, not yet.

"I very much doubt that, Enchantress." It's not what Sorin says, but how he says it, with such conviction, that raises the hair on my arms and neck.

Eyeing him for a moment, I try to push past the fact that he is standing so close. The warmth of his body radiates toward me so I take a step backward to rid myself of it, ignoring the scent of pine and firewood that drifts off of him.

Angling my face away from him, I fixate on a large tree near my cabin.

"Hypothetically..." When his eyes land on me, I stop and take a few more steps backward. Taking a deep breath through my nose, I let it out in a long exhale through my mouth. "Hypothetically, if the Stones still remained where I believe they could be—" I turn to face him, careful with my words to not reveal their exact location as I last saw them "—maybe I would consider finding them myself."

His smile reveals that dimple again. Forcing my gaze back toward the fire pit, I wait for his response.

"And you'd wish to do this alone?" Sorin asks. His jacket rustles as he pulls it off the rack where it's been drying for most of the day. Whipping my head back in his direction, I don't hide the frustration on my face.

"How typical of a man to believe his presence is necessary to accomplish anything at all. Is it so hard to believe? That I'd be able to accomplish such a task without you?" Heat rises to my cheeks as my mother's voice rings in my ears.

"Such a sour temper for such a beautiful girl."

She wasn't wrong about the temper part.

"Oh, I have no doubt of your abilities to do anything, love." Sorin laughs. "In fact, I'm certain you possess an arsenal of skills you have yet to divulge." With a wink and another smile, Sorin gets what he wants; a rise of my temper. Shooting him a warning look, I open my mouth to retort, but he cuts me off, slinging his jacket on and waving his hand loosely in the air. "I'm merely suggesting that if you don't go alone, the process may be faster. We all need an extra hand from time to time." Closing the distance I created between us, he invades my space again with his large frame.

Clearing my throat, I ask, "And why would you want to help? What would be in it for you?" I'm not sure if I'm asking because I'm considering this plan, or if it's more for curiosity, but I'm no fool to think he would help me find the Stones just for the sake of it. There is always something. Always a catch. A price. His eyes narrow and shift to the ground. Casually, he places both hands in the pockets of his dark pants. He gives a slight shake of his head, clearly fighting something internally. As if he's struggling to find the right words to say. The right secrets to tell.

"I've traveled the coast. I've seen the effects of the famine. Of the sailors lost at sea. And let's just say," he whispers, "there is something I seek to acquire in Valebridge. Something of value that I've sought for a long time." His gaze finally meets mine. Though, I can't read the expression on his face. "And seeing as how you're an Enchantress, I imagine you grew up there, as most Enchantresses do. So, who better to show me around?"

"You want me to help you get into Valebridge so you can... steal something?" I ask, shaking my head. "You may as well have led with that instead of all that fuss about saving people."

"Acquire," he says with a smile. "And you don't know me, so you have no reason to believe me when I say I'm truly worried about the fate of our country with Roman at the helm and the Mother pissed off. Valebridge is so heavily guarded after the uprising, it's impossible to get in without being on the king's roster." I want to correct him. Remind him that the uprising was falsified. An unjust coup to rid the Enchantresses of their freedoms. To lock them up. But before I can, Sorin continues, "Or the false uprising I should say."

"You...you know it was false?" My stomach drops at his validation. For whatever reason, hearing someone else confirm the truth lessens my burden only a little.

"Of course," he scoffs. "King Roman is a fool drunk on power. Any one with half a brain knows the Enchantresses didn't turn on him, rather, the latter." He runs a hand down his face, scratching at the dark stubble that lines his jaw. "It's a miracle you escaped."

My stomach sours at the word.

Escape.

I did anything but.

"I will help you journey to Kirsgard Mountain," he continues, pulling me from the spiral of thoughts that have begun to poke at my mind. "Help you find the Stones so we can prove to the Mother that we are on Her side, if you can agree to help me into Valebridge. There must be a way that's unguarded."

He isn't wrong. There are tunnels that lead under the castle, hidden and warded by use of magick. But the thought of returning to Valebridge, to the place where I spent the better part of my life, sends my heart into a flurry.

"I..." My words fail me as I try to speak, my fingers flex at my sides. "I...I haven't been there since... It's been a long time," I say, forcing the words out, wrapping my arms tighter around myself. "I'm sure much of it has changed." Panic creeps into my chest and up through my throat at the thought of coming face to face with anyone in Valebridge. The king, no less.

I've thought often of the Enchantresses who didn't make it out the night the king and his guards turned on us. Of the ones who were destined for an unwelcome life serving Roman against their will. Having their magick stolen from them and when there is nothing left to steal, likely their lives ending.

My concern for them while hiding safely in the forest has done nothing. Has saved no one.

Not to mention those far more affected by the famine than I've been. I knew things were shifting in the forest, more and more often food became harder to find. But I hadn't realized just how bad it's gotten in other parts of the country.

It's your duty to serve and protect the lives of those who reside in Teravie.

I may be without magick, but I am still my mother's daughter. The daughter of the late King Silas' most powerful Seer. I owe her this much.

Sorin steps toward me again, continuing this cat and mouse dance we've started. I dart my eyes to the smoke tendrils still rising in the night.

Looking past the smoke, the moon has begun its crest over the treetops casting wicked, silvery shadows on the landscape below. The usual crow sits perched on a branch of a nearby evergreen, its silhouette illuminated by the moonlight as it keeps a watchful eye over the creatures of the night.

"But you remember Valebridge, don't you?" Sorin's voice is a low rasp in my ear. My shoulders tense as the darkness tries to sweep in. Pushing against my temples, blurring my vision.

Stay here with us, the voices hiss.

Shaking my head, I tug lightly on my earlobe. "Yes," I say. Closing my eyes, images of crimson and steel flash behind them. "I remember it."

CHAPTER 6
ELORA

THE DENSE TREES ARE NEARLY SHAPELESS IN THE PALE gray light as we make our way to the river's edge the next morning. Waking before the sun, we packed as much as we could carry on our backs before setting off on foot. Before we left, I memorized the shape of my cabin, the pattern of trees near the ravine, and how the crisp morning air felt against my cheeks.

The sorrow of leaving another home washes over me. I can only hope I've made the right choice in trusting Sorin, on embarking on this quest to find the Stones. On possibly ending the blight that has affected our kingdom. Our country and home.

"Why should I trust you?" I asked last night, rubbing my arms to keep myself warm.

"I can't give you any great reasons," Sorin said from across my small camp. Shaking my head, I started heading back toward the cabin. If he couldn't give me any reason to trust him, I wasn't going to leave everything behind.

"You don't know me, and I don't know you," he said matter of factly. Pausing at the door's threshold, my fingers gripped on the wooden frame. "But I do know what has been happening to your kind for far too long," Sorin continued. "I don't know your

personal story, but I know that of many others. The pain, the injustices, the horrors. All at the hands of the bastard who calls himself king. I have seen firsthand the happenings around Valebridge. The crops that turn to dust and the fish that have up and disappeared."

He settled himself on the large tree stump by the firepit. "I can't make you trust me. But I can trust you as a show of good faith." Nothing but the noises of the forest floated between us for a moment as Sorin let his words suspend in the air. "You take the lead," he continued, "after we stop in my village, we follow your lead to the mountain. We can help each other, Elora. I don't know about you, but I think the fact we ended up in each other's company is more than just a coincidence."

I weighed the benefits of leaving the woods. The possibilities. I weighed the benefits of staying. I've lost so much, or rather, had so much stolen from me the past few years. My family. My life. All at the hands of King Roman and his thirst for power. For a magick he could never possess on his own. Maybe it's time to stop running. Stop hiding. Time to take a stand. To fight. For my mother. For myself. For any other Enchantress who has ever felt less than. For the people who are dying at the hands of an enraged deity, if what Sorin says is true.

"What do you mean, we?" I sputtered, loosening my grip on the doorframe to turn slightly and face him.

Sorin laughed quietly. "We'll need a crew of course. Think of them as an extension of myself. If you can trust me, you can trust them. We have a long way to Kirsgard, and we'll need the resources." His voice was weary, no doubt tired after today's events. "So, what do you say? Do you trust me?"

I let a few minutes of silence pass between us. "I trust you." My voice wavered, and I wasn't entirely sure if I meant what I said. At least not right now, but maybe I could. Sorin's eyes met mine through the darkness, and for a moment, he said nothing. All I could hear was the sound of my own breathing. My own heartbeat quickening.

"And I you," he said through a muffled yawn. "Now, you should get some rest, we'll be leaving before dawn." He moved to settle on the ground next to the firepit, rolling to his side, facing away from me.

Entering my cabin, I collapsed onto my bed. The weight of today crashed upon my body and mind. A heavy weight full of burden and grief pulled down on my bones. The guards. The wolves. The thief. And now the possibility of the Stones. The possibility that maybe I could help in some way. Right even just one of my many, many wrongs. Curling myself into a ball surrounded by darkness, I wept myself to sleep.

With everything I value strapped to my body, I give one final look to my cabin. My eyes prick with tears, but I quickly brush them off. Whispering a quiet thank you to the woods I leave the rest behind. I don't allow myself to linger because if I do, I will find a hundred reasons to stay. But the one reason to leave outweighs all the rest.

Hope.

"We'll make a stop in Copenspire, find some horses. That'll get us to the village by day's end tomorrow," Sorin says as he paces behind me. I made it a point earlier to lead once in the ravine to get us through as quickly as possible. Glancing over my shoulder I shoot him an amused expression.

"And by find, you mean steal?" I ask. "We made a pact to tell the truth, remember, no sense in padding what you actually mean now." I continue forward but can hear him huff a short laugh as he closes the distance behind me.

"Fair enough," he says. "Yes, we'll steal them. But trust me in this, we need them more than the guards do. They spend most of their nights in that bloody pub senselessly gambling away their coin like they have an endless supply."

The grin that spreads across my face feels unnatural, and yet, I can't stop it. "Ah, yes. The guards. That brings me to my next question," I say, stopping to take a quick drink of water from a babbling stream. "Just how many shillings did you *acquire* to warrant the chase of two royal guards through *The Ravine of No Mercy?*"

Sorin laughs again. "I'll have you know, love, I won those shillings practically fair and square."

I bark out a laugh, the unexpected noise making me jump. "Practically?"

"More or less." Sorin laughs as we trudge uphill into the densest part of the ravine. "I can't stand to see those smug pricks blowing their coin while others starve in the streets." Catching up to me now, we keep pace with each other as we crest over the hill. He continues, "I only meant to stop in Copenspire for the night. I was on my way back from a meeting with fishing merchants on the Galdosa. We work closely, the merchants and my village.

"Anyway, I got word of a lively card game happening at the local pub with several of the royal guards. Being the opportunist that I am, I couldn't shy away from a chance to line my pockets while draining theirs. The guards didn't see my hand coming, they went all in, end of story."

Nodding my head, I try to keep the smile that twitches on my lips concealed. Leading us over a large fallen pine and down the riverbank to the water's edge, I take a moment to appreciate the sunrise. Deep pinks and oranges streak the sky, casting a glow to the hillside. It won't be long before the sprites are awake, and after yesterday, I want nothing more than to avoid the nasty beings. Shuffling down the rocky hillside, we're met with a low rumbling of white rapids. The Galdosa River greets us with a shiver of cold.

"I've never understood gambling," I say between shuffles. "My friend, from back home, enjoyed it as well when we still lived in Valebridge. My mother, too, for that matter. Can't say my friend excelled at it though. He was always losing more than he could afford, but enjoyed it nonetheless." The memory brings a smile to my face. I can picture Cade pouting when he'd lost another shilling or two in a round of cards. My mother shaking her head as if there was anyone else to blame but himself. I realize I've let my smile linger when Sorin's eyes sweep over my face. Quickly changing my disposition, I point toward the path that leads directly to the river and steer us away from the hillside.

At the water's edge, Sorin stops to roll up his breeches, slinging his boots over his shoulders in an attempt to keep them dry. He takes the first step into the water, then another and another. I take a moment to look back at the ravine before heading into the water. This feels like a final goodbye, as if this journey will never lead me back here. My heart sinks with the realization. These woods have become my home. My sanctuary after so much loss. But if there is even a small chance the Stones still remain, I remind myself, I have to go. To find them and honor the Mother. To honor *my* mother.

"Are you coming?" Sorin shouts, standing a few steps in the water. I shoot him a narrowed gaze as I begin to unlace my boots. "Must you always scowl?" Sorin asks playfully, kicking at the water with one foot.

"That depends," I say, crossing my arms and joining him near the river. "Must you always speak?"

The river is crisp on my skin and the rocks are slippery beneath my feet making it a difficult trek across. Once on the other side, a crow caws in the distance. I search the skies before it flies into sight. Landing on the opposite side of the river, it perches on a piece of misshapen driftwood. Its eyes meet mine across the water for a brief moment, but long enough to have me second guessing what I see. The bird's eyes are different from any other crow I've seen, but with the great distance between us, I cannot make out the color.

A passive smile takes over my face, quickly replaced with a feeling of sorrow. This is it. No turning back. I muster all my strength before I reluctantly turn from the crow and the river. Turning from the ravine, a whisper of a howl dances along the trees. My heart races, but I pay the wolves no mind as I follow Sorin into Copenspire.

ENTERING Copenspire always feels like entering a different world, a busy contrast from the quiet of the Trinity Forest. While calm during the off seasons of Autumn and Winter, Spring and Summer has the town bustling with different shops and patrons. The Summer season is coming to an end, but the merchant ships are still docked, not yet departing on their voyage to trade the goods they've purchased. I pull my cloak's hood up and mask my eyes as we make our way in and out of the small alleys that are woven into the port city.

Coming to a stop between two stone buildings, I glance up to take in the massive structure. On the larger of the two, a thick group of ivy grows up the walls, gathering densely towards the top, skirting on either side and wrapping over the small windows. The breeze carries a hint of the ocean, mixed with the freshness of the foliage. The alley between the two buildings is still shadowed despite the sun's unforgiving glare.

"So, what's your plan exactly?" I ask, risking a glance at the opening at the end of the alley. "I don't even see any horses."

"Just wait," Sorin says as he holds a hand up toward me. Tapping my foot in equal parts impatience and anxiousness, we wait. Minutes drag until the faint chime of a church bell rings in the distance. Once, twice, three times the bell chimes a deep, low ring that echoes through the square. Like clockwork, the sound of hoofs click-clack against the cobbled stone on the street at the end of the alley. A beautiful cream mare with a golden mane comes into view in the small opening. I suck in a sharp breath as a royal guard shifts atop the horse. The hilt of his blade reflects in the sunlight, sending a bright beam of light into the shadows where we're hidden. The sudden realization of Sorin's plan crashes into me.

"You can't be serious," I whisper, cutting him an icy glare. He returns my glare with a smirk, his cheek dimpling causing my frustration to grow even further. Of course, he's serious. Turning myself, I rest my back against the wall of the larger building. "Your plan is to steal a horse from a royal guard knowing what *I* am and what they will do to me if we get caught?" I ask, fiddling with my daggers. Sorin shrugs and my eyes drift to the opening where the guard is still perched atop his horse. "What could possibly go wrong," I mumble.

Chuckling softly, Sorin positions himself to face me and places his hand on his chest. "Your doubt wounds me, love. Haven't I told you I'm an excellent thief?" Craning his neck to peer down the alley towards the guard, he takes a moment to look back at me. "Didn't I also tell you that no harm will come to you while in my company?"

Scoffing, I rest my hands on the hilts of my daggers. "You may have mentioned that a time or two," I grumble, biting down on the inside of my cheek. "Okay, thief," I say, giving him a quick nod, "time to prove what you're made of."

Without hesitation, Sorin takes off in long strides toward the exit. The guard is oblivious as he makes his approach, resting heavily atop his horse. On my toes, I follow behind Sorin, shifting my weight with each step to avoid any noise. The guard's focus remains on the bustling, busy square of the city. Locals and patrons intermix as they hastily make their way toward a looming, decaying white church at the square's center.

Keeping ourselves in the shadows but close enough to the exit to see our surroundings, I take a quick survey of the area and notice there aren't any other guards in sight. Just the one. With a town as small as Copenspire, it is no surprise they've only allotted one guard to be stationed at the square. Not to mention two others had suddenly gone *missing*. The memory of yesterday's gruesome events flash in my mind.

Turning to face Sorin, I open my mouth in question, but he stops me before I can utter a word. His fingers brush against my lips as he silently shakes his head. The warmth of his touch is almost enough to send me recoiling backward and away from him. Using the same hand that was just on my lips, he drops it lower until it lands on the hilt of my right dagger and gives it a tap. Meeting his gaze, I nod my head in understanding. He pulls the blade from its sheath and heads out of the alley.

Tracking his movements, I take a few steps backward, focusing on my breathing. I made it my mission the past three years since fleeing Kirsgard Mountain to remain in the shadows, to remain unseen. And here I am, about to steal a royal guard's horse in the middle of the day.

Sorin approaches the guard, and I brace myself for the worst, gripping the hilt of my remaining dagger, willing myself to keep it in its place until the opportune moment. I'm unable to make out the few muffled words between them, and before I can move closer to try, the guard willingly jumps off his horse. Extending his hand, he holds it out to Sorin and the two share a laugh. Confusion overtakes me as I watch the exchange unfold.

Told you not to trust him.

The voices buzz in my ear, and I all but swat at the air around me to make them stop. The guard heads straight for the alley as Sorin follows closely in his path. Swallowing deeply, I steady my hand and pull out my other blade. Holding it low to my thigh, I keep myself in place against the stone wall of the building. Was this his plan? Lead the guard straight to me without warning? So much for a great thief. Casting my eyes to the ground, I chew my cheek and wait for the guard to approach.

"'Scuse me miss, you must be the young lass that gentleman there was talkin' 'bout." Gesturing back to Sorin, with a wave of his hand the guard continues. "He says you're looking for work 'round here." The guard reeks of ale which is shocking considering it isn't even midday. Anger floods over me as I finally understand Sorin's plan. I must've let out some sort of noise because the guard laughs before continuing, "Don't worry, lass, you'll get your shillings—" Inclining my face, I unmask my eyes, letting them glow in the darkness of the alley. The navy blue of his uniform singes a hole in my chest as I take him in.

Navy and white and *crimson*.

A snowy mountain and my mother.

His eyes widen and lip curls as he reaches for me. "Filthy Enchantress," he snarls, but he isn't quick enough. Darkness encroaches my vision and before me no longer stands a man, but an enemy. Pushing myself off the wall, I grip the guard by his collar, slamming him into the opposite wall. My dagger moves swiftly, undetectable as I pin it neatly across the man's throat. Droplets of blood trickle down his skin, landing on the bear crest positioned on the center of his uniform. He gasps under my blade, so I dig it further in.

How long have I dreamt of redemption? My conscience battles with itself. *How long have I dreamt of revenge?*

Let him go.

Make him pay.

My pulse thunders in my chest, breaths short and angry. So, so angry.

Sorin's boots scuff against the cobblestone as he dashes toward us, but I don't care. My focus remains on the person before me.

Traitor.

"Elora." Sorin's voice echoes in my ears, but still my vision darkens. Nothing he says can save the man before me. Nothing he says can save *me* as I'm swept away. No longer in an alleyway, but atop a death filled mountain.

Snow falls in thick flurries, and my mother screams and screams and screams.

The guard attempts to speak, but I don't give him the chance, digging my blade deeper into his flesh.

"You will pay for what you've done," I hiss, though my

voice is not my own. Belonging to the shadowy dark that lives buried down within my soul. The monster I've kept locked up all these years feels for that break in armor, slithering out like a snake through a field.

A heavy hand on my shoulder snaps me back to the present.

Sorin's voice is steady. Calm. "Elora," he says again, and for a moment, the fog is lifted. For a moment, I'm not on a mountain fighting for my life but in an alleyway in Copenspire. The guard before me did not kill my family.

But he did not stop the others, either. He still serves the man that is responsible for the attack.

Kill him.

Spare him.

Then, the guard moves, tugging to free the sword at his side, and in that small instance, I am transported once more. To the mountain. To the night my life changed forever. All I see is red as I slit the guard's throat.

CHAPTER 7
SORIN

Blood spills from the guard's throat, coating
the stone ground and rolling toward my boots. My attempt to
pull Elora back had failed, her hands quicker than mine as she
sliced her dagger with precision and ease. Blood splattered
across her boots, her breeches. A faint ring echoes through the
alley as she drops her blade to the ground. Her eyes are frantic,
breathing uncontrollable. Recoiling from my grip she kneels
down, clutching her chest, she whispers to herself things I don't
understand.

Slowly, I approach her, crouching down, and I lay a hand
upon her shoulder as I had only moments ago. Before she killed
that man. "Elora," I whisper, squeezing her shoulder. Her
breath hitches. Spinning on my heels so that I'm in front of her,
I tip her chin up with my thumb and force her eyes up to mine.
She avoids my gaze, instead her focus narrows on the guard
slumped opposite us.

"We need to go," I whisper, sliding my hands away from
her. Reluctantly, she stands, pulling her hood up to conceal her
face. "Wait by the horse," I tell her. "I'll be out in a minute."

"What are you going to—"

"Just, go," I say. And to my relief, she does.

I wait for Elora to leave before I get to work. Salvaging what I can of the guard's uniform, placing his sword on my hip and doublet over my tunic. It will have to do. As I approach the end of the alley, Elora shifts uneasily on her feet. Her cloak remains tightly wrapped around her, despite the heat from the approaching midday. Though my plan was not much different, my heart sinks knowing she will live with the guilt of killing this man forever. Just as I have with every man I've ever killed. At my approach she whips her head towards me. The radiant glow of her golden eyes narrows in my direction leaving me unnerved.

"We have about ten minutes before—" I start to explain before she quickly cuts me off.

"Don't ever do that again," she hisses between her teeth, keeping her eyes narrowed.

"I would have never let him hurt you," I say as I move to the opposite side of the horse. I understand she's upset, the element of surprise of a royal guard was probably unfair given that she's an Enchantress. But it was the only way to get the guard away from the busy square.

My hands move quickly, untying the saddle bag to see what supplies the guard has left us with. Some bread, a half drunk bottle of ale, an empty canteen, and a few ropes. I roll my eyes and drag a hand down my face at the guards' incompetence. Can't even pack a proper bag. Closing the saddle bag, I redirect my focus to the square.

"That's not what I meant," Elora snaps. Glancing back at her, I fail to read the expression on her face. "Next time, tell me your plan," she whispers. The sharpened edge to her tone has me shifting uncomfortably in my boots. "Don't just *assume* I can't handle whatever it is you're going to do. Tell me so I'm prepared. Tell me so I don't—" Her voice waivers on the last words and I can tell it's a slip she didn't plan to make.

Shite.

I've underestimated her and whatever it is she's gone

through. My stomach roils, I should've known better but my drive to get out of Copenspire outweighed my common sense.

Stepping around the horse, she glances up at me, meeting my gaze as I tentatively place a hand atop her shoulder. "I'm sorry," I admit. And for whatever reason, I mean it. I've only just met the woman and her value to me is considerable. She is my way into Valebridge. My key to stopping Roman and this blight, if that's what we can call it. So, it's that very reason that has me willing to admit my wrongdoings.

Something I've never been good at.

"Next time, I'll tell you. I didn't realize..." I move my hand from her shoulder, suddenly unsure if touching her at this moment is the right thing to do. "I swear it, I'll tell you." I place my hand across my heart and offer her a small smile. She doesn't return the gesture; instead, she turns her head back towards the square.

"So, what's next?" she whispers, brushing her hand over her shoulder where mine had just been. "Where do we go from here?"

Taking a deep breath I gesture to the square. "We wait until the church bells chime again," I say. "Should be any minute now, and then once the villagers are dispersed, we make our break for it through the square. There's a path that will lead us up to the northern end of the Trinity Forest. We'll ride until sunset, then commence again tomorrow morning."

As I finish explaining our plan, the church bells ring out three times. Low and drawn out. On cue, people begin to flood into the streets from the church. Making their way to the various shops along the coast or back home to continue their daily routines.

"We really should go, love." I hoist myself onto the mare and extend my hand, wanting to give her time but needing her to move. Our window of opportunity is short before a second guard will come to switch rotation after the church service and every second counts. She eyes me for a moment as her brows pinch together.

"You expect us to ride all that way on one horse?" Her question is sincere, and I almost smile, but I'm sure if I do, it would just cause more hostility. Relaxing my hand to my side, I run it over the mare's silky coat.

"Well, seeing as how time is of the essence, it isn't possible to steal another horse," I say, extending my hand again, it feels heavy and awkward suspended in the air. But I don't drop it, I wait for her to decide.

Reluctantly, she places her palm in mine and heat spikes through me. Clearing my throat at the sudden warmness of her hand in mine, I pull her up and position her in front of me. Elora draws her hand away quickly, and I shake off whatever the hell feeling that just was.

Using one hand to take the reins and the other to hold her waist, I give her a quick tug backward until her body collides with my chest, that strange warmth spreading over me again. As if on cue, she casts me that signature scowl I've already come to know so well.

"For safety, love," I laugh. "Wouldn't want you falling off before our trip even gets started." With a quick wink I kick my heels into the mare and take off through the square before she can utter her argument.

Our horse gallops across the cobblestone with ease. Most of the people are already busy back at their shops or in their homes to notice a guard making his way through the square. Weaving through town, we exit by the docks at the Holden Sea. The salty breeze of the ocean brings me back to my childhood and all the supply runs I'd make with my father. But then, a shout has the hair on my arms raising and my mind snaps back to the present

"Stop that man!"

For fucks sake, I can't catch a break with these people. Elora's body tenses beneath my grip, she, too, having heard the shouts from behind us. I dare a glance, and two royal guards scramble to make their way back to their horses. So much for being subtle.

"Hold on, love," I whisper in Elora's ear, and to my surprise, she leans into my chest so I can wrap my arm around her further. Hooves against stone sound behind me and the men continue their demands, but I don't stop. Don't falter. Our mare remains steady and fast as we race through town.

The wind off the water is even more vigorous than in the square. Whipping wildly, a few pieces of Elora's blonde hair loosen from her braid, flying back into my face. Pressing my heels into our horse, we pick up speed and start the trek up the hill and into the woods of the northern Trinity Forest. The shouts from the men fade to the distance as we crest over the hillside. I steer our mare off the trail and into a dense group of pine trees, she obeys without question and to my surprise stays silent as the men catch up to us.

Elora's body tenses again as the royal guards come into view, her hand grazing mine briefly. The sensation catches me off guard, so I grip her hand and hold it tight as the guards search the surrounding area.

Slowly, they make their descent, not having a clue that we're only a few feet away, hidden by the vast trees.

Idiots.

Once I'm sure the men have made the trek back to town, we step out of the trees, our mare following my lead as though she too was trying to escape.

"Good girl," I whisper, letting go of Elora's hand to pat the horse's side. Then, we're off again, riding further north until the air turns cold and the trees more sparse.

The woods here are similar to the forests across the Galdosa River where Elora and I met. Though not quite as dense, the evergreens in these regions still grow wide and tall, jutting toward the sky as if reaching for the heavens; branches of deep green spreading vastly in all directions.

Stopping a few miles into the woods, once I'm sure no one

else has followed, we let the horse rest and drink from a nearby spring. The water trickles down off the mountainside and gathers into a small pool. My eyes catch on Elora as she strokes the horse. Her hands are gentle, but it doesn't match her face. A deep crease forms between her brows as she focuses on the horse.

"We'll rest here for a half hour, give the horse time to catch her breath. Then we'll continue our ride north," I tell her, though she doesn't bother to look in my direction. "There's a small cave a couple hours away. We'll camp there tonight and reach the village by the end of day tomorrow." Heading toward the spring, I settle down on a large rock covered with thick, spongy moss. Varying shades of green speckle the ground, and with the sun dimmed behind the curtain of trees it almost appears to be glowing.

"Will they continue to look for us?" she asks, her voice is distant and flat. Keeping her back toward me she focuses all of her attention on the horse. "Someone must have found that guard," she continues, "and the other two from yesterday will be noticed missing. Those two that followed us surely won't give up that easily." Turning to face me, she's unmasked her eyes again, the golden reflection catches my breath.

Standing from the spring, I take a few cautious steps toward her, but when I do, she takes a step backward.

"They will come looking for us," I say, keeping my voice low. "But I promise, you're safe with me. The guards in Copenspire are nothing but lazy, low-lying filth. Everything that has happened to them, has been deserved for one reason or another." I'm not sure if I'm trying to convince her or myself. I'm ashamed of the men I've killed to keep my village safe, and yet, if it came down to it, I would do it again. Maybe this makes me a dishonorable man, but I never claimed to be anything better. "You did just as I would have done," I whisper. The words are intended to be a comfort, and yet as soon as they leave my lips all I feel is ill.

Without a glance in my direction, she moves toward the spring, settling on a spongy patch of vibrant green moss. Ignoring the warring feelings inside myself, I turn to prep the horse for our journey. By this time tomorrow, we'll be riding into Loxley, and I'll finally be home.

CHAPTER 8
ELORA

THE CAVE SORIN SPOKE ABOUT YESTERDAY IS NESTLED deep in the woods, keeping us protected from the wind. Sleep eluded me most of the night, but I found myself drifting in and out, muddy images of the days prior stole the rest I so desperately needed. Faint howls echoed through the cave every so often, giving me even more unease. Though, Sorin didn't budge at the noise, and I'm beginning to believe they're in my head now too.

The ache in my skull is as sharp as a blade as we prep our horse for the final sprint to Sorin's village. The guard's face from the alley is now burned into my mind, along with the guard I killed on the river. Two more demons to join my already cursed soul. I replay the instance in the alley over and over again. How my hands betrayed me, how my *mind* betrayed me. I've never felt more scared than I was yesterday—of myself, of what I'd done.

Rubbing my temples to help soothe the constant throb, I shove down the image of the man, pocketing him with the other faces that reside in my mind, leaving him there to haunt me later.

"Water?" Sorin's voice breaks my spell as he hands me the

small canteen from the guard's pack. Greedily, I grab it from him and gulp it down. My throat is hoarse and dry and the water from the spring is so cold it burns as it slides down my throat. "Okay, then," Sorin snorts as I finish off what's left in the canteen.

"Thanks," I say, closing the cap, I make a mental reminder to refill it before we leave. Glancing down at my tunic, I make a separate reminder to wash the dried blood off my clothes. Turning my attention to Amis, I whisper hello to the horse. Of course, we don't know her given name, but Amis suits her. She nuzzles my hand in search of food as I stroke the velvety portion of her nose. Chuckling softly, I reach in my cloak pocket and fish out a small handful of salmonberries I scavenged the night before. We'd been lucky to find such a treat, but unfortunately it was all the food we were able to find and my stomach protests as I feed the last of the berries to the horse. Amis swallows them down, licking my hand for any remnants of the berry juice.

"You're welcome," I laugh and give her a final scratch behind the ear.

Breaking the silence between us, Sorin gathers the small amount of supplies we have left into the saddle bag positioned over Amis. "The ride to Loxley from here is only a couple hours, though the terrain gets pretty rough." He mounts Amis and reaches his hand down for me.

"I'm sorry, did you say Loxley?" I ask, grabbing his hand to haul myself up into the saddle. "As in the fabled village of Loxley from the schoolbooks? I wasn't sure that was even a real place. Especially considering all the stories surrounding it," I admit. Sorin lets his arm drape loosely around my waist, nothing like the firm grip he held me with the day before. Amis begins her soft trot north, taking us deeper into the woods.

Sorin's body shakes as he lets out a low, bellied laugh. "Oh yes, the unrighteous village of Loxley is very real," he says. "Full of outlaws and thieves, bastard children and adultery," he continues, chuckling softly as he steers Amis to the left, taking her up a narrow rocky path. "Well," he says softly, his laughter dissipating, "the schoolbooks are only partly true."

I tighten my grip around the pommel of the saddle as the incline steepens. "I have a hard time believing Loxley is as real as you say." I laugh nervously, surely sounding naive. As we breach the top of the hill, I unclench my shoulders and readjust in the seat. Peering to my right, the cliff face is jagged and rocky, leading down to the crashing white waves of an endless sea. Without thought, I lean back against Sorin. The height of the fall has my instincts begging to put as much distance between myself and the edge as possible. His arm tightens around my middle, and I stare at the engulfing waves crashing upon the shore below. Before we linger too long on the cliffside, Sorin pulls the reins and leads us back into the safety of the forest.

"Loxley is indeed real," Sorin says, "but it's only spun in half truths. Yes, Loxley has remained hidden from the rest of the kingdom for quite some time, the elders have done a great job of that. We're a village built on stubborn independence and diligent hard work." The crunch of Amis' hooves turns to a soft thud as the forest floor changes from rocky and rough to mossy and soft.

"As for the debauchery," he starts again, "it's mostly a myth. Loxley is made up of outcasts, sure. People Valebridge didn't have use for, or people who didn't have use for Valebridge but couldn't quite find their place elsewhere. Who wanted to live life freely. Openly. Without the strict guidelines of the king looming over their every move." I chew on his words but don't press any more questions.

"Growing up in Valebridge we were taught in school to fear the outliers," I admit. "That the mythical village of Loxley was nothing more than a breeding ground for the ruthless." Sorin laughs, but my mind flashes to yesterday, to the alley with that man. It sounds as though I'd be more suited with the fabled Loxley anyhow.

"And what of the Jade Guild?" I ask, adjusting in the saddle.

I've never been one to sit still for long. "Is it not in their jurisdiction? Surely they'd know of Loxley."

"Lord Thaddeus is an old man." Sorin sighs. "He knows of Loxley's existence but I'll be damned if he ever finds us." Sorin's grip tightens on the reins, his body shifting behind me like he's suddenly uncomfortable. "If I'm being honest, I'm quite disappointed by his lack of involvement since Roman took over. People this far north have suffered greatly the last few years with the blight and he's done nothing to stop it."

"You personally know Lord Thaddeus of the Jade Guild?" I ask, truly puzzled why a thief from a fabled village would know such a man of power. Though, with the recent rumors of the lord's solitude, I'm not sure how much power he truly holds anymore.

Sorin shrugs behind me. "We've been acquainted," he says. "My father was a well known man."

Was.

"If there was someone to know in the Trinity Forest," Sorin continues, "he knew them, and he made sure his children knew them as well. Family responsibilities to uphold and all that."

"And the other Guilds?" I ask, my mind wandering to a distant memory, a meeting of my own. "Do you know any of them? Do they also believe Mother Gaia is responsible for the famines?" It would make sense, I suppose. I knew the Jade Guild had been locked up, but being so far removed from the rest of the kingdom I haven't thought of the others.

"Can't say that I do," Sorin says. "Though, with their lack of response to Roman's new rules in Valebridge, I'm not sure I want to know them anyway."

Warmth blooms in my chest for our shared disdain for the corrupt king.

"What about you?" he asks, his arm sliding around my middle. Ignoring the feeling it sends to my stomach, I focus on the trees as we pass them by. "Did you meet any of the Guild members when you lived in Valebridge?"

The only time I've ever met a member of the Guilds, it was the start of the rainy season and the annual meeting of the Guilds for the first full moon of Autumn had just begun. My mother had been dressed in her finest dress of blue silk, various gems and stones adorning her waist and sleeves. Being the curious child that I was, I snuck out of my chamber to seek her out but before I could make it very far, I was stopped by a man I didn't recognize.

He was tall, much taller than the late King Silas if I remember correctly, donning black from head down to his polished boots. I recall his voice vividly as he bent down where I crouched low near the spiral marble staircase. Deep. Dark.

"Hello little one," he'd whispered, his voice rough around the edges. As if he'd spent his whole life screaming. *"What do you seek from hiding in the shadows?"*

"No," I lie, coming back to the present, my mind shutting down the memory completely. "They were always so secretive with their meetings. I wasn't allowed out of my chamber when they visited Valebridge."

Sorin grunts behind me. "Sounds about right," he grumbles. "None of the four Guilds have voiced their concerns for the blight. I imagine the other three have locked up their keeps just as Lord Thaddeus has. Protecting only those closest to them. Cowards." Sorin snarls at the last word.

If Sorin is right, that means the Guilds have also not been attending and celebrating the Autumn moon within Valebridge. Their apparent distaste for the new king could work in our favor when we take back the Stones.

While the Jade Guild is nestled within the heart of the Trinity Forest, the Cerulean Guild resides off the coast of the Holden Sea. The Bloodstone Guild, the southernmost Guild located within the Montrock caves, is rarely visited and I'm not quite sure how we'd even get a message to them. But the Onyx Guild, which is deep within the Kirsgard Mountain range, is the closest to Valebridge. And potentially our best bet at an ally if the need for it arises.

WE RIDE in silence for the next several miles, the only sound aside from the caw of the crows is Amis' occasional huff of air through her nose.

"Tell me something about yourself, Enchantress," Sorin blurts out, making me flinch in the saddle. "Anything," he says again, sounding desperate. Taken aback by the sudden request I turn my head and peer at him over my shoulder. "I hate silence, if you couldn't tell," he says through a smile.

"It's certainly not a surprise," I say flatly. "What do you want to know?"

"Well," he says, "what brought you to the Trinity Forest?" Steering Amis to the left, we pass a small green pond filled to the brim with toadstools. The deep croaks of the toads ring in my ears, and I squint my eyes against the radiant reflection of the sun, hoping to steal a glimpse of the animals. I'm unsuccessful as Amis breezes past it.

"Couldn't pick an easier question?" I ask, gritting my teeth. Amis picks up her pace again leading us over another steep hill. Sorin chuckles, wrapping his arm tighter around me to compensate for the incline.

"You've just piqued my curiosity, love. An Enchantress alone in the densest part of the Trinity Forest, curious is all." His voice is light, all the tension from this morning's conversation about the Guilds has melted away.

"All right." I let out a deep sigh and readjust in the saddle again, shifting my weight to try and get more comfortable. "The short story is that when Roman took the throne, a few of us escaped Valebridge. We fled to the Kirsgard Mountains. For whatever reason, my mother knew we'd be safe there. We managed to stay hidden until—" I cut myself short. Bracing my chest with my free hand and slamming my eyes shut, I focus on steadying my breathing. The panic that tightens across my chest spreads like wildfire.

Inhale. Exhale. Inhale. Exhale.

I'm not sure if it's intentional or because we're cresting over the steepest part of the hill, but Sorin's grip tightens around me even further, his palm grasping over the back of my hand. His hands are calloused yet warm. Strong yet gentle. His sudden touch snaps my eyes open, and I briefly look down at where our hands connect. That sting of heat leaves an invisible mark against my skin. Shrugging his hand off, I continue, "We managed to stay hidden until we didn't." Not giving any more indication as to what happened that night. He doesn't need to know everything.

Not yet.

"We lived there for a couple of years, a handful of Enchantresses and a few others. We thought we'd found peace in the mountains. Far enough from Valebridge, warded enough from Roman." My instinct is to stop. To not divulge any more secrets, because after all, I don't even know this man. But once I begin, I can't stop. The words on my tongue fall out quicker than my mind can decide this is a bad idea. "We made a mistake," I admit.

You *made a mistake*, the voices hiss.

My cheek begins to sore from chewing the last few days, but I press on anyway. "I'm the only one who made it off the mountain." My voice cracks at the admission. I risk a quick glance back at Sorin, but his face is neutral, eyes locked on the path ahead.

"I made my way to Copenspire." I decide to keep going, despite the gnawing feeling in my stomach to silence myself. "Gathered supplies and kept to the woods. Being alone has always been something I crave, anyway." His eyes snap to mine, and for a moment, his features soften, like he can relate to the sentiment. Though, nothing about Sorin strikes me as the kind of person who prefers solitude.

"And the wolves?" he asks, pulling Amis to a sudden halt. "How many times have you run them off?" His question is direct but not unkind. Still, I can't help the irritation it makes me feel.

Scoffing, I tug his arm off me. "I've never seen the wolves before that day," I admit, even if it's not entirely true. The day, two summers ago, when I *had* indeed seen them is still bright in my mind. "What are you implying?" So much for casual conversation.

Sorin's lips turn up as he dismounts Amis, offering a hand to help me down which I decline by crossing my arms. Sighing, he sticks his hands in his pockets. "I'm implying nothing, Enchantress." His voice is tired, and I'm beginning to wonder if he, too, didn't sleep well. "The wolves in the southern part of the Trinity Forest are notorious for being ferocious predators. I mean just look at the guards." He shrugs, and I'm reminded he didn't witness me killing one of the men. He must think the wolves killed them both. What would he think if he knew? We've only known each other a few short days, and in those days I've ended not one, but two lives.

Monster.

He takes a hand from his pocket to run it through his dark hair. "And the fact that you survived all that time without a single run in," he continues. "Impressive is all. I am *wildly* fascinated by you, Enchantress."

I roll my eyes, and remain seated atop the horse. "Your turn," I say. "Tell me something."

"All right," he says, stretching his arms above his head. My eyes snag on his arm again. Deep circular, swirls of black, somehow all connected and yet complete shapes on their own, are permanently inked on his skin.

. . .

"What does the mark on your arm mean?" I ask, craning my neck to get a better look as he stretches.

Sorin pauses, absently running a hand over his inked forearm. His expression darkens for a brief moment before brushing it off. "Ah this? A brash decision. Nothing more than teenage regret." He laughs. "I'm sure you understand."

I don't.

"My turn again," he says, offering his hand to me again. This time I accept it. My boots sink into the moist soil as I hop down from Amis. My legs ache from riding, but I don't mind. Pain has never been a stranger, rather an anchor.

"Ask away, thief," I say, mimicking his movements, stretching my arms over my head. Admittedly, it feels good to be out of the saddle.

"Your favorite color?" Sorin asks in the most serious tone I've heard him use yet. As much as I don't wish to, I can't help but laugh at the severity in his voice.

"Are we children?" I manage through a laugh, placing my hands on my hips and twisting my body. Hoping to stretch out any knots formed in my back.

"Most certainly not," Sorin's words are playful. Dangerous. I meet his eyes, swallowing down the unwanted feeling swirling in my stomach. "But I'm afraid if I ask anything personal again," he continues, "you'll have my head."

Good point.

I cease stretching to consider my answer. Had I ever thought about my favorite color? Maybe it's not a favorite, but the only one that matters.

"Black," I finally say.

"Black?" He laughs.

"Yes."

"Interesting."

"Is it?" I laugh again at how absurd our conversation has gotten. How one moment we're discussing my past and the next we're bickering over a color.

"Sure," Sorin says, taking a sip from the canteen. "I don't think I've heard anyone say their favorite color is black of all things."

"That is because everyone is so afraid of the dark." I smirk, grabbing the canteen from him and taking a deep gulp. "The unknown. The inability to see what's right in front of you." I wipe my mouth with the fabric of my cloak. "I find comfort in it. The deepness of it." I brave a glance in his direction, to the dimple on the left side of his cheek.

"Fascinating," he whispers.

DUSK HAS SETTLED as we reach a small clearing in the woods. The expanse of the trees becomes less dense, leaving room for small patches of moss and beautiful rich ferns to cover the ground. White birch trees line the clearing, their stark trunks an amazing contrast against the darkening sky.

My ears buzz with the faint hum of music. I frantically scan the woods for the source. Through the small line of birch trees, whimsical voices singing words I can't decipher carry through the forest. The softness of a flute floats through the air, the beautiful melody washing over my senses. As Amis steps closer to the line of birch trees, panic begins to settle in my chest as the noises become clearer, but the image of a darkening forest is all I can make out. *Where is the music coming from? Is it in my head?*

Sorin leads Amis by foot but halts her with a quick tug of the reins. "Through here," Sorin says, gesturing to a thicket of bushes nestled between two tall, skinny birch trees. The bush is covered in tiny green leaves with jagged edges, small red berries adorn each leaf.

Glancing between him and the thicket, I'm wondering what exactly I am supposed to be looking at. I shoot him a puzzled look, keeping my place atop Amis. Reading my mind, Sorin laughs as he pushes apart the thorny bush, creating a small tunnel. As he does, the music I thought I heard earlier grows louder.

"In we go," Sorin says casually as he gestures again to the thorny bush.

Hopping down from the mare, I give her a pat on the nose before heading toward the bush. "And what about Amis?" I ask, glancing over my shoulder to the horse.

"I'll send someone for her," Sorin says as he drops the branches of the bush, diluting the music on the opposite side. "She'll be safe here for now."

Taking her reins, he loops them loosely around a nearby birch tree. She happily bends down and begins grazing the ground for food. Walking back toward the thicket, Sorin parts the dense and prickly leaves again. "Are you coming?" he asks, holding out his hand. With a bit of reluctance, I reach out and intertwine my hand with his as we climb through.

Entering the thorny bramble feels similar to submerging into a pool of water. My vision clouds and ears become plugged as the pressure from the lack of oxygen pushes down against us. The music from before becomes briefly muddled as I fall through the other side of the bush. Then, in a tidal wave of noise, the sounds become clear and rich. Visions of orange flames from a fire flick through the air, and dull shapes of stone houses linger in the distance.

Rubbing a hand over my eyes, I attempt to make sense of what just happened. Clarity slams into me as I take in my new surroundings, hidden in plain sight. The village must be warded using magick. *Magick.* As if sensing my disbelief, Sorin dips his chin to my ear, sending a shiver down my spine as he whispers, "Welcome to Loxley."

CHAPTER 9
ELORA

WHAT LIES BEFORE ME IS MIND FALTERING. THE difference between this village and the one I was warned against all those years ago in Valebridge is astonishing. Women and children laughing and playing together. Men singing while strumming away on their instruments. A few dogs lay near the fire, music and laughter lulling them to sleep. So different from the outcasts and debauchery I'd been warned about.

Warm air coats my skin as the thrum of magick bounces off the trees inside the warded village. Meeting Sorin's stare, my eyes flicker in the darkness. I don't bother masking them. For the first time in a long time, I truly feel safe. I'm not sure if it's the sweet sounding music or knowing magick breathes here, but my lips begin to curve into a smile.

Heading toward the fire, I tense my shoulders as I wait for a sense of nervousness to wash over me. It's been years since I've been around so many people at once. Even on Kirsgard Mountain, our group was no more than a handful. Much to my surprise, the dread and nerves never surface. Instead, I'm met with a sense of calm. Contentment. Even a bit of excitement.

Sorin takes a slight turn and leads us to a small stable, lit dimly by a lantern anchored to the outer wall. He quickly discards the guard's sword and pulls on a cloak that's hanging in one of the stalls, concealing the bloodied uniform he still wears from days before. Stepping away for a moment, he leans around a wall, whispering to someone I can't see. But quickly, a boy rushes out from behind a stall—he can't be older than fifteen years, his hair a shaggy mess of blonde curls. Stopping briefly, he bends in a quick bow. Unsure what to do with myself, I attempt a curtsey, nearly tripping over my own feet. The movement feels awkward and foreign, despite growing up in a place that required such things.

"Thank you, Jacobi," Sorin says, dismissing the boy. "Amis," Sorin whispers, reading my question before I can ask it. Relief spills over me knowing she won't be left alone for long.

With Sorin more appropriately dressed, we head back toward the village, but my eyes catch on the people circled around the small fire. "They're not usually this rambunctious," Sorin laughs, noticing my gaze. "With the full moon approaching, sometimes they let their guard down." I dart my eyes up at him and am surprised to see how his face has softened upon our arrival. The smugness he's worn the last two days has morphed into something resembling contentment.

"I know what you're thinking and yes," he says, pausing his steps. "Even people no longer associated with Valebridge celebrate Mother Gaia and the full moons." While I'm ashamed to admit it, I've let the last three years worth of full moons go to waste, wallowing in self pity and grief. The idea of celebrating Her in the coming week sends a plume of anticipation through me.

"Well," I say, rolling my shoulders, attempting to unleash a bit of stress I've been carrying. "Is it too late for us to join them?"

Sorin's eyes widen as his brows jump to his hairline. "Are you sure?" he asks. "After yesterday, I thought you'd appreciate a moment alone. With all that's happened..." he trails off, letting his final words turn to a question.

While being alone *does* sound refreshing, I can't help but stare at the joyous people around the fire. Their laughter and singing sparks a remnant of hope in my chest. After that night on the mountain, I vowed to myself I'd live alone until my days ran out, or I ended them myself. More vicious words and thoughts begin to form in my mind, so I bite my bottom lip to distract myself. Glancing back to the people around the fire, I force a small smile.

"I'm sure."

CIRCLED around the fire are a few of the village elders. Eviey, Letty, and Agnes. Sorin introduces me to Eviey and Letty first, each of the women takes my hand in their palms as we meet. The warmth of their touch is like a sip of mulled wine. Familiar and comforting. So much so that I fight against pulling them in closer for a hug, but I keep my wits about me and draw back after our introduction.

"Eviey and Letty are twin sisters, if you can't tell, and the resident forest witches and healers of Loxley," Sorin explains. My smile widens as the two take their seats by the fire. I've never met a witch before. While witches and Enchantresses both possess certain magick from the Mother, they're also different in many ways. Witches are not born into their magick as Enchantresses are. They are born human and from practice and servitude gain simple magick. Their magick comes in the form of potions, healing, possibly a simple spell, like warding a village such as Loxley. It's not to say they can't be powerful, there is always a darker side to any otherworldly gift. But I detect none of that in their presence.

Both sisters wear their long, silver, hair in loose braids, several strands hanging freely around their faces. The only real difference I can spot between the two is that Eviey wears thin rimmed wire glasses, and Letty does not. Their wrinkles are deep against their sun-kissed skin, accentuated by the flickers of firelight and smiles adorned on their faces.

"So good to have you here, Elora." Eviey says, face beaming through the flames.

When I'm introduced to Agnes, the warmth and comfort I felt from Letty and Eviey settles and my nerves get the best of me. Unease brews in my stomach as we approach her. While all three of the women are elderly, Agnes wears much deeper lines around her eyes and face, showing she is the most mature. Her eyes, while dark in color, have flecks of honey brown that make them sparkle in the firelight.

Agnes' deep brown skin accentuates her silvery white hair that hits just below her ears, the tightly coiled curls springing in all directions. She wears a multilayered patchwork dress, different shades of green and blue billow down to the ground, accompanied by a green scarf draped loosely around her shoulders.

When she stands to shake my hand, the gold bangles lining either wrist clink together making music of their own. I am not a tall woman, but Agnes barely reaches my shoulder. Though her frame is petite, her hips are full, as well as her cheeks, softening an otherwise hardened face. I focus on her eyes. They give away the unrelenting strength she exudes. Sharp and alert despite the lines surrounding them, I have no doubts that she is the powerful village leader Sorin has told me about.

"Elora, welcome to Loxley." She grips both my hands in hers. A faint whiff of peppermint hits me as she speaks. The yearning to linger in the embrace of the witches is absent as I shake hands with Agnes, and I find myself withdrawing a little too quickly. I flash her a quick smile to make up for my abrupt release.

"I hope my son remembered his manners on your journey," Agnes says. "Whatever it is that brought you here, we're glad to have you." She peers into my eyes with a fierceness so deep I begin to worry she can see the demons that lurk beneath. After what feels like an eternity, she breaks our gaze and turns her attention to Sorin. Bending down before her, he places a quick kiss on her cheek.

I can't help but stare at the two of them side by side. Sorin stands easily a foot taller than her, and they bear no resemblances.

"Son? You're Sorin's...mother?" I regret the words as soon as they leave my lips. Scrambling, I try to correct myself as Agnes turns to look at me, narrowing her eyes slightly at my impulsive outburst. "Apologies," I say with haste. "I didn't mean to be rude. I just... it's just that..." Snapping my mouth shut, I clench my fists together at my sides.

You're an idiot.

Agnes' laugh bellows off the trees as she throws her head up to the sky. "My child," she chirps between laughter, "I like you already."

Turning from Sorin, she heads back in my direction. It's only then that I notice a slight limp in her walk. Pulling my hand as she passes by, she leads us to a few open tree stumps being used as seats around the fire. I dare a glance back at Sorin who meets me with a smile. The stubble that lines his jaw is much more profound since we met several days ago, and I'm not entirely sure why I've noticed such a detail.

"Unfortunately, no," Agnes says as she settles onto the tree stump. "Sorin is not my son by birthright." Eviey ushers over to offer her a thick, gray wool blanket, gently placing it across her legs. She muffles a quiet thank you before she continues, "Sorin's mother was a dear friend, she came to live with us in Loxley when Sorin was a small boy, maybe just barely four? Or was it five? I can't remember to be honest. The two of us, Celia and I, became good friends." Her eyes lose focus at the memory, her smile fades and morphs into something more somber.

Agnes shakes off whatever memory haunts her and glances at me. "She came to us in a moment of desperation. She must have known she'd find solace here, in Loxley. She brought so much to our village. Possessing a certain joy that was infectious, an appetite for life we could all admire," she pauses and glances around the fire at the fellow villagers. I follow her gaze. Everyone around the fire nods slowly and I get the impression there is more to the story than they are letting on. Something deeper rooted, but I won't press it. Not now, not tonight, when they've already dredged up this painful past for my sake.

I hold back from shooting Sorin another glance, itching to read his face, but I refrain. I want to let him know he isn't alone in this loss. That in all the ways we are not alike, this is one thing we share. But the words don't come. They are left frozen on my tongue, like bits of ice so cold they burn. Swallowing hard against the knot forming in my throat, I keep my attention locked on Agnes as she continues her story.

"When Celia arrived in Loxley, she was already ill. It was barely a year later that she passed. Eviey and Letty did their best to help her." Agnes glances in the direction of the sisters. "Unfortunately, it was beyond their abilities. The Fates had made up their minds and there was nothing any of us could do to stop it.

"Before she passed, she asked me to look after her boy. Raise him as my own." She lets out a soft chuckle then. "As if it was any question that wasn't my plan already." At that she looks over to Sorin, a smile returning to her face. Her eyes shift and fill with love and pride for this son she's inherited. He dips his head into a bow as a small smile creeps across his face. Though he wears a smile, his eyes tell a different story. My heart constricts at their obvious love for each other, and for the sorrow that haunts me for a mother I miss so dearly.

"I'm so sorry." Is all I'm able to mutter. I place my hand atop Agnes' but my eyes remain on Sorin. He dips his chin again but says nothing. Agnes pats my hand, giving it a tight squeeze before I move it back to my lap.

"Well," she says with a deep sigh. "I imagine the two of you are worn out from your journey. You came all the way from Copenspire, I assume?" She looks between Sorin and I. Her tone is questioning, prodding. Opening my mouth to explain, I'm quickly cut off by Sorin.

"You're right, as usual," he says, standing from his kneeling position and stretching his arms high above his head. "I'm exhausted." Shooting me a glance with eyebrows slightly raised he adds, "I think we'll turn in for the night." Walking over, Sorin stops and plants a kiss atop Agnes' head.

"I'm glad you're home, son." She turns her focus on me and gestures toward the line of stone cottages behind us. "Show Elora to the main house. There are extra clothes in Samaria's room she can borrow, as well as an extra bed until she returns."

"Ah, speaking of my dear sister," Sorin says as he reaches for my hand and pulls me from my seat. "Where is she and the usual lot?" A fluttering sensation invades the pit of my stomach as his calloused hand wraps around mine. That now familiar spark from his touch shoots up my arm. Not wanting to feed this growing feeling, I quickly withdraw my hand, fighting the urge to wipe it against my breeches to get the heat of his touch to cool.

"Hunting trip," Agnes says. Her eyes crinkle as she smiles at us before returning her face to the fire. "Let us hope this one is more fruitful than the last," she whispers. "They're expected back in a week for the full moon. Now don't let us keep you two."

She shoos us away with a gesture of her hands. Peering back at her over my shoulder, she sings lightly into the flames, "Sleep well, Enchantress."

CHAPTER 10

ELORA

Sorin guides me through the village. Small stone cottages line either side of the street, mossy roofs glow a deep green in the moonlight. Puffs of smoke from different chimneys float into the night sky but dissipate completely as they drift to the top of the ward that keeps the village hidden. Most of the cottages are dark inside, but a few have candles flickering in the windows, illuminating cozy kitchens and warm bedrooms.

We walk in comfortable silence as the faint sounds of music from the villagers whispers along in the night breeze. The air is starting to chill so I wrap my arms around myself to preserve heat.

"I truly am sorry about your mother," I find the courage to say. Sorin, keeping pace next to me with his hands tucked into his pockets, glances in my direction but doesn't stop walking.

"I appreciate it," he says, "but it was a long time ago. She was sick and suffering...all I can hope now is she's found peace in the afterlife." I rub my hands against my arms to warm them up and debate continuing this conversation. I'm not sure why I suddenly feel so cold, it's as if my cloak has evaporated entirely. Then, the warmth of something heavy drapes around my shoulders, as Sorin places his cloak over me. Startled, I glance up at him, halting my steps momentarily.

"Thank you," I say, not sure why it comes out closer to a whisper. He smiles and my stomach warms at his small gesture. Now would be the time to say something about how I understand his pain of losing his mother. How, no matter how hard you try, the hurt never really goes away. But, as usual, I say nothing for fear of showing my hand too early. For fear of showing any sign of weakness.

Coward, the voices hiss.

Perhaps.

When we reach the end of the dirt street, a larger home sits perched atop a small hill. Its bones consist of wooden logs, instead of stone like the other smaller cottages. The gaps in the logs are filled with dark moss and dried mud. A large, crooked stone smokestack puffs out gray whirls and the roof is covered in thick moss much like the rest of the homes we passed.

Leading me up the set of stairs, Sorin opens the tall wood door. Its weathered blue paint reveals chips of the natural dark wood underneath and it gives way with an ancient creak. Peppermint and pine greet me as we enter the dark foyer. It takes a moment for my eyes to adjust, the only light in the entirety of the home is a warm flicker from the hearth softly illuminating the narrow hallway.

As if hearing my thoughts, Sorin steps down the hall. His boots are loud against the grainy wood floors, but he returns quickly with a brass candelabra lit with three white pillars.

"Sam's room is just here, to your right." He points to a small archway and steps around me. I follow his lead into a neatly kept room. It's simple but comfortable. A wooden bedframe fills up most of the space, accompanied by a small faded red chest at the foot of it, closed tightly with a rusted clasp.

Next to the bed is a small shelf overly stacked with several books piled high on top of each other. The spines are cracked and the lettering worn, but I catch myself close to drooling at the sight of them. In Valebridge, reading was one of the few indulgences I often enjoyed as a child, and one that I haven't had the pleasure of in years.

"You're sure she won't mind?" I ask, creeping farther into the room. Peeling my eyes from the books, not wanting to disturb the peacefulness of the space but desperately wanting to lay down.

Sorin chuckles. "Hardly. If anything, she'd be upset that we didn't offer it up." He places the candelabra on top of the stacked books, which offers a little more light to the space. "Sam's a force to be reckoned with," he continues, moving himself to the foot of the bed. Kneeling down he opens the chest and pulls out an ivory nightgown. "Strong willed and slightly feral when it comes to those she loves," he says with a laugh, "but then again aren't we all." Still bent down, hands leaning against the wooden chest for support, he adds, "She's more decent than I could ever hope to be."

"Here." He straightens and hands over the nightdress. "You're about the same size. If you need anything, I'm just across the way," he says, gesturing out the door. I crane my head to see another archway across the hall directly adjacent to this one, no doubt leading to his room.

"You live here too?" I ask. "With your mother?"

Sorin's deep laugh makes my stomach coil into a thousand tiny knots. "Yes," he says, sticking his hands in his pockets, leaning heavily against the door frame. "But to be fair, I'm not home much."

"Where is it that you're always running off to?" I resist the urge to collapse onto the bed and fall straight to sleep.

"Copenspire, Wickersham, Davenport...anywhere there are trades being done with Valebridge merchants," he says, pushing himself off the doorframe.

"Well, thank you," I say, gesturing to the nightgown. The

fabric is soft, almost silky as I slip it between my fingers. Maybe it would be good to change out of these soiled clothes after all.

With a quick nod, he takes a few steps out into the hall but stops before he gets to his room. "Bread and apples are in the kitchen, down the hall and to the left. Help yourself." Without so much as a glance back to me, he enters his room and clicks the door shut.

To my surprise, sleep comes easily. Falling almost instantly into a deep slumber as my head hits the pillow.

THE CLANGING of metal pots and promising smells pull me from a comfortable sleep the next morning. Stretching out my limbs, I indulge in the softness of the quilt above me and buttery sheets beneath me. As much as I tried to mimic these same comforts in the forest, nothing could quite compare to this. I fold the nightgown neatly before placing it back on the bed and return to my dirty breeches and tunic. Quickly plaiting my hair into a messy braid, I head toward the sounds and smells of the kitchen.

Down the hallway, large windows adorn the outer wall of the house. I easily count six rectangular, glass shapes and am certain there are more on the sides of the room that I can't see. Warm orange sunlight spills through the glass, casting a glow to everything residing in the room. Though I walk on my toes, the wide planked floors creak beneath my bare feet as I inch toward the heart of the home.

At the end of the hallway, the house splits in two. On the left, there's the kitchen. It has a tall, long wooden table that runs almost the length of the room. Atop it sits several loaves of freshly baked bread in a dark woven basket and a bowl of fruit that appears to have been thoroughly picked over. My stomach rumbles in response to the delightful aromas, a reminder I haven't eaten since yesterday morning.

The clanging of pots I heard earlier are replaced by the sounds of the crackling fire from the stone hearth. I scan the rest of the room to find it also empty. To the right of the kitchen are the living quarters. A round, worn rug with varying spirals of faded red and blue takes up most of the floor space. Centered on the wall is a large tapestry woven with wildflowers and sticks. The loudness of the artwork, so out of place with the rest of the house's simple elegance. A few wooden chairs circle around a quaint table near the windows in the living quarters, the top stained with rings of brown. I smile at the circular tea stains, a testament that this table has heard many tales, many secrets.

Through the windows, nothing but bright sunshine and beautiful green trees span for miles. My hands twitch at the sight of the dense trees, a longing to be back in the woods.

"Good morning, Enchantress." Agnes' voice is soft and sweet as she makes her way into the kitchen. My heart skips a beat not only at her entrance, but because it's been so long since I've been addressed as an Enchantress. So long since I've been comfortable enough to keep my eyes their natural color. I smile, masking my nerves instead of my eyes as she joins me at the kitchen table. Normally I would scold myself for being caught off guard, but since I'm a guest in this house, I let it go.

Agnes wears a long brown apron covered in flour over a pale blue dress that's cut short at the sleeves. Delicate gold bangles from the night before still adorn each wrist, clanking lightly as she sways into the space. In the daylight, I can make out her features much clearer, the radiance in her honeyed eyes is fierce as I position myself across from her at the long table.

As she reaches for a loaf of bread, my eyes catch on her knuckles, each one marked with an intricate symbol. The ink is dark, much like that of Sorin's arm. She moves quickly, slicing the bread so I'm unable to make out what any of them are, and before I can ask, she catches my eye and casts me a smirk. Though they are not blood-related, I can see immediately where Sorin gets his signature look.

"They're for protection," she says, noticing my gaze. She sets down her knife and stretches her fingers. "An old legend, really. I've had them since I was a young girl. My mother swore they would keep me safe, so she had them etched into my skin. I'm not sure how much I believe in it now, but one can never be too careful, I suppose." She winks before returning to her work. Looking down at my own hands, I grimace at the dirt stains across my knuckles and under my fingernails.

"Is there somewhere I can wash up?" I don't know why I'm nervous to ask, maybe because Agnes' energy fills the room to the brim, it leaves little space for much else.

She gestures to a small room off the back of the kitchen. Inside of it houses a small bowl and pitcher with a cube of honey scented soap. I scrub at my hands until they are red and raw, then move on to my face and cheeks, making sure to cover every spot. The water from the pitcher is cold and refreshing as I splash it on my face and coat my hands. Most of the dirt from my hands has been freed, but I imagine how much more is lodged in my hair. A problem to deal with another time, I decide, heading back toward the kitchen.

"Smells wonderful," I say, motioning to the bread. Agnes shoots me a full smile, placing the slices of bread in a cloth before nestling it into a woven basket. Her lips are stained a deep berry which only accentuates the whiteness of her teeth.

Gesturing to one of the wooden chairs near the window she says, "Sit. I'll bring you some breakfast." I don't dare argue as I make my way to the table and plop myself down into one of the chairs, basking in the warmth of the sunlight through the glass. I'm unsure what to do with my hands, nerves of being in a foreign place pitting in my stomach. So, I cross them lightly in my lap to keep from fidgeting and hope the vibrant greens of the trees and yellow light of the sun will settle the panic that always lingers just beneath my skin.

"I appreciate your generosity," I say, drawing my eyes toward the kitchen. "Please know I'll repay you in any way I can." Agnes drifts over to the small table, the hem of her dress skims the hardwood floors creating a soft whooshing sound. Scoffing, she sets down a worn, silver plate and mug of hot tea in front of me before turning back toward the kitchen.

"Nonsense, child," she speaks over her shoulder as she busies herself with the rest of her morning chores. Dusting remnants of flour off of her apron, she says, "Any friend of Sorin's is a friend of mine. Let alone an Enchantress. Offering you what little we have is the least we can do." Distracted by the warm bread with apple butter staring up at me from the plate, I almost miss what Agnes says. *Friend*? Is that what Sorin and I are? Friends?

I'm unsure if it's the peppermint tea Agnes handed me or the thought of having a friend, but my stomach fills with warmth as I finally allow myself to bite into the bread. Still warm from the hearth, the apple butter creates sweet notes that dance along my tongue. I try to pace myself, but it's been years since I've had anything this delicious and I end up devouring it within three bites. Washing it down with a few gulps of the tea, I fail to notice Agnes staring at me from the kitchen.

"Delicious. Thank you." I smile, trying to hide my embarrassment. Inhaling my breakfast was likely not considered ladylike. I wipe a few droplets of tea off my mouth with the sleeve of my shirt, debating if I'm courageous enough to ask for seconds.

Silently, Agnes nods her head, her eyes still scouring over me. There is something in her stare that turns my stomach, and I fear I'll lose the breakfast I just ate if she looks at me like that much longer. Like she can tell my darkest secrets, see me for what I really am. What I've done.

Murderer.

Shifting against the hard wood of my chair, I turn my gaze

to the forest outside. "It's beautiful here." I attempt to lighten the tension building in the room, the energy palpable. As if I could run my hand through the air and touch it. "Where is Sorin?" I ask but am left unanswered. My knee bounces recklessly under the table, so I dig my fingers into my legs to urge them to stop. *Calm down*, I tell myself. *You're safe.* The voices in my head laugh. Of course I'm never really safe.

Agnes hums a tune as she slides into the chair across from me, setting her own mug of peppermint tea down on the wooden tabletop. Extending her hands across the table, palms up, I clench my fists at my sides before reluctantly sliding my hands into hers.

Before, I was never bothered by touch. A hug from a loved one. The brush of a lover's hand. But now, touch is almost painful. Unnatural. Having someone grasp so tightly onto my bare skin makes me clench my teeth. Though, admittedly, when Sorin touched my hand it was a different kind of uncomfortable. Burning. Confusing. But this, with Agnes, has my mind screaming at me to flee.

"Elora, Enchantress of the woods," she whispers, tightening her grip around my hands. Her smile spreads wide across her face, deepening the lines around her eyes and mouth. "There is hope for us yet," she muses. Puzzled by her words, I offer a quick smile in return. Sorin must have filled her in on our plan to retrieve the Stones, I decide. He said to trust him, and I was trying. I needed to try.

"I'm no one special, my lady," I reply, keeping my voice low to match hers. "It's just the Awakening Stones belong to the Enchantresses, and I believe I might know where they are," I say, swallowing down the fear that rises in my throat. Why am I suddenly so terrified of this woman who has shown me nothing but kindness?

"And with the troubles I've heard of hunting and farming lately..." I fidget under the table, my nerves getting the best of me. "I'm only trying to do what's right by the Mother," I continue. "I'm not even sure I'll know how to retrieve the Stones but..." My voice waivers so I quiet myself. Vulnerability is a fickle beast. Show too much, and you're considered weak. Show too little, and you're considered cruel. I glance toward our connected hands and desperation to pull away gnaws at me. I want to tuck them safely back into my lap, but her grip is relentless.

She smirks before her eyes narrow and lips fade into a thin line. "You have no idea just how important you really are, Enchantress. Do not let the actions of others diminish what you are destined to do. Who you were *born* to be." My fingers ache as I unsuccessfully attempt to free my hands from Agnes' grip. "There is strength in overcoming your fears, Elora." Her voice has raised from a whisper to a dull roar and the panic that rose earlier has unleashed inside of me.

Get out! I yell at myself but am drowned out by Agnes' roaring voice. "There is power in facing the demons that live within you. That have buried their way deep into your soul. We all have them, but few find it in themselves to confront them," she says, her voice now closer to a shout. "You will do right by those you feel you have wronged."

Her eyes bore into me, the usual honey tone now milky white and devoid of color. My hands slick with sweat, and I wiggle them to free myself from her grip. Her nails dig deep into my skin as her voice turns into a low growl.

"Crowds will kneel before you, but not unless you face what it is you fear the most." My focus remains on freeing my hands but her words hit their mark. What is it I fear most? Everything I have ever cared about has already been stolen from me, surely she is mistaken. I have nothing left to lose.

Ripping myself from her grip, her nails drag against the back of my hands, leaving streaks of red against my pale skin. Struggling to catch my breath, I remain frozen in my chair. "You may be our savior, Elora Leigh," she whispers, "if only you should choose to be." Placing her hands delicately around her green mug, she takes a slow sip, as if nothing out of the ordinary has just happened.

"How do you know my surname?" I ask, my body trembling in my seat. The milky white that overtook Agnes' eyes moments ago has faded, revealing their true honey color once more. Standing, she disregards my question, and makes her way back to the kitchen, humming the same tune from earlier. One I cannot place but know in my heart I've heard it before...

"You're a Seer." The words feel like ash in my mouth. "An Enchantress," I whisper, clutching my hands to my chest. Seeking proof my heart is still beating. I need to get out of this house. I need air. Stopping at the long table in the kitchen, she doesn't bother looking in my direction when she huffs her quiet reply.

"Indeed, little *susi*, you're catching on."

RUSHING OUT THE FRONT DOOR, my lungs ache but it's nothing compared to the weakness in my knees. A *Seer.* Agnes isn't only an Enchantress but a Seer. My mother's face plants itself at the forefront of my mind. She was the Seer to King Silas before...

Before.

It's unheard of for Enchantresses to live outside of Valebridge. With magick so strong, we've been kept in confinement of the castle walls. Of course, until King Roman staged the uprising all those years ago and a small group of us fled.

Agnes is an Enchantress, living in Loxley for what appears to be a very long time. Are there others outside of Valebridge? Others within Teravie hiding and living on, despite the cruelties our people are facing? How had Agnes ended up here in the first place? Unscathed and protected while others are tortured and dying at the hands of a malicious king. Heat boils in my stomach, a white rage I know so well begs to overtake. The same rage that reared its monstrous head in that alleyway in Copenspire.

Picking up my pace, I head toward the trees behind the house. I need to lose myself in the woods, let them wrap around me and drown the voices pounding inside my head. The forest has been my sanctuary. It healed me after that night on the mountain, heard my cries and swallowed my tears, and I want nothing more than to be surrounded by it.

As I make my way into a dense grove of trees, the air turns cool and thick. The rich, green canopy shields most of the forest from the morning sun, leaving shadows around every turn. Sitting myself down at the base of a large pine tree, I rest my head against its trunk. Squeezing my eyes shut, I try to steady my breathing. *In, out. In, out.* But still the voices come.

Give up, Elora.

Join us. I press my eyes tighter as flashes of Cade and my mother dance behind my lids.

Cade.

My mother.

The guard on the river.

The guard from Copenspire.

In, out. In, out.

Slowly, my breathing begins to steady as I force the demons into silence, using every last bit of will I have against them. Down, down, down. I bury them deeper and deeper. As my breathing slows, Agnes' words become clearer in my mind.

You will be our savior, Elora Leigh.

The ache begins to set in my temples, like needles on already tender flesh, pulling me from Agnes' vision. I rub my fingers in meticulous circles along my hairline, but I know it won't be long before the pain takes over the entirety of my head. Surely whatever Agnes thinks she knows, she's wrong. I am no one's savior.

I am no *one*.

Forcing my shoulders to relax, I lean into the darkness behind my eyes, willing the pain away. Willing the anger toward Agnes and the others here to subside. How could they go on living in peace and merriment while Enchantresses stuck in Valebridge suffer? But then again, wasn't I doing the same thing in the Trinity Forest? Hiding? I, too, have stood idly by.

I'm not sure how long I sit against the tree with my eyes pressed tight before the hair on my arms and neck raise. I don't have to open my eyes to know I'm not alone, but I do anyway. Pushing past the blurring of my vision, it takes a few moments for things to come into focus. The brightness of the forest, even through the canopy of trees, is sudden and sharp. Dropping my hands to my sides, I strain my eyes as I take in the shape before me. As I reach for the daggers I placed at my hips this morning, I keep my movements slow and intentional. Dipping my head low, I wait.

Narrowing my gaze at the beast before me, the wolf's gaze narrows back.

CHAPTER 11

SORIN

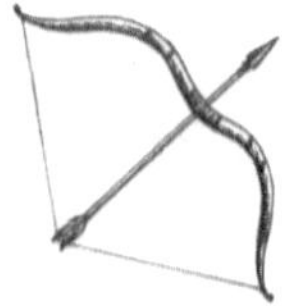

I should've known better than to try and sneak out of the house before dawn. I barely make it three steps before Agnes' voice drifts down the long, narrow hallway.

"Leaving already, son?"

Spinning around, she stands at the end of the hall, apron on, no doubt already preparing bread for the day. The image casts a smile across my face. Despite the abundance of work I need to do around the village, there's always time for her. The sun still sleeps quietly behind the stars, leaving the only light in the house from the hearth. Creeping toward her, I'm mindful of my steps. Tiptoeing as best I can in my boots so as to not wake Elora.

Reaching the end of the hall, I give Agnes a tight squeeze. Peppermint and sage fill the room. Just as it always has. It smells of home. Pulling back, we both turn for the kitchen. "Just figured I should get a head start around the village this morning. I was gone a little longer than expected." My voice trails off as I wait for the inevitable. Her gift of sight isn't always predictable, especially with her age and varying health ailments. The magick comes and goes these days, so there isn't a sure way to know exactly what she's already Seen.

She huffs a small laugh, coating her hands in flour. Something warm settles within me as she methodically begins kneading the next loaf. I haven't realized how much I missed home until this moment.

"Your stop in Copenspire was successful." She doesn't stop working the dough as she glances up at me. I know what she's asking, but I'm not entirely sure how to explain this deal between Elora and me. Not without her disapproval. The last thing she'll want me to do is journey to Valebridge.

"Yes," I say, sitting myself down on one of the stools at the large table. Tossing a grape from the fruit bowl into the air and catching it with my mouth. "The meeting with the merchants went well," I continue, "nothing out of the ordinary to report. Trades should go undisturbed so long as they work with clipped tongues and we provide the pelts they desire." I cup a handful of grapes and lean my elbows on the table, savoring the warm crackle of the fire and the sweet juice of the fruit. "You do think Sam will get the pelts this time? With everything going on with the blight—"

"I trust your sister," Agnes says, continuing her work on the bread. "You should too."

Sighing, I roll my shoulders. The last year has proven more and more difficult to uphold our bargain, and without it, Loxley will cease to stay hidden.

The fishermen in Copenspire have been allies for years. Trading us whatever fresh fish they have for copious fur pelts from the animals that reside in the Trinity Forest. Their allegiance dates back to when William, my adoptive father and Agnes' husband, was the head of Loxley. Though the merchants and fisherman we work with don't reside in Loxley, our goals are common. Take down the rich and feed the poor. The trades they make with us are not trafficked through the kingdom, as most others are. Strictly between us, we're able to get a great deal of goods for nearly no cost and absolutely no tax to add to Valebridge's fortune.

But lately, the animals are more sparse, the fish more evasive. If we don't stop this blight, this punishment from the Mother, I'm not sure how we'll survive.

Pausing her kneading, Agnes crosses her arms and eyes me from top to bottom. I bite down on my tongue, preparing for what's coming next. "And the Enchantress? Care to tell that story?"

I pop another grape and consider my words. Bringing Elora here was a risk, I knew that the moment I offered her my help. Agnes left Valebridge under King Richard's rule, the ruler before Silas and long before Roman. That's where she met William. As a member of the royal guard, it was forbidden then to have any interactions with the Enchantresses. Or with anyone, for that matter. A chaste life meant no distractions, which meant more dutiful and determined armies for the king.

Or that was the idea anyway. So much changed under Silas, and as much as it pains me to say, he was a decent king all things considered.

Agnes has told me the story a dozen times, and yet this morning, it feels fresh in my mind as I think of Elora and our journey to Valebridge.

Despite the restrictions of the kingdom, Agnes and William couldn't help falling in love with each other. They lived in secret for years. Small glances in the halls of the castle. Shadowy meetings in the darkest corners of Valebridge. But after years of insurmountable hidden moments, they decided they needed more. Wanting a simpler life together, a life without rules, without forbiddance, they left.

The moon was full the night they fled Valebridge, and Agnes' magick was strong. She had a vision of the Northern Trinity Forest. A clearing in the center of the trees. She saw stone-built homes and plentiful bounties of animals and berries. Children laughing around the firelight and dogs chasing their tails. She didn't know it yet, but she had envisioned Loxley. Sneaking away with only whatever they could carry on their backs, they left Valebridge and never looked back. Together, they built Loxley from the ground up.

Many others from Valebridge eventually made their way to the village, and when Eviey and Letty stumbled upon what they'd built, they warded it, and it's been that way ever since. Grown to what it is today. Loxley is a haven for those who want to live outside of religious boxes. Outside of the demands of a king who cares so little for who he deems the lesser man.

After some time, King Richard no longer felt it necessary to waste any more time or resources looking for the traitorous guard and Enchantress that up and left in the middle of the night. He had bigger issues dealing with the threat of an uprising from the Enchantresses in Valebridge.

With the wards heavily in place, the hunt was fruitless and eventually Agnes and William became forgotten. Nothing more than a myth to those who journey this part of the forest. Who claim to hear voices and music but see nothing but trees.

I can hear my father's words clear as day, "*Until the last star burns in the night sky and in all the darkness that comes after, I am forever yours.*" A declaration he often made to Agnes, which always guaranteed an eye roll between Sam and me.

"Dumb luck," I say to Agnes with a wink before standing and walking around the kitchen table.

Leaning down, I wrap an arm around her shoulders. "You've always said it yourself," I whisper, "nothing happens by chance." Pulling back from my embrace she greets me with a mix of emotions. Warmth and wariness battle behind her eyes, and it's then that I realize my suspicions are true. She already knows. She knows why I brought Elora here and it will devastate her when we go. But she knows better than to suggest otherwise because she is my mother, and she knows me best. Knows what my heart has desired for too long.

Revenge.

The word catches on my tongue so I grab a mug from the

counter and fill it with tea that sits in a kettle atop the hearth to wash it down.

Agnes has denied every request to take me to Valebridge. Growing up and learning the truth of what happened to my mother, it was my only wish, albeit it was a wish for blood. But she knew the dangers. The risks. With her health failing after William passed, the hope I had to avenge my mother dissipated. I let it die with him so I could focus on Loxley and caring for my family. I had moved on.

Until the blight started. And my mind began to replay the anger of watching my mother die all those years ago. I can't let Valebridge sit back and do nothing as the people are stripped from their crops, their hunting, their livelihoods.

I knew I had to make a move, to try and stop Roman. I just didn't know how. I didn't know where to start.

And then I met Elora.

A sudden drop in my stomach sends me into a fit of panic. I want to explain to Agnes. Explain that this is my best shot at getting into Valebridge. Explain that even though we'll be leaving, this is my home, and I *will* make it back safely. Agnes knows what I plan to do and still she doesn't protest. She lets the silence hang between us before offering me a small smile.

Placing her hand on my heart, her voice is soft. "Just come back, my son. Don't forget where you belong." Without another word, she removes her hand and turns her attention back to the bread.

LOXLEY IS JUST as I left it a few weeks ago, only now the trees are beginning to change with Autumn looming at the seasonal door. The evergreens will remain, but the maple trees that line Loxley will soon lose their green color and trade in for rich oranges and reds. It's my favorite time of year. And this year, I'll miss it.

I take my time strolling down the small main street, flipping my lucky Queen of Spades through my fingers before placing it securely in my breast pocket.

Along with the maple trees, the main street is lined with the small homes of our locals and a few merchant shops. Each of the homes look the same. Small stone cottages with mossy covered roofs, vibrant after the recent rain. Most of the stone chimneys are puffing out light gray swirls of smoke, turning a deep purple as it mixes with the dim light of dawn.

I cross the street and head toward Ulric's. I have no doubt he'll be up at this hour—an early riser, just as I've always been. I need to check in on my bow. Seeing the shops lining the streets makes me think of my father. My stomach twists recalling one of our last conversations.

"While the foundation of Loxley was built on freedom and dreams, the backbone and walls are made from the work of the opportunists, Sorin."

"Opportunists?" I laughed, leaning over to sharpen my blade. "You sound like Sam, trying to make something out of nothing."

"Maybe opportunist is a slightly exaggerated term. Thieves is probably more appropriate, as I'm sure your mother and sister would agree," William said, joining me in my laughter. "But always remember, son, we never steal from anyone with the same misfortunes as us. If the king himself is fine letting the people who live in the outer villages starve, then we are fine taking from those who have more than what they need. More than they deserve. Steal from the rich..."

I smiled, striking my blade against my whetstone, "Even more from the richer."

Reaching Ulric's, I stop, smiling at the familiarity of the building. A sense of nostalgia sweeps over me as I reminisce the many days spent in the back of the shop learning the various trades Ulric is fluent in. A wooden sign reading *The Lazy Anvil* hangs low from a chain and directly underneath it, a smaller sign. *Closed.*

I have to duck to make it to the doorway, but I press on despite the *Closed* sign. The nostalgia fades as the reminder of why I'm here slams into me. I need my bow and arrows for our trip to Valebridge and all the places we must stop along the way.

I would be a fool not to admit I'm nervous about this venture. Nervous that I won't be returning to Loxley at all. Nervous that I've put Elora in more danger than she was back in the woods alone. But the risk is worth the reward. The risk is worth everything.

Opening the shop door, the heat of the fires hit my cheeks instantly, and the clang of steel against hammers leaves a familiar ringing in my ears. Walking up to the counter that sits to the left of the shop, I crane my neck around the corner to try and get Ulric's attention. Cupping my hands on either side of my mouth, I yell towards the blacksmith, "S'cuse me sir, don't you know it's rude to keep a customer waiting!"

He mumbles a curse before tossing his hammer down. I take a few paces backward and wait for him to take notice, placing my hands in my pockets, I rest my back against the shop door. His voice is laced with irritation as he rounds the corner to the front of the store. "The sign says we're closed—" he cuts himself short when our eyes meet. "Bloody hell, man! I didn't know you were back in town!" All the irritation from before sweeps away as his laughter fills the air.

Ulric is older than I am, if I had to guess I'd say he is in his late fifties. He found Loxley after being released from the royal army for a devastating injury to the leg. Once he was deemed "untreatable" they tossed him out like last night's garbage. No mind he served King Silas his entire adult life, they threw him to the streets when he was no longer considered useful. Without any family, he had nowhere else to go, so he sought refuge in the forest, hopeful the myths of Loxley would be fruitful. A mysterious village nestled deep in the woods, making itself known to only those who are deemed worthy of entry. Luckily for him, and us, those rumors are true.

He's been with us for ten years now. Letty and Eviey patched him up as good as they were able, aside from the permanent limp he now walks with, he's in decent shape. He stands several inches shorter than I do, but then again, I'm taller than most. His hair is cropped short and almost all gray now, matching his eyes. The smile he wears intensifies the roundness of his reddened cheeks. The color, a byproduct of working so close to the flames. Closing our distance, he wraps me in a tight hug.

"The prodigal son returns," he laughs and I return his hug before breaking away.

"Please," I say, rolling my eyes at the nickname. "Don't start with that nonsense." I know he's jesting but it's a nickname from William and it never felt right. "I'm glad to be back." Moving to the stool behind the counter, he removes his long leather apron before sitting down.

"How long are you here for this time?" he asks, but my eyes snag on his hands as they rub his right leg, no doubt stiff from standing too long. Breaking my eyes away, I refocus them out the window of the shop. The sun has almost risen, bright orange and pink flood a cloudless sky. Villagers are beginning their day, sweeping stoops and setting up for the daily market. A trade of goods and services that's tradition during the Summer months.

"Not long, I'm afraid." I finally answer and meet his gaze. "Business to attend to farther...north." I know many questions linger on his lips but to my relief, he doesn't ask them.

Ulric leans back on the stool and rests his body on the wall behind him. Crossing his arms, his brows furrow. "You know that mother of yours had one of her visions while you were away. Saying something along the lines of change, and possibly...a girl." It isn't a question, but at the same time, it's definitely a question. His smirk and my silence say more than enough. "It's no matter though," he continues, throwing his hands in the air. "She's always speaking in circles, anyway."

"Spending a lot of time with her, are you?" I raise my eyebrows and Ulric's laughter bellows through the shop.

"Touche', Sorin," he laughs. "I'll stay out of your business, if you stay out of mine."

"Be careful, Ulric," I say, letting out a low whistle. "Not many who lay with dragons live to see the next day."

He laughs again, throwing his hands up. "I imagine you want your bow," he says, changing the subject.

"Indeed. Is it safe to assume it's nearly fixed? We'll be staying until after the full moon, so I'd like to have it before then." I purposely leave out our destination, though I have no doubt he already knows. He eyes me for a moment before his features soften.

Standing again, he braces himself on the counter as his legs threaten to wobble beneath him. I'm on my way to his side in an instant, but before I reach him, he holds out a hand. "I'm fine, Sorin. Just a little stiff is all." I know the snap in his voice isn't intentional, so I stop in place and nod. Gritting my teeth, I watch him struggle to regain balance. He's as stubborn as Agnes. Maybe they're meant for each other, after all.

It pains me to see them both this way, and the idea of them bearing the burdens of Loxley alone for even longer makes my stomach churn with guilt. "And your bow is near ready," Ulric huffs, "give me another day to finish her up and she's all yours."

"Thank you, Ulric." I take the last few steps toward him and grasp his outreached hand. He dips his head quickly before heading back to the shop.

Warmth shrouds me as I make my way through town, whistling and stopping every few minutes to chat with the villagers. I've missed being home. Missed this. The simple mornings, the Summer markets, Loxley in general. I decide to swing by Marian's to pick up some huckleberry jam for Agnes' fresh bread. I make a mental note as I head back to the house to bring Elora into town today. She should see Loxley for what it is, not what she's been told it is. My heart lightens and pace quickens as I begin to steer myself toward the main house.

Nearing the end of the main street, something in my gut turns and the memory of what Ulric said about Agnes' vision whispers into my mind. The sky shifts, the harsh light of the sun swiftly replaced with gray. The breeze changes direction and a few leaves tumble from the maple trees on either side of the street. Something inside me tells me to run.

So, I run.

Sprinting down the rest of the street, I make it to the house with my heart slamming in my chest. Pushing through the front door, I head straight for Sam's room. The bed is made and the nightgown folded neatly at the end of it. Undisturbed and empty. I round the corner and sprint down the hall to the kitchen. Another empty room save for the sliced bread on the counter and a couple of half empty cups of tea. I drop the jam on the counter before heading to Agnes' room.

"Agnes!" I shout but am left unanswered. Panic courses in my chest making my feet move quicker than my brain can think. I let them lead the way out the back door. Let them guide me into the woods behind the house. To her.

A howl pierces through the trees, solidifying what it is I fear. Picking up my pace, I run as fast as I can, my breathing heavy as my boots slam into the forest floor.

The wolves have followed us here.

CHAPTER 12
ELORA

THE WOLF KEEPS HIS DISTANCE AS HE THROWS HIS head back and lets out a long howl. Likely signaling to another wolf that he's cornered his prey.

Prey.

Keeping my eyes locked on the animal, I clench my daggers, not daring to move from my spot against the tree. Pushing my back against the trunk, the bark scrapes against my spine. Dampness fills the air as several gray clouds block the sun, promising rain.

The wolf stands several feet away, pacing back and forth between the trees. His heavy breathing is frantic and erratic as he glances between me and the ground. Almost as if he's waiting for something. Even from a distance his massive frame takes up most of the space between us. His claws dig deep lines in the ground, flinging loose bits of dirt with every step. Something snaps in the woods behind the wolf, and he whips his head instinctually toward the sound.

Now.

Hopping up on both feet, I ready my daggers into a fighting position. Keeping my steps light, I move silently across the forest floor. With the beast distracted, I decide I need a better vantage point. Across from me lies a large fallen log that I could easily hop on top of. Without a second's hesitation I dart across the clearing toward the log.

As fast as I think I am, the wolf is faster.

The ground vibrates as his paws thunder closer. Spinning at the last moment, I turn to face the beast. His approach is stunningly quick, but to my surprise, the moment I turn to face him, he comes to an abrupt halt. With only about a foot between us now, my breath catches in my chest. Though, quickly I realize it isn't fear that paralyzes me. No. Definitely not fear. But something different. Familiarity?

A voice deep inside me tells me to straighten myself. A voice I don't recognize. Not those of the demons whom I carry with me every day, but something older.

You're safe.

My hands tremble as I straighten myself, the clutch on my daggers loosening. The wolf sniffs the air around us, but makes no move forward.

"You're not going to hurt me, are you?" I whisper. Am I really speaking to a wolf? I'm not sure if my mind is playing tricks, or I've truly gone mad, but the wolf dips his head in my direction. My eyes widen as I watch this massive animal soften and bow before me. After straightening himself, he takes a final stride in my direction. Anticipation beats against my rib cage but still, I'm not afraid.

Cautiously, I place one of my daggers back at my hip and use my free hand to reach for the wolf. Instead of shying away from my touch as he did by the river, he closes the distance between my hand and him.

The fur on his nose is short and coarse, the wetness of his snout is cold against my clammy hand as he nuzzles deeper into my touch. A low vibration exudes from his throat as I stroke the bridge of his nose a few more times. My hand moves up to scratch behind his ear, the thick fur is lush against my palm.

"What are you doing all the way up here?" I whisper, disbelief still making me doubt that this is truly happening. Wolves are only known to roam the southern forest, but maybe he got lost. Turned around somehow.

Licking my hands, the wolf whimpers as I begin to pull away. Taking a step back, I get a better gauge of how large he really is. Standing on all fours, he reaches just below my shoulders. I graze my hand over the top of his head and down his back. His fur, perfectly woven gray and white. No matted blood as I last saw him by the river.

"Do you have a name?" I ask, as if it's a completely sane thing to be doing. Then, before I can question my sanity further, a word splays itself across my mind. In a flash it's there, and even quicker, it disappears.

"*Alaric*," I say the name aloud as the wolf bows his head, bumping me under my chin with his snout. My laugh startles both the wolf and myself, we both jump back which only makes me laugh harder. Entranced by this powerful animal, the sharp snapping of branches coming from behind us draws me from my haze.

"Elora!"

Sorin's voice cuts through the woods, the crunch of leaves loud and prominent as he makes his way closer. I open my mouth to shout that I'm okay but the moment I do, the wolf bolts in the opposite direction and down the hill.

"Alaric, wait!" I whisper after him, but I'm too late. His figure disappears down the hill and into the deepest part of the woods.

Sorin's breathing is heavy as he reaches me. Did he run all the way here? I don't bother turning around as he approaches, my mind transfixed on what has just happened. I can't tear away from the direction the wolf ran to.

A new voice pops into my head.

"*Follow him,*" the angelic voice whispers in my ear. Ethereal. Ancient. Without giving it another thought, I take a step toward the hill. Only, before I can make it any further Sorin's hand wraps around the back of my arm.

"Elora, I heard a howl and—" he cuts himself short, noticing my hesitation. My eyes drag from his, down his body, landing where his hand grips my arm.

Stammering, he drops my arm. "I...I'm sorry, I just thought I heard a howl and when I couldn't find you at the house I..." His voice trails off as he tucks his hands into his pockets. He wears his worry the same way he wears all his other emotions. Blatantly.

"Something told me to come here," he continues, running a hand through his hair. His face truly looks perplexed, but I can't find it in me to care at the moment. "That I'd find you. I can't explain it. I just felt..." He shakes his head, letting loose a long breath. "So, are you all right?"

Relaxing my face, I attempt to let go of my frustrations. He is genuinely concerned about my wellbeing. Likely to ensure his guide into Valebridge stays intact, but concerned nonetheless.

"I'm fine," I offer. "I came out here because I needed some air and then..." I let my words linger, glancing toward the ground. How absurd will it sound if I explain that I ran into the wolf from a few days ago and instead of ripping my throat out, it nuzzled my hand and let me scratch its back?

He'll think you're crazy.

I let out a long sigh as the voices in my head return. The weight of their burden resting heavily on my shoulders once again.

"Then I heard something, a howl, like you said. I was just on my way back to the house." Guilt lines my stomach as I lie to Sorin. I want to trust him and for him to trust me. But whatever this is with the wolf, I need time to figure it out on my own first.

Studying me for a moment, he gives his head a quick nod. "I'm glad you're okay." He appears genuine, despite how harsh I was just moments ago. Turning on his heels, he heads back in the direction of the house. With a final look to the hill where the wolf disappeared, I reluctantly turn to follow him.

Glancing back over his shoulder, Sorin says, "I was coming back to the house to look for you anyway." I lock eyes with him briefly before he turns his head away. If he hadn't followed me into the woods, I could have followed the wolf. Could have found...

There's nothing for you here, Elora.

"I was thinking I could show you around Loxley before we have dinner together." Sorin's words catch me off guard.

"Dinner?" I snap, frustrated to have an obligation to attend to later. Frustrated I have so many questions from today and no answers. First Agnes, then the wolf. And now, a dinner of all things.

Stopping, he looks back at me and lets out an irritated sigh. "If you have something better to do, by all means. I'm sure Agnes wouldn't mind the company." His smirk reveals that damn dimple and I have to stop myself from tripping over a branch at the sight of it. *Get it together, Elora,* I tell myself. I push my way past him, taking the lead on the final stretch through the woods.

A day alone with Agnes after this morning's encounter sounds about as enjoyable as a day spent with a fire throwing sprite. "That all sounds fine," I grumble, keeping my eyes to the ground.

CHAPTER 13

ELORA

WE STOP BRIEFLY BACK AT THE MAIN HOUSE TO DROP off our cloaks now that the clouds have burned off. Sorin disappeared to his bedroom, giving me a few moments of much needed silence as I recoup in Sam's room.

My mind races thinking of the wolf in the woods. *Alaric,* I remind myself. This connection with him is unlike anything I've ever felt before and I begin to doubt what I actually experienced. Did I really hear his voice in my head? Or was that just another trick my mind so often plays. And the other voice? Where did it come from?

A sudden rap at the bedroom door draws my attention. On the opposite side of the threshold, Sorin waits for me. Casual, as usual, in his black pants and white linen shirt, rolled up to the elbow, showing off his inked forearm and tanned skin.

"Ready?" he asks with a smile while stepping back to open the front door of the house. I nod in reply and squeeze past him, leaving the house first.

The walk toward town is mostly silent. Birds sing loudly, their voices carried and amplified by the slight summer breeze. Keeping pace with each other, neither of us breaks the silence hanging in the gap between us. The closer we get to the town's main center, the sounds of nature are distilled and, instead, turn to sounds of a sleepy village coming to life.

As we walked to the main house last night, I could make out faint lines of stone cottages, but in the light of day, Loxley is much more magnificent than I had imagined. The cottages line either side of the dirt path, each one with different shades of ivy growing up the sides, creating pockets of green over the stones. The small front stoops on each house have different potted plants and flowers. Tomatoes and berries, bursting with vibrant reds.

My stomach flutters as I take in the villagers next. Most are in comfortable clothes, breeches and loose tunics to accommodate the heat. Some women wear simple linen dresses, the length of them long enough that the hems sway in the dirt. Their bare feet take no mind to the soft beds of dirt that line the gardens.

My heart warms as I watch a mother and her two children tend to their small garden just off the side of their house. The mother bends over to pick a few weeds as the children bicker on who gets to use the watering can next. The normalcy of their actions confounds me. With the talk of the blight, how is it that everything here feels so easy?

"It's market day." Sorin's voice interjects my thoughts, and I break my gaze away from the woman and her children to look up at him. "Every month during the warm season the villagers set up a street market to trade goods."

As he speaks my eyes wander down the street and it's only then that I notice people setting up tables in front of their homes. Most tables are filled with various vegetables and a few fruits and loaves of bread. Though, some house different items such as small wooden trinkets, fishing nets and wires, woven baskets and swatches of fabric.

"Where do they..." I start but stop myself short. I'm not sure how to phrase my question without coming off as impolite.

And before I can piece together what I'm trying to ask, Sorin speaks again.

"They have no money. Money isn't an object in Loxley." He continues to explain as we pass a table with a basket of overflowing peaches. My eyes catch on the beautiful fruit. "It's all about trade," Sorin continues. "What you give to the town, is what you'll receive back. We've found that once money is involved, greed is knocking at the door before we can stop it. The council and I provide the bare essentials. Seeds, flour, oil for lamps. What the villagers do with those goods is up to them. Most tend to gardens, others as you can see, have talents with woodworking. Some of the men and women who have joined us over the years come from various trades. Blacksmiths, butchers, healers, you get the idea. Letty and Eviey have done a wonderful job teaching others their craft of potions. Helping women with childbirth and various hunting injuries."

He takes a few steps backward and plucks one of the peaches from the basket. The woman behind the table, not much older than I, has dark hair braided neatly in a crown around her head. She blushes as Sorin thanks her for the fruit and passes her a packet of seeds in exchange. She's pretty in a soft way, and I don't know why, but for the first time in a very long time, I'm envious. Of the ease in which she does her job, trading fruit and conversing with the townsfolk. Of the way she doesn't flinch when she takes Sorin's hand, or hide the fact that it caused her to blush.

"In fact," Sorin continues, bringing my attention back to him. "I'm sure there's a thing or two you could also teach before we leave. You did an excellent job stitching up my head, as thick as it is." He winks at me before continuing down the road.

"So, if the council provides the bare needs, where does the council get their funds from? I can't imagine you provide such supplies for an entire village by scamming royal guards in card games," I say, watching Sorin as he inspects the peach a little too thoroughly.

"A fair question," he says, tossing me the fruit. I catch it clumsily and quip my head to the side. "Eat it." He gestures to the fruit. "They're the juiciest this close to Autumn." I eye it for a moment before taking a bite. The skin is velvety and sweet, almost tart. The juice drips down my chin but I don't care about how I look at the moment. It may be the most delicious thing I've ever tasted. I make myself take one small bite at a time, savoring every moment along the way.

"To answer your question the short way," Sorin says, peeling his eyes from me, "the council and I work with different merchants along the ports of the Holden Sea. We trade fur pelts, smoked meats, and other various items. Our goods that the forest so fruitfully provides, are traded for other items we don't have access to outside of the Kingdom's rations." He stops to smile at me. "And yes, sometimes the additional coin from a game of cards comes in handy."

I listen while I chew on a piece of the peach. It makes sense, using only trade and not money. Money is the next evil after power. And the two of them combined make for monstrous outcomes.

"Recently, however," Sorin continues, "hunting has been meager. Our trades have been low and therefore, new goods haven't been as plentiful. Luckily, the people of Loxley have come from mostly lower class. We know how to stretch a shilling, get the most out of what we have. And for whatever reason, the crops are doing okay here." He stops, glancing to his right at a small field of corn. "But I can't imagine we'll be that lucky for long. I'm not willing to bet on it."

Nearing the end of the road, I discard the peach pit into the field where the fire raged last night. As I wipe my hands clean of the remaining juice on my brown breeches, my breath catches as I narrow in on the last table at the end of the road. Letty and Eviey sit perched on two wooden chairs, light blankets draped over their knees despite the heat. Sprawled out on their table are beautifully crafted, leather sheaths. The colors of the leather are deep and rich. Burnt oranges, earth browns, and forest greens. But there are two in particular that have caught my attention. Not waiting for Sorin to finish his conversation with a man named Ulric, I make my way toward the twin witches.

"Good day, Enchantress," Eviey says, setting down her mug of tea. "Tell us, how has your stay been thus far?" I barely register her question as my hands trace two deep green sheaths that are displayed neatly across the table.

"It's been lovely," I reply, still distracted by the leather. Noticing my distant response, Letty clears her throat, causing my gaze to finally break and meet hers. "These are beautiful," I say, picking up one of the sheaths, "they remind me of my mother." I almost choke on the word as my fingers grip the supple leather. Etches of leaves and foliage dance across it, I trace them all with a delicate finger.

"If she was any bit as beautiful as you, I would not be surprised that such a lovely piece reminds you of her." Letty's voice is higher than Eviey's, but just as honey filled.

I offer a faint smile, heat rising to my cheeks at her compliment. "Actually I meant the sheaths itself. She often wore one just like it." Suddenly the leather feels too heavy in my hands. My body, too hot. Dropping the sheath back on the table I clasp my hands together to keep from fidgeting. The memory of my mother sheathing her blade on her hip before our departure that night sends darkness into the corners of my vision. But before I can spiral, a hand placed lightly on the small of my back jerks me back to the present.

"Morning, ladies." Sorin's voice is smooth and low, as usual. I don't flinch away from his hand that lingers on the small of my back, I sink into his touch despite myself. Letting it ground me in the moment, the way it briefly did in the alley. The three of them chatter amongst themselves. The weather, the rest of the crew arriving in a few days, the upcoming full moon celebration. But my mind is far, far away. Trapped on a snowy mountain, eternally surrounded by screams and clashes of iron.

Chapter 14

Sorin

I try my best to keep my eyes on the road and not on Elora as we reach the house. But this woman, this Enchantress, has a hold on me that I can't explain. She's stubborn and fiery, absolutely beautiful and absolutely terrifying.

My eyes drift toward her again as a few loose strands of her blonde braid sway lightly around her face, framing the scatter of freckles that don the bridge of her slightly bent nose. And those eyes. A golden hue that rivals the intensity of the sun, a glorious benefit of being an Enchantress. My eyes drift even lower as she turns to walk up the steps of the house. *Mother above I need help.* I'm so lost in my train of thought I don't realize Elora has stopped at the top of the steps and is now the one staring at me.

Her gaze is flat and unamused, and I can't help but laugh as her eyes narrow further. Clearing her throat, I close the distance between us and make it up the few steps to the porch. As she crosses her arms, I laugh again. "I was just admiring those daggers," I say, tapping the hilt of one of the blades.

She counters with a small smile of her own, though I know it isn't genuine. "Right," she says, nodding her head slowly, "the daggers." The hint of a grin is now gone from her perfectly pink lips as she turns the knob of the door and disappears into Sam's room, leaving me on the porch like an absolute idiot.

THE REST of the day is spent in and out of meetings with the council. Getting updates on our supply stock and taking note of what needs to be replenished. Though our small fields of crops are doing okay, foraging outside the warded walls hasn't been fruitful. My stomach turns with each new revelation that if something doesn't change, we may not have enough in our reserves to get through Winter.

No one knows of the plan to travel to Kirsgard Mountain and then to Valebridge, best kept to ourselves until our strategy is set. In my absence, Ulric will take over provisions with the help of a few other merchants, including Thomas. Thomas is young, closer to Elora's age. But I use his inexperience to my advantage, teaching him the ropes of running things on the trade, making sure he does things the way I'd like them to be done.

"I won't let you down," he says with a smile. His auburn hair is ruffled, like he's just gotten up. Shaking his extended hand, I head out for the day.

This isn't the first time I'll be gone from Loxley for an extended period, but it is the first time I'm unsure of when, or if, I'll be back.

I make my way back to the house, my hands full of vegetables and other ingredients I traded the villagers for. I breathe in deeply as a quiet house welcomes me. Elora is busy bathing and changing, and I mentioned to Agnes earlier that Elora and I would be dining alone to discuss our strategy, and with a few eye rolls and laughs she conveniently had plans with Eviey and Letty to begin the preparations for the coming full moon celebration.

The entire house smells divine as I finish preparing the last of the food. A typical fishing day would usually yield between three and five fish but today, I was lucky to catch just one.

Baked trout smothered in butter and herbs. Potatoes fresh from the garden, a handful of carrots roasted with leeks. I attempt to act casual, despite my quickened heartbeat, as I wait for Elora to meet me in the dining room. I'm not sure what it is, but I can't keep my composure around her. I'll blame it on the presence of her magick. Of her being an Enchantress. Because there aren't any other logical reasons for me to act like a complete fool whenever she's near. Though if Sam were here, I'm sure she'd argue I'm a fool, regardless.

Agnes insisted Elora borrow one of Sam's dresses while her tunic and breeches get a fresh wash. Elora had protested, naturally, but eventually relented, realizing arguing with Agnes is an uphill battle. One that is rarely won.

As Elora enters the room, my lungs freeze in my chest. What I thought was a quickened heartbeat before is nothing compared to how it rages now. Her hair is bound in the usual braid she often wears and draped across her shoulder, a few rogue waves hanging around her face. The dress she picked is a deep orange that brings out the flecks of gold in her eyes, illuminating them even brighter in the dim light of the candles. The sleeves are flowy and loose. Though the hem is several inches too long, it fits snugly on the curves of her hips, making my chest tighten even further.

"Smells incredible," she says, passing me by without a second glance. Closing her eyes she takes a deep inhale, practically salivating over the food displayed across the large table in the kitchen. "Did you make all of this?"

"I did," I say, laughing at her surprise as her eyebrows jump to her forehead. "We've been...fortunate to have crops remain strong despite what's happening just outside the wards." Her eyes meet mine and there's a look in them I can't place. "Only the best for you, Enchantress," I say with a wink, feigning casualty despite the thudding in my chest. Her cheeks flush, and for a moment, I think I've earned a compliment. Then, her eyes narrow in my direction and the moment is lost.

"Speaking of Enchantresses," she says, scooping heaps of the food onto her plate, "you failed to mention Agnes was an Enchantress. Interesting how that didn't come up when you formed this plan to retrieve the Stones." The icy wave of her stare hits me before she turns to seat herself at the small table by the window. She eyes the bread and licks her lips softly before biting down and reclining in her chair.

Clearing my throat, I grab a plate of my own. "Loxley is hidden in the woods for a reason." I scramble to focus on our conversation and not Elora as I fill my plate. "Agnes and William made sure of that. It would be treasonous of me to go around telling our secrets to a stranger." With my plate full, I make my way to the chair opposite her, braving a quick glance in her direction to gauge how much trouble I'm in. She keeps her focus on her food, but her shoulders are still, her eyes narrowed.

She finishes her piece of bread before reaching for the wine and pouring us each a glass. "What about the whole 'trust each other' business you were so *passionate* about back in the woods," she says before taking a long sip from her cup.

"I trust you," I state, forcing my eyes down to my plate like a coward. Keeping conversation between bites of fish and potato, I continue, "That doesn't mean everyone else will right away." I'm not lying when I tell her this. I do trust her. Everything in me says I should, but the people of Loxley have faced their hardships, life in the woods isn't so easily lived. But of all people, I suppose Elora already knows that. Despite her similar situation, Agnes will be an especially hard wall to break.

"Then tell me," she starts again between sips of her wine. "If Agnes is an Enchantress, surely she's been to Valebridge at one point or another. The fact that she's here outside the castle walls is amazing enough. Why wouldn't she just take you there herself to seek whatever it is you're so desperately trying to obtain." I can tell she's baiting me as she draws out the last few words. She wants to know about Agnes, but she really wants to know what my motives are. And rightfully so. I'll tell her, I will. But I'm not ready for that conversation yet.

Leaning back in my chair, I cross my arms and contemplate where to begin. With my stomach full and head beginning to feel a slight buzz from the wine, I fear I'll let too much slip, so I choose my words wisely. "Agnes is...well, Agnes." I uncross my arms and let them lay loosely in my lap, resisting the urge to fiddle with the ring that I wear on my index finger. It was William's. A thick silver band with a black stone in the middle. I've worn it every day since his passing, an heirloom of my adoptive father I cherish deeply. "What brought her here from Valebridge is her story to tell, not mine. And as a mother, her only wish is to keep Samaria and me safe. Dragging her back to a place that despises what she is isn't a fair ask."

"And yet you ask it of me," she counters, quick and harsh and exactly what I deserve. Her brows furrow, and I immediately want to take back my words.

I let loose a sigh while my mind tries to catch up. "It's different," I finally say, knowing it's not enough. Leaning forward, I prop my elbows on the arms of my chair. She peers out the window, into nothing but a black forest, the last of the sunset already disappeared back into the earth.

"It's different," I say again, drawing the word out, "because you and I have an arrangement. There's something in it for both of us. I help you find the Stones; you help me get into Valebridge unnoticed. For Agnes it would be nothing but painful memories and another loss."

"A loss?" she asks, turning to face me again, the ice slowly melting around her edges. I refill our cups again with the dark red wine and she watches as I pour. Placing the empty bottle down, I twist the ring on my finger, contemplating just how much to say.

"Who knows what can happen once we're there," I say, peering past Elora and at the stone wall opposite the kitchen. A tapestry hangs across it, a smile tugs at my lips as I recall Sam and I poorly making it for Agnes one year. We wove together different twigs and mosses we'd found in the forest. Sam dried the wildflowers between stacks of her books, I'm amazed they've survived this long. It fascinates me how it is the smallest items that make a home rather than the home itself.

I bring my gaze back to her. "It's not a risk Agnes was willing to take is all." She shakes her head, but to my relief she doesn't push it any further.

"So, you mentioned earlier you had something to tell me, that was your reasoning for dinner was it not?" Elora asks, taking a long sip from her wine, her empty plate pushed to the center of the table. Deep pink flushes her cheeks, the lids of her eyes heavy. "So," she says again, her voice is quiet, but not quite a whisper. "What is it you need to tell me, Sorin?" she asks, leaning back into her chair.

Hearing my name from her lips sends a chill down my spine so I bite my bottom lip to keep from saying or doing something I shouldn't. She tilts her head to the side as if sensing the change in energy, lifting the corner of her mouth in a small smile. Elora with her guard down is an entirely different specimen. Intoxicating as she was before, I can't draw my eyes away at how casually she sits across from me.

A smile tugs at my lips as I down the last of my cup. "The full moon celebration is a week away, Samaria and the rest of the crew are expected back then. I'll meet with them first to fill them in on the details and then—"

"No." Setting her now empty cup down a little too harshly, causing the table to rattle, she pinches the bridge of her nose with her fingers.

"No?" I question, trying to keep my composure as she quickly appears to lose hers.

"No," she says again, long and drawn out. "You will not

meet with them first." Tucking a piece of hair behind her ear, she tries to focus her eyes as she sits forward resting her elbows on the table. "If we're to trust each other there's nothing you can say to them that I can't be a part of," she says. I attempt to conceal my amused smirk as she continues, it isn't often I'm the one being told what to do.

"We tell them everything together," she says. "You promised you'd keep me in on your plans." My mind flashes back to the guard in Copenspire and our conversation thereafter. How defeated and angry she was that I used her as a pawn instead of a player and how poorly that ended for everyone.

Leaning forward on the table, I mirror her posture by propping myself on my elbows. As I hold her gaze, I watch her, and she begins to toy with her fingers and hands under the intensity of my stare. Maybe I'm not the only one feeling this connection after all. Fascinating.

"Okay, fair enough," I say, tapping my fingers against the tabletop. "When they're back, you'll meet the crew. Then, after the full moon celebration, we'll explain the Stones and the plan for Valebridge. And *together* we'll all come up with a strategy." I settle back in my chair and study her as she contemplates this.

"Together?" She challenges me, raising her brows. The orange of her dress and gold of hair makes her appear ethereal in the candlelight.

"Together, I swear it." I raise a hand and dip my head in a quick bow. This seems to satisfy her as she lets out a deep sigh, relaxing her shoulders. Slinking low in her chair, she rests her head on the back of it, staring up at the ceiling.

"I have another secret," she whispers. Her words come out in a slur, and I can tell she's fighting to keep her eyes open. How much wine did we drink? The dull ache forming in my head tells me it's been too much.

"Well do tell, Enchantress," I say, keeping my voice low as I scoot my chair back. Crossing around the table to her side, she rolls her head and looks up at me from her chair as I approach.

Her eyes slide down my face and stop on my lips, cheeks reddening as she drags her eyes back to mine.

Lazily, she lifts her hand and grabs my shirt, tugging me down to her. Dropping to my knees I succumb to her request. She pulls me closer, bringing my ear to her mouth. The smell of wine on her lips is intoxicating but all I can think about is how close our bodies are. How hot her breath feels against my skin. How, without the wine, she'd likely have a dagger to my throat if I attempted to get this close.

"Promise you won't think I'm crazy?" she whispers.

"Promise," I whisper back through a smile. She lets out a small laugh before rolling her head away from me, letting go of my shirt and facing the ceiling again. Her eyes close and her breathing starts to slow.

"The wolves," she slurs, "they followed us here." She goes silent for a moment and I fear she's fallen asleep. Until she whispers something that raises the hair on my arms and neck.

"And this time, I spoke with them."

CHAPTER 15
ELORA

"GO, SUSI." MY MOTHER'S VOICE DIDN'T WAVER AS she placed a kiss on my head. "We have this handled, you need to run."

"I won't leave you! I can fight!" Reaching for her, I beckoned for my newly awakened magick, but it didn't come.

Cade reached for my arm, dragging me backward to the hidden path beneath an underbrush of trees. "Go, Elora." I opened my mouth to protest but before I could say a word, his mouth met mine. The kiss was brutal and desperate, my heart sinking when he pulled away. "You must go. Wait for me by the large pine tree," he said in a hurry. "The one with the crooked trunk, do you remember it?"

I nod, of course I remembered. How does one forget your first kiss? Or the first time Cade's hands ran over my bare skin. The first time we allowed ourselves to be together.

"Good," he whispers, "wait for me there. Don't move. I'll find you, I promise." The thought of leaving sent bile up my throat, but I did as he said. Kissing him quickly again, I ran for the path.

As I began the descent down the mountain, something in the pit of my stomach stopped me.

As I turned, my mother's silver eyes were shocking in the dark-

ness. The others scrambled around her, calling upon magick they hadn't used in years. Magick that wouldn't aid them. Wouldn't help them survive. What they needed was to train. To learn to fight. But of course, they never had the chance.

Arrows from hunters whizzed through the air as shackles slammed around any wrists they could find.

I need to fight. I have to fight, I told myself. And yet, I was frozen in place. My heart slammed against my ribcage. I called for my magick again and again, but I was met with silence. We'd only just performed the Ceremony, and I'd failed to wield it. I failed.

Failed.

A thick layer of static bounded through the air before my mother met my eyes again. And still, my feet lodged in the snow. I dared one last glance, crouching between the bushes, concealing myself the best I could, I begged the Mother to bring me my magick.

Cade fell to his knees, as guards surrounded him. Biting down on my tongue, I covered my mouth so as not to scream out his name. He was a fighter and yet my heart lurched as the snow quickly turned red.

Legs wobbling, I was determined to make my way back to him. But I didn't make it far before swarms and swarms of men spilled onto the mountain in every direction. Swatches of blue, the Valebridge colors, against the shining white and now crimson snow.

We were outnumbered. How were we so outnumbered? A high shriek drew my attention. My face found my mother's just as she pulled her blade, pushing off a guard. She smiled at me, just once, before her eyes closed and she sliced her own throat.

My head lolls as firm hands shake my shoulders. I come to my senses slowly, eyes struggling to open. Sorin's voice wafts through the haze between unconsciousness and reality, but I'm stuck, drifting between the paralysis of my nightmare and the reality of the present.

"Elora, wake up." Sorin's voice again. "It was a nightmare, Elora. You're safe." Slowly, the haze lifts and my eyes open. Blinking away a few remaining tears, I slide out of Sorin's grip and sit up, resting my back against the headboard of the bed.

"Take a deep breath," Sorin commands, sliding his hands onto his lap.

Placing my hand on my chest, I feel for the erratic *thud thud thud*. Proof I am in fact alive and breathing. *I am not on a mountain*, I remind myself, looking around the small room. *I am in Loxley. I am safe.*

"I'm sorry," I mumble, avoiding eye contact as I use both my hands to twist my hair off to the side. The back of my neck is drenched in sweat, stickiness coating my skin down to my toes. *I am safe. I am safe.* I remind myself over and over until the touch of Sorin's hand breaks me from my spell. He tucks his hand under my chin, lifting my head so I meet his gaze.

"Don't apologize," he whispers. "Not for anything," he continues, "but especially not for this." Taking his thumb, he brings it up to my cheek, wiping away the tears now freely falling. I stifle a cry, the way he's looking at me right now with such worry, such concern, is so undeserved. If he knew what I did, he wouldn't be looking at me like that. Wouldn't be soaking up my tears and doing his best to comfort me. If he knew I was the cause of my own nightmares, he'd walk away, leaving me in the darkness alone, just as I should be. Just as I was in the woods.

Murderer.

Tilting my head to the side, I press my ear into my shoulder. Trying anything to suppress the voices. I could tell him, right now. Could tell him the truth like we swore we would. That I don't deserve this. Don't deserve any of this kindness, this hospitality. I don't even deserve the chance to find the Stones, but I convinced myself it wasn't for me. That I would find the Awakening Stones for *them*, the Enchantresses, the people across Teravie who are suffering.

Though, in my heart, I know. While I am doing it for them,

I'm also doing this for myself. Retribution for what happened that night. As if the blame for what happened could fall to anyone but myself. As if bringing the Stones to the Enchantresses could ever right any of my wrongs.

Swallowing thickly against the knot in my throat, I meet Sorin's gaze. Straightening myself all the way up, I reach for his hand that is now draped lightly on my knee. I lace my fingers in his. The hitch in his breath as our skin connects leaves me wondering if he feels the same energy I do whenever we touch. No words break the surface, though, I'm not sure I want them to.

So instead, I squeeze my hand tighter around his and bring it up to my lips. Placing a soft kiss to his calloused knuckles, I let my lips rest there for a moment too long. Allowing myself to take a deep inhale through my nose, soaking in his warmth, his kindness. I hate that I'm unable to stop the tear that rolls down my cheek. At that, I disconnect our hands and before he can open his mouth, I cut him off by turning away. With my shoulder blocking him, I lie back down to face the darkness and demons alone once more.

THIS PAST WEEK was spent preparing for the full moon celebration as well as the return of Samaria and the rest of the crew. Tonight is finally the night. I gladly volunteered this morning when Eviey and Letty asked for help in the gardens. Late Summer doesn't leave much to harvest other than a few root vegetables. Mostly, the witches needed help preparing the garden for the change of seasons, managing the pesky weeds and setting up for the upcoming cold.

I spent most of the morning rooting for potatoes and yanking out the occasional carrot in Letty's garden. Sweat beads across my brows as the sun drifts to its highest point in the sky.

Standing, I gather my vegetables and turn to head uphill toward the cottage.

I've forgotten how wonderful it feels to put my hands to use. I've missed it the last week being away from the woods. Living alone, there is always something to be done. Hunting, trapping, fixing my cabin, an abundance of busy distractions to keep my mind from wandering down a less pleasant path.

Not to mention, I would do anything to avoid Sorin. I've managed pretty well this last week. I moved myself to Eviey's after she offered up her guest room. I've only seen Sorin when having our meals with Agnes, Letty, and Eviey. His eyes burned into my skin last night as we were the last to leave the table, but before he could get a chance to speak, I left. Staying with Eviey has proven much less distracting, anyway.

The night Sorin and I had dinner together was an intimacy I haven't felt in years and shouldn't have let happen. Especially letting him see me after my nightmare. Pushing the feeling of his hands on my chin deeper and farther away, I bury those feelings in the dirt, where they belong.

He would never want you.

The voices are right, he would never want me. No one would. So, I shake off the thought and continue back up to Letty's cottage, needing a refill of water and a break from the heat.

Letty's house sits between Eviey's and Agnes'. It's smaller and stone like the others in town, but radiates warmth and coziness even from the outside. Large, flat stones line the path from the garden up to the cottage. An array of brightly colored wildflowers decorate either side of the cobblestones. I drag my hand, letting my fingers graze the tips of the petals as I pass by. The smell of lavender hangs heavily in the air, a natural refuge for the buzzing bees surrounding the plants. Delicate wind chimes dance lightly in the breeze, letting off faint pitches of music into the warm air. Surely, I could stay perched in the garden with the breeze and the wildflowers forever.

But, alas, I cannot, because tonight is the full moon.

The aromas from the cottage as I open the rounded door set my stomach into a fit of audible rumbles. Peeking around the corner, I place my basket of vegetables on the small wooden table at the entry and watch as Letty and Eviey busy themselves in the kitchen.

"I told you, you added too much sugar!" Letty drops a dirty spoon on the worktable as Eviey laughs playfully, scooping what looks to be cobbler filling into a baking dish.

"Oh, relax sister," Eviey says, "you've always been such a rule follower. Live a little." She shoots Letty a wink who responds with a shrug and a wave of her hand.

The kitchen is much smaller than Agnes' but brightly colored. The walls are splashed with turquoise; the wooden table tops streaked with pinks and orange. A small work table at the center is lined with different shaped baking dishes. A sink with a small, round window centered above it overlooks the wildflowers below. Herbs and dried flowers of all colors hang from the ceiling, the mixture of aromas is strong but not pungent. I set my empty canteen down on the worktable with a *clink*. Eviey looks up from her cobbler, apron dusted with flour, a grin splitting across her face.

"Elora, you've been out there all morning," she says. "Please come sit." She gestures to the stool next to where she works, making the sweet smelling desserts.

"Thank you," I say, sliding onto a stool. "I think I managed to get most of the weeds pulled. There's just a few more on the southern end. I only needed a quick refill." I point to my canteen, and before I can ask where to fill it myself, Letty saunters over and begins pouring water from a pitcher, doing the task for me.

"You've done more than enough," Letty says as she tops off the bottle. "We appreciate the help. Working bent over in that garden in this heat...We're not as young as we used to be." Letty and Eviey share a laugh together, and I can't help but smile as well. Their love for each other is endearing. It would be diffi-cult, I imagine, for anyone not to be swept away by it.

While they are twins, the more I look at them, the more differences I can see. Letty wears her hair in a braid and the texture of her dark silver locks is much straighter. Eviey switches her hairstyle often, sometimes in a braid and other times, like now, in a knot on the top of her head. A few loose, silver curls hang down at the nape of her neck. And of course, Eviey wears the small, rounded spectacles. Both sisters have deep lines around their brown eyes. Their tanned skin is weathered from a life under the sun, though the creases along their mouths are a sign it's been a life well lived.

Letty crosses back over, handing me the canteen. I don't hesitate to take a greedy gulp before wiping my lips with the back of my hand. "It's really no problem at all," I say, refas-tening the lid. "I quite enjoy working outside and appreciate the solitude." The twins shoot each other a look, raising their brows.

Me and my damn mouth.

"I just mean, I lived alone for so long, being around other people, no matter how *lovely*," I emphasize, "is still an adjust-ment." My cheeks begin to heat with the threat that I've offended them, so I glance around the kitchen for a change of conversation. It isn't as though I haven't enjoyed the company, but a part of me will always need to be alone. At least in some capacity. Nothing like Sorin and his exuberance for life and revelry.

As I'm about to point out the magnificent collection of teacups Letty has displayed in a small cabinet, I'm interrupted by the sudden touch of Eviey's hand on mine. Bringing my attention back to her, I'm met with a kind smile by both sisters.

"Whatever happened to you, Enchantress..." Eviey's voice goes distant for a moment before continuing. "Whatever hard-ship you were forced to endure, the tragedy I'm sure you went through that brought you here, I hope you know what a blessing you are to us. It's not every day we meet an Enchantress such as yourself." My brows knit together as confusion splays across my face. What is it that they think I can do? First Agnes and now this.

Parting my mouth I intend to ask her what she means, but I flounder to find the right words. I don't know what these people expect of me. It may be that they think I possess a useful kind of magick and can help them in some way. How disappointed they will be to know the magick I possess is absolutely nothing at all. Or is it that they think I have yet to obtain any? It could be possible they're holding out hope for when I retrieve the Stones.

Another disappointment.

But the way she and Letty gaze at me with such admiration makes me keep my thoughts and the truth to myself. Let them think the latter. That I have yet to complete my Ceremony. No good will come from the realization that a magickless Enchantress is after the Stones.

Clapping her hands loudly together, Letty's sudden cheeriness makes me startle in my seat. "Now," she exclaims, standing from her stool. "Enough serious talk. We're merely glad to have you here Elora." She clasps her hands together at her chest as a beaming smile spreads across her face.

I let out a small laugh. "I'm happy to be here. It's my pleasure to help with anything for the celebration tonight." I hope the change in subject will be enough to break their gaze away.

"Ah, yes." Eviey draws out the phrase. "The full moon celebration is a wonderous time indeed." She drags her eyes from the top of my sweat matted braid to the toes of my dirt caked boots. Her face splits into a wild and wicked grin. "And what exactly do you plan to wear tonight, my child?"

CHAPTER 16
ELORA

I STRUGGLE TO BREATHE AS LETTY AND EVIEY tighten the laces on my dress.

Eviey explained earlier that the people of Loxley celebrate the full moon just as the rest of Teravie does.

Every month, a beautiful feast is laid under the moon, thanks is given to Mother Gaia for all she provides. Music and dancing are essential, though, my stomach churns at the thought. Never been much of a dancer. It's not so much the act of dancing itself, but the attention. I despise any activity that would land too many eyes on me at once.

Letty happened to have a particular dress close enough to my size, and I gladly slipped out of my dirt covered clothes into it. The gown is a stunning ivory with a thin, gold trim. Stitched wildflowers in deep magentas, vibrant blues, indigos, and yellows adorn the bodice. The corset cinches at my waist, giving the illusion of a much larger bust than I actually have. While the neckline scoops low, leaving my entire chest on display, and the sleeves fit snugly on my arms but widen at my elbows, hanging loosely at my fingertips. The rest of the ivory fabric flows delicately from my hips down to the floor in a soft cascade. It's truly beautiful and I insisted several times that it was too much. To which Letty replied with a scoff, "Nonsense. For you Enchantress, it is barely enough."

With Eviey's help, we detangle my hair after I took what felt like the most luxurious bath since living in the castle in Valebridge. The steaming water mixed with various herbs from the garden were nearly enough to lull me to sleep. Eviey has pinned one side of my hair back, leaving the rest falling down my back in blonde waves. Plucking a pink wildflower from her garden, Letty stops to tuck it behind my ear.

The three of us balance the food dishes from earlier; a rather large quantity of blackberry cobblers, carrot and potato stew, and a few other cooked green vegetables from the garden. Taking a slight turn to the main road, a small gasp escapes me as I take in Loxley as dusk begins to settle over the town. The small stone cottages that frame each side of the dirt road have been decorated in an abundance of varying foliage.

Beautiful wildflowers sit atop the windowsills and porches in huge, overflowing bundles. Lavender, daisies, and buttercups bring a beautiful brightness of color to the green ivy that naturally grows up the sides of the homes. White pillared candles line the road on either side, each one flickering to illuminate the path towards the center of the small town. My mouth gapes at the lit plumes. There must be hundreds of them and miraculously, each one remains lit. Letty notices my gaze, chuckling softly as she gently grabs me by the elbow.

"We may not be Mother blessed with Enchantress magick," she whispers, "but we have a few tricks up these old sleeves."

In the center of the road there's a row of large wooden tables, the same tables I realize were used at the market yesterday. On top of each table sits stunning piles of pink and yellow flowers in varying glass jars and vases with candelabras at the center, each full of long, tapered candles. I'm dazzled as I watch the flames flicker softly in the late summer breeze, the soft pulse of magick in the air sends a chill down my spine, and my throat aches from the cry I refuse to let out.

It reminds me of her.

It reminds me of home.

Following Letty and Eviey as they head toward one of the tables, we set down our offerings of food and my eyes drift again over the town. It is beautiful. So very beautiful.

"I'm going to go check on Marian and see if she needs help with the bread." Eviey excuses herself and turns to head across the street.

The children of Loxley busy themselves with a game of make believe. Running around the tables, playing with their wooden swords and bows. The sound of their laughter brings me back to our first night here and how it felt when I saw so many happy people gathered around the fire. My heart sinks at the memories their sounds bring up. The memories of my own childhood.

"Let's play a game," Cade insisted, pacing back and forth in the dimly lit library. Even at fifteen, he had too much energy for his own good. Always pacing, running, playing, fighting.

"I am tired of games," I said, flipping through another book I'd pulled from the shelf. Reading was the only pastime I preferred, but the look in Cade's hazel eyes, I could never say no. "Fine," I replied, tossing the book down. He pulled me to my feet, his blonde hair cut too short from his newly begun military training. "But no poker. This time," I laughed, squeezing tight to his hand, "I get to choose the game."

Before I can get too lost in my train of thought, a familiar voice catches my attention at the furthest end of the table.

Sorin.

He is dressed in his usual black pants and a loose-fitting black linen shirt, the laces unraveled slightly, revealing his tan chest underneath. Silver rings adorn each of his fingers now, more than the one he typically wears on his index finger. I surprise myself that I've noticed such a small detail, but I ignore it and watch as he sips casually from his chalice.

I recognize the man he chats with, Ulric, I believe. They

appear comfortable next to each other, though I've yet to meet anyone who isn't comfortable or pleased to be in Sorin's presence. His wavy dark hair is swept back on the top, the sides cropped fairly short. His stubble accentuates his sharp jaw and full lips, and in the glow of the late evening sun, he is magnificent.

I don't realize how long I'm staring until his eyes lock with mine from across the tables. Dipping his chin in my direction, I scramble to find focus elsewhere. Anywhere. I catch his body out of my peripherals and heat blooms across my cheeks and neck as he saunters toward me. Biting the inside of my cheek, I prepare myself for the unavoidable. I hardly knew how to be around him before, and now that he's seen me at my most vulnerable, his presence is overwhelming.

He makes it about halfway in my direction before Agnes steps in. Grabbing his arm, she pulls him down to meet his ear. Dressed in a beautiful gown of deep purple with golden flowers etched into the fabric, she is glowing in the growing moonlight. The two of them whisper back and forth a few times, and I crane my ear, eager to know what they're discussing. Letty's warm hand on my elbow pulls my gaze downward.

"There's someone you should meet," she whispers, nudging me around. Reluctantly, I turn, and as I do, Agnes bounds past me.

Sorin follows Agnes, and as he passes me, his hand grazes my lower back. His touch is brief before he moves on but my stomach dips instantly. The lingering heat of where his hand was placed burns clear through my dress as I watch Sorin follow Agnes through the crowd of people down the street.

The group headed toward us is led by a giant man. His skin is as pale as his hair which is shaved bald on the sides, the rest is knotted loosely atop his head. A neatly cropped beard lines his jaw, and even from here, his blue eyes stand out among the crowd. Standing easily six inches taller than Sorin, I imagine he weighs double as well. His sculpted muscles are easy to identify even through his loose white shirt. Squinting my eyes, I try and fail to make out the swirling marks of ink that twist and turn around his forearms and up the collar of his shirt, covering his throat and stopping just below his chin.

Sorin catches up to the man and the two of them embrace in a violent hug, nearly toppling each other to the ground. An ear-to-ear grin splits across Sorin's face, and I hate the weakness that smile brings to my knees. Breaking apart from their hug, the taller man bends down and touches his forehead to Sorin's. What they whisper to each other, I can't make out.

"Who is he?" I whisper to Letty, keeping my eyes locked on them. It isn't often men show affection to each other this way, the same way I would assume siblings would.

"That big one there," she gestures, "that's Jarek." Tugging my arm, Letty leads me to a small round table that houses carafes of wine and chalices. *Jarek*, I note. By the looks of their embrace, I imagine they're close. Must be one of Sorin's crew he mentioned. Letty pours us each a glass of huckleberry wine before my attention refocuses to the group heading our way.

It's only when Jarek steps aside to grab his own chalice of wine that I notice the woman behind him. She walks with her arm linked with Agnes', her beauty so intense I fight the will to keep my mouth from falling to the ground.

Her skin, a deep brown, matches Agnes'. Their resemblance now glaringly obvious as their distance between us grows smaller. Tightly coiled curls spring from her head, grazing just above her shoulders, the color a deep and shining black. She's tall, but it's the way she moves with such confidence that shrinks me to an inch.

Her slim fitting, dark blue dress clings tightly to her curvy hips, the long sleeves, the same style as the ones I wear, are tight in the arms and flowing loosely past the elbow. The energy in the air shifts as she draws nearer. An energy I'm all too familiar with, one I'm ashamed I missed the night I met Agnes by the fire. The energy of an Enchantress.

"Samaria!" Letty's voice booms through the evening sky. "So glad you've returned safely to us once more! Was the hunting trip a success?" Letty asks cautiously, gripping Samaria's hand.

"Glad to be back, Letty," Samaria says. Her voice is soft, barely a whisper as she bends down to kiss Letty on either cheek. "And it was as successful as it could be, given the circumstances." Letty's gaze bounces between Agnes and Samaria, a look of understanding shared between the three women.

Her smile fades slightly as her attention is pulled toward me. I begin to shift under the weight of her stare, but to my surprise, my nerves settle quickly as our eyes meet. "And you must be the Enchantress?" Her question is more of a statement. I hold her gaze and am relieved to find no judgment there. Only curiosity peeks through her glowing eyes, much like the color of flames. Clearing my throat, I extend my hand in her direction.

"Yes," I say as confidently as I can muster. "I'm Elora. Sorin and Agnes have told me nothing but wonderful things about you, Samaria." She smirks as she places her hand in mine.

"Oh, I'm sure they've reserved the *best* stories for when I'm here." She turns, dropping my hand to grip Agnes by the shoulders. "There's nothing these two love more than to embarass me." She chuckles softly. "And please, call me Sam."

THE CANDLES MELT to waxy pools of white, dripping lazily on the tabletops as we enjoy the humble but delicious meal. Rich spices filled the air as carrot and potato stew are passed around with baskets of freshly baked rolls still warm from the hearth. Roasted rabbit accompanied by a spiced glaze Marian had made herself, is so tender and decadent it falls apart in my mouth. Guilt ticks at my insides for burdening Loxley with another mouth to feed during the famines, but no one says a word. Everyone laughs and speaks their gratitude for the Mother, even if what she's been able to provide is far less than usual. Letty offers me a second helping of cobbler, and because I can't help myself, I accept it.

Copious amounts of wine flow freely from the carafes as all the people of Loxley, and myself, sit together along the row of long tables. As the meal comes to an end, Agnes leads us in a toast.

"To our lovely village of Loxley," she says warmly, peering over the crowd still seated at the table. "And to our even more lovely guest." She turns her focus on me and without thought, I shrink into my chair as dozens of eyes find their way to me. "We must give thanks to the Fates for introducing Elora to my Sorin, your company is our honor." Swallowing thickly, I pick at my nails under the table before smiling at her, nodding my head just once.

"And above all," Agnes continues, finally breaking our gaze, "to the Mother. For all she gives. For all she does."

"To the Mother," the crowd echoes before everyone, myself included, takes a sip from their drink.

I've managed to avoid Sorin for most of the night. Every time he caught my eye, I made myself busy cleaning up or chatting with one of the twins. I'm not sure how I ended up here, but Agnes and I sit alone at the table. Fighting the urge to fidget, I recline back in my chair as she speaks, wishing desperately to rip this corset off here and now. Breathing has begun to feel like a chore, though I don't mind the rest of the dress. It's quite nice to feel pretty for once.

"About the other day," Agnes starts but her eyes draw past me, watching Sam and Sorin as they laugh about something Jarek is enthusiastically explaining. "My visions are more and more sporadic," she explains. "Ever since William passed, they've never been the same. And with my health..."

"It's not a worry." I cut her short, saving her from explaining any further. "While it was certainly a surprise, I understand the visions are not something to be controlled." Something I know all too well given my mother's gift of Sight.

"I know why Sorin didn't tell me about your gift or Loxley," I continue, "I understand." Feeling brave, I reach forward and squeeze her hand. With no more than a few pleasantries, Agnes gives me a small smile before excusing herself for the night. Ulric appeared all too eager to walk her home, and the two slipped silently through the crowd, arms linked and faces beaming.

With Agnes gone and the twins occupied by the relentless dancing around the large fire, I find myself a quiet corner near a smaller fire at the edge of the clearing and away from the dancing. My body screams to rest after a day in the garden and socializing. Sitting myself down, my ivory gown falls into a puddle of fabric all around me. Though the corset is still cinched tight, I attempt to relax my shoulders and close my eyes, taking in the sounds of revelers and music, a smile dancing on my lips.

You shouldn't be here.

Drawing my eyes open, I let out an exasperated sigh. The voices never let me rest for long. I'm not sure why I thought tonight would be any exception. "Do piss off," I say aloud, hoping by some miracle they'll listen.

"Well, that's one way to greet a friend," Sorin says as he sits down next to me, carefully balancing two chalices of wine in the process.

My body jolts, his approach catching me completely off guard. "I'm sorry," I say, frustration lacing my words at another missed moment of solitude. "I didn't realize you were over here." He chuckles lightly before nudging my elbow. Turning to him, I don't hesitate to take the glass of wine he's offering.

The sweet smell of huckleberry overwhelms me before I even take a drink.

"If that greeting wasn't meant for me, who was it for?" Sorin asks, taking a sip of his wine.

Shaking my head, I take a long pull of the wine in an attempt to delay my response. Wiping my lips with my thumb, I shoot Sorin a glance. "Just thinking out loud," I say.

He smiles but says nothing before taking another drink. We sit together in silence for a few minutes, sipping our wine and watching the villagers dance and sing around the large fire. If this is the closest I can get to a moment alone, I suppose it isn't so bad.

"I'm sorry I woke you the other night," I say, deciding not to tiptoe around the subject any longer. "The nightmares... they're not as often as they used to be but they're just as vivid." I focus my attention on the flames. Dizzying spirals of heat shoot to the sky, and I'm hypnotized by their constant movement. Not to mention, I don't want to see the pity that is no doubt forming in Sorin's eyes. Pity and weakness go hand in hand, and weakness is not something I'm comfortable with, even if it's something I often feel. I set my empty cup on the grass and let the wine stream through my system, working its magick to help unclench the last of the tightness I carry between my shoulders.

"Didn't I already tell you not to apologize?" Sorin's voice is playful, so I turn my eyes to him. He downs the rest of this cup, throat working, before giving me that signature smirk.

"Hmm, I vaguely recall that statement." Though it doesn't change the fact that I'm still uncomfortable with how vulnerable I felt that night.

"Really, it's fine, Elora. We all have our demons," he says with a shrug. His eyes and voice house no pity. Only warmth and understanding. A relief, albeit small, a relief nonetheless. "Is that why you've been avoiding me?"

Huffing a laugh, the wine makes me braver than I feel. "One of the reasons," I say, avoiding his eyes.

"And the other reasons?"

Turning to face him, his eyes are dark, but there's a sparkle in them. A curiosity.

"Maybe being here makes me feel things I haven't felt in a long time," I whisper, turning my attention back to the flames, leaving out what I truly want to say. That his presence, that *he*, makes me feel things I never thought I'd feel again. "It's a bit overwhelming."

Before I can say another word, Sorin jumps up, the movement so sudden it takes me a moment to register he's no longer sitting. He grabs my arm, pulling me up to my feet.

"What are you doing?!" I protest, swaying slightly, the earth feels as though it's going to move beneath me.

"You can't celebrate the last full moon of summer without a dance," Sorin says, pulling my hand in the direction of the fire and the dozens of people still dancing around it.

"Oh no, no, no." I jerk my hand out of his. "I do *not* dance." My words are clipped, my heart racing at the thought of dancing. "I haven't danced since I was a child, and even then it was a sorry excuse for it." Stepping closer, he ignores me. Grabbing my hand again, his fingers lace with mine as he tugs me forward. It must be the wine getting to my head, because I don't struggle as he pulls me close to him.

Perhaps it *is* the wine or the lightning I feel with every touch of Sorin's hand is more than what I think. Perhaps, I like the way his skin feels on mine. Perhaps, I think of it far too often and for far too long. But then again, perhaps it's just the wine.

"You're allowed to be happy, Elora." Sorin strokes the back of my hand with his thumb, the sensation bringing a flurry of butterflies deep in my stomach. He dips his chin lower so his lips rest just at the bottom of my ear. "Despite what you think you deserve. Despite whatever happened in your past. It took me a long time to accept that. That I could be happy, but I did learn. And it's time you do as well."

His lips brush my earlobe, the rasp in his voice only enhances the swirling heat now in my stomach. He pulls back, but only slightly. "Besides, you look way too beautiful to be sitting here all alone. That dress should be a sin." He smiles. My cheeks heat but I still don't pull away.

His words may cause me to blush, but they soothe the ache in my chest I've lived with for so long. I should pull away. Tell him he doesn't know what he's talking about, because truth-fully, he doesn't. But I say nothing.

Swallowing the knot in my throat, I look past him to Letty and Eviey swinging in each other's arms. Tossing their heads up and faces beaming as they sing loudly to the moon. Then my eyes drift to Samaria and Jarek who sit nestled together near the fire. Their bodies intertwine as they sway to the beat of the music.

My conscience and heart have been at war for so long, and here Sorin is, laying it all out in front of me. Saying the things I've wished to hear. As if he somehow knows exactly what I'm thinking.

I want it all, of course. To live joyfully, free of the demons who have claimed my mind as their home. The problem is, I don't know how. How can I live happily when my family is gone? When, if it wasn't for me, they'd be here. Guilt is the heaviest armor I bear. A shield crafted of steel, meticulously built over the years to keep me from enjoying the things I simply do not deserve. Because I'm here, and *they* are not.

But maybe this once, I can be that person behind the armor. Maybe just for tonight, I can simply be Elora. With no past. No demons. No burdens.

My gaze drags back to Sorin, his hand still holding mine. His eyes never left my face, I realize.

"You're not..." I whisper, dragging my eyes to the ground. "You're not afraid of me?" Embarrassed by my actions in

Copenspire, I've avoided the question for fear of his answer. He should be afraid. Any sane person would.

Sorin squeezes my hand, and I glance up at him. His eyes are so dark they reflect the bits of orange cast from the flames. "Not for the reasons you may think, love." I don't know why but his words make my heart race. My lips curve into a half smile as I force the demons down, down, down. A ritual I'm all too accustomed to.

"Fine," I say, breathing deeply so the crisp night air stings my lungs. "Just one dance."

CHAPTER 17

ELORA

A SMALL GROAN ESCAPES ME AS I PRESS MY PALMS into my eyes, attempting to block out the natural light flooding the room. The pounding in my head is incessant, my throat coarse and dry. My desperation for water outweighs the harshness of the light so, reluctantly, I sit up and force my eyes open.

I've spent the last several nights in Eviey's guest room. Her small four post bed faces a lone window and the walls are made of stone. I've become comfortable and familiar with the space. Only now, my blurry gaze rests upon a wooden planked wall, not a window. The window sits slightly off-centered and is much larger. The wall before me is adorned with a small canvas and several other pictures pinned neatly in a row. I tilt my head to the side and squint my eyes to get a better look. Is the canvas a constellation or a map?

Already giving up my attempt to make out the pattern of the canvas, I close my eyes again, using my fingers to massage my temples. The pounding in my head is fierce and unrelenting, likely the result of that last cup of huckleberry wine. I agreed to one dance, and it ended up being at least an hour of swinging and laughing under the moonlight. I don't remember the last time I let myself have that much fun.

The night was beautiful despite the now glaring conse-
quences. Forcing my eyes open again, I refocus on the room.
The bed is similar to the one at Eviey's but no nightstand. The
quilt is a deep gray rather than her vibrant patchwork. My eyes
draw forward toward the fireplace in the room and a small settee
that sits in front of it. Covering my mouth to muffle a gasp,
clarity hits me like a ton of bricks. I'm in Sorin's room. In
Sorin's bed. And there is Sorin, asleep on the settee near the
fireplace.

Glancing down at myself, I drop my hands from my
temples and pat over my chest and stomach. Fully clothed in
breeches and a tunic, certainly not my own. Regardless, I slump
back on the pillows, relieved that I'm dressed. After the last cup
of wine, the rest of the night is a blur. We danced and ate and
sang. But do I remember even walking home?

This isn't your home.

Clasping my hands over my mouth, I suppress a laugh
because for once, the voices are right. This isn't my home. I'm a
guest. A guest who is in the bed of her host while he sleeps
cramped up on a small settee.

I pull back the quilt softly before dropping my feet to the
ground. The ivory gown I'd worn the night prior is discarded in
a pile near the end of the bed. A memory from the night before
forces itself behind my eyes. Diluted images of Sorin and myself
come into view as I struggle to find my balance.

*"I don't need help," I hissed as Sorin offered his hand to
unlace the back of my gown. Except, I definitely did need help.
Samaria and Jarek left us, turning in early long before dawn.
I'm not sure what brought me to Sorin's room and not Eviey's, but
I didn't question it at the time. All I could focus on was removing
the corset still cinched around my waist.*

*Pulling his hands away, Sorin took a step backward. "As you
wish, Enchantress."*

*Fumbling with the strings for a few moments, my shoulders
slackened in defeat. "Fine," I mumbled, dropping my hands to*

my sides. "Can you please undo the back of this Mother forsaken gown?" Gripping the end of the bed to steady myself, not trusting my own ability to balance. The room spun as Sorin's laugh filled the air. His fingers worked the laces slowly down the back of my dress with expert precision.

I ignored the small touches of his skin on mine, focusing all my energy on keeping myself upright. But as he got to the final lace, he stopped. Tracing a line up my naked spine with his finger. Goosebumps erupted over my exposed skin, but I didn't move.

Then, before I could urge him to continue, he removed his hand, undoing the final lace before turning the opposite direction. I slipped out of the gown and into the borrowed breeches and cotton tunic. My mind wandered momentarily, as I studied Sorin's back. I pondered how it might feel to run my fingers through his dark hair. How his hands might feel wrapped around my thighs. I debated whether or not I should pull him closer, just to feel the energy of his touch again.

Instead, I bit my tongue and clasped my hands together to keep them from doing something impulsive. Curling into the bed, I tugged the quilt up to my chin and pressed my eyes shut, hoping the stars that danced behind them and the ghost-like lightning of Sorin's touch would soon subside.

The memory creates a tight knot in my stomach and the need to leave this room is now desperate. Darting my eyes around for my boots, I spot them laying by the door.

Convenient.

Tip toeing over the wooden floors, I make my way towards the exit. As I reach down for my boots, I dare a final look at Sorin. Still sound asleep and in his same clothes from the night before, his fully unbuttoned shirt leaves his sculpted abdomen on display. My throat feels thick as I attempt to swallow. His dark brows are furrowed as if in deep thought, and I can't help but smile at how ridiculously large he looks on the tiny sofa. Peeling my eyes away, I grab my boots and head silently out the door.

Chatter from the kitchen and the rich aroma of coffee and baked bread wafts down the hallway. Raking my fingers through my hair to free it of tangles, I'm greeted by a mischievous grin from Agnes as I enter the kitchen. The smile reminds me of my mother so much that I take a step backward, stumbling slightly on my feet. The all-knowing smile of a mother who knows what you're up to without being told.

"Good morning, Elora." Agnes draws out my name as she and Sam share a look. Opening my mouth, I'm immediately defensive and eager to explain nothing happened between Sorin and I, but before I can speak, Jarek hands me a mug of steaming hot coffee.

"Figured you might need this," he whispers with a wink before settling into the stool next to Sam. His accent is none of which I've heard before, and though we haven't been properly introduced, I already feel a sense of comfort in his presence. He places a quick kiss to Sam's cheek before taking a sip from his own mug. Sam peers over to me with the same mischievous smile. She looks casual in a pair of dark breeches and a velvety cream blouse. Her eyes ask a million questions but I'm grateful her lips do not.

"Thank you," I mumble, raising my mug to Jarek before moving and settling into the chair by the window. Agnes bids us all a good day before leaving through the back door.

"So," Sam says as she moves around the kitchen, pulling plates from different cabinets. "I imagine Sorin's still passed out on the settee? He's always been quite the lightweight." Her laugh is melodic and so intoxicating that even I find myself letting out a small laugh of my own. Though her words are lighthearted, I'm relieved it's known that Sorin and I didn't share a bed.

"It's true," Jarek chimes in as he bites into a piece of bread. "Once, at a full moon celebration, he barely made it to midnight before he was face first in the dirt," he says between bites. "Could never handle his wine."

"I promise you, I can handle my wine just fine," Sorin grumbles, entering the room with narrowed eyes. Rubbing at his temples he adds, "I'm just tired is all." He's changed out of his black attire, and swapped for a pair of dark brown pants and a forest green shirt.

Sam and Jarek exchange a look before breaking out in a fit of laughter. Ignoring them both, Sorin smiles in my direction. "Good morning," he mouths before swiping Samaria's coffee out from her hands. The incredulous look she shoots him doesn't last long before she's getting up to fill a new mug.

"I appreciate the coffee," I say, taking a long sip of the thick brown drink. Letting it rest on my tongue a moment before swallowing it down. "I haven't had it in years." The slip isn't intentional, but the words are out before I can stop them. Breaking my eyes away from Sorin, Sam's grin lights up her entire face, dark curls circling her face like a halo. Placing a plate of jellied bread on the table she motions for everyone to eat.

"It's our pleasure, Enchantress," she says. My gut wretches at the kindness in her voice. The sincerity. She lets loose a long sigh. "Besides, it's my understanding that my brother has a proposition for us." Her dark brows draw upward as she passes a glance to Sorin then back to me. "If that's the case," she continues, "I assume abundant amounts of coffee will be necessary this morning."

"LET ME GET THIS STRAIGHT." Jarek stands to stretch his enormous arms over his head before craning his neck to either side. The dark ink that swirls up his arms is even more defined with his movements.

We've gone over our plan three times already, the sun now high in the sky indicating its nearing midday. "Your plan is to find the Awakening Stones on Kirsgard Mountain," Jarek continues. "Which, by the way, is one of the most notoriously brutal mountains in all of Valebridge, weather so unpredictable nothing survives there." A crack pierces my chest at his words. *We survived there*, I want to say, until we didn't. Sorin glances at me for a moment, then returns his attention to Jarek.

"Not to mention," Jarek says, "the guards that may still be stationed there looking for the Stones themselves. Then, you plan to just waltz into the castle and—" He cuts himself short and shoots a quick look in my direction before continuing. "Do whatever it is you plan to do."

I force myself to look away as he begins to jog in place. The spinning in my head is only made worse by his quick movements. Sorin kept his plans for Valebridge a secret from me, and despite our promise to be truthful, he has yet to divulge any information.

You're keeping a secret too.

"More or less, yes. That's our plan." Sorin's tone is just as relaxed as his posture. As if we aren't discussing an impossible idea. He reclines back in his chair as he crosses one leg over the other, placing his hands lightly in his lap. The movement is subtle, but I watch as he twirls the ring on his index finger several times.

Samaria and I move to the floor to stretch out our limbs, sharing a plate of various fruit and crisps. The pounding in my head has subsided, at least, as I fill my stomach with water and food.

"Doesn't sound crazy at all," Sam mumbles before stuffing another grape in her mouth. I toss Sorin a look, the worry I feel I'm sure is obvious across my face. Maybe we hadn't thought this through enough. Finding the Stones is already a risk and we haven't even discussed how we'll get into Valebridge. But Sorin's expression remains unbothered as he finishes his second mug of coffee.

"Shouldn't we wait for Galen to get here?" Jarek's voice is winded as he drops down next to Sam from his exercise. "He is coming, is he not?" He reaches over and helps himself to the remainder of the grapes from our bowl. Sam and I send him the same narrowed gaze as he tosses half of them in his mouth, with a wink.

"He'll be here." Sorin's voice is assured, though when I glance up at him, he doesn't hide how his knee bounces under the table.

"My apologies," I say, standing to head to the kitchen for another glass of water. "But who is Galen?"

Sam's burst of laughter startles me so much that I spin around on my heels. Jarek and Sorin wear the same smile, clearly I've missed something.

"Galen, Galen, Galen," Sam muses, snatching back the last few grapes from Jarek before he gets a chance to eat them himself. "He's Sorin's best mate. The brains behind every one of Sorin's plans. Though Galen finds Loxley unworthy to reside in," she says, rolling her eyes. "He lives in Ramshire. Studies there under the scholar...oh what's his name? Leland?" Jarek shrugs in response, piling the remainder of the crisps into his mouth.

Sorin scoffs, "I like to think I'm the brains of at least some part of the plans." Standing from his chair, he joins me at the large kitchen table. My shoulders release their tension at his closeness.

Jarred memories of the two of us intertwined while dancing make my skin heat in the brutal light of day. How his hands felt on my waist. How, when we danced as the music slowed, his mouth had grazed my neck. How badly I wished he hadn't stopped our touches on the dancefloor and even more so, how desperately I wish to get the memory of it out of my mind.

"Studies what?" I ask in an attempt to clear my mind of Sorin. And Sorin's hands. And most importantly, of Sorin's hands on my body.

Sam hums for a moment. "Arithmetic for one," she says. "But Leland, I think that's the scholar he studies under. Damn,

I can't remember. Anyway, he's best known for the history of magick." She cuts me a glance, and I arch my brows, curiosity fully piqued. "And Galen's been studying under him for years now," she continues, "isn't that right Sorin?"

Nodding, Sorin places the porcelain pitcher back on the table between us. "Yes. Well, everything aside from the Loxley part. You know he has never looked down on Loxley. He's an opportunist like us, Sam. He just so happens to find his opportunities in a less unsavory way." Sam rolls her eyes while Jarek gives her arm a quick squeeze. "Where I'm the big picture man, Galen is the details man," Sorin continues. He brings his fingers to his temples again, rubbing around his hairline. "He'll be the one to fine tune the logistics of our plan. Tell us if we're completely mad for attempting any of this."

"Oh, we're mad. There is no question about that." Samaria lets out a laugh as she scoots herself onto Jarek's lap.

"Ah," Sorin says before downing an entire glass of water. "So, you're saying you're in?" He sets the glass down and crosses his arms. His lips curve into a lethal smile, showing off that dimple I've come to admire too much. Sam and Jarek share a look, their communication so fine-tuned they don't require words to understand each other.

"Of course, we're in," Jarek says, grazing Sam's cheek with the back of his hand. She leans into his touch with no hesitation, and for a moment, I wonder what that must be like. To embrace the touch of another and not have guilt and fear swallow you up. "We're always in."

WHILE SORIN and Jarek clean the dishes from breakfast, Samaria helps fetch my freshly washed tunic and breeches so I can change out of the clothes I borrowed from Sorin. Back in her room, I quickly braid my hair while she thumbs through a book on her bed.

"The Stones." Her voice is quiet, almost a hum. "Do you know how to wield them? It's rare to meet any other Enchantresses aside from my mother. It's embarrassing, really. How little I know about...any of it." Fastening my hair with a band of leather, I reposition myself at the foot of the bed.

"You have nothing to be embarrassed by," I say. "Your life..." The words catch on my tongue. "Loxley looks like a beautiful place to grow up. I'd be lying if I said I wasn't a little envious." Sam laughs, low and sweet. "And yes," I continue, "I have a general idea of how to use them."

My knee begins to bounce, responding to the anxiousness growing in my stomach. "If I'm being honest," I say again, "I've never done a full Ceremony before. It was something my mother and the older Enchantresses performed, but I've attended several." I meet her gaze at my confession. "I'll do my best. If it means helping you awaken your magick, I'll try." I offer a small smile.

"And what about you? In what ways has your magick manifested? My mother is a Seer but outside of her, I don't know much about what we're...capable of," she says, her eyes scanning my face with curiosity. I bite my lower lip, glancing down at my hands. "If you don't mind me asking, of course," she says, reading my shift in disposition.

"I haven't completed my Ceremony," I say. "No magick to be had, yet." The shame of not possessing any brings me to lie, and I'm instantly guilted by doing so.

"And where are they now?" Sam asks, setting her book to the side. "Your mother? The others?" My body tenses. Opening my mouth, I quickly snap it shut. My knee ceases to bounce as I clench my hands into fists. Pushing deeper until there's a sting of nails against flesh. I don't mind the hurt. I need it. It's a small reminder to myself I'm in the present, so I don't get caught up in the past.

"I'm sorry," Sam says. "I didn't mean to be blunt." She scoots closer to me on the end of the bed. Furrowing her brows she says, "Sorin hasn't told us much about you. I don't mean to pry."

She reaches her hand over to place it on mine. Slowly unrolling my fingers, I place my palm flush with hers, surprising myself by not flinching away. She has every right to be curious about the person who has suddenly shown up in her life, asking her to risk everything on a slim chance of success. I owe her at least an explanation of where I've come from.

"They're...gone. My mother, the Enchantresses that escaped Valebridge with us, and a few others. They're gone." I swallow a little too loudly as I recall the night but find myself grateful for Sam's closeness despite having just met her. "We fled to the base of the Kirsgard Mountains five years ago, right after King Roman took the throne and staged the uprising.

"When King Silas died, everything happened so quickly. Then when Roman took over, there was so much other noise with the turning of the throne that no one took notice of the small changes he began to make. One day, Enchantresses weren't allowed to practice magick after a certain hour. The next day, we weren't allowed to practice magick at *all*. Of course, we were upset. Outraged. Those who lashed out against the king did out of defense. That's all it took for him to change the narrative and poison the minds of the people into believing that we struck first."

"Then what happened?" Sam asks, her grip on my hand firm and assuring.

"The people of Valebridge have been through uprisings before," I explain. "Have seen what happens when Enchantresses are pushed too far. The last time it happened was long before you and I were born, but the stories were told to us every day in our schooling. How Enchantresses unleashed their magick against those in the kingdom, killing anyone who stood in their way.

"King Richard changed the laws after negotiations were made. He gave us more freedom, more of a life. But the scar of the last uprising remains, people don't easily forget fear, and when the stories are repeated day after day, it didn't take much to convince them it was going to happen again. Roman's lies spread like wildfire through Valebridge. So, when the Enchantresses began to question the new rules, the people saw it for what they wanted. An uprising."

"It wasn't long after the banishment of magick that Enchantresses began to go missing. Pulled from their beds, taken off the street, and all the while, King Roman became stronger. Smarter. More skilled than any other king."

"He's been harvesting magick," Sam whispers as if in disbelief, bringing her hand to her mouth.

NODDING, I continue, "My mother led a handful of us to the base of the mountain before Roman could take full control. I'm not sure how she knew we'd be safe there, but with her ability of Sight, it's likely she knew exactly where to go." It's only now I'm questioning the many years spent untouched on the mountain. How is it that no one from the Onyx Guild found us? They controlled all of the Kirsgard Mountain range and yet we lived peacefully for two years. Maybe they didn't care to look just as the Jade Guild has ceased caring in the forests.

Pushing away thoughts of the Guilds for a moment, I continue, "The moon was new and its light was faint that night." Clenching my fists, I focus on my breathing. "The snow was the heaviest I've ever witnessed. No one could see—" Pausing, I bite the inside of my cheek as the darkness dances along the corner of my eyes. Any moment and they'll start.

Murderer.

Murderer.

The voices come ceremoniously, using the darkness as their opening to strike me when I'm at my most vulnerable. "We couldn't see—" I attempt again but come up short. Ripping my hand from Sam's, I grip my chest to soothe the ache. "I'm sorry." It's all I can say before bolting out of the room.

"Elora, wait!" Sam's voice trails behind me as I sprint from the house, pressing my palms to my ears to muffle the word still echoing there.

Murderer.

I'm so focused on the ground as I descend the final porch steps, I don't see the figure standing at the bottom. My face collides into something firm yet warm, sending me tumbling backward and onto the ground. Shooting my head up, I glare at whomever it is that stands in my way.

Wearing black from head to toe, his pale blonde hair is a shock of light against his obsidian attire. Long legs and slim torso dressed immaculately in form fitting pants and a long sleeve shirt, laced loosely in the front. His blue eyes pierce into me as I straighten myself, suddenly very aware of his proximity. The expression on his face is cool, borderline annoyed as he watches me get ahold of myself. Not so much as offering his hand to help me up, as if I am the one inconveniencing him, not the other way around. A pile of papers and books are tucked neatly under one arm as he looks down at me. His high cheekbones give his face a certain sharpness that makes my stomach turn.

"Going somewhere?" His voice is low as I wipe the dirt from my breeches and pull myself to my feet.

"Well, I was trying before you decided to get in my way," I snap at the arrogant stranger. He flashes me a quick closed mouth grin, clearly amused by my frustration. I open my mouth to excuse myself but am not given the chance before Sam rushes out of the house.

"Elora, please, come back inside." The worry in her voice is displayed across her face. Her widened eyes scan over me, surely I look completely disheveled after my fall.

My options are minimal; stay here with this cold stranger,

walk aimlessly through town before ending back up here anyway, or save myself the trouble and just go back inside now. I sigh, steadying myself before I take the few steps up to the house. If I want to stay and do this, this journey, I'll have to face my demons and truth some time or another.

Samaria pulls me in for a hug, her body wrapping me up in a tight embrace. I lean into her closeness rather than fight it. My heart rate returns to a normal pace and slowly, the voices fade.

"We'll talk later. Whenever you're ready," she whispers, pulling herself away. I cast her an appreciative smile before the sound of the man clearing his throat catches both of our attention. Sam grins, turning toward him. "Well, I see you've already met Galen."

CHAPTER 18

SORIN

"So, it's settled, then," I say, handing Galen a glass of wine before sitting across from him on the settee.

"No," he says, drawing out the word and rolling his eyes. He sets down his glass, a soft thud as it hits the wood. "It's not settled. What you're attempting to do is ridiculous. Do you have any idea just how many guards could be stationed on Kirsgard Mountain?"

I shake my head.

"Exactly," he sighs. "It's an uncalculated risk, and a huge one." He drags a hand down his face as I settle on the couch beside him. With Elora helping Sam prepare dinner, I snagged some time alone with my oldest friend. However, if I'm being honest with myself, I wish Elora would join me in my room, not Galen. Though, it is good to see him. It's been far too long this time.

Sipping my wine, I brace myself for the battle. "I understand it's going to be difficult—"

Galen's laugh cuts me short. "Difficult is an understatement, Sorin. What you're asking is impossible," he says before taking a small sip of drink, his lip curls into a snarl, his distaste for wine has always amused me.

I tsk, wagging a finger toward him. "Now, now. Just because you're an educated scholar doesn't give you the right to speak down to the rest of us." I laugh, though his eyes narrow in my direction, and I know I've gotten under his skin. I flash him a wide grin that he promptly ignores. Pushing his blonde hair out of his eyes, he relaxes back into the sofa for the first time since we've sat down.

"Fine," he says. "If we're looking at it logistically, it's not *impossible*. But there are so many risks. The journey, the terrain, actually removing the Stones, not to mention the royal guards." His voice becomes flustered as he throws his hands up. "And we haven't even touched on actually getting into Valebridge. What is your plan when you finally confront King Roman?" He pauses, a flicker of curiosity flashes across his face. My suddenly tensed posture doesn't go unnoticed though, and Galen's tone softens. "All I'm saying is, we need to be practical about what you're asking of not just the girl, but Samaria and Jarek as well."

"Elora."

"What?" he asks, sounding rather exhausted and pinching the bridge of his nose with his thumb and index finger.

"The girl's *name* is Elora." I sit forward, placing my elbows on my knees. We stare at each other for a moment, and it's only now that I wish Galen didn't possess the ability to read me like a damn book.

"Please don't tell me..." His head dips back as he lets out a low laugh. "Now it's all making sense. You should have just said you care for the girl and saved me the hassle of trying to talk you out of this ridiculous idea."

He continues to chuckle as I toss one of the small couch pillows in his direction. Of course, I can't hide my feelings from him, even if I'm not entirely sure what those feelings are yet. He's been my best friend, aside from Sam, since I was a young boy. He grew up in Loxley, but his parents moved to Ramshire when we were fifteen. I don't blame them for seeking a place to raise their son that held more opportunities. He's always been so smart, nose in a book, rather than out hunting like the rest of us. He's done well for himself, too, but always finds his way back to here, as most do. Loxley tends to have that effect on people.

"So, what if I'm interested in her company? It makes no difference, the goal is the same," I say, settling back into my seat. "Besides. it wouldn't be the first time we've done something reckless on account of one of our hearts." His laughter ceases, and I know I hit my mark. *That one stung.*

"That's low," he grumbles, taking a decent sip of wine this time, and to his credit, he doesn't snarl as he gulps it down.

The memory is one I'm so fond of, I can see it clear as day. Galen and I were maybe seventeen when he got his first, and only, broken heart. Separated from the boy he admired so much, we took it into our own hands to justify the situation. The scholars in Ramshire did not take lightly to two students being romantically involved, whether it be two men or a man and a woman, it was forbidden as an academic. Galen's partner was kicked out of the program, his own brilliance the only thing saving him from the same fate. The scholars couldn't risk not having him under their wing, so he was spared. Though, that only enraged him further. Two house fires and a night in jail later, Galen and I accomplished nothing trying to mend his broken heart all those years ago.

"I'm sorry," I say through a laugh, "but you can't deny the truth." I flash him another wide grin before drinking down the rest of my wine. "Besides, this isn't just about her. She can help Samaria. And if the suspicions are true about the Mother being responsible for the blight and storms, this could change everything."

Galen nods, and I know I have him beat. The positives outweigh the negatives.

"And despite what I may or may not feel," I continue, "Elora knows Valebridge better than any of us. I have a hard time believing our crossed paths weren't destined by Fate." I consider my next words carefully. "If there was ever a time to do this...to confront Roman, it's now." I absently run my hand over the ink that lines my right forearm.

Galen watches me for a moment then lets out a long breath, rubbing his palms down the top of his legs. "I thought you were past that," he whispers.

"I thought I was too," I say, letting loose a long breath. "But, with all that's happening around Teravie and along the coast, we can't just sit back and let this continue. People need our help."

Sighing, I lean back, crossing my arms. I've let so much crucial time go to waste. I built a wall around myself, closing myself in and narrowing my sight of the world to just Loxley, denying the hardships of everyone else around me because I felt *content*.

I'm done feeling content.

Neither of us speak for a moment, letting the memories of our past fill the gaps between us. "And you're sure she can retrieve the Stones?" Galen asks, breaking our silence. Clicking my tongue, I lean back and mull his question over.

"She can," I say.

"How can you be sure? If she isn't a—"

"I believe she is," I whisper. Though, of course I can't be certain.

Galen strums his fingers against the edge of the settee a few times. "And you're sure you want to go to Valebridge, Sorin? You're sure it's worth it?" Galen's brows furrow, waiting for my response. I know he's worried, but he's always worried.

"I'm sure," I finally say.

Then, without another word he pulls himself to his feet, gathering his books in silence and heads for the door.

"Where are you going?" I ask, leaning forward.

He turns to face me. "If we're to venture on an inevitably doomed mission with our closest friends and *Elora*"—my heart dips slightly in my chest at the sound of her name—"then we need to stop pissing around in your room drinking wine." He waves his hand dramatically. "I need some time to think and review my books. Surely there's something of use about the Awakening Stones in here," he says, holding the stack lovingly to his chest. "Not that I doubt your lady's ability to retrieve them or find our way into Valebridge, but any piece of information will be helpful," he adds and without so much as a smile he spins for the door. I catch him before he reaches it, grasping him in a tight hug.

"Thank you. You know how much this means to me." I let him go and step back a few paces to give him the space I know he needs. Brushing his hand down the sleeve of his jacket, he straightens the wrinkles I've created before turning to the door again.

"Why do you think I'm doing it?"

CHAPTER 19

ELORA

THE NEXT DAY IS SPENT GOING OVER THE LOGISTICS of leaving for Kirsgard Mountain. Galen and Sorin have left town for a supply run, while Samaria has busied herself with Agnes and the other elders to make sure duties around Loxley will be tended to while she and Sorin are gone.

That leaves Jarek and myself. Sitting together outside of Agnes' home, the sun is shining brightly again today, but the breeze leaves a chill across my bare arms. Jarek has set up to train, and since I have nowhere else to be, I've agreed to train with him.

"Have you ever thrown an ax?" he asks, moving a large rounded tree stump several feet away from us. The center of the stump has been painted with a red circle, dents and cuts litter its surface.

Shaking my head, I stand to stretch my limbs. "No," I admit. "Mostly just dagger work and some with the shortsword but there wasn't an option for weaponry training when I lived in Valebridge."

I'm sure it was intentional for the kings of Valebridge to keep weapons out of the hands of Enchantresses. We are powerful enough when our magick has awoken, so I can see now that it was just another tactic to hold us down.

Lucky for me, Cade was willing to train me. His year in the royal guard before we fled Valebridge taught him enough skills that he passed them onto me. Jarek finishes pulling the stump in place before returning to stand at my side.

"Let's see how you do with those daggers of yours before we get into ax throwing," he says with a smile. I'm not sure I've seen him speak *without* a smile.

Nodding, I step up to the line he's drawn in the dirt, leveling my shoulders and unsheathing both of my daggers.

"It's been a long time since I've trained," I admit, suddenly nervous. His presence looms behind me so I glance over my shoulder. Crossing his arms, he strokes a hand through his short, blonde beard.

"There isn't any pressure," he says in his soft, soothing tone. "We don't have to train if it makes you uncomfortable."

My heart warms and the nervousness consuming me moments ago washes away. "No," I say, spinning my daggers in my palms. "I want to." Jarek smiles again, nodding his head, encouraging me to start.

Turning back toward the target, I close my eyes for a moment. Grounding myself, I press the tip of the blade between my thumb and index finger while listening to the world around me. I breathe in slowly through my nose and open my eyes to find the target. I wait to exhale until the last moment before I throw my first dagger.

It glides through the air, spinning with ease, before it lands just off-center of the target on the stump with a loud *thud*. A low whistle sounds behind me, glancing over my shoulder Jarek nods in approval.

"Not bad," he says. "Now this time, angle your right foot slightly above your left." Frowning, I turn back toward the target and do as he says. Breathing in again, my second dagger slips free and this time hits directly at the center of the target.

A grin spreads across my face as Jarek's hand lands upon my shoulder, giving it a squeeze. "I'm impressed," he says with another laugh.

"Thanks," I whisper, unsure how to take the compliment. I walk over to grab my daggers sticking out the stump, smiling as I reach for the one lodged in the center. It takes me a moment to yank it free before I turn back to Jarek. "So how about that ax?" I gesture to the large weapon strapped across Jarek's back. He smiles, his eyes crinkling as he does.

"Let me show you first," he says as I step to his side. His tall frame hovers over mine as he reaches back to unstrap his ax from its holster. Squaring his shoulders before spinning the ax in one hand, he somehow looks taller than before. The sweat along his muscled forearms glistens from the morning heat. Without any notice, he twirls the ax handle in his hands again before throwing it with expert precision, landing on the stump with a loud *crack*, slightly off target.

"Impressive," I say, clapping my hands together. "But you missed." Jarek glances down at me and laughs, running a hand down his face.

"You remind me of my youngest sister, Cora," he says before walking to grab his ax. "She was always the better fighter, the only reason I had the upper hand was because of my size." Rejoining me by my side, he hands me the ax. It's large and heavy in my hands, completely unfamiliar. "Your turn, smart-arse, show me what you've got."

Smirking, I step up to the line. It feels good to have a challenge.

AX THROWING with Jarek proved to be much more difficult than he made it look. I wasn't able to land the target, even after a dozen tries, but he never laughed. Never made me feel bad about my poor attempts. He only encouraged me to try again, showing me the proper way to hold the weapon while telling me tales of his sister Cora and how her fiery spirit is so similar to mine.

My arms are sore and shoulders tight, but the salve Sam applied after she returned from her meetings has helped slightly.

Now, the five of us sit crammed around the small table by the windows of Agnes' home. She, according to Sorin, is occupied for the night. He doesn't disclose where but after the full moon celebration last night, I imagine she's with Ulric. The two appear to be inseparable.

"Now," Sorin's voice is boisterous as he slams a deck of cards onto the table. "The rules of poker are simple." His eyes find their way to mine as if speaking only to me. We haven't had much time alone together since last night, and I fight the blush that creeps over my skin from his stare. "First, you'll need to underst—"

"What makes you so sure I don't already know how to play?" I cut him off, reaching across the table and snagging the deck from his hands. Sam laughs and Jarek joins soon after. "Maybe I can teach *you* a thing or two." The cards glide between my fingers as I begin to shuffle them. Memories of my mother dealing hand after hand, playing into the wee hours of morning.

Sorin smiles in my direction as he reclines back in his chair, tossing his hands up. "I have no doubt of the things you could teach me," Sorin says, his voice dropping low, snapping my attention back to him. "My apologies for assuming you didn't already know the game." He casts me another quick grin before I start dealing out the cards. "But I'm afraid you don't know *our* rules," Sorin continues, "so allow me to be your guide."

Stopping, I let a card linger in my fingers before tentatively placing it down in front of Galen. Jarek slams a bag onto the table, one I recognize immediately from the day I met Sorin on the river. The contents jingle as Jarek pours the Copenspire guards shillings onto the table. My stomach turns sour remembering that day, and the day after…

"And what are your rules?" I ask, furrowing my brow, pushing past the memories of what I've done.

Sam laughs again before taking a slow sip from her tea. "Every time you lose a round or someone calls you on your bluff, you must drop an article of clothing."

My cheeks heat and my grip on the cards hardens.

"What?" My voice shakes, nerves settling into my gut. The earlier wine from dinner now, apparently, a very bad idea. I glance at each face around the table, but I'm only met with grins. They can't be serious. "I'm not stripping my clothes." Setting down the pile of cards, I cross my arms.

"Well, there won't be any need to," Sorin says, leaning forward so his elbows rest against the table. "If you're as good a player as you say you are, there's nothing to worry about." His smile makes the erratic thumping in my chest beat even harder.

"Are you always so arrogant?" I gruff at Sorin as I pick up the cards to deal the rest of the hand.

"Yes," Sam, Jarek, and Galen say in unison.

Sorin laughs it off, scooping up the pile of cards I've dealt before him. "Are you always so angry?" he asks, keeping his eyes on his cards.

Yes, I think to myself. But instead of voicing it, I roll my eyes and turn my attention to Sam. "You play this way every time?"

"Not always," she says, setting her now empty mug onto the floor. "But, seeing as how we leave in a few days, and there won't be much time for relaxation, I don't see how a bit of fun could hurt."

"Just remember," Jarek whispers, leaning around Sam so he can meet my eyes more clearly, "Sorin's got a reputation for a reason. Don't believe him for shite."

"I heard that," Sorin deadpans before flicking his attention to me. "So, Elora, are you in?" His eyes meet mine from across the table and the challenge in his tone has my competitive edge flaring up. I think of this morning, when Jarek challenged me to throw the ax. Even further back my mind goes, to every challenge Cade insisted on as we trained together. I curse myself for being so stubborn as I square my shoulders. I don't break his gaze as I deal the final card. If he expects me to back down, he has severely misjudged my character. Besides, I know how to play the game, I've played it all my life. Perhaps it's him who should be nervous.

"I'm in," I finally say.

"I'm not." Galen's voice tears my gaze from Sorin, he's been so quiet I almost forgot he was there.

"Oh, come on, mate," Jarek groans, as if Galen's unwillingness to play is a usual occurrence. "We're all here, it's just a bit of fun."

"I have work to do, or have you all forgotten we're leaving in a few days?" Galen pushes his cards away, glaring at Jarek as he does so.

"All the more reason for one last hurrah!" Sam says, her bright smile splitting across her face.

"No," Galen says, pushing back his chair and standing abruptly.

"Sit." Sorin points to his chair. "Indulge in something exciting for once in your boring, scholarly life," he says through a laugh. As if reading each other's minds, Sorin, Sam, and Jarek all break out into a chant.

"Galen! Galen! Galen!" The trio yell in unison, timing the pounding of their fists onto the table. This continues several more times, and the smile that threatens my lips takes over completely.

Galen pulls his chair back before raising a hand to stop the outburst of chants. "Fine," he grumbles. "I'll play one hand."

It doesn't take long for Galen to lose his first article of clothing. As soon as he dropped his vest, he folded his next hand and excused himself for the night. Sam has somehow managed to lose every round, leaving her in just a camisole and undergarments. I'm not sure why she kept bluffing, maybe she thought if she *believed* she could win, eventually she would.

She didn't.

But now, she's out of the game, having lost her share of shillings we divided.

Jarek studies his cards, holding them close enough to his face I can't see his eyes. "I call," he says, pushing the last of his shillings onto the table.

"Confident, are we?" Sorin laughs, crossing his arms across his bare chest. The sculpted muscles of his arms flexing as he does.

"Oh aye," Jarek says, mocking Sorin by crossing his arms. "Let's do this brother." I sit at the end of the table, already out this round, leaving just Sorin and Jarek. The five cards dealt onto the table don't leave much to work with, but before Sorin flips his cards his hands linger in his lap. His brows furrow before he leans down to gather his discarded shirt, frantically patting it.

"Looking for something?" Jarek asks with a smirk, I'm completely lost as to what is happening but with the two men shirtless, it's difficult to pay attention anyhow. Sorin glares at Jarek as he lays a Queen of Spades onto the table.

"You cheeky bastard," Sorin says with a laugh. "How the hell did you steal it this time?" Jarek joins in on Sorin's laughter, and soon Samaria does as well.

"You were awfully generous with your hugs last night," Jarek says, tossing the clearly old and used card in Sorin's direction. "You made it too easy for me." Sorin catches the card, kissing it before tucking it lovingly back into his pants pocket.

"I don't understand," I finally say. Sam, Jarek, and Sorin all turn to me, smiles lining their faces.

"It's a silly prank these two have had for years," Sam explains, standing to refill her mug of tea from the kettle. "The Queen of Spades is a sacred card, and for some reason, these idiots always steal it from each other."

"Says my sister with love," Sorin mumbles, strumming his fingers across the table. I smile at their childish joke.

"Now," Sam says, sitting back down with her tea, "show us your actual hands so we can wrap this up."

At the same time, the two men flip their cards, and despite Sorin not having his lucky queen, he still wins the hand with a full house.

"Pay the price," Sam says in a sing-song tone before Jarek groans and slips off a ring from his thumb, leaving his breeches intact.

"Boo!" Sam says, drawing out the word. "How disappointing."

"Nothing you haven't seen already." Jarek laughs, pulling Sam in for a quick kiss.

Swallowing thickly, I cast a glance at Sorin. He and I remain in the game, and frustratingly enough, the only clothing he's lost thus far is his shirt. I glance down at myself, grateful the tunic I remain in is long enough to cover my backside. Sam deals us another hand and with each pull of my cards, my stomach sinks lower and lower. After a few minutes of contemplation, Sorin speaks first.

"I'm all in." Sorin's confidence is evident in his voice as he pushes his pile of shillings into the center of the table. His dimple deepens as he smiles at me. My brows pinch together before I refocus on my cards.

Five cards lie face up on the table. Jack of Hearts, Four of

Clubs, King of Diamonds, Two of Hearts, and an Ace of Spades.

The only decent card in my hand is a Four of Hearts, giving me a one-pair. It's not nothing, but it certainly isn't great.

I can either fold and lose or match Sorin's bet and hope he's bluffing. I flick my eyes upward again to assess Sorin's face. He has yet to bluff tonight, earning him the luxury of keeping most of his clothes. But as I watch him across the table, his fingers twitch, strumming a melody against the wood. Could he be... nervous? Maybe all that fidgeting is his tell and maybe he *is* bluffing this time.

"What's it going to be, love." My stomach somersaults at Sorin's use of the nickname.

Taking a deep breath, I place my cards face down to conceal the cards I've been given. I have no clue if Sorin lies about his hand, but my need to prove him wrong gets the best of me. With absolute uncertainty, I lock my eyes with him again.

"I'm all in," I say through gritted teeth. Sorin's grin widens as I push the sum of my shillings into the center of the table, matching his bet.

"Moment of truth!" Sam shouts, throwing her hands up in a show of enthusiasm. "Sorin first."

Flipping his cards, my stomach drops as he reveals his cards including a Jack of Spades and a King of Hearts. Combined with the Jack of Hearts and King of Diamonds already on the table, he's lined up a two-pair.

Blowing my one-pair completely out of the water.

My gaze slides from the cards to Sorin's face. He quirks his head to the side and raises his brows as if prodding me, pushing me to reveal the hand that I have.

Or lack of.

Tossing my cards onto the table with a shrug, I let out a long sigh. "You win." To my surprise, Sorin offers no quick retort, no snide comment. Rather, a faint hint of pink blushes across his cheeks and over the tips of his ears.

"Off with that shirt, Elora," Sam says through a laugh, her coiled curls bouncing lightly as she does. "Join the rest of us losers." My stomach knots when I realize I have no jewelry on to shed as Jarek just had.

Sam's voice is jovial, splendid, even. But for whatever reason, I can't take my eyes away from Sorin. The determination to prove he hasn't bested me, despite my poor hand, overpowers my usual need to blend into the shadows.

Slowly, I stand. My chair scrapes loudly against the wood floor as I push back. Feigning as much confidence as I can muster, I pull the hem of my tunic up, revealing my bare legs, then my abdomen. Sorin holds my gaze and even when my body starts to heat under his stare, I refuse to break eye contact first.

Sam and Jarek's laughter and banter between them has faded to the background. It's as if they have left completely and only Sorin and I remain. A muscle flexes in his jaw as I raise my tunic higher still, until finally, I pull it up and over my head completely. Leaving me in nothing but my undergarments.

The thin fabric of my camisole feels obsolete as my skin ignites under Sorin's gaze. His eyes narrow to scan and scour over every inch of my now exposed skin. I stand there, like a fool frozen in time, letting him look. Maybe wanting him to look. The flesh on my skin rises while somehow still heating. The memory of his hands on my hips while we danced makes my stomach flip. Just as I'm about to begin fidgeting under his stare, Sam's voice draws our attention.

"Here, here!" she shouts, jumping from her chair and grabbing her mug of tea. I shake off the heat of Sorin's lingering gaze and smile at Sam. "Let me be the one to officially applaud your *valiant* attempt at triumph. Unfortunately, my brother here, withholds his reputation as card master." Rolling her eyes at Sorin, she turns to me again with a smile. "No matter," she laughs before clearing her throat and switching to a more serious tone. "Elora, welcome to the crew."

CHAPTER 20

SORIN

WITH GALEN TUCKED AWAY IN A CORNER WITH HIS books, and Sam and Jarek occupied in her room doing who knows what, I'm relieved to have some time alone with Elora. We agreed she'd stay with Eviey again tonight where she feels most comfortable, and Galen will take the spare room at Letty's.

In the meantime, Elora and I sit in contented silence back in my room. She's stretched out on the settee by the fireplace, cupping a mug of peppermint tea and reading a book she borrowed from Sam, while I pretend to thumb through a book I stole from Galen.

"So, according to Galen we'll be leaving in a few days?" she asks over her shoulder, my eyes catching on her golden hair. She's let it down after our game of poker and it falls in waves down her back.

"Yes," I say, clearing my throat and wandering thoughts of Elora in her camisole. "The sooner the better." Tossing the book onto my bed, I join Elora on the settee. "The weather will start to change soon and it's best we make headway before the rain starts." She straightens herself to make room for me, a simple gesture that feels almost intimate. Like we've sat together and had tea, reading books a hundred times before.

She nods, taking a small sip from her mug before closing her book. "You're watching me," she grumbles, shooting me a look. Huffing a breathy laugh, I recline and rest my head on the back of the couch. My gaze redirects to the ceiling.

"I don't mean to," I admit. Counting the beams of my ceiling silently in my head. *One, two, three, four...* Anything to distract me from this Enchantress. "Where did you learn to play poker?"

Elora chuckles as she sets down her mug on the side table. The pressure dips on the couch as she scoots herself closer. Rolling my head to the side, she sits only a few inches away, studying my face the way I've often studied hers. Her brows furrow when she reaches my lips then quickly redirects her attention towards the fireplace.

"My mother taught me," she says. "Along with my friend, Cade. The two of them loved playing together. It wasn't my favorite way to pass the time, my body was always too busy to sit for that long, but I do miss their faces whenever we'd play. So full of life and mischief." She smiles, letting her eyes drift from the fire back to my face. My hand twitches, wanting to reach for hers, but she speaks again before I get the chance. "So, Galen is interesting," she says, changing the subject.

"He grows on you," I offer. "I know he can come across as a bit...hostile. But he's a good man. Loyal. Not to mention incredibly smart." She hums quietly and I can tell she is chewing her cheek again.

"I've been thinking—"

"Sounds *very* unlike you," she quips, catching me off guard and flashing me a bright smile I've rarely seen. Her attempt at humor warms my chest, and I find myself letting out a small chuckle of my own. Losing all control of my hand, I reach out and tuck a strand of her hair behind her ear. She watches me with widened eyes, but doesn't move away.

So neither do I.

"I'm glad we met," I say, reluctantly placing my hands in my lap. The lingering heat from her skin, still burning my fingertips.

"I am too," she whispers. "Lucky for you, our paths crossed by the river." Crossing her arms, she tilts her head to the side. "Whatever would you have done without my help?"

"We need to help *each other*," I remind her, casting her my widest smile. She rolls her eyes, but I catch the smile dancing on her lips. So stubborn. Leaning my body forward, I angle myself even closer. I tilt her chin up with my thumb, but still, her gaze doesn't meet my eyes. She lingers on my mouth, making the pounding in my chest loud enough to drown out the crackling of the fire. She stares at me with the same intensity she had earlier as she slipped out of her tunic. "But maybe there's another reason we met. One other than to help each other," I whisper. "Maybe the Mother has grander plans for us after all."

All I would have to do is tilt my head forward a few inches. Mere inches. That's all that separates my mouth from hers. Inches that feel like miles. The courage from the earlier wine leads my next movements. Dipping my head, our foreheads touch, and I relish in the warmth of her skin against mine. I bottle up the way she sounds as she sucks in a sharp breath before she quickly reclines, leaving a cold spot on my skin.

A sudden knock at the door causes us both to jump, nearly sending Elora toppling off the couch. Throwing her hands up to her mouth, she laughs. *Laughs.* A delicate high-pitched laugh that bounces off the walls of my room. I can't help but join in her laughter before standing and walking to the door. Sam waits on the other side with her hands on either hip.

"Am I interrupting something?" she asks, stepping up onto her toes, attempting to peer around me.

"Yeah, kind of. Do you mind?" I glare at her as I pull the door closer to my chest, narrowing the gap so she can't see in.

Always such a nosey big sister. Her smile is playful as she steps backward a few paces, crossing her arms behind her back.

"Please let the Enchantress know I have some spare night-clothes for her." Sarcasm rolls off her tongue, turning from me as she crosses the hallway back to her room. "That is if she still needs them," she says over her shoulder with a wink before closing her door behind her.

Pressing my door shut, I take a large breath before turning around to face Elora. She still sits on the couch with her knees brought up to her chest. All playfulness from moments ago slipped away, burning with the logs in the fire.

"It's getting late," she whispers, standing from the couch. Stretching her arms over head, she speaks through her yawn. "We should probably get some sleep." Nodding, I drag a hand along my jaw as she makes her way toward the door, trying desperately to ignore the disappointment that settles into my gut.

As she brushes by me to reach for the door knob, our hands briefly meet. The softest graze where our skin connects has my stomach flipping. I take a chance, gripping her hand, tugging her into me. The movement is quick and jarring for the both of us as she collides into my chest. She takes a sharp inhale, and I half expect her to slap me or stumble backward, but she doesn't. She stays pressed against my body, dragging her eyes up to mine. Heat spreads across my chest where Elora is firmly planted, our fingers interlaced. Leaning down, I press our foreheads together again. Then, moving slowly, I take my time dipping my head even lower, tracing my nose along her skin before planting a soft kiss against her jaw.

"Good night, Elora," I whisper, my lips brushing against her ear, before sliding my arm behind her to open the door. She's momentarily frozen in place, pressed against my body with her mouth left slightly agape. Until those perfect lips curl into a wicked smile that sends my heart lurching and all the blood in my body rushing to places it does not need to be. "Good night, Sorin."

CHAPTER 21

ELORA

THE SUNLIGHT IS STILL HIDDEN AWAY BEHIND THE grayness of early morning as I wake from yet another fitful sleep. I tossed and turned all night again, only the last few nights, it hasn't been a nightmare keeping me from my rest. Replaying the feeling of Sorin's lips on my skin over and over again, sleep has eluded me.

My mind is fixated on how his touch caused my stomach to dip and heat to pool inside of me. How I wanted nothing more than for him to do it again. Squeezing my eyes shut I push the feeling and images away. The last thing I need is a distraction, yet every time my eyes close, there he is. The image of his dark hair and stubble pressed close to my neck and his smell clouding every inch of my judgment. The past few nights have all been the same repeated images. Every time I close my eyes, he's there.

I've finally succumbed to sleep this time when, what feels like minutes later, Eviey gently shakes my shoulders to wake me up. Groaning, I stretch my arms and reluctantly dress before heading over to the main house to meet with the others.

Today's the day we leave Loxley and a part of me mourns having to do so. I've grown fond of the village and people here. Even Agnes has warmed up a bit, offering to teach me how to make bread and telling stories about when she lived in Valebridge. I haven't asked if she knew my mother. Though, it's crossed my mind more than once.

Settled in Sam's room while she finishes getting dressed, a light tap at the door catches both of us off guard. Apprehensively, she opens it. I can't see beyond her who it is but her smile broadens. Without an exchange of words, she closes the door and faces me, arms juggling a rather large, black box.

"For you," she says, a grin still splitting across her face as she places the large box next to me on the bed.

"What's this?" I shoot her a puzzled look.

"A gift," Sam says coyly, sliding the box closer until it bumps my leg, "from Sorin." Without another word, she slinks out of the room, clicking the door shut behind her.

Once alone, I trace my fingers along the edges of the box. It's long and narrow, but not incredibly heavy. The shiny, black wrapping paper is silky to the touch. A wide, black ribbon is tied across the top, so neatly I almost don't want to disturb it. Black wrapping. Black ribbon. Despite his natural arrogance, Sorin remembered my favorite color.

Curiosity finally gets the best of me, and I unwrap it quickly, tucking the ribbon into my pocket. Inside the box lies a new, black cloak, a fresh white linen shirt, black breeches, and sturdy soled boots. And at the very bottom... My hands freeze over the objects. Tears threaten to overspill as I pull out the last items from the box. The dark green leather is butter smooth in my grip. Tracing the lines of the etchings, my fingers take their time as my eyes soak in their beauty. The sheaths from Letty and Eviey's table at the market fit perfectly on my belt loop, and my daggers slip in smoothly as if they were made just for me.

Sorin's gift is more generous than I could've imagined. Is this where he snuck off to the other day when I trained with Jarek?

Layering my new black cloak atop my shirt and breeches, I clasp it shut despite the warm weather I'm sure we can expect from today's ride. Stepping in front of the small mirror in Sam's room, I take a quick glance at my reflection. Not half bad now that I've been able to bathe properly the past week and a half. My eye catches on a reflective bit of wool in the mirror. So small and delicate I almost missed it. A small arrow has been stitched into the fabric just above my heart.

GATHERING OUTSIDE THE HOUSE, we take a moment to say our goodbyes. Letty and Eviey both give me a kiss on the cheek before insisting I take an extra loaf of bread in my pack. Agnes holds Samaria and Sorin in a close embrace. Her faint sniffs have me averting my eyes, guilt settling in me that she has to say goodbye to her children. That we can grant no indication on when we'll return.

If we'll return.

A thick hand on my shoulder is a welcome distraction. "You ready for this?" Jarek's deep voice is a comfort to my growing nerves.

"As ready as I'll ever be," I say, offering him a genuine smile. His blue eyes are soft and assured as they meet mine. It's only then that I realize he wears a matching cloak—black wool with an identical arrow stitched in the fabric. Over his heart. I glance around at the rest of the crew. Sorin, Sam, and Galen, all wear the same cloak.

"What's with the matching ensembles?" I ask, his eyes remain locked on Sam as he answers me.

"Sorin likes the way it looks whenever we have to venture into other villages. United. Strong." He taps above my heart. "The arrow," he says, "is for alliance. A reminder we're all in this together." I trace the stitching with my fingers and replay the word in my mind as warmth spreads through my chest.

Thinking of the dinner Sorin and I shared together when we first arrived here. A promise made.

Together.

ONCE THROUGH THE ward that keeps Loxley hidden, we gather the horses we prepared earlier in the stables. There are five of us, and only four of them. Amis nuzzles my hand as I feed her a fallen apple from the ground. When Sorin suggested he and I ride together, I couldn't find a good enough reason to fight him about it, so I didn't.

I'd be lying to myself anyway if I said I wasn't excited to be so close to him again. After our night in his room a few days ago, we haven't had much time alone, and while I'm not sure what our growing friendship means, I've become quite fond of his company. Excessive chatter and all.

Seated atop Amis, Sorin pulls me close into his chest, a swarm of butterflies flutter in my stomach as his thumb caresses the back of my hand. "Ready?" he whispers so only I can hear. After a deep inhale, my body relaxes further into him and I nod my head. Jarek, Sam, and Galen ride up next to us and position themselves in a half circle with Sorin and I in the middle, as if they're waiting for his lead.

"We'll ride until nightfall." Sorin's voice is authoritative but kind. "That should get us to the edge of the Trinity Forest. We'll plan to set up camp there and continue east first thing tomorrow morning. We should reach Wickersham by end of day tomorrow if the horses allow." His voice is confident but the way he tightens his grip ever so slightly around my waist gives me an indication he's nervous. "Once we make it to Wickersham, we'll rest for the night and leave the horses. The rest of the journey needs to be on foot. More inconspicuous that way. "And that should lead us"—his hand flexes on the reins as he lets out a long sigh—"through the Wicked Wood."

"What!" Sam's voice booms as she and Jarek exchange the same wide eyed glance.

"It's the fastest route, Sam," Galen chimes in as he positions his horse between Sam and Sorin. My eyes bounce between the friends and I dare not say that I have no clue what they're talking about.

Sam's brows furrow as she grips tighter on her reins. "Fastest route or not, we can't go ba—"

Sorin cuts Sam off, his grip around my waist even tighter than before. "We've made it through before, Sam. We can do it again."

"But Sorin you—"

"The decision is made." He cuts her off again, his body flinching as he does, as if it hurts him to do so. "We can't risk the alternative route, you know that."

Not giving the conversation another second, he gently presses into Amis with his heels, and we take off in a slow trot, leaving the other three behind us. Peering back over my shoulder, Sam and Jarek exchange words I can't quite hear as he attempts to comfort her from his horse. Ripping her arm away, Sam shakes her head before trotting in our direction. Galen and Jarek follow suit and our four horses form a single file line as we ride into the Trinity Forest.

"I guess this is a bad time to ask," I say, pulling my hood up and over my head to shield myself from the wind, "what exactly are the Wicked Woods?" Sorin's arms stiffen around me, his chest pushes into my back as he takes a deep breath.

"The Wicked Woods are a small grove of trees between Wickersham and the Kirsgard Mountains," he says. "It used to be a well-traveled route by the fishing merchants traveling from the mountain to Davenport but now all the merchants travel around the grove, adding over a week's time to the journey."

"I don't understand," I say. "I've traveled those woods and

never heard such a thing. What has deterred so many people from entering?" I ask, repositioning myself in the saddle. Trying anything to get more comfortable though nothing seems to work. Most of my memory from fleeing Kirsgard Mountain is a blur, my mind's natural defense mechanism. Keeping me shielded from so many painful nights alone. But I do remember the woods and never once do I recall anything like the Wicked Wood Sorin explains now.

"The Wicked Woods are home to a woodland nymph, Grawgeth." Sorin continues his story as Amis leads us through the dense pines of the northern forest. "The story is that Grawgeth fell in love with one of the fishing merchants off the coast of the Holden Sea many years ago. When he was called to fight in the Geode War, she waited years for his return only to find out he had fallen in love with a human woman in Davenport. With a broken heart, she called upon the dark parts of her magick, cursing all those who entered her woods, stealing the souls of travelers who failed to pass her tests or pay her price upon their entry." Sorin hasn't disclosed how or why Sam had entered into the forest before, but if I had to guess by Sam's reaction, it didn't end well.

"If we stay close together, keep our wits about us, we'll make it through. I have no doubts."

"Don't you think you should have told Sam your plan? Clearly, she's upset," I say, resting my head back on Sorin's chest. I have given up all attempts at keeping distance between the two of us and right now any bit of comfort is worth more than my pride.

"If I told her the way we were going, she wouldn't have come, and we need her with us." His voice sounds tired, and half of me wishes I could comfort him, while the other half is frustrated that he withheld a part of the plan from all of us. All but Galen it would seem.

"Well," I say through a yawn, "it sounds to me like she has every right to be concerned." His silent reply is an indication that the topic of conversation is over. Too exhausted to push it any further, we ride the rest of the day in silence.

THE SUNSET CASTS a pale pink glow to the horizon, airy wisps of purple scatter across the trees leaving me breathless as I watch the changing hues. Setting up camp in a small clearing, I'm impressed we managed to make it this far on the first day of riding. Though, the ache in my legs tells me this kind of stamina won't last long. Sam has remained silent as she tends to the horses while I build a fire. She and Sorin haven't looked at each other since this morning and the tension creates an ache in my stomach.

With Sorin hunting with his bow for dinner, Sam joins Jarek at a nearby creek to try their hand at fishing. Settling around the makeshift fire pit to indulge in a bit of silence before their return, I stretch my limbs over the flames. Only, it doesn't last long before Galen's cold energy looms over my shoulder.

"Do you need something?" I snap unintentionally, glancing up at him. I don't mean to be so curt, but my mind itches for solitude after a day spent practically glued to Sorin's chest.

"I do, actually," he says. Standing to face him, I toss a stick to the fire and wait. "Sorin's been through a lot," he says, peering down at me with blue eyes as cold as ice. "He wears his heart on his sleeve and like the true romantic he is, he's been known to put everything on the line for people who may not deserve it."

Taking a step back, my tone is intentional this time as I hiss through my teeth. "What are you implying?" I'm not sure if I'm upset that Galen doesn't think I deserve Sorin's attention or upset that he assumes we are more than friends in the first place. But are we more than friends?

"Whatever is going on between the two of you," he steps

closer, placing his hands in his pants pocket, "just know that it won't last. He has bigger plans than this one, and the last thing he needs is a distraction from them. I don't mean any disrespect, I'm just trying to set your...expectations."

Grinding my teeth, I square my shoulders as I step closer. Galen appears to be the kind of person who takes immense pleasure preying on the weak, and I will not be his next victim.

"I appreciate your concern, Galen." I brush a bit of dirt from his shoulder, and he recoils away from my touch. "But I'm old enough to manage my own expectations." Smirking, I take a few steps backward before turning and heading to my tent.

CHAPTER 22
ELORA

MY HAIR IS SLICK WITH SWEAT AS WE RIDE INTO Wickersham the next evening. The late summer sun is brutal and no breeze has graced us since yesterday. As Sorin takes Amis to the stable, I peel off my wool cloak, grimacing at how my shirt underneath sticks to my skin. We've been riding for two days and already I miss the comforts of Loxley. I curse myself silently for how low my tolerance has become. Only two weeks ago I was living in a cabin alone, and now I can't stand a bit of sweat on my shirt.

With the horses tied off, the five of us head towards town in search of a few rooms for the night and a meal. I send a silent prayer to the Mother, hoping by some miracle Wickersham hasn't been affected by the blight as bad as Copenspire and the rest of the coastal cities.

The wood slab that reads Mahaffey's Pub hangs slightly crooked, the hinges rusted and barely functional. I'm surprised at how loud my stomach growls with the promise of food. On instinct, I mask the color of my eyes, hiding their golden glow, before entering the pub.

Inside, the sound of drunkards laughing fills the air. The floor is sticky beneath my boots and a pungent aroma of sweat and ale makes me cover my nose and mouth as we move further into the pub. We pass a lone barkeep who stands behind a long, honey colored countertop pouring ample amounts of dark ale into much-too-large tankards.

Sorin leads us to a dark wooden booth in the back corner of the pub before he and Jarek turn to approach the bar. Piling my hair into a high knot to keep it off my neck, my eyes rake over the establishment. The pub consists of several round wooden tables, a few scattered in the middle, and two large ones in either corner. A wooden bench lines the wall where our booth is placed. Once my hair is secured, I slide into the booth while Sam takes a seat in the chair opposite me. Oil lit lanterns line the walls offering light to the room and despite the lack of windows, it's pleasantly cool, almost as if being underground.

My eyes catch on Sorin as he shakes hands with the barkeep. "Do they know each other?" I ask Sam as she hangs her cloak on the back of her chair. She glances over her shoulder briefly before redirecting her gaze to me. I realize then, she hasn't masked her eyes. Their flame-like color burns brightly in the pub, and I can't understand why she hasn't taken the necessary precaution to shield herself.

"Yes," she says. "That's Park Mahaffey, he owns this place. We've done business here before, many years ago and as of recently, just started again. Besides, Sorin's not someone people often forget." She winks before reclining back in her chair. "Glad to get out of that damn heat for a few minutes."

I can't help but agree. I dare a quick glance to Galen who has said nothing since we sat down. His eyes remain focused on a piece of parchment, and I don't bother making conversation. As Sorin and Jarek make their way back to our table with hands full of ale, Galen excuses himself to see about any rooms at the inn next door.

"Not much for socializing, is he?" I ask, grabbing a tankard from Sorin and taking a sip. When the ale hits my tongue, it isn't quite warm but definitely not cold. I've only ever had the huckleberry wine from Loxley, and I can tell by one sip of the ale, I much prefer the wine.

Sam tips her head back in laughter. "Absolutely not. Galen is the complete opposite of Sorin in that regard."

"Never has been social, I imagine there's no sense in him changing that now," Sorin says, scooting closer to me in the booth. "It's not personal, it's just who he is." As much as Galen intimidates me, maybe he and I have more in common than I thought.

As Sorin slides closer, our thighs touch under the table. Heat floods my system and I'm taken back to the night we spent dancing in Loxley. To our game of poker where he watched me undress. To his lips against my skin in his bedroom.

He sets the rest of the tankards in the center of the table and Sam snatches one, taking a deep gulp, clearly unphased by the taste and temperature. Wiping her mouth on the sleeve of her dark brown shirt she places the half empty mug down on to the table.

"Thanks for the ale." Her voice is sincere but her eyes still narrow in Sorin's direction.

"Does this mean you've forgiven me?" Sorin asks coyly.

"It means I'm *tolerating* you," Sam says, scooting herself onto Jarek's lap as if her own chair isn't good enough to sit in. Jarek chuckles as he brushes a few of Sam's curls away from her face.

"You know it'll take more than some piss poor ale to win her back, mate," Jarek says, raising his tankard in Sorin's direction, "but cheers for trying."

Sam pinches Jarek's arm as he shoots her a toothy grin. Right as I open my mouth to ask a question, a tall woman with stunning red hair comes over to our table, carefully balancing a tray of what appears to be hot stew. The woman sets down a bowl in front of Sorin and me first. Holding my breath, I wait for her reaction as she places a bowl of food in front of Sam.

Surely, she will notice her eyes, and with that realization, she'll know she's an Enchantress.

But the woman says nothing, doesn't so much as flinch as she sets down the bowl.

"We appreciate the meal," Sam says to the woman. Nodding, the woman tucks the empty tray against her side.

"It's our pleasure," she says, her eyes drifting to each of our faces. "I'm sorry it isn't much, but it's the least we can do for you." She's pointed at Sorin when she says this, and my eyes bounce between the two of them. My stomach turns. Is there anyone Sorin *doesn't* know?

"Has everything been faring well, Jeanette?" Sorin asks before taking a sip of his ale. Jeanette blushes, her cheeks deepening to match the red coloring of her hair.

"We're getting by," she says quietly. "The last year has been...meager. But Park's smart with the crop and the trade, we'll be okay. If there's anything else you need, let us know." She offers a smile at each of us before returning to her post near the bar.

"So," Sorin says after a few moments of weighted silence, "does a *meal* gain me any points toward winning back the affection of my dearest older sister?" Sorin's sarcasm drips off his tongue and I would roll my eyes, but they're too busy now fixating on the bowl of food that's been placed before me. Sam's muffled laugh is indication enough that, yes, the hot food has earned him back some points.

Bringing the spoon up to my lips, I realize it's more broth than stew. The liquid is thin, and a few potatoes and carrots dance along the bottom. My heart sinks. Wickersham is being hit with the blight and here we are, taking food from their rations.

"How long have you two been...together?" I ask Sam, turning my thoughts away from the people of this town and the struggles they're to face. Hunger gets the best of me as I dive into my soup.

"Hmmm," Sam ponders, pinching her brows together. "I'm not sure I remember just how many years. Could it be three? Four?" she asks Jarek who simply shrugs, clearly not remembering either. "Jarek arrived in Copenspire on a ship headed for Valebridge," Sam continues. "He was to be enlisted in the royal army. Sorin, Galen, and I were there gathering supplies for our next job when we ran into this giant man," she pauses to squeeze Jarek's arm. "He was making a run from the docks."

Jarek laughs, low and rough. "I was not about to enlist in an army to serve that despicable excuse for a king," Jarek says, shaking his head and polishing off his bowl of stew. "The ships had come to our homeland, Scandavi, and every man old enough to wield a weapon was to be enlisted. Most of us were taken against our will, removed from our families in the middle of the night. I tried to fight them off, but there were far too many. I haven't had the chance to speak to my mum or sisters since I was pushed upon that ship.

"I know they'll be all right without me. They're the strongest women I know. Scariest too." He laughs, though his eyes cast a sad shadow. "But it doesn't make it any easier, being away from them. It's the not knowing that breaks my heart."

Silence hangs heavily around the table as we all tune into Jarek's words. His story is not so different from mine and here I've been wallowing in my grief, not thinking for a second what the others around have gone through. I think of his sister, Cora, who he spoke so highly about. Sorin's eyes turn down, looking at his hands while Sam runs her fingers through Jarek's hair. She watches his face, never once letting her attention falter.

"So," he continues, "once our ship docked in Copenspire, I took the first chance I got to flee. Was supposed to be gathering supplies to move up the coast and that's when I bumped into Sorin."

"Quite literally, bumped," Sorin says with a laugh, breaking the rising tension. "I was minding my own business leaving a poor excuse for a tobacco shop, when out of nowhere, came this giant oaf of a man barreling into me. He almost knocked me on my arse."

Jarek's laughter is deep and infectious as it bellows through the pub. "A moment I'll never forget," he says. I finish off my bowl of soup and push it to the side, silently wishing it would somehow refill itself.

"I'm sorry, Jarek. I had no idea about your family. I'm sure you miss them terribly." My apology is weak in comparison to all he's been through, but it is all I can offer right now.

"Of course, I miss them. I have to believe I'll see them again." His eyes go distant for a moment, lost in a sea of memory. "No matter where I land, though," he says, bringing his eyes back to mine, "it'll be home so long as I'm with her." He squeezes his arms tighter around Sam and she leans into his embrace, resting her head against his shoulder. My heart swells at the sight, how the two of them have found each other despite all odds.

"Here we go," Sorin mutters under his breath before taking another drink. Sam shoots him a sly smile, her brown skin radiant in the golden light of the lamps.

"Jealousy doesn't suit you, brother," she says with a smirk.

"If anything, I'm nauseated," Sorin counters, snarling his lip and laughter breaks out between the four of us.

"For what purpose does the king need to enlist men from Scandavi?" I ask, changing the subject back at the risk of sounding naïve. This might not be new information but living on the mountain and then in the woods has shielded me from most news from other parts of the world. "Scandavi, if I recall correctly, is several months away by ship. I can't wrap my head around the purpose of King Roman expending such resources."

"Not just Scandavi, I'm afraid," Sorin says. "Men from Dunbrink, Hofin, and Narasavik have all been rumored to be arriving by ships as well." Sorin wipes the corner of his mouth and sets his spoon in his now empty bowl before continuing.

"King Roman's building his armies, for what we haven't quite determined. Park, however, has confirmed there aren't any more royal guards stationed on Kirsgard. So, at least we have that going for us."

Sam and Jarek nod, as if it's completely understandable that a barkeep would know such a thing.

"And no word from the Guilds?" I ask. How is it that the four Guilds have remained silent in the wake of such change?

Sorin shakes his head as he spins his tankard aimlessly, the liquid sploshing the sides but not spilling. "From what I've heard, the only Guild that has been in contact with Valebridge since Silas died is the Bloodstone Guild. Likely because of the ruby trade they partake in every year. The Jade, Onyx, and Cerulean Guilds have been locked up for the last four years. Silent. Even their annual meeting for the Autumn Moon has halted." Sorin glances at me briefly and I don't bother hiding my disbelief.

"I have my suspicions as to what Roman is up to, but we'll get to the bottom of it once we make our way to Valebridge. All of the extra men, not to mention the countless Enchantresses he's forcibly taken...the hunters..." I shoot him a quick glance, and his hand finds mine under the booth. "Whatever it is he plans to do with these armies," he says, giving my hand a squeeze, "we'll get to the bottom of it. Just as we'll get to the bottom of this blight."

"How do the hunters sense magick?" Jarek asks, scooting Sam farther onto his lap. "We don't have these hunters back home, it makes no sense to me."

Sorin shrugs, casual as always. "Last I heard in Davenport there's a potion they take. Allows them to tap into magick being used in nearby areas." I watch Sorin intently as he speaks, never having known myself exactly how the hunters can sense such a thing as magick. "One of the fishermen, Quinn was his name, told me about a group of hunters who passed by several years ago. Posted up at the Blackwind Tavern for a few days.

There was talk then about a drink they all were required to take regularly."

"I've never heard of such a thing," I whisper, and by the look of Sam and Jarek's face, they haven't either. A potion to sense the use of magick. My body shudders at the thought and the dark magick that must have been used to concoct it.

I take a sip of the stale ale and refrain from puckering my face as it slides down my throat. The more we speak on the matter of Valebridge, the less confident I become that coming here was the right choice. What do I have to offer to help the situation besides a faint memory of where the Stones are located and the knowledge of a tunnel leading to the castle?

Swallowing the rising regret in my throat I focus on the people in front of me. Sorin's hand is still placed on mine, the heat of his touch pulses up my arm and into my chest. Leaving tiny trails of static across my skin. The immediate urge to pull away has subsided and now I find myself dizzied by his touch.

Sam and Jarek are working on their third round of ale when Galen saunters back to our booth from the inn across the street. He remains standing despite the empty chair at the end of the rounded table.

"There are three rooms." He sounds tired as he takes in the empty tankards and spilled ale across our table. The snarl of his lip says more than his words need to. Most of the other tavern patrons have left, leaving us alone to discuss our business. Sorin assured me Park and Jeanette would remain quiet about any details overheard, and I'm inclined to believe him given their friendly nature earlier.

"And you reserved all three?" Jarek asks before downing the last of his ale, and then mine. I chuckle despite myself as he drinks down the brown liquid before slamming the tankard on the table.

Galen shoots him a look before rolling his eyes. "No, Jarek, I insisted we only needed one." Pushing his hands in his pockets, he leans back against the wooden beam next to our booth. "Clearly, yes," Galen says, closing his eyes, "I reserved all three."

"What crawled up his arse?" Jarek mumbles under his breath. Sam chokes her ale as she breaks into a fit of laughter. Standing to collect the empty tankards, Sorin plays peacekeeper as I imagine he so often does with the four friends.

"Sam and Jarek take one, Galen and I will bunk in another, and Elora can have the third. Easy enough." My stomach sinks and I struggle to come to terms with why. I tell myself it's because I don't want to be alone, not because I want to be with Sorin.

Liar.

Tipping my head to the side, I give my earlobe a light tug. Galen tosses Jarek a key with a wooden toggle attached, then does the same to me. The toggle is shaped like an arrow, with a number two burned into the wood.

My eyes drift to Sorin as he crosses the pub over to the bar, juggling the empty tankards before setting them down on the bartop. Park greets him with a smile and shakes his hand in a way of thanks.

The gold shimmers against the oil lamps as Sorin slips the man a handful of shillings, far too many for what our meal and drinks could be worth. The two of them begin a hushed chatter that I know I won't be able to make out, but I try anyway, leaning slightly forward on the table.

"You know…" Sam's words are drawn out as she leans across the table, "rather than watching him all night, you could just kiss and get it over with."

I imagine the look on my face is somewhere between surprise and embarrassment as I jolt backward away from her. Heat flushes over my cheeks, and I bite the inside of them to keep myself from spewing some ridiculous excuse that I know she won't believe.

Sam's laugh echos through the empty pub, and I fight the urge to kick her under the table. "Relax," she says between laughter, "I'm just teasing." She reaches for my hand, and I let her grab it despite my embarrassment. "Unless, of course, you do want to kiss Sorin," she whispers. "Which..." She squints her eyes at me for a moment, contemplating her answer. I pull my hand away a bit too aggressively, the memory of Sorin's lips on my skin making my cheeks redden even further. Slapping her hand down on the table as if she's just solved a mystery she says, "Yes. I believe you do want to kiss him, and if that's the case might I suggest—"

"I believe that's our cue." Jarek laughs as he cuts her off. Standing, he swings Sam over his shoulder as if she weighs nothing at all. "Off to bed, my queen," Jarek says, patting her across her arse, making her laugh even louder than before.

"We'll meet at the stables at morning's first light," Sorin shouts across the pub as the two of them head out the door. Rejoining us at the booth, Sorin slams down a bowl of soup in front of Galen. "Thank you for taking care of the rooms. Eat."

Galen sighs, but doesn't argue as he leans in and starts on the soup.

EXCUSING MYSELF A FEW MOMENTS LATER, I leave Sorin and Galen at the pub. My body aches in agony from the multiple days on horseback not to mention how desperate I am for a bath.

The Sherwood Inn is located just across the cobblestone streets of Mahaffey's Pub. The two stories that make up the building have a slight lean to them. The mossy coated roof reminds me of those in Loxley, which brings a sense of comfort I wasn't expecting. An elderly woman by the name of Anne greets me and insists on escorting me to my room. Even though I can clearly see the number *two* marked on the door that matches my key. Unlocking the door, she guides me into the room.

"If you need anything, Enchantress, don't hesitate," she says, making her way back toward the front of the inn. Surprise lodges in my throat as I realize I've let my mask fall, showing my eyes true color. Then again, Sam hadn't masked hers at all and no one took notice. Perhaps Sorin has more allies than he's let on.

Once inside the room, there isn't much to see. A simple bed that sits atop a dusty patterned rug, a small end table with a lit lantern and across from the bed is a window that overlooks the streets of Wickersham. I pull the heavy, floral drapes closed to conceal the view, not that there are many onlookers this time of night. Waves of dust disperse from the fabric and I cover my mouth to avoid inhaling anything unsavory.

The fireplace isn't lit, but with the air still warm outside from summer, I don't bother starting a fire. Tossing my cloak in the chair adjacent to the fireplace, I head for the bathing chamber that's attached to my room. It consists of a chamber pot, pitcher and bowl, and to my delight, a deep, soaker tub.

Once out of the bath, I shake my hair free and let it hang loosely down my back. Pulling on my tunic, I decide to forgo my breeches since the room is already warm from the sticky, summer air. The quilt on the bed has various patchwork patterns, swirling purples and deep oranges in different shapes, and in the center a spiraling flower. While it appears just as dusty as the rug underneath the bed, it's soft and warm, so I climb in and pull it up to my chin. Taking a few deep breaths, I ignore the musty smell and focus on relaxing my shoulders. Sleep isn't far off as I jerk myself upright.

When a second knock raps at my door, my heart stammers against my chest.

CHAPTER 23
SORIN

"Are you even listening to me?" Galen's voice cuts through me like steel as I lean my head back against the wall with a sigh.

"Yes." Closing my eyes, the exhaustion from the past few weeks seeps into my bones. My travels down the coast have been mentally draining. Ramshire, then Davenport. Both cities are typically prosperous and eager to trade under the king's nose, but with the blight, the pickings were slim. "But also, no," I admit halfheartedly. Galen's glare burns through me, even with my eyes still closed.

"Just go," he growls.

"I beg your pardon?" I manage to say through a laugh, amused by not only his shortness but his command. I don't often take commands, rather, I never take commands. Whipping his head toward me, he slams down his book.

"You're distracted and we both know it," he says, pointing an accusatory finger toward me. Well, he is right about that. "And I think we've known each other long enough to be honest, yes?" he asks as I sit and wait for what I'm sure is to be the chastising of the century. "So just... go," he says, throwing his hands in the air. "Go tell her how you feel. Get it out in the open. Not only is it annoying to be around the two of you, it's distracting for everyone. So, just go." He leans forward placing both elbows on the table, his blonde hair is ruffled and out of place, frustration displayed between his dark brows. It isn't often Galen lets himself show so much emotion, even disdain.

"I'm sorry to have annoyed you," I laugh, standing a little too quickly from the booth, squeezing his shoulder as I walk by.

"You always annoy me," Galen gruffs. "She's in room two."

THE WALK down the hall of the Sherwood Inn stretches for what feels like miles. Several times, I make it halfway before turning and stomping back to the front door. I have no doubt the kind woman at the front thinks I'm mad, but my heart and my head can't agree on what the fuck I'm actually doing.

Letting out a long sigh, I run a hand down my face. I should let her be. Let her rest. But as I turn a final time to head back across to the pub, my boots skid to a stop. My heart races, and before I know it, I'm back outside of Elora's door.

When I finally get the courage to knock, Elora opens the door with her hair still wet from the bath, and it takes me a moment to realize she's wearing nothing but a tunic, her bare legs smooth as ivory. My heart skips a beat, thinking of the last time I saw her legs bare. The poker game where she almost bested me. I've never had to fight to keep my composure before, and her taking off her tunic that night almost did me in.

"Is something wrong?" she asks, cracking the door open, allowing me to see that she's carrying one of her daggers. She catches my eyes on the blade, and relaxes her grip as she opens the door further. She gestures for me to come in, so I do. Taking a seat in the small chair by the fireplace, Elora sits on the bed, covering her lower half with the patchwork quilt, tucking her dagger into its sheath atop the bedside table. I smile, noticing she's using the sheath I traded Eviey and Letty for.

"So..." she says then stops, chewing the inside of her cheek, her hands toying with the edges of the quilt. What the hell did I even have to say? Why did I come here?

"The other night"—standing, I cross the small room in a few steps, sitting myself on the foot of the bed—"I just wanted to commend your poker skills. It would appear as though I've met my match."

Idiot.

"You still beat me," she says, a smile tugging at the corners of her mouth. Her cheeks flush but then, in an instant, her eyes turn weary as she tilts her head to the side, pressing her ear into her shoulder. A gesture so small, and yet I've seen her do it often. I'm beginning to wonder if it's more than what it appears. Despite it, I could live in these moments. Where Elora lets down her guard. Her playful quips. If I hadn't witnessed magick outside of this room, I'd swear this was it.

"True." I smile and to my surprise, she smiles back. A full, wide grin I've seen only once before, back when we first entered Loxley. A smile that'll be sure to damn my heart, keeping it her prisoner until she decides to let it free. Though, would I want her to? I trace my eyes along the freckles that skirt across the bend of her slightly crooked nose, up to her golden eyes, back to her full pink lips before scooting myself closer to her.

"Whatever this is between us," I whisper, twirling a lock of her damp hair between my fingers, "I hope you feel it too." I let my hand rest on her shoulder for a moment but as I pull away she reaches up, intertwining our fingers.

"And what feeling is that?" she asks, her smile gone and brows furrowed.

I *hmm* for a moment, savoring the heat of our joined hands and her touch. "It's difficult to put into words, isn't it?" I laugh, stroking the back of her hand with my thumb. My skin lights up with every touch, and I hope to the Mother she feels it too.

"Like a bolt of lightning during a dry storm. The kind that cracks across the sky, leaving sparks of heat in its place." I stroke the back of her hand again and she flinches, but doesn't pull away. "The kind of lightning that is so distracting, so beautiful and foreign, it could easily destroy everything it strikes."

She says nothing for a few moments, letting my words fall heavily in the air. A confession, more like it. I begin to doubt coming here when, finally, she chuckles. "Are you a poet as well as a thief?"

Huffing a laugh of my own, I grip her hand firmer. "I guess one could say that I am."

"Maybe I like poetry," she whispers, breaking our gaze and glancing down to our connected hands. "Maybe I like you, too." Her words leave my stomach swirling but it's her face that leaves my heart in a flurry. I can't help but think how beautiful she is at this moment. The armor she always has wrapped so tightly around herself, cracked slightly. Only for me. If I achieve anything in this life, it will be to tear her armor completely. Or rather, give her no reason to wear it at all.

"I won't lie, that's a bit of a relief." I smile, clearing my throat. Nerves getting the best of me. "I was worried you'd tell me to piss off again."

Her features soften, but her eyes still hold a hint of worry, maybe doubt. Whatever it is, she doesn't voice it. I force myself to stay absolutely still, fearing I'll blink and she'll scurry away like she's done before.

"You have a lot of feelings for a lowly thief," she says, making me smile. "And maybe I would agree with you that whatever *this* is"—she gestures to our hands—"doesn't feel like anything I've experienced before."

"And what does this feel like to you?" I ask, not entirely sure if I even know that answer. Not sure if Elora liking me is the same as the magnetic draw I feel toward her.

Leaning closer, she readjusts, uncrossing her legs. As she does, the quilt shifts revealing the bare skin of her thighs. She makes no attempt to cover herself, and it takes every inch of restraint not to slide my hands over them, grip the backs of them and pull her onto my lap. Leaning into me, her lips brush against my ear as she whispers, "It feels a bit like fate."

Breaking our hands apart, my fingers trace along her jaw, before I wrap my hand around the back of her neck, pulling her into me. I hesitate, only for a moment, giving her a chance to tell me to stop, to say no. But instead, her hands slide around my waist, anchoring herself to me.

I start slowly. Planting a small kiss to her collarbone. Then, when she gasps lightly, I move along her neck and over her scar before dragging her earlobe softly between my teeth. Continuing, I work my way along her jaw, eliciting small gasps from her that leave me needing to readjust my pants. Finally, my lips hover over her mouth, the smell of jasmine invades my senses leaving me with a dizziness that rivals intoxication. Dipping my forehead down so it meets hers, my words come out more breathless than I imagined they would. "You can tell me to stop, Elora." I'm not a praying man, but I pray she won't.

She slides her hand up my back then combs her fingers through my hair before gripping the back of my neck. "Don't."

CHAPTER 24

ELORA

SORIN'S HANDS ARE ROUGH AND CALLOUSED AGAINST the smoothness of my skin. With one hand gripping the back of my neck and the other resting on top of my thigh, we sit in momentary silence, sharing each other's breaths. I lean into the weight of his hand on the back of my neck, letting it sear me like a brand. I almost told him to stop, that this can't be what he wants, but my selfishness kept my mouth quiet.

My breathing is already ragged and the intensity of his kiss catches me so off guard, any breaths that come next are now an afterthought. The initial shock of his lips, soft and full, turns to fire, molten and destructive. Every part of me is ignited by his touch, even the parts of me that have laid dormant for so long begin to rouse. As if he is the only one who could break me from the hazy fog I've been living in. Or maybe it's us together that awakens those parts of me. A pang of familiarity shoots through me. Like my body knows his in all the ways it shouldn't.

His grip on my neck is firm as he pulls me into him, leaving his other hand to wander my body before grabbing me by the hips. I move to wrap my legs around his waist. Hoisting me up with one hand, he positions me so I'm straddled across his lap. The firmness of him presses between my legs, and I bite down softly on his bottom lip to stifle a moan. All sense of rationality is lost on me and in this moment, he is all I see.

Hear.

Taste.

Our mouths never leave each other except for quick breaths between kisses. As if separating would break the spell we're under. Heat spears down my spine and it isn't long before it settles between my legs. Rolling my hips forward, Sorin scrapes his teeth along my neck, dragging his tongue followed immediately by a kiss. Then, my collarbone. My chest. The pounding of my heart is practically audible as I run my hands through his thick, dark hair then down across his broad shoulders and over his chest.

"Elora," he starts but I move quickly, pressing my hand to his mouth. There is so much to say, so much we haven't told each other. But even if this means nothing, even if it's only this moment, I want it. Whatever it is. We can simply be two adults, getting lost in each other's company. Tonight will not be for talking. Sliding my hand from his mouth, Sorin's smirk and dimple greet me. Only, now, I allow myself to do more than just admire him.

This time, I lean forward and kiss his dimple before moving to his mouth. Kissing him deeper and harder than before. Whatever happens to our friendship after this will be tomorrow's problem. Letting my instincts take over, my fingers fly to his shirt, unlacing the front before pulling it off him completely. His skin is toned and strong under my palms as I run my hands over his chest, down his arms. Tracing over the ink that resides there, relishing how his breaths change every time my skin touches his.

Sorin grabs my hands, bringing them to his mouth, kissing my fingertips. Taking his time, he mirrors my movements, tracing lines down my body. Across my chest, down the curve of my hips. Tracing the edge of my tunic, he runs his hands over the top of my thighs before gripping the back of them.

His mouth finds mine again, and I suck in a sharp breath as his hands, excruciatingly slow, find their way up my shirt. He traces my bare skin, my breasts, all while I continue to kiss him feverishly, focusing all my energy on his mouth. His neck. His shoulders. His hands stop below my navel, and I can sense the question form on his lips. I don't give him the opportunity to speak before I press my hips forward and bury his mouth with my own.

He lets out a small laugh against my mouth but doesn't stop his hands from running them over the tops of my thighs, moving slowly between my legs. Slumping forward so my head is resting on him, I graze my teeth against his shoulder earning a soft moan. The noise sends a thrill up my spine, so I do it again.

"Elora, you are—"

"You really do always speak, don't you?" I laugh, pushing back to meet his eyes. His smile only intensifies the fluttering feeling in my stomach, and his hands move to my back, bracing me as he leans me backward onto the mattress. His body hovers over mine so I pull him closer, letting the warmth and weight of him encompass me.

"I can be quiet," he whispers, pushing my legs apart before settling between them, leaving me gasping at the sudden friction, "but can you?"

I let out a laugh as my hands explore the muscles in his torso, dragging my nails slightly over his chest. He kisses me again, a clash of tongues, a jolt of heat. More, more, more. It's the only thing I can conjure to think at this moment.

Then, without any warning, they start.

It's quiet at first, a soft thrumming in the back of my mind. So soft it takes me a moment to make out the word. Then, like a clap of thunder, my ears are splitting as the voices in my head scream and scream.

Jerking myself sideways, I push Sorin off me in the process.

The shouts in my ears so deafening I cover them both with my hands, slamming my eyes shut to stop the images I know will come. They always do.

Murderer.

Liar.

Murderer.

Sorin shakes my shoulders, making no attempt to be gentle. "Elora!" He succeeds, breaking through the invisible barrier, releasing me from the torment. At least, momentarily. My hands tremble as I pull them from my ears. I let them hang at my sides as my chest heaves and vision spins.

In.

Out.

I hate the way I flinch away as Sorin slides his hand toward me, but I hate even more the look of hurt in his eyes after I've done it.

"I'm sorry." My voice is as weak as my apology.

Weak, weak, weak.

"Don't do that," he says, still a little breathless. I refuse to meet his eyes, but I know he's watching me. "Whatever this is, whatever is going on. You can tell me. But don't apologize for it." He inches himself closer but hesitates, pulling his hand back into his lap. "If it was something I did—"

"No." I stop him, whipping my head up. Pushing my hair back over my shoulders and out of my eyes, I lean forward. "This has nothing to do with you. Or with...us." I'm not sure why the word catches on my tongue. Why does it leave a bitter taste there like berries that aren't ready to be picked?

Us.

I never thought there would be an *us* with anyone again, and saying it aloud rattles me to my core. "I *will* tell you," I say, reaching out for his hand. He takes it and scoots closer, though the way he reclines his body slightly away doesn't go unnoticed, making my heart sink in more ways than one. "I just can't tell you yet," I whisper. Because everything will change between us when I do. There's that word again.

Us.

Gripping my hand, he brings it to his lips, brushing a soft kiss along the back of it. "Whatever it is that's going on inside your mind," he says, "whatever darkness inflicts you there, it will never be dark enough to scare me away," he pauses, delicately placing my hand back onto the bed. "Nothing will." Inclining his head, I part my mouth but he cuts me off, turning to leave. "I'll let you rest," he says. "We have an early morning."

With every step toward the door, my heart sinks further and further. I curse the demons in my head, but aren't I the one who keeps them there? As he reaches for the door, my heartache turns to panic so I sit up and jump from the bed.

"Stay!" I shout, just as his hand grasps the doorknob. Pulling his hand back, the muscles flex as he balls his fingers into a fist, then straightens them again. My heart races, and for a moment I've convinced myself he'll say no. And he has every reason to.

There is nothing easy about the person that I am. There is nothing light. I am not a happy maiden whose days are blissfully spent sitting idly by, even if some deep part of me longs to be just that. I am the monster who keeps the maidens up at night. Who lurks in the shadows with demons in her head and blood on her hands. If I were Sorin, I too would hesitate. Would turn and never look back.

Just when I'm beginning to regret my words, Sorin spins around. His dark eyes scan my face. Searching, longing. He steals my breath with his stare alone, and I know, at this moment, nothing will ever be the same.

I'm not sure how long I've been awake, but I don't dare move. The warmth of Sorin's body and tangle of limbs as we slept intertwined with each other...a comfort and contentment I thought I'd never feel. Shouldn't feel. The butterflies in my stomach quickly sour as my mind drifts. Even while Sorin's deep breaths strum against my back, the need to hide from the joy I've allowed myself to feel, even briefly, is all consuming.

Sun peeks through the bottom of the heavy curtains casting slivers of distorted light across the room, and with it, a memory. So sudden and jarring. So fast and raw and real, I couldn't stop it if I tried.

Our small room in Valebridge comes into view. Marble walls. A large four post bed, and of course, *her*. The picture is painted in my mind as clear as the day I lived it.

"Tell me again," I begged my mother. My braided pigtails hung below my shoulders. My favorite blue and ivory nightgown had begun to fray at the ends, but I refused to wear anything else.

She laughed as the sunset filtered through the drapes that hung over the carved windows, shining onto her radiant onyx hair, sending a mix of shadow and light dancing up the marble ceiling of our room. Her hair was silky and black as a crow, spilling over one shoulder in loose waves. "Once more," she said. "Then, you must sleep, susi.*"*

I was five-years-old and she was the only world I knew, so one more chance to hear her voice, I eagerly took it. Curling up into my bed, she sat at the end, rubbing my legs idly as she began her story again.

"Once upon a time, there was an Enchantress—"

"Was it you, mama?" I asked through a yawn as my head sank further into my large pillow. She smiled and leaned forward, brushing a kiss to my forehead.

"Shhh, Elora. Listen," she whispered against my skin.

I nodded my head as I rubbed the sleep from my eyes, but it was no use. I was too tired to fight what was to come.

"Once upon a time, there was an Enchantress, who loved a little girl very much..."

As always, the memory stops short. The end ripped away, leaving me feeling cheated by my own mind. The soft drop of a tear lands upon my pillow. Blinking the rest away, I peel my eyes from the sun drifting under the curtains, suddenly desperate for rain.

Isn't it funny...the memories we keep, sealed away inside of us like tombs? Protected and guarded only to be cracked open by the most mundane instances. The smell of tobacco or the hum of a childhood melody. Sun filtering under the curtains. Memories linked to those we love and those we've lost. Grief rears its head as swiftly as water destroys. Slow and quiet, then all at once, insurmountable.

Sorin rustles behind me, his muscled arm wrapping around my middle, pulling me deeper into his chest. Wiping my eyes, I roll to face him. Sleep still lines his eyes, his hair a mess of brown waves, the scruff along his jaw dark and more pronounced. He smiles and despite the war inside myself, I force a smile back.

"Good morning, love," he whispers against my hair. Reaching down, he finds my lips, his kiss feather light. Sweet as honey, smooth as silk. When he pulls away and heads to the bathing chamber, I miss the heat of his body instantly. The rhythm of his heart.

So, it's now, with the light filtering through the curtains, and sleep lining Sorin's eyes and the brush of his lips and the memory of my mother that I decide what I must do. Today, I will trust Sorin wholly, and today, I will tell him my secrets.

GATHERING BACK at Mahaffey's for breakfast before our journey, Sam, Jarek, and Galen sit at the same booth from last night when Sorin and I arrive. Sam's body is slumped over onto the table, a jumble of black curls that takes up most of the space. Jarek and Galen sip coffee in contented silence as I slide into a chair across from them.

"Morning!" Jarek's voice booms through the pub. This early there aren't many patrons, the sun beams through the door that remains propped open, illuminating remnants of dust and last night's debauchery on the tabletops. I turn to my right expecting to find Sorin but realize he's wandered to the bar.

"Please, Jarek." Sam doesn't bother to lift her head from the table as she grumbles in his direction. "Can you find it in yourself for once not to be so damn joyful in the morning?" Her voice is hoarse and craggy, I press my palms to my mouth to cover my smile. Maybe the third round of drinks was a bit much after all. "At least not before I've had any coffee," she groans.

"Sorry, my queen," he laughs. "Just eager to hear from the happy couple is all." Jarek shoots me a wink, downing the rest of his drink. The chipped ivory mug looks comical in his large hands, as if it were meant for a child. Jerking up off the table, Sam tucks her tight black curls behind her ears, a few pieces springing freely around her face. A hint of a blush scatters across her cheeks.

"Well now, that *is* interesting," she muses. Tilting her head to the side, she swipes Galen's coffee from the table without so much as looking in his direction. Opening his mouth in a retort she cuts him off. "Trust me"—she holds a hand up in his direction—"I need it more than you." To my surprise, Galen doesn't balk, rather, smiles and shakes his head before returning his focus to his book. After taking a deep sip, she peers over my shoulder toward the bar, cupping the mug with either palm.

"So," she says, raising her eyebrows in question, redirecting her gaze to me. "Did you two—" Galen's elbow bumps her arm, causing the hot liquid to spill over the cup and onto the table.

"Hey!" Sam shoots him a snarled look, and I bite the inside of my cheek to keep myself from smiling.

"Manners, Samaria," Galen says in his usual monotonous

tone, picking his book back up. Before burying his nose in it, he glances at me briefly giving the slightest dip of his chin. Warmth spreads over me at the subtle gesture, and I will be sure to thank him later. Maybe we can be friends after all.

With stomachs full of oats and the last of the seasonal berries, we head on our way. Checking in at the stables, I'm riddled with guilt as I venture toward Amis' stall. I want so badly to take her with us, but I know Sorin and Galen are right about keeping low to the ground as we get closer to Kirsgard.

Running my hand down Amis's velvety nose, I lean in and kiss it quickly. She nuzzles my hand as if she knows what I have brought with me. Tilting her head up and down several times, she coaxes a laugh out of me as I sneak the small handful of blackberries from my cloak pocket. "We'll be back," I whisper before rejoining the group.

Each of us carries a pack with various supplies that the barkeep provided to Sorin this morning. Explains the ample schillings he paid him last night, I suppose. Mine holds my ration of bread and jam, cured meats from Loxley, and a canteen of water.

Sorin's bow and quiver are strapped to his back, the black arrows glinting brightly under the morning sun. Jarek wields two axes strapped with a leather harness, the tips of the metal engraved in various swirls and markings I don't recognize but admire anyway. Samaria has a similar bow to Sorin's; only hers isn't black.

Her ivory bow is beautiful and appears to be feather light as she flips it around a few times before securing it. It's only then I realize Galen bears no weapons, at least none that I can easily see. Three rolls of canvas are secured on his back in a row, along with a pack of his own slung over his shoulder. I pat my hips out of habit, ensuring my daggers are in place, hoping I won't need them.

"We'll make our way through the outer edge of the forest," Sorin says, readjusting the straps on my pack, helping tighten them. "Karos Falls is about a day's hike from here. We'll camp there for the night. The closer we get to Kirsgard, the more subtle we'll need to be, just in case. Galen and I think it's best to utilize the falls as a natural noise barrier," Sorin explains before turning to Galen.

"THIS PART of the Trinity Forest holds many creatures that will not be thrilled with our presence," Galen says. A vague memory of Sam telling us Galen studied magick under an esteemed scholar raises the hair on the back of my neck. I've had my fair share of run-ins with forest sprites, but my palms sweat with the idea that other creatures may be watching us. Not to mention hunters of magick, though they'll be disappointed to know I bear none. My mind snags on the last time I stepped foot upon Kirsgard. The swarms of hunters. The blood and chains and screams.

"Tomorrow," Sorin interrupts my thoughts, "we'll leave at first light to make it to the Wicked Wood before nightfall." The four of us nod in understanding, though my stomach churns with unease. I risk a glance at Sam, but her face is turned away from me, peering at the horses lined in the stables.

"Ready?" Jarek's hand lands on my shoulder, making my stomach tense further. Clearing my throat, I nod and fall in line next to Sam as we head toward the edge of town. I shake my hands out at my sides, clenching and unclenching my fists, trying to regain my focus on the tasks at hand. Make it through The Wicked Woods. Lead us to the Awakening Stones. Perform the Ceremony and help Samaria gain her magick. Then show Sorin how to get into Valebridge.

Easy enough.

Fool.

CHAPTER 25

ELORA

THE WALK THROUGH THE FOREST THIS MORNING feels like a homecoming. The melodic song of a lonely bird follows us with every step. The pine trees bend with the weight of the needles. Their heavy limbs dipping low into our path. Bowing. Leading the way. I've missed the woods. The sounds, the smells. During our night in town and my stay in Loxley, part of me felt incomplete. While I can certainly appreciate the warmth of the baths and a proper bed, the woods have earned their way into my soul. I cannot be me without them. The moment we step back into the trees, an itch of magick thrums against my palms. I flex my hands quickly and close my eyes. Hope spears through me for a moment, but as always, nothing manifests.

"You are the magick, susi.*"* My mother's voice rings through my ears. The same phrase she'd said to me throughout my childhood. I trudge forward, keeping my pace with Sam, focusing on my steps and not the disappointment that washes over me that I'm useless. Over a fallen log, around a bush of thorny vines. Anything to keep my mind clear, anything to keep it from drifting toward memories of her.

Sorin, Jarek, and Galen lead us through an overgrown path

of brambles. Thick, leafy branches that are riddled with ivy, I'm certain they're the poisonous kind, so I pay extra attention to each step, tugging my cloak tightly around myself to avoid exposing too much skin.

Sam and I keep close together near the back of the pack. The farther we venture north, the more changes I notice from the area of woods I called home all those years. The trees are more densely sprouted, leaving very little visibility ahead of us. Jutting toward the sky, it's almost impossible to see the tops, and while the trees back at my cabin are enormous in width, they would be dwarfed next to these. Easily five times larger around than my arms could wrap, the ancient sentinels demand respect as we delicately tiptoe through their home.

"I didn't mean to be presumptuous this morning." Sam breaks our comfortable silence once the boys have gained some distance in front of us. "I'm sorry if I offended you," she admits, casting me a sorrowful glance. Worry displays across her face as her brows pinch together.

"Please, Sam," I say with a shrug. "Haven't we gone over this? You could never offend me." My smile is genuine as I wrap an arm around her shoulder. "Besides," I continue, "you weren't totally far off assuming something *may* have happened last night." Whipping her head toward me, her worried brows are now sprung up near her hairline. The sudden change in demeanor is too much, and I can't help but tip my head back in laughter.

"Do tell more, Enchantress." Her voice is teasing as we duck around a fallen tree, taking our time catching up with the boys.

"Just a kiss," I speak through the smile on my face though the confession causes my cheeks to flush. I'll blame it on the heat if I must.

"Oh, I'm sure it was more than that." Sam laughs. "I wish I could show you the grin you have plastered on your face." I should've known she'd see through my vagueness.

"It was really just a kiss." I attempt to convince her again, which only makes her laugh harder. Our laughter catches the attention of the boys for a moment, the three of them stopping to turn. Sorin cocks his head to the side, his smile bright even from this distance.

Wiping the grin off my face, I smooth my features back into their typically neutral demeanor. I'm not entirely sure why I feel embarrassed admitting my kiss with Sorin, it's not like he's the first man I've been with.

Cade.

His name hits me like rock. A weight tied to my soul. I silently damn myself for allowing myself to forget, to move on. My boots grind against the forest floor as I come to an abrupt stop. The pain in my chest spreads like a wildfire, and I know it won't be long before the dark floods my vision. Gripping my chest, I force the voices down. Push the memories away. *Just for a little longer,* I tell them, *let me get through today.*

"Elora?" Sam's grip on my arm is a tether back to reality. When I look up I'm grateful the boys have busied themselves with their canteens and chatter while they wait for us to catch up.

"Sorry," I say, attempting a laugh but all that comes out is something strangled and weak. "Caught up in my own thoughts again." Pulling my hood back, I take a huge gulp of the forest air. The sun is warm, so I tilt my chin up, letting it kiss my skin and push the demons further down. Always down, down, down. Sam's gaze burns against my back.

"Sometimes," I whisper, "I have flashbacks. Memories, I guess, of my life before." Walking in unison now, Sam reaches for my hand and I let her grab it. "And sometimes," I continue, "the memories are so vivid they feel very real. As if I'm living the night I lost my family over and over again. When those memories arise, it makes it difficult to decipher what is present and what is past." Stopping for a moment, I catch my breath. "It's as if I'm stuck in some in-between reality from the night I lost them," I continue, Sam's grip doesn't falter, her touch soothing.

"It's as if I don't belong here, but I can't belong there. Because here is to be without them, and *there* no longer exists."

"And you've not explained this to Sorin?" she asks. Shaking my head, my words fail me yet again. "The weight of losing your family can't be light, Elora," Sam says, squeezing my hand in the reassuring way I've found she often does with all of us. "You needn't bear this alone. You can trust Sorin, and you can trust me." I struggle to hide my wince as she speaks, her words too kind. Too unassuming to who she is speaking to. "He was there for me," she whispers, "there for all of us when our father died. He knows grief. We all do in some way."

Her words jolt me. Stopping, I grab her arm. "I've been selfish," I admit. And I have. Acting as though I'm the only person to experience loss.

Shaking her head, we continue on. "You are anything but selfish," she says. "Just trust him, okay?"

"I have every intention of explaining...*this* to Sorin," I say, gesturing to my head. To the mess that is my mind. "I just..."

"You underestimate him, Enchantress," she says, picking my hand back up. "Don't let Sorin's sunshine and roses facade fool you. Just because he wears his burdens well, doesn't mean they don't exist. I know more than anyone they're much heavier than he's willing to admit." She stops, chewing her bottom lip for a moment before dropping my hand. "Tell him what's going on and let him help you. Help *each other*. Nobody should wade through the dark alone, perhaps together you can find the light."

I mull her words over as we continue our walk.

Find the light.

But what if darkness is all I've grown to know? What if darkness is to me what light is to everyone else? When everyone craves to get through it, I thrive within it. Hidden from sight. Alone. I want to tell Sam that it isn't so simple to explain you're the reason your loved ones are dead. Maybe I deserve every bit of my despair for I'm at the root of it.

CATCHING UP TO THE BOYS, Sam and I prop ourselves against a tree, opening our canteens for a drink. I'm quickly learning that no matter how hard I try to conceal my emotions, Sorin somehow knows when something upsets me. He tilts his head to the side as he studies me. Avoiding his gaze, I'm surprised when he approaches, but rather than asking how I am or what bothers me, he lets the words go unsaid.

Bending down he places a kiss to my forehead, his lips linger longer than necessary and my stomach dips in response. It's the smallest act of kindness, not to pry or demand an answer for someone's woes, but instead to simply exist in the same space as another. Dragging my eyes up to his face, his smile melts another layer of ice around my heart. The change is swift as it thaws, leaving more and more space to welcome him in. As if reading my mind, he grips the back of my neck and draws me in for another kiss atop my head. My shoulders unclench at his closeness, and I begin to wonder if that is *his* magick. Making me feel at ease in a way I've never felt before.

"We have another two hours before we reach Karos Falls," Sorin says, repacking provisions into his bag, "Once we—"

His words are cut short as our attention turns to the deafening howls that sound from all directions. A murder of crows shoots out from the trees in a flurry of black. Their caws send a warning signal through the sky a moment too late. Hope fills my chest at the promise one of the howls belongs to Alaric, but fear overrides it as I realize my companions may not be as welcoming to a giant wolf approaching as I would. Tugging at my ear, we wait for another howl.

"Was that what I think it was?" Sam asks. "Wolves?" Her voice is shaky but her hands are anything but as they reach for her bow before pressing her back into Jarek's so they're flush.

"That's not possible, is it?" Jarek eyes the woods around us as another howl shoots through the pines. Ripples of fear and adrenaline cascade over my body as I watch my friends react to what I know now is definitely Alaric. His howl is distinct, and for whatever reason, I can decipher it. Jarek steps away from Sam for a moment to reach an arm up and behind him to unsheath an ax from his back. The movement is so smooth and natural, his arm cutting through the air like butter.

"It's not *impossible*." Galen's voice remains unbothered despite the current circumstance. "But it *is* unusual." The heavy weight of his gaze sends a shiver down my spine despite the summer heat. "We haven't had wolves in this part of the Trinity Forest in centuries," Galen continues, stepping toward me now. "How peculiar, wouldn't you say, Elora?"

Swallowing thickly, I don't miss the way Sorin steps slightly closer to me. "I wouldn't know," I finally say. Galen's eyes scan my face, but for the first time, I see softness instead of scrutiny.

"You two can discuss the details later," Jarek says, unsheathing his second ax and pressing his back against Samaria again. Her bow has an arrow nocked and ready to fire as her eyes drift through the woods. A true hunter in every form. The two of them look somehow both lethal and completely comfortable in this position. Two halves to a whole. "Please just shut your mouths for a minute," Jarek whispers again. "The *susi* are likely planning an attack as we waste time bickering."

My stomach lurches. His accent isn't heavy and typically I forget it is even there, but the dialect he uses on one word is strong and pronounced. Unmistakeable.

Susi.

"What did you say?" The accusation in my tone is one I immediately regret as four sets of eyes land on me. Pushing past Sorin, my chest heaves as I glance up at Jarek.

Relaxing his axes momentarily to his sides, his voice is much softer than before. "I asked if you could quiet your—"

"No, not that part." Shaking my head impatiently, I drag my hands down my face. "The word you used...*Susi*." Closing my eyes briefly, I do my best to ignore the others stares boring into my skin. My body heats under their gazes but still, I stand my ground. "What does it mean?" I demand again.

For a moment, the ground beneath me has been uprooted. Turning. Twisting. The trees disappear to ash as the skies darken to near obsidian. Songbirds cease, their melody replaced by howls that swiftly turn to screams. Stumbling backward, I bump blindly into Sorin. I recoil away from his touch like a serpent pinned in a corner desperate to escape. Dropping to my knees, I press my hands to my ears and will myself to slow down. To breathe. To remember that the world is in fact, still spinning. That my heart still beats.

But the word echoes inside my head over and over again. The same word my mother had given me as a nickname from birth. The word Agnes had used the day she had a premonition in the kitchen. The word that haunts every nightmare since my mother's death. The word that holds more value than I could explain and yet I never knew its true meaning until this moment.

Susi.

Wolf.

Part two:
The
Wolf

CHAPTER 26

ELORA

"ONCE UPON A TIME, THERE WAS AN ENCHANTRESS *who loved a little girl very much. But the little girl did not know her power."*

"*Here comes my favorite part.*" I giggled, eyes heavy with sleep. The sunset had long since passed, replaced by silver slices of moonlight. My mother shushed me, running a delicate hand over my cheek.

"*One day, the little girl will grow big and strong—*"

"*Like you mama?*"

"*Even stronger, yet,* susi. *Can you guess? How strong will you be, Elora?*"

"*As strong as an ox?*" I managed to ask through a yawn.

Leaning down, her lips brushed against my brow. My eyelids were too heavy, but I managed to lift them in time to see her dark hair fall forward, encasing me momentarily.

"*No, my girl,*" she whispered against my skin. "*Stronger yet.*" I tried to keep my eyes open, fighting against the call for sleep to admire how her silver eyes glow in the dark. But I was only five and I was so, so tired.

"*You, Elora Leigh,*" she whispered, the warmth of her body

slowly faded as she drifted from my bed, moving toward the door of our room. "You will be as strong as a wolf."

"ELORA, WHAT IS IT?" Sorin's at my side in an instant, though he makes no attempt to touch me again. Having learned quickly I'm best left alone in my moments of panic.

"My mother." My voice waivers as I drop my hands to my sides. I make no effort now to conceal my pain. Little by little that guilt ridden armor has been cracking since Loxley, and little by little my confidence builds in its absence. I shouldn't feel the need to hide from my pain. From my past. Not here, with them. Not with myself. The air that fills my lungs is sticky and warm, but I let it be a reminder that I'm still breathing. I'm still *here.*

"She used to call me *susi,*" I explain, my breathing erratic. "From the moment I was born. I thought it was just an endearing nickname until the other day." I flash my eyes past Sorin to the rest of the group. "The other day when Agnes had a premonition in the kitchen, she called me *susi* as well." Shaking my head, I glance toward Jarek. "I never knew the meaning...until now." His solemn expression hardens when another howl bounces around us.

"I don't understand," Sam says, keeping her back pressed against Jarek, her weapon glistening in the sunlight. Such a beautiful thing to carry with such a devastating purpose. "Elora, what does the word wolf have to do with you?"

The ear splitting howls from earlier transform to low growls as the wolves move closer.

"Whatever is going on, Enchantress, you realize you aren't alone in this?" Galen's voice has softened as he steps around Sorin toward me, but before he can make it any further, the shape of a familiar predatory beast blocks the sun from behind me, casting a shadow large enough to engulf the two of us.

Everyone, save for Sorin and myself, let out audible gasps as Alaric hops down from the fallen log behind me. I dart my eyes between the wolf and Sorin, then to Sam and Jarek. Finally, to Galen who stands before me. A second wolf hops atop a fallen log adjacent to me. Her coat, black as night, with bright green eyes that burn against the summer sun. The same wolf that had been with Alaric on the riverbank, I realize.

The hair on Alaric's back stands straight on end as he hunches his body toward the ground. His low growl drips with warning as he narrows his focus on Galen, elongated canines peeking out through a snarled snout. To Galen's credit, he doesn't move a muscle. Doesn't show an inkling of fear as the wolf stares him down. Wielding both his axes, Jarek steps forward, surprisingly light on his toes, placing himself between the wolf and Galen. Without thinking, I move to position myself between the wolf and Jarek.

"What are you doing!" The terror in Sam's voice is unnerving but I keep my calm.

"Just trust me, Sam," I say. Looking up at Jarek, Alaric inches closer to my rear, brushing me slightly with his nose. "Lower your axes, Jarek." Holding my hand outward, I gesture for him to drop them. He begins to shake his head when Sorin steps in, placing a hand on Jarek's back.

"Listen to her," Sorin says. It isn't a request. Jarek frowns but he does as Sorin says. As I say. He lowers his axes to his sides.

"He won't hurt you." I wish my voice was more convincing as I unclench my fists. I hadn't realized I'd balled them up so tightly, little crescent moons dented into my palms. "He won't hurt any of us."

Alaric takes the cue and straightens to his full height before dipping his chin down to nuzzle the side of my neck. Sam gasps, her face horrified and before I can reassure her that he is not harmful, Galen takes a step toward the wolf and me. The black wolf who has been perched upon the fallen log stands attentively, her massive frame taking up most of the tree trunk, as Galen closes the distance between us.

Alaric's sharp canines peek out again, the sight of them enough to make Galen halt his steps. But as I pat the wolf's side, he relaxes, snapping his jaw shut and lowering his haunches. Galen must see this as an opportunity as he makes the final step toward me.

"Elora," he says softly. I shoot a look towards Sorin and see that he's retreated with Jarek to a nearby tree. Leaning against it nonchalantly, as if everything happening is completely ordinary. "What you say next is very important," Galen continues, reaching his hand out cautiously toward Alaric. The wolf sniffs the air around Galen before turning his head, dismissing him as any sort of threat.

"Have you ever..." Galen's voice trails off as he pulls his hand back from the wolf and places it on my shoulder. It takes me a moment to realize what he was doing. He asked the wolf's permission to touch me. Be near me. I glance at his hand on my shoulder. "Have you ever spoken to these wolves, Elora? Whether it be aloud or...in your mind?"

The knot forming in my throat is painful, but I push past it as I nod my head. Galen frowns, but only for a moment, before sliding his hand from my shoulder. "And you've heard them speak back to you?" Another shameful nod as my secrets become public. "Right," Galen says, the usual flatness of his tone returning. "We're all good here then." Spinning on his heels, he heads back toward Sam.

"What do you mean?" I shout. He halts, turning to face me again.

"I mean these animals are not a threat to us as long as we're not a threat to *you*."

"You aren't making sense, Galen." Sam's voice is still shaky. Jarek has returned to her side, sliding his hand down her arm and coaxing her to relax her bow. Galen lets out a long sigh, a show of his usual disdain for having to explain anything at all. As if all of us should know exactly what he means at all times.

"What I mean is, Elora here is a Dyrsjel. And so long as *we* do not harm or threaten her, the wolves will not harm or threaten *us*."

"No, that can't be, she hasn't completed the Awakening Ceremony," Sam says before I get the chance to speak.

Again, four sets of eyes land heavily on me, and I fight to keep the heat from crawling over my skin.

"Something to tell the group, Elora?" Galen steps forward, but Sorin stops him with the wave of a hand. I brave a glance at Sam, my heart sinks at the shock on her face. That I've lied to her. That I have completed my Ceremony. That I do possess my magick. Though, to be fair, I thought it a waste. That the Mother skipped me. That I was nothing.

Galen sets his pack onto the ground and pulls it open. The wolves have settled now, both laying down observing the five of us. "Dyrsjel magick is descended through bloodlines," Galen explains. "Enchantresses are gifted this ability through the Mother, only to those possessing Dyrsjel blood. There are only a few bloodlines in Valebridge history that have been reported to be of Dyrsjel magick—"

"My mother was not a Dyrsjel," I cut him off a little too defensively. Confusion swirls in my stomach as I dart my eyes between Galen and the wolves.

"It could have easily been your grandmother," Galen says without missing a beat. "It's coursing through you just as naturally as the blood you bleed, whether you deny it or not." He continues rummaging through his pack.

Finding whatever he was looking for, Galen saunters to me and slides a book into my hands. It's delicate and small, the spine cracked and peeling. I flip it over to read the title that is etched in gold filigree across a faded green cover, *"The Natural History of the Dyrsjel."*

"Wait," I say, shoving the book back into his hand. "You're

telling me all this time, I've had this ability? To speak to them? *That* is my magick?" I gesture to the beasts at my side.

"Yes, after your Ceremony of course," Galen replies, a hint of a smirk on his lips at my secret revealed. He gestures to the giant beasts, the black wolf releasing a low rumble in her throat as he does. "If your mother never explained what a Dyrsjel is, it's likely she didn't want you to know. Perhaps to protect you." He studies me for a moment before shoving the book back toward me. I take it, though uncertainty and disbelief make me want to drop it and run away.

"The magick you feel pushing against your skin," Galen says, his voice returning to the soft calm I was so surprised to hear earlier. "As if it's trying to claw its way out..." I glance at Sam and then to Sorin, my nerves more and more exposed and raw with each word. "*That*," Galen continues pointing a finger at me and then to the wolves, "is *them*." A heavy silence drifts through our group as I consider everything Galen's told me. "You must let them in. Accept that this is part of you, otherwise the bond is pointless. It won't work unless you allow it."

Anger boils within me and with it, a swift kick of guilt. Anger that my mother withheld such valuable information from me, keeping me from accessing my magick. And guilt because if I know her as well as I think I do, I know she kept it from me to keep me safe. Keep me out of King Roman's hands.

"So...this magick, this Dyrsjel magick, is from the wolves?" Sorin asks and I am grateful he has spoken, leaving me more time to catch my breath.

Galen pinches the bridge of his nose, clearly bored of the topic already. "No, it isn't always wolves. The animal varies depending on the Enchantress, but an animal, no less." He turns his gaze back to me. "You could consider the wolves more like your guides. Partners, even. Dyrsjel at the very root means *animal soul*." I nod, only once, my mind going through waves of disbelief, then anger, then back to disbelief.

"Dyrsjel blood runs as deep as the trees," Galen continues.

Sam has lowered her bow, though I don't miss how tightly she still clutches it at her side. "As old and ancient as the dirt we walk on, thus, giving you access to a much deeper pool of magick." His brows furrow for a moment, as if he's conjured a thought before returning to his natural smooth disposition. "The caveat," he continues, shrugging off whatever question popped into his mind, "is that it won't manifest until you make the bond with your guides as I said before." He glances again at the wolves and my heart races.

"But my mother was a Seer," I say, disbelief lining every word. I stand frozen, opening and closing my free hand repetitively at my side. "I don't possess that gift as far as I know."

Galen chews his bottom lip for a moment, eyes raking over me but I don't feel the judgment as I did before in Loxley. Only curiosity.

"That is why they're here," he finally says, pointing to the wolves. "To help you. Guide you to your magick, whatever it may be. A Seer or maybe a Healer. We'll know once you've made the bond. The magick you possess is much stronger than the magick of any other Enchantress, you'll need their help to control it." My eyes drift to the wolves, then back to Galen. "And as a Dyrsjel," he continues, "you alone will have control of the Stones."

There it is.

The *truth*.

My mother was the only one in Valebridge to perform the Ceremonies for as long as I can remember. The only one who was able to escape with the Stones when King Roman turned against us. She was, without a doubt, a Dyrsjel. As her mother was before her and so on. The Leigh family is one of the last Dyrsjel bloodlines.

And I am the last of the Leighs.

"Isn't that what the Awakening Ceremony is for?" Sam asks, snapping me back to the present.

"The Ceremony unlocked Elora's connection with the

wolves, but her magick will need to be coaxed out," Galen shoves his hands in his pockets before he shrugs. "Whatever magick it is you have Mother Gaia knew well enough that you'd need help. Just as *your* mother likely needed help perfecting her gift of Sight. The wolves will help guide you, once bonded."

My laugh is nervous and borderline manic as I take in this slew of information. My mother was the Head Enchantress, a powerful Seer. But how powerful must she have been to also be a Dyrsjel if what Galen says is true? The night of my Ceremony she was unable to see the attack coming, how is that possible if she was as powerful as he says?

"I have never even *felt* magick before." The admission deflates me even further. "All this time I thought…"

Useless.

Worthless.

"Why are they coming to me now?" My question isn't pointed at anyone in particular but the rising anger in my chest catches my breath. "Why weren't they there when…" I let my voice trail off, the shame of having this gift and not knowing how to wield it is too much to bear. I could have saved them. Or worse yet, my mother *knew* I possessed this ancient magick and purposely withheld the information from me.

"It's different for each Dyrsjel. You haven't had any encounters with them since your Ceremony?" Galen asks, pointing again to the wolves resting lazily at my sides. I bite my tongue as reality slams into me. All the times I hid from the wolves in the forest. Every moment I heard a howl, how quickly I ran. Shaking my head, shame and frustration lodge in my throat, leaving me speechless.

Galen glances around the group, his blue eyes narrowing slightly before ending the conversation by turning his back and making his way to the nearby stream. Sam and Jarek follow suit without muttering a word, keeping their eyes on the wolves as they head after Galen toward the water.

Sorin clears his throat, grabbing my attention.

"I truly wanted to tell you about speaking with the wolves, about having already gone through my Ceremony. I just wasn't sure how," I say, bending down to pat Alaric lightly on the head. A deep, contented sigh escapes him, causing me to smile despite the confusion still swirling in my gut.

"Oh, you told me about the wolves, love," Sorin says as he bends down, holding his hand out to the wolf. Alaric sniffs his hand before settling back down in the dirt.

"What? When did I tell you?" I ask as I rack my brain trying to remember the day in Loxley I spoke with Alaric. How Agnes' premonition had sent me spiraling through the woods. Sorin's fingers graze my neck as he brushes my braid over my shoulder.

"That night in Loxley we had dinner together. You told me just before you passed out and I had to carry you to bed." His fingers trace along my shoulder before his hand drops to clasp mine. "And to think," he continues, "everyone doubts *my* ability to hold my wine." A smile splays across his face before he dips his head to kiss me softly on the mouth. Nothing like the kiss we shared last night, but just as magnificent all the same. If I hadn't been so shocked by what he just said I may have begged for more.

Scoffing, I step backward, pulling myself away from him. Stumbling over the giant canines at my feet in the process. "You should have said something!"

"I thought it was a drunken tale." Sorin laughs. "Besides, I had a suspicion you could be a Dyrsjel that day we met on the river. Something about the way the wolf seemed to bend to your will. It isn't common, if you didn't realize, for these massive beasts to protect anyone but their pack."

Confusion plagues my face. "You've heard of the Dyrsjel?" I frown, heart racing again as if I'm the only one not in on another secret.

Sorin *hmms*, before he simply says, "Yes."

I wait for more of an explanation why he would've heard of such a thing while I had not. Then, the fog lifts from my mind.

Like a gray mist dispersing as it hits the ocean horizon. "It's common knowledge, isn't it?" I ask, though I don't need him to speak to know his answer. He nods his head, placing his hands in his pockets, the dimple that now possesses my entire heart hidden away behind his solemn expression. "It's common knowledge," I say again, "and my mother kept it from me."

Sorin says nothing as he steps forward. Wrapping his arms around my waist, he pulls me flush with his body. I lean into his chest and soak up the heat of him. The smell of him. Pine and firewood. I relish in it, even if it's just for now. Even if I don't deserve it. My mind reels against the new found truth. That my mother was full of her own secrets. That she chose to keep such a huge part of me hidden. In all my studies in Valebridge, this large part of the Enchantress history was left out of it.

"As Galen said, it's believed that only Dyrsjel's have the power to call upon the Stones," Sorin whispers, holding me close to his body. "Maybe she was protecting you? Having that sort of ability would put you even more at risk with the king."

Anger rears its head again as I attempt to pull away, but Sorin's hands are planted firmly against my back. "And that is why you pushed for me to join you?" Tears prickle my eyes, my body's response to this overwhelming betrayal from my mother. From Sorin.

"That was part of it," he says, finally easing up on his grip. I step back to meet his face, my brows furrow together and when I'm about to say something, Sorin brushes his fingers down my cheek. "Don't look at me like that," he whispers, placing a hand over his chest, "it'll break my heart." Crossing my arms, I take another step back. Despite the anger, the confusion, the look he's giving me softens the blow. Which only angers me more.

"I knew you were an Enchantress," he says, taking a timid step forward. "But when we met the wolves on the river that day—"

"The day I saved your life," I say, boots rooted to the ground as he steps even closer.

"Yes, to which I am forever in debt." He rests his hands on the tops of my shoulders, giving them a squeeze. "Something told me you were different. Something told me that maybe you were exactly who we needed to get to the Stones. To help Sam. To help the other Enchantresses still locked in Valebridge. To end this famine...this blight."

"You didn't tell me about your suspicion."

"I didn't," he admits. His arms wrap around me again, pulling me flush to his chest. I fight back, leaning away from him, but he steps closer, forcing me into him. "When I realized you'd never met the wolves before that day, I thought you didn't know. If it was true that you were a Dyrsjel, you needed to figure it out for yourself. It wasn't my place. Besides, I wasn't sure, not until just now."

I push against his chest again, attempting to put some distance between us. He lets me go, but I don't make it far. I don't want to be far from him despite how frustrated I am.

"To be fair," he continues, "you didn't tell me about your Ceremony. All this time I thought you were without magick." His hand moves from my back and slides to the back of my neck, gripping me there so I'm forced to look up at him.

"I didn't know," I whisper, guilt lining my insides. "I didn't know I had any magick, I thought I..."

"It's okay," Sorin whispers, resting his chin on the top of my head. "I would have asked you to come with me, either way," he says. Bending down, he presses his forehead into mine. "Enchantress or not. Dyrsjel or not, I would have asked you to come with me, Elora."

"And why is that?" I'm not sure why I ask, maybe it's a selfish question. Maybe hearing that he simply *wanted* me to come will help ease the truthful blows that hit me today.

"Because you enraptured me," he laughs. "How could I resist that life altering scowl? There is no way I was leaving those woods without you, you fiery thing." I smile into his chest, ignoring the voices in my head that say I don't deserve him.

"I don't know where to go from here," I say through a sigh. "It's been years since my Ceremony, and I've not *once* felt magick possess me the way it had my mother." He runs a hand down my spine, twisting his fingers in the ends of my braid. I leave out the rest, that knowing I've had this magick all along makes losing them an even heavier burden to bear. I had all the weapons at my disposal and yet, I did nothing. "I'm sorry I lied to you," I whisper, swallowing down my grief. The guilt. "About having completed my Ceremony."

His idle hands stop against my back. He says nothing, but he doesn't need to. I tip my chin up as his fingers grip my jaw, pulling me into a deep kiss. "And I'm sorry I didn't tell you about my suspicion that you could be a Dyrsjel," he whispers against my lips before kissing them.

A low, growl interrupts my wandering thoughts. We both direct our attention to Alaric. The wolf has moved from his position on the ground, sitting upright, eyes focused on where Sorin and I touch.

"Well," Sorin muses in my ear, "it appears as though I have competition."

THE WOLVES FOLLOW my every move through the woods. When I stop for water, they stop behind me. When I trip over a covered root, Alaric is there before I can hit the ground. I'm baffled by how they can anticipate my next step, and the farther we walk the more attuned they become. The black wolf keeps her distance behind us as Alaric and I walk in unison. I attempt a few times to reach out my hand for her, as I've done to Alaric, but unlike Alaric I'm met with resistance. I'm not sure how to get through to her, but maybe with Galen's help I'll be able to speak with her in time.

"So, we know the big guy's name is Alaric, right?" Jarek says from over his shoulder as we trudge through a swampy part of the woods. My boots slosh in the spongy moss that covers the forest floor. Water seeps up from the ground with every heavy step threatening to soak my boots entirely. Jarek and Sam have kept their distance from the wolves, and by the wary look on Sam's face, I'm sure it'll take longer for her to come around. I can't blame her caution. I've witnessed these very wolves kill without a moment's hesitation. But then again, so have I.

"But what about that one there?" Jarek gestures to the black wolf at our rear. She lowers her head in Jarek's direction. Her perfect white canines peek through her snarled lip, and Jarek shudders at the sight. Pausing my steps, I let the black wolf catch up to me, ignoring the water seeping through the soles of my boots. While she doesn't allow me to touch her, she paces anxiously from side to side in front of me. As if my sudden stillness causes her some sort of unrest. I catch her green eyes for a moment and everything around us falls into silence. The forest shifts as the trees still their movements. The crows cease to caw and the only sounds left are my heartbeat and hers.

As bright as lightning, her name appears in my mind.

"Ruse." The word pours from my lips in a soft whisper. Turning back toward the rest of the group, I can't help the grin that splits across my face. "Her name is Ruse."

Jarek's laughter bounds through the otherwise silent woods causing Ruse to jump. Sorin beams with what I hope is pride as Sam offers a faint smile. The hair on Ruse's haunches raises as she continues to pace behind me. Her eyes, however, lock on Galen, not Jarek as I would expect.

"I'm not sure I'll get used to that any time soon," Jarek laughs again. "Speaking to the *susi*."

MY MAGICK PUSHES against my fingertips as I drag them over the rough bark of a fallen tree branch. The intensity grows stronger the longer I'm with the wolves. They flank me on either side as we trudge up a steep incline. Their silent paws are undetectable as we make our way over the moss ridden hill. How an animal of such size can be so quiet moving through the forest baffles me.

Emerging on the other side, my chest heaves from the effort of the climb. The rest of the group descends the hill, but I take a moment to catch my breath. Kneeling, I take a long drag of water from my canteen before a nudge at my elbow causes the water to spill over the sides.

As if encouraging me to stand, Alaric nudges my elbow again, and this time, I let out a laugh. Tightening my canteen, I place it back in my pack.

"Okay, you big beast. What demands so much attention?" I pat his side and he yips, tossing his head toward the bottom of the hill. Such an innocent gesture for such a giant animal. Redirecting my attention to the landscape below, I suck in a sharp breath at the magnitude of beauty that awaits us.

We've made it to Karos Falls.

CHAPTER 27
SORIN

KAROS FALLS IS UNLIKE ANYTHING ELSE IN THE Trinity Forest. Surrounded by dense pine trees lies a vast pool of shimmering emerald water. The water pours from the falls in silky waves that are velvety to the touch. The thick canopies of the trees above us let in very little sunlight, the light from the water casting an effervescent glow to the surroundings. At the center of the pool is the massive waterfall from which it's named. The tidal wave of raging white spills into the emerald pool, the noise creating a natural barrier from predators.

My eyes lock on the falls, memories of my last time here pushing against the back of my mind. Sprites buzz wildly at the water's edge, their bodies offering a twinkling of light as the day grows darker. It's their light that brings a smile to my face, despite knowing generally they're up to no good.

"Have you been listening to anything I've said?" Sam hisses as a rock collides into the back of my arm. Whipping my head around, I shouldn't be surprised to see her smug expression.

"Well that was rude," I say, bending down to bundle several pieces of wood into my arms. Galen, Jarek, and Elora left to scan the area to hunt, leaving Sam and I to collect wood for the fire.

"But you must admit my aim was impeccable," Sam says, the same smugness on her face dripping into her voice. I laugh as I continue to gather sticks.

"Don't flatter yourself, we're less than five feet apart," I say, tossing a stick in her direction and missing.

"What I was asking," she starts again as we make our way back to camp, "is if you're ready for tomorrow?" Her question brings me to a halt.

I am certainly not ready for tomorrow.

"Sure," I lie, picking my pace back up.

"You're a terrible liar." Sam laughs, though I know it's laced in fear. "Is shaving a week off the trip really worth going through the Wicked Wood? Surely it can't make much of a difference."

Stopping again, I spin to face her. She's tall, only a few inches shorter than I am. Her fiery eyes are intensified by the growing circles of dark under them. "We can't risk you or Elora that close to Davenport," I tell her. "Going around the Wicked Wood would lead us straight into the city and they yield a much larger guard station, it isn't worth the two of you being seen."

"But facing the nymph is a better option?" She steps toward me, fury creasing her brows. "How is *that* worth the risk?"

"Because I, dear sister, have a plan." I toss her a wink, though my stomach knots with dread. She chews her bottom lip for a moment. Stepping closer, I bundle the firewood into one arm, using the other to reach for her shoulder, giving it a squeeze. "Trust me, Samaria."

"I trusted you before."

"And I made damn sure you made it back safely," I clip out, hating my voice.

"Sorin—"

I cut her off, shaking my head and squeezing her shoulder again. "We'll get through Sam," I say, softening my tone. "The faster we get the Stones, the faster we can get to Valebridge." My eyes drift downward, stomach still a frenzied mess.

"It's not your fault, Sorin," Sam whispers, taking a step toward me. She gives me a wry look before cocking her head to the side. "Have you told her? About any of it?" she asks, reaching out and giving my arm a squeeze.

My jaw flexes but I say nothing. Sam shakes her head, brushing past me to take the lead back to camp. My knotted stomach only coils further. I have many secrets of my own, but I can't bring myself to see the look on Elora's face when she discovers them. Not with the way she looked at me last night.

Selfish, I hear my mother's voice.

Reckless, William used to say.

Coward, my own voice pops into my head.

I am all of those things and still, I bite my tongue.

"You are better than that, Sorin," Sam says over her shoulder as she begins to walk away. "*Be* better than that."

DUSK HAS SETTLED as I hike up the nearby hill, leaving Galen, Jarek, and Sam to tend to the fire after our dinner of snared rabbit and salmonberries. The rabbit is small, hardly enough for the five of us to share, but it's all the forest was willing to give tonight. So, we'll gratefully take it. The orange flames of the campfire mix with the emerald light of the pool cast a yellow haze around our camp. Elora didn't join us, even though she is the one who caught the rabbit.

"Not hungry." Was her only reply, but I won't stand for it.

"I hope I'm not interrupting," I say, approaching her with caution. She's been inseparable from the wolves since this afternoon, and I can't say I blame her. The power radiates off of them. Ancient. Deep. A bit terrifying.

"We were just talking about you, actually," she teases, casting Alaric and Ruse a glance. The wolves take note of our closeness but don't move from their spots. I have no doubt they can sense my nerves, so I try my best to calm my heart rate as I slide next to Elora.

"Well, hopefully only the best things then. I have a feeling these two don't give out second chances often." Alaric yawns, showing off his pointed teeth. Elora nods at the two of them before they both stand and retreat down the hill and into the deepness of the woods.

I force Elora to take the rabbit leg I brought with me and a handful of salmonberries. A loud huff of air is her only protest, but despite her stubbornness, she takes it and scarfs it down.

"I know Galen said this was something that should come naturally…" Her voice drifts, shaking her head before wiping her mouth clean with the sleeve of her shirt. "But I don't know where to even begin with my magick. It's like it's just beneath the surface, but nothing I do makes it come forth." The sense of defeat in her voice is palpable. "And communicating with the wolves is so sporadic. Like their voices are muffled through layers of fabric."

Her shoulders are tight as I place my hands there. I let them trail down to her waist, pulling her into me. The tension in her body melts as I hold her and something settles inside of me that I didn't realize was at unrest.

"Give it time," I say, kissing the top of her head. "I imagine it will take practice just like any other skill, and Galen said he's studied the Dyrsjel before. He will help you figure this out. The wolves, your magick. You can trust him."

"We don't have much time," she counters as she rests her head on my chest, welcoming my closeness instead of fighting it. "If there's a way to utilize this *ability* I have with the wolves," she continues, "I imagine it could be quite useful once we reach the Wicked Woods. Or better yet when we make it to Valebridge." Her body tenses again, and I don't have to see her face to know she's chewing her cheek. "All this time I've had this magick and I have wasted it," she whispers. "I feel more powerless than I did before."

That defeated tone again breaks me. I hum quietly, resolved to help as my hands work their way up her back, coaxing the worry out of her with each small slide of my palm. She lets out a soft sigh before nuzzling deeper into my chest, warmth blooming there with every crack in the armor she often wears.

Pulling her back, I tilt her chin towards me so she's forced to meet my eyes. "Can't you see, love?" I say, brushing her braid off her shoulder, letting my fingers glide down the jagged scar on her neck. "How the moon and the tides fight for your attention?" Bending down, I place a kiss on the small space between her neck and jaw. "How the owls turn and the wolves bow..." Another kiss. "How my knees weaken with a single touch?" Pulling back, her eyes are glazed, their golden glow beaming in the darkness. "You don't need anyone to tell you how powerful you are, Elora. Open your eyes, and look for yourself. The magick you wield is in you, the walls you've built are sturdy. Strong. And once, I'm sure, were very necessary. But maybe it's time to let them down, even just a little."

A tear slips down her cheek, and I'm there in an instant to dry it, to soak it up. Standing on her toes, she cranes her neck to meet my mouth, pulling me into a deep kiss. My stomach dips and swirls as our mouths connect, and for a moment, I don't think I'll be able to break apart. For a moment, it's just Elora and myself and nothing else in this Mother forsaken world matters.

But reluctantly, we separate. Breaths heavy, I wipe away any last tears from her eyes.

"What did I do to deserve your attention?" she whispers, lacing her fingers with mine. My chest cracks and I'm unsure how to respond. How to explain that I am the one on the undeserving end. Especially with all I have yet to tell her. But whatever this thread of fate that's been woven between us is, I won't deny.

"I want to show you something," I whisper, leaving my thoughts in my head as I tug her in the direction of the falls.

KEEPING ELORA'S hand in mine, we skirt our way around the emerald pool, stepping lightly on the large stones that border the water. The raging waters muffle the world around us, the constant *whoosh* plummeting into the pool below. Standing at the entrance of the waterfall, I tug Elora's hand, gesturing again to a small opening. She hesitates for a moment, but as I make the final step into the cavern, she follows.

The small cavern is a byproduct of years of erosion from the icy waters. It's mostly dark aside from the glow of the pool beyond the backside of the waterfall and small flickers of iridescent light bouncing off the embedded crystals that lay within the rock.

"This is beautiful." Elora's voice echoes off the cavern walls, not realizing that while inside we are protected from the water's raging sounds. Startling herself she brings her hands up to her mouth.

"Much quieter in here." I laugh, spreading my cloak on the cavern floor and patting the ground for Elora to join me.

"I take it you've been here before?" She mimics my movements, removing her cloak and setting it down next to mine before joining me on the stone ground. We sit facing the wall of water plummeting down in front of us, the sound of raging rapids replaced by a soft trickle.

"Once," I admit, pulling her closer to me by the waist. "Sam and I have traveled past the falls before." The memory of the two of us caught in the Wicked Woods flashes into my mind. Sam's limp body as I slung her over my shoulder. The blinding pain. Her earlier words.

"It brings me peace," I say, shaking off the memory of almost losing my sister. "The water," I clarify. "There's something reassuring about the constant flow of it." She exhales quietly before resting her head on my shoulder. If I could freeze time, it would be this moment. In a cavern of starlight, with nothing but the gentle rush of water, Elora tucked next to me.

"Tell me something." Her voice breaks my trance as she pulls away from my shoulder, leaving a spot so cold I run my hand down my arm. The same words from our ride into Loxley.

"Like what?" I ask. Resting my arms behind me, I lean back and place my weight on my palms.

"Anything," she says through a sigh. She watches me, placing a hand delicately on my thigh. "Everything." This time her voice is a whisper, and I watch her intently for a moment. The shape of her nose, the slight bend it has in the middle. The freckles that dance along the bridge of it. The roundness of her cheeks and pink of her lips.

"You are beautiful." A rush of childlike embarrassment washes over me as the words leave my lips, but it is the most truthful thing I've ever said. She is absolutely beautiful. Tipping her head back, her laugh bounces off the cave walls.

"Now you tell me something," I say, reaching for her hand, pulling her close.

"Anything in particular?" Her voice is still shaky with laughter.

A few beats of silence pass between us before I whisper, "Tell me about that night, love." I know it's a risk to ask, but it's a question that's laid heavily on me since I woke her from her nightmare. All playfulness leaves her face and I immediately regret my question.

She slips her hand from mine and redirects her attention to the water. "You've told me it was memories that keep you up. But not what the memories are," I press further, wanting to ease some of her burdens by taking them on as my own. Her silence sends a prick of needles rushing down my arms as I wait for her to decide what she's going to do. What she will say. Pulling herself up to her feet, she begins pacing back and forth, chewing on the inside of her cheek, clenching and unclenching her fists.

"When I tell you what happened the night my family

died..." She turns to face me. The color drains from her face with each word. "You'll no longer see me as beautiful." My brows pinch together as I listen, but I remain silent. "You'll look at me, and no longer see Elora. You'll see this...this selfish monster." She resumes her pacing, her face shifts from the soft, beautiful one I've become so familiar with, to something troubled. Something unsettled. Something dark.

"So, then let me see," I say. "Let me see this monster you claim to be. Let me see and let me choose you anyway." Elora's eyes rake over me as she halts her methodical pacing. "Because I will," I say, standing and taking a step toward her. "I'll still choose you." Like a skittish deer, I know it won't take much to send her darting through the cave looking for an escape.

"We barely know each other, Sorin," she says, clicking that armor back into place, little by little, her walls go up and her eyes go distant.

"That may be true for this life, love. But I have no doubts that we've known each other in every other life before this. Or that we'll know each other in every life after." I stop just before her and place my hands in my pockets. How can she not feel the same? The kiss we shared was proof enough our bodies recognize each other in a way I can't explain. "Wasn't it you that said, this feels like fate?" I continue, taking another step forward. "Why hide what we feel? Why lie to ourselves, to each other? Time is not relevant. It could be weeks or a year, my feelings for you are the same."

I reach for her hand, and she lets me grab it. Interlocking our fingers, I dip my head down, letting my forehead rest on hers. "You can keep denying the way you feel," I whisper, "but it won't change the way I do. If more time is what you need to tell me what happened, then I will wait. Whatever you need, let me be the one to give it to you."

I take a step backward, removing my forehead from hers so I can see her face in its entirety, giving her the space I know she needs. Her features have softened but the unmistakable ink of dread still lies in her eyes.

She steadies herself, taking a deep inhale, clenching her hands to fists at her sides. "The reason I have the nightmares," she shakes out, "is because I'm the reason my mother and Cade are dead." Her eyes line with tears, but her face is firm.

"You can't blame yourself, Elora—"

She shakes her head, cutting me short. "You don't understand."

"Then make me," I challenge.

She whispers her painful truth and it pangs through the hollowness of the cavern. The flickering crystal light washes out as I process what she says.

"It's my fault they're dead."

CHAPTER 28
ELORA

MY WORDS LINGER IN THE AIR AS IF THEY ARE suspended in time, floating aimlessly through the cavern and piercing my heart a hundred times along the way. Sorin says nothing, and because the cave is now so dim, I can hardly make out his face. The faint rush of water is the only sound between us, aside from the steady pumping of my overworked heart.

"Say something," I whisper through the painful silence.

"What do you mean, exactly?" The softness of his voice sends a shiver down my spine. Is this the calm before his storm? The momentary peace before a certain exile? I take a deep breath and let the memories of that night create a flood through me. All the images I've pushed away for so long come rushing back in an aggressive sprint, happy to be free from my constant barricade.

"The night of my Awakening Ceremony, my twentieth birthday, was the heaviest snowfall we'd ever seen on the mountain." I push down the threat of tears, swallowing thickly before continuing. "We had been safe there for two years. And with the snow, I thought it would be difficult for the hunters to trace us."

"For two years our small group stayed that way, hidden in

the mountains. For two years we made a life for ourselves despite it all. But then, I turned twenty," I pause, taking a deep breath before forcing myself to continue. "I wanted my magick more than anything. And because we had been unscathed for so long, I insisted we do the Ceremony. Insisted it would not be a risk. I *made* my mother use the Stones despite her warnings. I may as well have drawn a map and led the hunters straight to us." My words come faster than my mind can think, a brush of Sorin's hand against my own steadies me from the darkening spiral that threatens.

"Keep going." Sorin's grip on my hand tightens, his voice a soft caress sweeping over my skin.

"Cade and I..." The words fight against me, refusing to be spoken. Using my free hand to grip my chest, the ache of betrayal spreads quickly to my heart. "We were to be married after my Ceremony. We...grew up together in Valebridge. And being on the mountain together, we were all we had." The gut-wrenching pain it takes to speak his name aloud is one I didn't expect. A swift kick to the stomach that has me wishing to keel over, as if my body has been slowly poisoned for years and the effects have just now caught up. I draw in a long breath before continuing. "On my Awakening Ceremony night, my mother thought she had a premonition, but she wasn't feeling like herself. Wasn't well. I ignored her, I didn't listen..." The tears flow freely down my face as I recall my mothers' words to me that night.

"Anything for you, my susi.*"*

Sorin says nothing as he draws my face into his hands. Doesn't balk when I meet his eyes. Maybe he's used to seeing monsters. Maybe, like me, he welcomes them.

"I acted as if I was a spoiled child being told no for the first time that night when she questioned my Ceremony," I continue, scraping my teeth against my bottom lip. "I thought my mother was just being difficult. I ignored her and decided gaining my *own* magick was more important than the safety of those I loved. It was my selfish stupidity that led everyone up that mountain. It was my own greed that blinded us from the hunters that met us there." My knees threaten to buckle, but Sorin is there to catch me before I fall. "If I had listened to her—"

"Then she would likely still be gone." Sorin's words leave me baffled.

"What?"

"Whether or not you went up the mountain that night, it sounds like Roman's hunters were already on your trail. They would have found you one way or another, there was nothing you could have done differently. It was a matter of time." I try to shake my head, but he grips either side of my face. So, instead, I bite down on my lip. So hard I wince, so I bite harder against the sting. Another small punishment.

"You want to blame yourself, Elora, because you lived. But it is not your fault that you escaped."

"Except I didn't escape." My voice raises and reverberates off the cavern walls, and I hate the way it sounds as it bounces back at me. Pulling free from his grasp, I take a step backward. I have no reason to be upset at Sorin, and I'm not. I am upset with myself. Always, with myself.

"I managed to make it off of Kirsgard because the two people I loved the most put my safety before their own. Because I had no idea how to wield this magick that was suddenly bestowed upon me. And I hate myself because I did not do the same for them. Worse, I didn't even try." Throwing my hands up, a broken laugh escapes my lips. "I ran. I turned and ran and now they're gone and every day I'm haunted by shame because I didn't fight for them."

"Cade did everything he could to keep me safe, and I sat there as he was beaten and dragged away like he was nothing. I let fear paralyze me. I am useless and pathetic. And my mother..." I stop, taking a deep breath before I find the courage to speak of her.

"Everyday I wake up and wonder what it's like not to be plagued by darkness. I wonder how it is not to hear your mothers screams as she slices a blade across her throat to save herself from capture. To wake up from a night's sleep not drenched in sweat from the terrors that feel so real. So real, that even when I wake I can't decipher the present from the past." I brush my hair back from my face. Sorin's eyes haven't left me, he stands absolutely still as I continue.

"Do you have any idea what it's like to wake up each day and not know if it's the day the voices will win? That it may be the day the war is finally lost and the demons take over every last inch of your mind? The final parts of you that you've battled to keep whole. Because that is my reality, Sorin. I didn't get away. I didn't escape. I live that night over and over again, and I fear I will until the day I'm finally laid to rest. Either by my blade, or another's."

Silence.

Deep, deafening silence weighs down on me and for a moment I consider running away from this cavern. Running back through the woods until I find the safety of my cabin where I can spend my remaining years being invisible, just as I always planned. But to run would be to leave him. And as much as it terrifies me, every word he spoke to me earlier matches my own feelings.

"Don't say that. Don't ever say that." Sorin's voice is sharp as he closes the distance between us. "I won't try to tell you how to feel or convince you that you've done no wrong. We have *all* done things we regret in this life. And we are sure to have regrets in the next." Sorin's hand grazes my cheek as his other wraps around my waist pulling me tightly to him. "But I will tell you this. That even with all you've said...with every dark part of your mind and past exposed, I still choose you. Monster or not."

I drink his words in. Letting them wrap around me as they caress every inch of my blackened soul. They seep into the darkest parts of me, the parts I closed off a long time ago. Though his words are not enough to heal the most broken parts of myself, maybe letting him choose me is a start. Letting myself choose him, a new beginning.

"Thank you," I whisper against his mouth before kissing him. Heavy arms wrap around me and I sink into their weight. Resting my head on Sorin's chest, the steady rhythm of his heart is the greatest reminder of what life can bring when you aren't stuck in the shadows of your past.

I'M NOT sure how long we stand that way, embracing each other in the faint light of the cavern. My secrets spilled upon the ground. The burden of their weight lifted ever so slightly. Then, Sorin loosens his grip around my middle, and I peer up at him.

"Dance with me," he says, not quite a question.

"Here?"

"Why not?" He shrugs, glancing around.

I scan my eyes around the cavern. "Well, there's no music, for starters."

"Isn't there?" he asks, running his thumb along my jaw. I pull back to question him again, but he's quick to silence me, running his thumb over my lips, parting them slightly. "Listen," he whispers.

Closing my eyes, I take a deep breath, and listen.

The subtle whoosh of water from the falls.

The faintest buzz of fireflies.

My heart beat.

His.

"Dance with me," he says again. Opening my eyes, I glance up at him before he tightens one arm around my waist, while the other finds my arm and clasps our hands together.

Then, we dance.

Just as we did in Loxley. Slow and steady, our bodies flush, the heat between them growing more intense with every move.

But it isn't the same as it was then.

This is different. Completely, utterly, aligned with one another. Our bodies move in perfect synchrony. I no longer fear his touch. I crave it.

"Why didn't you tell me about the Ceremony?" he asks, dipping me slightly.

"For obvious reasons," I say as he straightens us out, spinning me on my heels before pulling me back close to him. "I was ashamed I didn't have any magick. Or so I thought. And besides, I wasn't sure if I could trust you."

"And now?"

"Now," I drag my hands along his muscled back, "I trust you." He bends down, kissing the top of my head. Our swaying continues as we move to the rhythm of the falling water. "Do you trust me?" I ask, trying desperately not to trip over my own feet as he twirls me.

He laughs again, pulling me back into him so my cheek is nuzzled against his chest.

"Without question," he says, sliding his hand from my waist, painstakingly slow, up the center of my back. "I have many fears, many doubts," he says, his hand drifting from my back until it hits the nape of my neck. "But none of them, this." Continuing upward, he wraps a fistful of my hair. A light tug is all it takes and I know I'm at his mercy. "I am undoubtedly yours," he whispers against my ear.

Tilting my head up, his kiss is deep and unrelenting. I take no time opening my mouth, giving him exactly what he wants. What we both want. Our swaying ceases as our kiss completely engulfs us.

Sorin nips and kisses along my neck. Over my scar. My chest. My mouth. His hand slides up my throat, dragging his thumb up the underside of my chin until it reaches my lower lip. The mix of teeth and tongue against my skin sets my senses on fire. He scoops me up, my legs wrap around him as he continues kissing me. Biting softly on my lower lip. My neck. I drag my nails through his hair, squeezing my legs tighter around him, forcing his body close to me.

But it isn't close enough.

Pushing me up against the cave wall, my back is pinned between the cold stone and Sorin. I catch his eyes for a moment, and I can't help but whisper his name. When I do, it makes him press himself against me even harder. The cold rock bites into my back and I relish in the hint of pain, so I say his name again, hoping he'll do it a second time.

"Sorin."

CHAPTER 29
SORIN

ELORA SAYS MY NAME AGAIN AND THE SOUND OF IT IS equally unholy and divine. At that moment, I know there is no sin I wouldn't commit just to hear her say it again. She traces my bottom lip with her tongue before planting a soft bite there, forcing a moan from my lips. Her hands work up and down my chest as her hips push forward against me.

"I like the way my name sounds on your lips, Enchantress," I tease before pressing her harder against the wall, raking my teeth along her throat. Pulling back to gauge her reaction, I'm met with that mischievous grin I've come to adore. Her eyes flicker as she wraps her legs tighter around my waist, a silent plea. Shooting her a quick grin, I tear her from the wall and carry her back to where our cloaks lie on the ground.

"I won't lie," I set her down softly, "this isn't where I pictured us being together for the first time."

Snorting lightly, she rolls her eyes. "Always such a gentleman."

"Hmm," I bite her neck just hard enough she gasps, then I kiss the hurt, while my hand pushes her tunic up until I graze the peaks across her breast. "Not always," I say against her skin.

She moans softly before I kiss her again, sending a shiver coursing down her body underneath me.

"Do you want me to stop, Elora?" Pulling back, I catch her gaze. Lids heavy, mouth parted. Before she answers, I hesitate. Only for a moment. I need to tell her the truth. My Mother-damned conscience is making me second guess myself. Telling me to stop this now.

"No." She pants out, finally answering my question.

There goes my conscience.

Bending forward, I scrape my teeth against the soft flesh of her neck again, relishing in the way her body responds every time I do.

"*Good*," I say. Then, our lips are ravenous and unrelenting. I keep my mouth locked on hers as we work in unison to remove her pants and then her tunic. She tugs at my shirt unsuccessfully, her frustration showing across her face. Laughing, I sit up and pull it up over my head, tossing it to the side before she greedily pulls me back down on top of her.

The heat of our bodies flush with each other is enough to put me on edge. Every part of her body molds perfectly into mine. Every dip and curve. I swear to myself, I will tell her everything. I want to tell her everything. But as her nails dig against the bare skin of my back and chest, my mind can only think of her.

Pulling her into me, I grip her wrists in both my hands, holding them firmly above her head. "Keep them there," I say. She makes no attempt to argue.

I kiss her throat, switching my grip on her wrists to one hand, using the other to slide downward over the soft plane of her stomach. My hand wanders over her inner thighs, her skin soft and smooth before I slip it between her legs. She tosses her head back, letting out a moan as I brush my fingers just above her center. A whisper of a touch. She inclines her hips so I give her what she needs, dragging a finger through her. Leaning over her, I bite down on her lip before taking another kiss. My hand works the apex between her thighs as I let go of her wrists to grip her hair, tugging just enough so it stings.

"*Sorin*," she says through a moan again, so I tighten my grip, wrapping the hair at the base of her neck, still working my fingers on my other hand.

"You're gonna have to stop saying that, love, or I'm not sure I'll be able to behave myself."

Breathlessly she pants, "Maybe I don't want you to." Letting go of my grip on her hair, I slide my body down between her legs. I take my time tracing my fingers lightly over the inside of her thighs, across the beautiful curve of her hips. Pressing my lips everywhere except right where she wants me to.

"Sorin, *please*," she says again, but this time it's lined in frustration as she grabs a fistful of my hair.

I shoot her a look, and immediately, she places her arm back above her head, chest heaving as she lies completely at my mercy. It's those two words that are my undoing. My name and a plea. I would never make her beg, but *fuck* if the sound of it doesn't drive me absolutely mad.

Chuckling, I finally dip my head between her legs and drag my tongue through her center. My hands grip her arse, lifting her hips to get a better position before she grabs my arms, pulling me toward her. I look at her again, she's glowing in the flickering light of the cavern. Without a word, she grabs for my pants and begins working my belt. Reaching for her hands, I grip both her wrists at the same time and pull them back up above her head as I lay her back down. I know what she wants, and I'd be lying if I said I didn't want it too. But I can't. Not yet.

"Tsk, tsk, Enchantress." She shoots me a look, somewhere between confusion and frustration. "Keep your hands above your head, I won't say it again."

CHAPTER 30
ELORA

SORIN'S GRIN IS WICKED AS HE HOLDS MY HANDS tightly above me. He leans forward, planting a kiss so deep I swear I see stars dance behind my eyes. My mind is blank with the exception of him.

Us.

And this time, the thought of us makes my stomach swirl in all the right ways. My mind focuses on how rough his calloused hands are as they explore my body. Even better, how they felt between my legs. As if reading my mind, Sorin releases my wrists, wrapping his arms around me.

As he clasps his hands together, I fight the urge to run my fingers through his hair. Over his bare chest. Gripping me firmly by my backside, he pulls me closer as I arch my back. He kisses down my neck, over my breast, his tongue dancing down the softness of my abdomen.

I gasp as Sorin kisses his way down the inside of my thigh, his tongue dragging again over the most sensitive area between my legs.

Sorin is as breathless as I am as he says, "Don't you dare hold back." The low rasp of his tone has my stomach in a frenzy and desperate to obey. Heat pools between my legs as he works his way down my other thigh, the tantalizing drag of his tongue then nip of his teeth.

I've spent the last few weeks denying our connection, but here in this cavern, it's no longer deniable. Sorin's tongue meets my center again, his fingers digging into my skin, and I embrace the ache it causes. I ignore his demand to keep my hands above my hand. Dropping them, I drag my fingers through his hair as a wave of pleasure begins to form. Settled deep in my core, it spreads throughout my entire being. Then, his fingers. The tension building in my body has my stomach tightening, coiling and my chest heaving.

Slowly, he swipes his thumb over the sensitive bundle of nerves again and it's the final friction I need to let go. The aching pressure explodes through me as I push my hips against him until my legs go limp.

Carefully removing his hand and then, eventually, his mouth, he takes his time to kiss every inch of me on the way up. He moves himself over top of me again, caging me in his presence. His beautiful, dark eyes reflect everything I've been avoiding for years.

Hope. Future. Fate.

Sorin dips his head, so our foreheads meet. Each equally damp with sweat. I reach for him, but he stops me. Saying nothing but shaking his head before kissing me again. Breathing each other in, our lungs working in unison. Hesitantly, Sorin rolls himself off to the side and wraps one of our cloaks around me. Cupping my chin, he kisses me softly, stealing my breath once again.

"What is it?" I ask, as he watches me. Suddenly very aware of what we've just done and how naked I still am.

"Nothing, love." He kisses me again. "Just thinking that meeting you must've been some accident written by the Fates." I frown and he takes his thumb, smoothing the crease between my brows as he continues, "Nothing I've done in this life that has ever been good enough to deserve you."

I close my eyes as his words sink into me. Swallowing down the guilt that I get to live this life, with him, while *they* didn't get to live at all. Opening my eyes again, I trace my fingers down the lines of his jaw, the dark stubble now more profound since leaving Loxley. Over the lines of his full ups, across the bridge of his nose.

"Well let's just hope they make the same mistake twice," I whisper, "because any other life without you in it would be rather dull without all that talking."

He chuckles, his firm hands wrapping around me, his mouth finding mine and kissing me deeply again. And again, and again.

HEADING BACK TO CAMP, I cling to Sorin's arm as we weave through the darkness. A flurry of crows flies gracefully overhead, their silence more menacing than the caws that typically accompany them. The flickering light from the campfire in the distance sets my nerves on edge. Of course, everyone is still up. I imagine Galen's look of disgust as Sorin and I walk back together. I shake the thought from myself as Sorin wraps his hand in mine.

"You're disappearing again."

Startled, I glance up at him, his eyes meeting mine through the darkness. "Just in my own head, as usual," I say, keeping my tone casual but Sorin's grip on my hand tightens anyway. His thumb traces the back of my hand as he leads us towards camp. He opens his mouth as if to say something, but stops himself short, pulling me closer as we walk through the woods.

Approaching our camp, Alaric and Ruse pop their heads up in unison. The thundering wag of Alaric's tail is laughable compared to Ruse's stoic demeanor. I nod in their direction which has the two of them lowering their guard, settling in next to the fire.

"Well, you've been gone awhile." Jarek draws out the words, slow and intentional. Sam nudges his side with her elbow, and he flinches before releasing his typical boom of laughter. Biting my bottom lip to hide a smile, Sorin and I sit side by side, his arm draping heavily around my shoulders.

"So, tomorrow's the day." Galen's voice is distant, and I hardly notice him perched opposite of us against a giant pine tree. His hood is pulled up, concealing his face, arms crossed tightly across his chest. His words hang thickly in the air. Tomorrow we'll face the Wicked Woods, and from there our fates will be sealed.

"We leave at first light," Sorin says, playing with the ends of my braid. "We'll want to make it there before dusk. That stretch of the forest is not one I like to venture into without daylight." A shiver courses down my spine in anticipation.

"Will you tell us what happened?" I ask Sam, feeling bold. "I understand if you don't want to...I just would like to know what we can expect."

Her eyes dart to Sorin, his body tensing against mine at my question.

"That's the thing though, Enchantress," Sam says, her voice tired. A sense of sadness also plagues her voice, and I immediately feel guilty I dragged her back to a place she clearly despises. "No passage through the Wicked Woods is ever the same," she continues. Tossing a bundle of sticks into the fire, she crouches near the flames to warm her hands. "What Sorin and I experienced all those years ago could be completely different from what we'll experience tomorrow." She leans back and settles in next to Jarek again, her eyes directed at me through the flames. "What happened with Sorin and I—"

"That's enough." Sorin's voice is low, quiet. A whisper that holds the power to still even the flames. Sam and Sorin stare at each other for a moment. A silent exchange of words only siblings would understand before Sam breaks and lets out a breath.

"All I'm saying," she continues drawing out the last word, "is whatever fear you have in your heart, she will find it and she will use it against you. That much I know will be the same." A few beats of silence hang around us until she mumbles under her breath, "I hope all this is worth it." My heart sinks and the guilt I felt earlier about bringing her here is now justified. She doesn't want to be here, and because of Sorin and I, she is. And for whatever reason, Sorin is still hiding something from me.

We told you not to trust him.

"Sam, this will help you get your magick," I start, ignoring the voices that have returned in my head, but before I can say anything further, she stands and walks toward her tent, leaving the four of us in silence.

"She'll be okay," Jarek whispers. "She's just afraid. And when Sam's afraid her only response is anger."

A response I can relate to all too well.

The sudden hop to my feet has the wolves alert and jumping from their sleeping positions.

"Where are you going?" Sorin glances up at me from the ground then over to the wolves who are now loom over him. I give a quick shake of my head to let them know I don't need their help and head towards Sam's tent.

"I need to speak with her," I say over my shoulder as I pass by the fire.

"We're supposed to train," Galen says, but I don't care about that right now. All I care about is making sure Sam is okay.

Hovering at the entrance of the canvas tent, I'm unsure of what to say or how to approach her.

"Are you coming in or not?" Sam says through the small opening. Taking a quick breath, I duck into the tent. She's wrapped up in her cloak, laying on her back and peering at the ceiling of the tent. She doesn't make any attempt to look at me as I drop down next to her. We lie like that for a while.

"When Sorin's mother passed," Sam whispers, her voice barely audible against the fierceness of the wind. Rolling, I face her. "Agnes and my father, William, adopted him without a moment's hesitation. He was young, you know, and my mother made it her mission to care for him. To make sure that despite his hardships he would know what a mother's love felt like." My stomach dips, and as much as I don't want to, my mind wanders to my own mother. How she also took in Cade when his mother passed.

"She wanted him to know what it was like to have a family despite all odds," Sam continues. "In doing so, Agnes inadvertently left me out of a lot of things. I know she didn't mean to, but it doesn't change the fact that she did. He was so young, so fragile after everything. All of her focus went to caring for him. Making sure he was okay. We're only three years apart, but I felt such a *massive* responsibility to take care of him as well. Even now, everything we work for is for him." In the dim light of the tent, she bites her lip. "It's not that I don't want to help, because I most certainly do. And Sorin is the best person I know. He cares about this kingdom..about change. It's just..." Her voice trails as she rubs her fingers against her temples.

"You just want to be a part of the initial conversation," I say, mimicking my own words to Sorin after the guard in Copenspire.

She smiles, though it's weak, tired. "Exactly."

"Deal," I say. "No more secret plans." I hold out my hand for a shake and she bats it away. I smile at my friend, who I've come to adore so much.

"Deal," she says, the playful tone returning to her voice. Warmth settles over me as we lie next to each other, the wind whipping wildly against the tent. "So," she continues, "are you going to divulge what you two were doing in that cavern for so long?" Sam's mischievous grin spreads across her face. I'm glad to see she's bounced back so quickly.

"It would appear you already have an idea." I laugh, tucking my arm under my head as a cushion. She raises her eyebrows before letting out a laugh of her own.

"And what happened last time," she says, ceasing her laughter. "In the Wicked Wood...it really is best to hear from Sorin. I was unconscious most of the time anyway."

I chew the inside of my cheek. The walls of the tent behind Sam start to ripple from the wind. A pool of white dancing in the darkness.

"Do you believe the Fates are still at work?" I ask, picking at the ends of my braid.

"Do you?" Sam asks, her voice laced with sleep.

"I can't honestly say if I do. I remember learning of the Fates in Valebridge. How fickle they were with sharing their visions."

"I can only remember one story," Sam says with a smile, "of King Bastian and Queen Solei. Agnes told me their story many times. Their love and passion and drive is what created Teravie. And eventually it was split up to form Valebridge and the Guilds, correct?"

"Yes," I say. But, so much power woven on such a thin thread causes too much weight and eventually, the thread snaps. So, after the king and queen confronted the Mother about the magick of the natural world being too great a burden, the Mother created Enchantresses to restore the balance. Help lighten the weight the Fates bestowed upon the king and queen. Gifting Enchantresses magick to aid those without, we are meant to bridge the gap between the natural world and the beyond.

When the Enchantresses were aplenty, the Fates became quiet. The balance was restored, and I suppose there wasn't much need for them. King Bastian and Queen Solei bore no heirs, and thus forth the throne was passed down to the highest and eldest council member, Cornelius Rudhek. King Silas' great, great grandfather. It's the Rudhek bloodline that has ruled Teravie since.

"I'm not sure if the Fates are still at work," I admit through a yawn. "But it appears as though they must be. How else is it possible that Sorin and I met? That we both...care for each other when we are so different."

"Hmmm." Sam repositions herself again to face the ceiling. "You have feelings for him?" Her question is simple and yet it holds so much force. So much power. I used to love a lot of things but loving another person... The betrayal of my own thoughts cuts me short.

"I don't know," I admit. I do know that I care for Sorin. But that doesn't make it any less complicated. Confusing.

"You have every right to wear your grief as long as you need to," Sam whispers. "You've lost so many. But that doesn't mean you're not allowed to be happy in their absence." She rolls to her side to face me. "Whether the Fates are working again, whether they have destined you to be together or not, the moment Sorin brought you to Loxley, he knew what he was doing. He chose that, not them."

"And what was that, exactly?"

"He brought you to us, Enchantress." She stretches her hand across to grab mine. "He brought you *home*."

The word stings like a thousand bees over my skin.

Home.

Grief and guilt go hand in hand. One can not exist without the other. To move on is to let go. And to let go, feels like forgetting. I've been so caught up in my own guilt and grief I haven't considered anyone else's. Every kind word and gesture from Sorin the past few weeks has been met with a wall of ice and reluctance. How selfish I've been to believe I'm the only one who is allowed to experience loss. I grab her hand and kiss the back of it before jumping to my feet.

"I need to find Sorin. I need to tell him..." I bite my bottom lip. I'm not certain I know what I feel, but I do know he is what I want at the end of this. At the end of each day and night, I want it to be him. Sam smiles and nods. I suck in a deep breath, hoping the extra oxygen will give me courage, before I duck out of the tent.

CHAPTER 31
ELORA

THE WIND HAS GONE FROM LIGHT AND AIRY TO A wild unseen force whipping through the forest. Branches snap and pine needles are thrown through the air so densely it resembles snow, if snow were green. I tighten my hood around myself before making my way back to the fire. Or at least, where the fire had been. Nothing but smoldering embers are left in the pit, the thick plumes of smoke swirling in all directions as they pull upwards into the night sky. Turning, I scan the other tents but I see no sign of the others. Alaric and Ruse stretch before sprinting toward me. Reaching up, I scratch Alaric's nose. Ruse skitters back a few steps as I attempt the same, just out of reach.

"Where did the boys go?" I whisper, hoping by some miracle they can understand me. As if in answer, Ruse and Alaric take off in a bolt past the fire pit and through a small grove of pines. I follow suit after them, adrenaline pumping at their sudden response. My hood is pulled back by the whipping wind, the cold bites against the flesh of my cheeks. It takes me a few minutes to catch up to the wolves, they sit patiently, waiting for me to arrive. Alaric turns his head toward an opening in the center of the grove. Squinting against the wind, three figures come into view.

Galen, Sorin, and Jarek stand together to form a circle, their faces dimly lit by the light of the moon and small torch Jarek holds. Their attention is pulled to a few books and maps Galen has sprawled onto the ground. What are they hiding? Crouching low next to the wolves I watch, trying desperately to hear what they're saying through the snapping wind around me.

"Once Elora leads us into Valebridge, we won't have long until we have a decision to make." It's difficult to see their faces from where I crouched, but I recognize the flat tone of Galen's voice.

"I thought we already established a decision." Jarek's low voice rumbles through the wind. "I'll take the King down myself if I have to." His normally gleeful tone comes out deeper than usual. Leaning forward, I rest my weight on my toes and attempt to angle my ear toward them. Thankful for a small pine tree to brace my hand against to keep me from slipping.

"No," Sorin says, his voice cutting through the approaching storm. "That will be for me to handle." I narrow my eyes as Sorin pulls something from his breast pocket. I can't make out what it is, but he pulls it to his face to study it closely.

"It's imperative we force Roman before the royal council at their meeting of the first Autumn moon, otherwise this will all have been for nothing," Sorin says. "The Guild leaders haven't been present at the last few meetings so it will have to be before them, though our luck would be greater if the Guilds decide to show up," he pauses, gripping tighter to the parchment.

"But the leaders of the council have been in place as long as the Guilds. They worked directly under Silas, and whether they want to admit it or not, they knew my mother." His voice turns sour as he folds the parchment and places it back in his pocket. "They are the only ones who will be able to verify me as the rightful heir to the throne. This decree of birth won't be enough," he continues, patting his pocket. "No one lays a hand on Roman until then. We need him alive." He runs his hands through his hair. " Until we don't."

My heart sinks in my chest as I suck in a sharp breath of damp air around me.

Sorin is the heir to the throne of Valebridge.

A million questions rip across my mind as I choke on breath after breath, struggling to balance myself.

"He won't go easy, Sorin," Jarek speaks again, turning abruptly just as my foot slips, snapping a branch in half. The flame from his torch casts an orange glow over his pale skin, and for a moment, I think he sees me. His blue eyes like chips of ice, but if he does, he makes no indication. He returns his gaze to Sorin.

"I'd expect nothing less than a fight when it comes to my little brother," Sorin says, his confidence evident in his tone. "I can handle him. *You* just need to keep control of yourself." He gestures toward Jarek who rolls his eyes, muttering something under his breath I can't make out.

"And the Enchantresses?" Galen closes his book before standing and scanning the woods as if sensing being watched. My eyes widen as my heart thunders wildly. "What will you do with them?"

Stumbling backward, the three men begin to walk in my direction. "I'll do whatever I see fit," Sorin snaps. "It's not your concern." I've never heard Sorin speak so bluntly and it sends a shiver of cold sweat dripping down my body. He is related to Roman Rudhek. The King of Valebridge and one responsible for the murder and abuse of Enchantresses. My heart races even faster, my ribs beginning to ache.

I need to flee.

Now.

A perfectly timed snap on the opposite side of the woods has the three men turning their heads. Jarek extinguishes his torch, leaving them in total darkness save for the moon. I glance at the wolves behind me, finding only Alaric. That tug in my chest pulls lightly at first, then, stronger and firmer. Swallowing the knot forming in my throat, I nod as Alaric nudges my elbow.

As if on cue, Ruse appears through the trees. She caused the snap across the clearing, giving me the distraction I needed to run. Clever. That tug in my chest pulls tight again as I meet her emerald eyes. So, I do what my deepest, most primal instincts tell me to do.

Run.

With Alaric to my front and Ruse at my rear, we run against the brutality of the wind and sprinkling of rain. Through the dense pines and over the thick mossy ground. We jump seamlessly over fallen logs and roots spread along the forest floor like a map of veins. To my surprise, even in the growing darkness, I stay my course. As we race through the trees, my mind jolts between Sorin and the Awakening Stones.

He lied to you.

To my mother and to Cade.

Murderer.

I play through all of the moments that have led me here. That led me to this. My pity turns to rage as we run and run and run. I told Sorin everything and still he kept this from me. What is his plan? To take Roman's place and free the Enchantresses? Unlikely, considering the amount of the people who still believe us evil. My legs are strong as we turn and sprint uphill, the ache in my chest eases with each step.

And soon my thoughts transform again.

I've spent the last few years in hiding, trying to forget who I am. Trying to forget my past and my history. I drowned in my grief and let it consume me. But I'll have it no more. Because to be here, in these woods with the wolves, is to be who I was born to be. And there is no greater power than accepting yourself for who you really are. Even when the reflection is difficult to look at, it's mine.

I'm not sure how long we run before my legs give out and I

collapse. Ruse and Alaric stand over me, panting heavily, their breaths puffs of white smoke in the cold air. Pulling myself into a sitting position, I rest my head against the trunk of the pine tree. Breathing in through my nose, out through my mouth for several minutes, forcing my lungs to slow their pace. The burning with each breath acts as a reminder of how far I've come.

Peeling my eyes open, I glance up at the night sky. The moon has begun to wane but the sight of her brings a sense of hope. I keep my eyes locked on the moon, sending out a silent plea to the Mother for a sense of direction. Wiping a rogue tear from my cheek, I curse myself for allowing it to fall in the first place.

Sorin is the rightful heir to the throne of Valebridge, to our country of Teravie.

And I am his key into Valebridge, and from the sounds of it, nothing more.

He'll lock you up.

He'll take your magick.

My heart cracks at the thought, the pain so real I grip my chest and inhale sharply. A soft cry escapes my lips as I force the tears not to spill from my eyes.

He purposely withheld his identity from me, even after I told him everything. I trusted him with my darkest secrets. We're only days away from retrieving the Stones, and yet still, I haven't been deemed worthy of knowing his plan. All the more convincing I was never to be a part of it in the first place.

My sorrow turns to anger as I dig my fingers into the dirt and moss. The cold damp earth lodges itself under my fingernails as I dig deeper. My knuckles whiten as that spark of anger forms into an internal rage as I grip onto the loose dirt. Only the rage isn't internal as the moss beneath my fingers changes. Instead of the dampy spongy green, it disintegrates to smoldering embers, hot to the touch. Unclenching my fists, I stare at what's left at the patch of moss in disbelief.

Alaric interrupts my thoughts, nudging my arm. I shake off the embers I've created from the dirt and lift my arm. Alaric takes the opportunity to nuzzle in and rest his head on my lap, the size of it taking up the entire space. My shoulders unclench themselves as I take a few steady breaths. Shaking the dirt and ash from my palms, cooling them down, I stroke his thick, shimmering gray coat and contemplate my options. Ruse sits nearby, her back toward us, watching the woods.

I can't leave now, I decide. I've come too far to turn back and no matter what Sorin's plans are, Samaria deserves her chance at an Awakening Ceremony. And the Stones don't belong to anyone but the Enchantresses. Sorin, included. If I get them in the hands of an Enchantress, a Dyrsjel, *my* hands, then maybe Mother Gaia will end the blight. If I leave now, that eliminates that possibility and I can't stand the thought of not even trying. I can't repeat my same mistakes.

I won't.

In the midst of a growing storm, a plan begins to form. I will obtain the Stones, perform the Ceremony for Sam. I'll bide my time until I can do what I do best.

Disappear.

Closing my eyes, I think of Galen's earlier words on how to tap into the Dyrsjel part of my mind. He made it sound so easy, as he makes everything sound so easy.

"Consider the wolves your guides."

My guides.

As I lay there with my eyes closed, I envision my mind opening, splitting in two. I picture Ruse and Alaric stepping into it from either side. I see their thick coats; Ruse's pure obsidian and Alaric's gray and white. Their long limbs and enormous paws. I imagine their eyes; amber and a pair of green. I hear myself speak to them and watch as they obey my every command.

I envision us running.

Running through the woods as we just had. The three of us

in perfect unison as we make our way up and over the obstacles of the forest. My heartbeat thunders in my ears but it isn't just mine. Three heartbeats pounding in sync with one another, molding together as one.

My breath catches as my eyes snap open. The two wolves stare down at me. I hadn't noticed they'd moved until now. Running my tongue across my bottom lip, it's still puffy and I wince at the memory of the cavern. Of Sorin's mouth on mine.

Standing, I shake off the memory before stretching my hand toward Ruse. A pull of resistance stretches taught in my chest. She doesn't budge. So, I don't budge either.

Pushing away the rising defeat in my heart, I raise my hand and close my eyes. Again, I envision Ruse in my mind. She steps closer, I see her thick coat glisten under the moon. Another step. I reach my hand out and picture running it over her back. In my mind, she doesn't shy away.

Opening my eyes again, I put my hand out and this time speak aloud, "Come, Ruse." I keep my eyes locked on her. Standing my ground, just as she stands hers. Sweat begins to form at my upper lip and around my temples despite the cold. The mental strain reaching out to Ruse sends a shiver over my body. Yet, I hold strong. Narrowing my gaze, I lower my chin slightly. She shifts her weight between her paws, her eyes darting away from mine for a moment.

Then, a movement so subtle I nearly miss it. A step forward. Then another. And another. She creeps forward until she's close enough to bend down, meeting me face to face.

She dips her large head down further until it rests upon the hand I still have suspended in the air. I let out the pent up air stuck in my lungs and crack a weak smile. The tug I've become familiar with whenever the wolves are around intensifies at Ruse's submission. The resistance I felt earlier snaps, a rush of energy shifts in my chest. As if my blood has changed course, like a river suddenly flowing backward. My fingertips glow an iridescent white as I rake them through her thick coat.

Then, a voice.

The same angelic voice that spoke to me in Loxley. The one that told me to follow Alaric.

Her voice.

Ruse.

The bond has been made.

A smile dances on my lips, but I'm too tired to give way to the elation I feel. But as Ruse nestles into me, her memories flood me in a tidal wave of emotion. I see them both watching me in the forest, outside of my cabin. Their anger for the guards on the river makes my legs shake. How badly they were afraid for me, then how badly they wanted to kill those men. I stumble backward, the new emotions and memories too much for my body to handle.

Sinking to the ground, the memories continue to flash behind my eyes while Ruse and Alaric settle in at my sides. Their howls are broken and winded in my mind as I watch myself leave my cabin and head to Copenspire with Sorin. Their cries break my heart, as they frantically search the woods for me. Until finally, Alaric is in my mind. Showing me how he found his way to Loxley. How, despite the wards, they were able to break through, stopping at nothing until I'd been found. The panic they felt when they thought I'd disappeared again when we left for Wickersham sends my own heart in a wild flurry of beats. Turning to face him, I scratch behind his ears.

"I'm here now," I whisper. He licks my cheek. "And I'm not going anywhere without you."

MY BODY still screams for more rest as Alaric nudges me awake. The blackness of the night sky slowly morphs into the dim gray of twilight. Rubbing the remaining sleep from my eyes, I stretch my aching limbs before rising to my feet.

Despite the morning dew coating the moss and ferns in tiny water droplets, I find myself warm and mostly dry. A benefit of two large wolf companions, I suppose. I reach out for Ruse and am relieved that she allows me to stroke the top of her head. *Wasn't a dream*, I tell myself. Then my mind crashes to the night before. A tumbling of highs and lows.

Sorin in the cave.

Samaria in her tent.

Sorin's secret.

My heart lurches but the ache quickly dissolves to anger. Another hidden part of the plan. But I remind myself that today, I must play nice. For Sam. For her, I will make it through the Wicked Wood and retrieve the Stones. For the Enchantresses I've failed to help all these years, I'll do my best to be cordial.

Following Ruse's lead we make our way back toward Karos Falls, and ultimately, back toward camp. About halfway there faint shouts in the distance halt my steps.

"Elora! Ruse! Alaric!"

The multitude of voices are easy to decipher; Sam, Jarek, and Sorin all shouting our names at different times. Dread ripples over me at the sound of them. My stomach twists and I'm uncertain if it's because of the guilt for letting them worry, or if I'm dreading seeing them altogether.

As we crest the hill and peer down toward the falls, I spot Sorin first. His brows are furrowed and eyes lost as he shouts across the way to Galen. Something about going to check the caverns again. I watch Sorin for a moment, his hair is disheveled and darkness encircles his eyes.

My traitorous heart skips a beat as he runs toward the cavern. I consider leaving now. With the wolves, I could easily make it back to my part of the Trinity Forest in a week's time. I could quickly turn and run, swift and soundless, with the beasts at my sides.

As suddenly as the thought comes, it escapes even faster as Sam pulls away from where she was buried against Jarek's chest.

My heart sinks. I can't leave her like this. She deserves her chance with the Stones just as much as I did. Possibly even more. The wolves pace impatiently at my sides until I reluctantly give them the go ahead to head to camp. As they come bounding down the hillside, Sam shouts Alaric's name. Rushing toward him she draws her eyes upward until they meet mine. Something resembling relief settles over her face as she takes off in a sprint up the hill. Slowly, I make my way forward.

"Thank the Mother!" Her voice is hoarse, maybe from shouting, and her breathing heavy as she grasps me in a firm hug. I wrap my arms loosely around her waist as she squeezes a little too tightly around my shoulders. Pulling back, she cradles my face in her hands. "You're okay?"

I nod in reply, not trusting myself to speak just yet, offering nothing more than a pathetic smile I know she'll see through.

"We were so worried. When the boys came back to the tents...we couldn't find you," she trails off for a moment. "What happened?" she asks, scanning my face. Likely looking for any ailments, any injury, any reason I may have gotten held up in the woods. But she'll find none. None on the exterior anyway.

"The wolves and I went for a run." I skirt my way around the full truth. I want to trust Sam but after knowing how big a secret Sorin kept, the weight of his betrayal hangs over all of them. "Just trying to get a feel for each other," I say, gesturing toward Ruse and Alaric. "We got caught up by some fallen logs up over the hilltop. Lost track of time, but I'm fine. I swear it." I smile again before making my way around her.

As I glance down at the camp Sorin stands breathless from running back from the cavern. Galen and Jarek are pulling down the tents but halt as they notice my return. My skin itches from looking at them, and the betrayal and hurt I buried within myself last night comes rushing back. But I pull myself together, linking my arm with Sam's as she catches up to me.

Sorin starts in our direction but, for whatever reason, stops. The smile he shoots me is weak, and despite my plan to keep my cool, I don't send him one in return. I veer toward the emerald pools of the falls instead.

Cupping the water in my hands, I splash it over my face and rub at my eyes. The chill of the freezing water shakes the rest of my senses awake. Inhaling the crisp morning air, it wraps itself around my chest. It's cold this morning. So cold the air stings as it hits my lungs. I take another deep breath, then hold it to the point of pain before letting it loose, long and slow. As I stand to meet the others, a deep crashing noise shatters through the woods from where the wolves and I just came.

Silence falls over the remnants of our camp. Frozen in anticipation, no one moves, myself included. I meet Sorin's eyes briefly and my stomach dips, he opens his mouth to say something but before he can, I redirect my attention to the hill. Alaric and Ruse, at my side, hunch over. Their barred teeth and low growls crawl over my skin. My hand drags to my dagger. But a voice—not those of the demons that thrash against my mind, but Alaric's—reminding me, I don't need the daggers anymore.

I don't know what magick I'm supposed to wield. I argue through our new bond. Last night when I turned moss to smoldering embers, I wasn't even trying. How am I supposed to know what to do now?

Trust yourself. Alaric's voice is low, rumbling, but assuring nonetheless.

Another deep split of a log followed by a low guttural moan crests over the hill. I cut a glance to the rest of the crew. Sorin and Sam ready with their bows, Jarek with his axes. Galen is hunched behind a tree, opening his pack low to the ground.

The ground rattles and I snap my attention back to the hill and to the large animal bounding down it. The sharp hiss of an arrow through the air is the only other sound. It lands directly in the animal's chest.

Sorin.

Another arrow.

Following its flight line, my eyes widen as the giant half decaying moose makes its way straight toward the others. The beast is massive, at least ten feet tall, dwarfing the wolves that stand at my sides. Moss and thorns drip from its skeletal antlers, its skin is sallow and rotten. Decay sinks where its eye sockets should be. But the animal's pace is strong, despite both of Sorin's arrows protruding from his chest.

Another whiz of an arrow. It takes me a moment to realize it is actually two arrows. Sam and Sorin shoot in perfect harmony, landing blows against the moose, or what is left of it, with precision. Yet, its pace doesn't falter.

The moose lets out a higher pitched moan this time as an arrow strikes just below his jaw. Half of its face is rotted down to the bone. Flesh drips down the other half, almost as if it's been melted off. The stench of decay fills the air as the animal makes its final steps down the hill.

"He's got Deathcap!" Galen shouts, reaching inside of his pack and pulling out a vial.

I click my tongue and without question the wolves and I bolt toward the crew and the moose.

Stay back. Don't get bitten. I warn them as we near the infected animal.

It's been a long time since I've had any lessons, but Deathcap is not something so easily forgotten. An infection of the bloodstream from ingesting poisonous mushrooms located in the thickest parts of the forest. Transferable by bite, we'd have minutes to live before our skin would be melting from our bodies, just as the moose is now. The larger the animal, the longer the effects would take to set in. And by the size of this moose, he's been infected for quite some time and no doubt gone rabid from the sickness.

Reacting on instinct, I move to the rear of the moose.

Keeping myself low to the ground, Ruse slides next to me on my right, her thick coat grazing my arm.

I draw my hands to my daggers again, desperate for the weight of them.

Use your magick, Elora. Ruse's sweet voice is clear amidst the chaos. *You need to help them.*

The moose has cornered the rest of the group, arrows whiz through the air while Jarek aimlessly swings his ax.

Trust yourself, Ruse says again. *We are with you.*

Moving my hands away from my daggers, I take a quick breath to ground myself. Whatever magick I conjured last night, it was fueled by rage. And I have plenty of that still brewing. I hang my hands by my sides, and just as I'm about to open myself up to whatever magick I possess, whatever magick the wolves are coaxing out of me, I freeze.

The moment I use this magick, hunters will sense it. Panic replaces fear and I quickly close my palms as the moose bellows out another howl.

I have been here before. Frozen in fear as the people I care for face danger. My eyes dart between the group and the moose.

No.

I will not be afraid again.

Listening for Alaric and Ruse's direction, they stalk the animal on either side.

Ruse's voice fills my ears.

Listen to the forest, Elora.

Listen.

I have seconds to take in my surroundings. Sorin and Samaria continue their tandem shooting, landing each arrow to the moose, though with its massive size, it is not enough. Jarek's ax lands a blow against the beast's leg, causing a low yell to pierce through the woods.

"You need to aim for his heart!" Galen yells, tossing his bag aside, he approaches Sorin.

Listen, Alaric says.

"We've hit it a dozen times!" Sam yells, her voice strained as she reaches for her last arrow. The moose lets out a deep, long, bellow as it charges, filling the gap between them. Jarek swings his ax again, but this time, he isn't fast enough. The moose lowers his massive antlers. Bone and rot and earth collide with Jarek's chest, sending him backward into a tree with a loud *crunch*.

Listen.

My heart races, but I sense it. An itch against my palms. My *magick* filling my palms. Magick I have no idea how to wield, but I do as Ruse says. For a split second I tune out of the chaos and I listen to the forest.

A breeze. The rustle of leaves.

A faint call of birds in the distance.

Scraping and swinging of branches.

Branches.

"Don't get bitten!" Galen shouts in my direction as Sorin readies another arrow, but it will not be enough.

None of it will.

I click my tongue, alerting the wolves. Ruse and Alaric sprint forward and flank the infected animal as I make my approach to its backside. The moose lets out a low wail as he veers toward Sam, cornering her between himself and a tree. The wolves move swiftly to cage the animal in. Magick stings against my palms, scraping down the corridors of my mind. It whispers against my skin, calling to me. Yearning like lovers that have been separated for far too long. My mind opens to the elements around me until there is only one beaming at the forefront.

Earth.

Branches.

A thick branch riddled with pine needles lies above Samaria's head where she's trapped against a tree. The moose dips his head again, scraping and prying with those wraith-like antlers as Sam burrows herself deepening into the tree's trunk.

Sorin shoots his final arrow, though it lands, the moose doesn't so much as balk. Galen has pulled Jarek out of the line of attack, checking him over for injury.

I focus on the pine needles, honing in on the rage of yesterday when I set the moss aflame.

Lifting my hands, I close my eyes. Little by little, the magick expels from my palms, an invisible force weaves through the air. My body slicks with sweat as I pour every ounce of energy into the branch with pine needles, into my magick. I sense the wolves at my sides without even looking. Sense their own magick, ancient and sentient. I lean into their presence, allowing them to guide me, just as Galen said. Closing my eyes, they're there. Alaric and Ruse are with me, guiding and pulling my magick toward the branches. It pushes through the air, through Sam's screams until it reaches the branch and wraps around it.

The transformation is like a snap in my chest. A tether being cut in two. Whipping my eyes open, the branch that once was, is now completely frozen. Twisting my palms, I no longer hesitate. No longer deny the gift bestowed upon me.

Wielding the Earth, the pine needles turn to ice. Sharp and poised, hundreds and hundreds of shards aim for the moose below. Using the last bit of strength I can conjure, I twist my wrist and slam the hundreds of shards of ice into the animal's body.

All that has been given life, shall have an end.

CHAPTER 32
SORIN

ELORA RISES FROM BEHIND THE RABID MOOSE AND MY heart stops. What is she doing? Then, one moment the animal is feral and attacking Sam, the next it's dropping to the ground. A wash of blinding light overtakes the entire forest just before the moose falls. A thousand shards of ice hover in the air before crashing into the animal's skull with a sickening crunch. Blood and black rot spill from the moose's head as it takes its last, short, desperate breaths. I shoot my last arrow, landing in the moose's neck, letting it rest in peace.

Elora has figured out how to call upon her magick. My heart swells with pride despite the gory scene before me. Despite her distance from me since last night.

Last night.

My heart snags on the memory as Elora moves around the moose. Her golden eyes glow wildly against her sweat streaked face as I take her in. A frantic energy radiates off of her. Her magick fills the air like static. Every inch of moss her boots land upon parts, like water. Carving a path for her to walk. My skin crawls as she passes me by, but I'm not afraid. Curious. But not afraid. I could never be afraid of her.

She meets my eye but only for an instant before turning to

the wolves. Without a word, they head to the emerald pool, each step in perfect unison.

Turning to Galen, I see he's given Jarek a tonic for the pain. Corking the empty bottle, he tosses it back into his pack. "Some bruising on his back, but otherwise should be okay," Galen says.

"Speak for yourself, this hurts like hell." Jarek winces as Sam helps him sit up, rolling her eyes as she does so.

"It could have been a lot worse," she says, peering past me toward Elora at the pool. She meets my eyes again, the same worry I feel inside of me she wears across her face.

"Gather the supplies." My voice is harsher than it needs to be, but with what just happened, we need to move. Quickly. "We leave in ten minutes." I hate the way it sounds like an order, but the luxury to be leisurely has long been abandoned. The moment Elora used her magick, I'm certain hunters sensed it.

Perched atop a large rock, Elora sits stiffly, cupping the deep emerald water into her hands and working it over her face and hair.

"Need some help?" I ask, keeping myself an arms length away.

Pausing, she doesn't look up before continuing with the water. Dipping her hands in again, she splashes her face, blood and rot slick off of her skin and into the pool.

"What you did back there," I say, gesturing behind me, "was impressive. You saved our arses." This grabs her attention. Her eyes are hollow as she snaps her gaze to me but still, she says nothing.

"Do you want to talk about it?" I ask, desperation lining my voice. Last night when we couldn't find her, I almost went out of my damn mind. And now, with the distance between us growing with every moment, it's as if solid ground is being pulled from under my feet. It's possible she regrets our time in the cavern. Dread coils in my stomach as I watch her with unease.

"Talk about what, exactly?" she asks, squeezing the excess water from her braided hair before standing to face me. "Talk about how I just killed an infected moose using Elemental magick I didn't know I possessed? Talk about how hunters are likely headed in our direction as we speak? Or shall we discuss what you've been keeping from me, Sorin?"

Her words spill out so quickly, I have no chance to intervene. "You should really consider discussing your secrets in a better place than a clearing in the woods where anyone could stumble." She scowls before jumping down from the rock. Crossing her arms, she leans her weight on one hip. I must wear my shock on my face, because it earns a terrifying chuckle from Elora. She heard us last night and now she knows. My stomach sinks. I should've told her sooner and I'm a fucking idiot for not.

Throwing on her cloak, she pushes past me, leaving me no chance to speak. Heading towards the others, the wolves follow in her steps.

"Excuse me, Your *Highness*," she snarls, bumping my arm as she goes by.

"Elora, wait—" She doesn't bother stopping. Doesn't bother looking back as I call her name a second time. There were so many chances I had to explain my role in Valebridge, but the fear of her rejection held me back and now I've compromised her trust. My heart beats erratically as she joins the others, and despite the swell of emotions rising within me, I swallow them down and follow suit.

"We'll set off through the bog, it'll be messy but it's the quickest route," Sam calls out as I sluggishly make my way back. She eyes Elora for a moment, but being as she's the smarter sibling, chooses not to press questions like I stupidly did.

"Looks like the rain will be starting soon," Jarek chimes in, "so we better get on with it." He walks with a slight hunch, but otherwise is unscathed from the infected beast.

The silence between Elora and I is excruciating as we make

our way around the bog. Every few steps there's a hurdle to maneuver around; wet patches, sunken moss, rotted branches. Not to mention the theoretical hurdle I've created for myself. I've messed up and now I don't know how to make it right. She was vulnerable with me. Telling me what happened to her family was not easy, and I blew the opportunity to tell her who I really am. I just couldn't face the fear of judgment. Couldn't see the look in her eyes when she found out I'm directly related to the man who had caused her so much pain. Directly related to that *monster*.

Sam leads the pack around the swamp. Jarek and Galen trail close behind while Elora, the wolves, and myself lead up the rear. "Elora, slow down," I say for the fifth time, reaching for her arm. Ripping it away, she trudges on through the dark, murky water. "Let me just explain," I try again and this time she whips her head back to me. Relief is a fleeting feeling as she places both her palms against my chest and pushes me backward.

"You withheld something from me," she seethes between her teeth, pointing a finger in my direction. "*Again.*" The last word lands its blow, directly to my heart. I straighten myself, taking a few cautious steps toward her.

"I know," I say, holding my hands up like I'm a prisoner. In some ways, I suppose I am. A prisoner of her heart, and she is the only one with the key.

"It was *you* who demanded we trust each other. Tell each other the truth," she hisses, though her voice cracks at the end.

"I know," I say again, taking another cautious step.

"I told you everything. I let you see the darkest parts of my being and yet you still kept this from me." Her voice drops to a whisper, but she doesn't back away as I finally approach.

"I know. I know and I'm sorry." Regret weighs heavily on me as I reach out my hand again, grabbing her elbow to draw her closer. Her brows knit together as she resists my grasp before giving in. "I should have told you about Roman. About who I am."

She meets my eyes. The fury in her shifts. Softens. Only for a moment until that steel armor clicks back into place. She's retreating with every breath. Building her walls. "But you of all people must understand how terrifying it is for the world to know who you truly are." She flinches but still holds my gaze. "We were born into what we are for a purpose. Whether you believe that to be true or not, you cannot deny the magick you wield at your fingertips, just as much as I cannot deny the title that is rightfully mine. Despite the men who have claimed the throne before me, please know that I am *nothing* like them."

The clouds have parted and the droplets of rain quickly turn to sheets of water. We'll be soaked in a matter of minutes if we don't head for the trees. The pitter patter of the water hitting the ground fills the silence between us.

"I'm sorry I didn't tell you," I say it again. I'll say it a hundred times. "I didn't know how you'd react knowing I was related to...*him*. After everything he's done." She wriggles from my hold and takes a few steps back, leaning herself against a leafless birch tree. Using the sleeve of her cloak, she unsuccessfully wipes at the water falling onto her face. I can't determine if it's tears or rain but my heart drops. I've hurt her again, and I hate myself for it.

"What is it with you not letting me decide what I can and cannot handle?" she asks, crossing her arms. "I'm not some broken thing you're responsible for fixing."

Her voice is muddled through the heavy rainfall but her words pierce me just the same. I open my mouth to grovel. To beg. To do anything I need to do to get her to understand that keeping my true identity from her was more for her protection than anything else. But before I can, she cuts me off again. "Why convince me I meant something to you when you already had my word I'd help you into Valebridge?"

Baffled, I shake my head in confusion. "What do you mean?" I ask.

She says nothing in return. Staring her down, I scan her face. The hurt so blatantly displayed there. Had she thought I was insincere in my admission? That I didn't care for her? The thought strikes me straight through my chest.

"Elora, I meant every word I said in that cavern." Reaching up, I sweep her hair off her face. It's matted from the rain, I tuck it behind her shoulder. "I would never hurt..." I stop myself. I can't finish the sentence because it is untrue. Because I have hurt her. Taking a deep breath, I push my soaking hair back from my face, the dripping rain blurring my vision. My boots sink into the soggy earth as I lean closer to her. "I swear to you, I meant every word I said."

"Or is it you just need something from me?" She shakes her head before continuing, "A pawn in your scheme to take the throne. You may as well add liar to your list of skills along with *thief*. I heard what you said to Galen. What do you plan to do with us when you're in power?" She grits her teeth, and pushes against my chest with her fists. "You act as though you're so much more righteous, but I'm beginning to see all the similarities between you and your brother after all. Lying, stealing, doing whatever suits *you* best."

All these weeks, I thought Elora could see me for who I really am and not just for the things I've done. The things I do. I never proclaimed I was a decent man, though I'd argue my reasons for doing the things I've done make me less of a monster than *him*.

I step closer, placing my hands on either side of her head, caging her against the tree. Against my chest. Her chest heaves as she watches me. Her narrowed eyes like daggers thrown against my skin.

"I do what I have to do in order to keep my people safe," I grit through my teeth, "for that I will never apologize." I dip my head low enough to graze her ear. "If my methods make you uncomfortable, love," I say, brushing her ear with my lips before pulling back to meet her eyes, "then by all means, *leave*. No one made you come here." I don't mean it, of course, but comparing me to Roman is just about the worst thing she can do, and I believe she knows it.

"Is that what you want, Sorin? For me to leave?" Her voice waivers, a flicker of doubt passing over her face.

Keeping my hands on either side of her, I don't move and she doesn't try to get away. Doesn't use her magick to throw me across the bog like I'm sure she easily can. Instead, she watches me with a steady, unnerving calm. Of course I don't want her to leave. I curse my pride for even saying the words.

Shaking my head in frustration, I expel a long breath. "Of course not I just—" Before I can finish a sharp pain pierces my right calf. Shock transforms my features as I glance down to see Ruse latched onto my leg. Through the rain, I didn't hear her approach. Her teeth don't quite sink into my skin but she flexes her jaw, as if to show me she'll snap it completely shut any moment she deems fit. Drawing my widened eyes back to Elora, she meets me with a small, closed mouth grin.

Pushing my hands off the tree, uncaging her, I let them drop to my sides. Elora stays there for a moment, with her back pressed against the bark. Watching me. She doesn't break our eye contact before she whispers, "Release."

In an instant I'm free from the wolf's grip. I let out a ragged breath but remain still, unsure if there's another unspoken command I need to brace myself for. Pushing herself off the tree, Elora steps onto her toes to reach my mouth.

Her breath is warm against the cold bite of the rain as she pushes her lips so close that we're almost kissing.

"The next time you lie to me," she whispers, her lips brushing mine, "I will *not* be so generous." Her words are clipped and fierce as she pushes her way around me, Ruse follows obediently.

I wait until she and Ruse are out of sight before I reach

down and push my pant leg up to quickly assess any damage to my calf. There's a few precise indentations that are sure to bruise but nothing more. Straightening myself, I roll my shoulders back before turning to catch up with the others. The sting of pain everytime I put weight on my right leg causes me to laugh.

Of course, the woman I've chosen has a pack of vicious wolves at her disposal and the ability to alter the elements. I suppose I wouldn't settle for any less.

Chapter 33

Elora

The rain has ceased, leaving a blanket of gray to cover the dusk sky. An ominous caw sounds from the circling blackbirds above, their silhouettes ghost-like in the graying evening light. It's as if they know we will never return the same. That is, if we ever return at all.

The wolves pace frantically at my sides, sensing what sinister presence lies just beyond. The five of us and the wolves stop at the entrance of the Wicked Wood. The trees whisper their sinister warning as the wind whips rapidly, tearing my hood from my head, stinging my eyes and exposed cheeks.

The residual dampness from the rain transforms into an eerie, mist-like fog. The once beautiful green pines we've been surrounded by are replaced by graying birch trees, their trunks etched with symbols I don't understand. Black sap seeps from their peeling bark, the branches turn in on themselves creating a tunnel of darkness, no light from the moon to lead the way. Swallowing deeply, I will the voices to stay down. I'll need all the clarity I can get before we enter. Despite my frustrations, I don't pull my hand away as Sorin cautiously slips his fingers in mine. A silent offering of apology.

Anger still bubbles under my chest from earlier. He withheld something so important from me, although I also had been withholding. Even through my rage, he is right that we can't deny the force between us and with whatever lies through the Wicked Wood, I'm glad he's by my side. As his fingers wrap around mine, the tightness I've been carrying in my chest lessens.

Collectively, we all take a last shuddering breath before stepping forward, inching closer to the opening of crooked trees. Swaying branches tickle along my skin. A breathy, "*Welcome,*" hisses in my ear, sending the hair on my arms up, despite the thickness of my cloak.

Arriving at the Wicked Woods is like entering a feverish dream. The kind where you're unsure if you should wake yourself up or endure the nightmare until daylight pulls you out. Though, there is no daylight to save us here. Only foolish hope and blind trust.

Loosening his grip on my hand, Sorin leads us into the tunnel of darkness. A faint howl echoes from the wolves as they trail us and it's the last thing I hear before the all-consuming black drowns out the rest of my senses.

There is no going back.

Shuffling feet and the occasional exasperated breath are all I can hear once we're inside the twisted trees. My eyes struggle to adjust as we inch our way forward. Little by little. Step by step. Hand in hand, with Sorin in the lead. A sudden flash of white illuminates the inside of the tunnel of trees, I throw my hands up to shield my eyes. A wicked echo of laughter bounces off the invisible walls of the wood.

There at the end of the tunnel stands who I can only assume to be Grawgeth. Her slim, naked figure appears slowly in smokey waves then all at once. Her height towers over us, making even Jarek look small. Sharp nails come to a point at the tip of each finger as she taps them against her long legs. Her sallow, gray skin blends into the eerie mist that coats the tunnel of trees and thick patches of bark scatter across her body. Like she herself is made from the forest.

My eyes catch on her obsidian hair that hangs low below her breasts, emphasizing the sharpened features of her face. Black eyes watch with hunger as we come to a halt. Her thin lips open in a cruel smile revealing too many pointed black teeth. Terror rips through me but Sorin's grip on my hand anchors me. Without it, I'm sure to be lost.

"Well, isn't this lovely." Her voice echoes through the hollow of trees, though it's not one voice, but many all at once. Deep and low, yet high and piercing. She strides forward, her elongated limbs taking graceful steps over the leaf littered ground. "Sorin Rudhek, no longer the boy I remember. It is not time to repay your debt," the nymph with many voices growls. "Tell me, what brings you back to my woods so soon?" She inclines her head to Sorin, flicking her eyes to Sam with another wicked grin.

My mind snags on one word, and one alone.

Debt.

"We're only looking for passage through." The uncertainty in Sorin's voice does nothing to settle my nerves. He squares his shoulders despite the fear I sense in his voice.

Tsking, the nymph shakes her long, pointed finger. "You, of all, should know it isn't that simple, Sorin of Loxley." Hearing his name on her lips ignites a flame inside me. She must read my emotions because her black eyes snap back to mine. Narrowing them, she scans me from top to bottom. "Interesting," she says. Thrumming her elongated fingers along her naked thigh. "Another Enchantress." She glances back to Samaria, flashing another glimpse of her too sharp teeth. Instinctively, I step to the left, blocking her view of my friend. "But you," she says, returning her gaze to mine, "you yield a very unique power. A Dyrsjel. Dare I say, the *last* Dyrsjel? Tempting, very tempting," the nymph muses.

The last Dyrsjel.

"She's off the table," Sorin grits out. "As they all are." The nymph says nothing as we wait in uncertainty. Voices seep through the trees, different whispers itch against my skin. I'm used to voices other than my own plaguing my mind, but this is different. It's as if the voices are trapped in the trees, begging to be let out. Distracted, I lift my hand and run it down one of the mutilated trunks. The bark scrapes along my fingertips as I press them into the tree. Flattening my palm against the bark I suck in a sharp breath as the voices boom through my ears like thunder.

Get out!

Get out!

Get out!

Pulling my hand back, I fist my palm, daring a glance to Sam, Galen, and Jarek before turning back to the nymph. We shouldn't have come here.

"You already know what I require." Grawgeth's voice rises as she slides forward along the forest floor. "I was robbed of my life when my love was stolen from me. My soul broke in the same way a heart does. So, the thing I require now is the same as I required of you last time, dear boy." Dipping her head to meet Sorin's ear I shudder at her words. "A bargain." I glance back to the trees, their muted pleas forever ingrained in my mind. Sorin's face is unamused as he takes a slight step back from the nymph.

"The trees," I say. Voice shaking and heart pounding. My fingertips trace the lines of the bark. "They're souls?"

"Merely payment for the passage through," Grawgeth explains, her dark eyes like slits as she watches me.

"Our souls are off the table, so name another price," I demand. Sorin's grip on my elbow tenses.

"Oh, so she doesn't know?" Grawgeth's menacing laugh wraps its way around my spine, scraping like talons on each vertebrae. "I wonder," she says between laughter, "why take my woods at all? If Kirsgard is what you seek, the way round is a matter of weeks. Time must be of the essence? Or is it discretion you seek?" She clicks her tongue, corners of her mouth twitching upward in a cruel smile. "Interesting, indeed, but you know my price," she says again, speaking to Sorin but her eyes remain on me.

"A year sooner." Sorin's voice cuts through the unsteady silence, breaking Grawgeth's concentrated attention, she snaps her gaze to him.

A year sooner? Panic floods my bloodstream. I can't breathe. Or think. The voices from the trees grow louder, creating a thicker haze in my mind. Surely everyone else can hear them? Looking over my shoulder, I take a breath as Sam clutches her chest, but Jarek and Galen remain calm. Steady. The wolves are farther back, pacing frantically but not daring another step toward the nymph.

"Leave the others' souls out of this," Sorin says again. "Take a year sooner and let that be enough."

Grawgeth says nothing, considering his offer. I grip Sorin's arm, tugging him closer to me.

"You are bold to assume that would be enough," the wraith says in her many voices, her pointed teeth peeking through a sinister smile. "One year sooner, and *you* are mine Sorin Rudhek," she repeats Sorin's offer, a wicked smile dancing on her lips. Sorin squeezes my arm, slowly dragging his fingers against my cloak as he slides his hand away from me. As if he doesn't wish to let me go. Pushing the sleeve of his shirt up he reveals the ink that is marked upon his forearm.

"Deal," he says, his voice unwavering, though his hunched shoulders give way that he is not as confident as he sounds. The black swirls on his arm glow and shift under the bright white light. As Grawgeth steps forward, she traces lines with her long, pointed nails around his arm, just above where the current ink resides. Beads of red bubble up from Sorin's flesh and after a few moments, she steps back, revealing another intricate set of black swirls.

Then it strikes me.

His words from our ride to Loxley weeks ago. The way he laughed it off as we spit questions back and forth to each other.

"Ah, this? A rash decision. A teenage regret."

My head pounds from the voices of the souls trapped in the trees. From the voices trapped inside my head. From what Sorin has done.

Sorin bargained his soul to save Sam all those years ago.

It's why she was so sickened about coming back here. It's why he has been so withholding with me. And now, he has agreed to give it to her another year sooner. Give *himself* another year sooner.

Himself.

My eyes snap to Grawgeth to find her already staring at me. Her smile exposes not one, but two sets of razor-sharp teeth.

"Ah, so now you see, Dyrsjel," she says. I grimace as she drags her bony fingers down the side of my cheek. Her sharp nails prick against my skin but I refuse to flinch. "You can keep your soul, Enchantress," she whispers as if to comfort my nerves, "but *his* is already mine. In a short time, he will belong to these woods. But before you go, you and I," she whispers, bending down so she's inches from my face, "let's have some fun. It is not every day I meet a Dyrsjel."

"That wasn't part of the bargain," Sorin says, stepping between the nymph and me. My pulse quickens as my chest heaves. Lungs burning with exertion, I reach for my magick but nothing greets me back. Whatever wards Grawgeth has on the Wicked Wood has dampened my magick. Even my bond with the wolves is hazy. Their voices muffled through the swarm of others now thrashing in my mind.

"You said I couldn't have her *soul*," Grawgeth growls. "Not that I couldn't have *her*. Next time, be less reckless with your terms." She laughs, snapping her fingers before Sorin can mutter another word. A second flash of blinding light encompasses the tunnel. Then, with no warning, I am transported from the woods and into nothing but pitch black.

THE FORCE of whatever magick the nymph used leaves me crashing onto the damp ground. I wince as my hands take the impact on the rough stone floor.

"Sorin! Alaric! Ruse!" My voice echoes through the darkness. Pushing myself up, I wipe my bloodied hands along my cloak. My eyes work unsuccessfully to adjust to the deep darkness, so instead of straining them, I slam them shut. Focusing on my breathing, I reach my hands out before me to get a grasp on my surroundings. I call for my magick but am met with silence.

Alaric? I try the bond between the wolves and I, but it's eerily quiet. I can't feel them as I usually do.

Nothing but jagged stone lies before me. Slowly, I move my hands along the rock wall, careful not to push too hard against the cuts now lined along my palms. I drag my hands until they meet a corner, then I pivot my body. Repeating this motion over and over, I feel for any change in texture. Any opening.

Panic crawls over my skin as my eyes open, adjusting slightly to the darkness. There is no way out. Totally encompassed by stone, I am trapped. My lungs burn with panic as my breathing becomes ragged. Uncontrollable.

I am in a cage.

Caged.

Breathe.

Breathe.

Breathe.

I command myself. Over and over again. "This is a test," I tell myself. "Panicking isn't going to help you accomplish it. Get. It. Together," I grit the words through my teeth. Sure enough, I begin to regain my composure.

Breathe.

My fingers trace the lines of the stone cage again, looking for any weakness, cracks.

Nothing.

Alone once more.

My hands freeze against the stone as the familiar voices in my head grow louder. The voices I've pushed down and silenced for years, now let loose. The invisible wall I built to keep them and the memories out crumbles to bits and any last control I've had over them is gone.

I let out a scream. An animalistic, barbaric scream, covering my ears to mute the voices. Another voice. Another scream. And another, and another. As the memories become clearer, my screams turn to sobs. Cade's body being dragged away. My mother's throat. Blood upon freshly fallen snow. My dagger as it slices through that guard in Copenspire.

Murderer.

Murderer.

Murderer.

Dropping to my knees, I forget the ground beneath me is no longer the soft pad of the forest. The rough grit of the stone rips my breeches at the knee. I feel for my magick. For the now familiar pulse beneath my skin.

No magick. No light. No wolves. No one.

We've been waiting for you.

How nice it is to no longer be pushed away.

Pulling my hands from my ears, I rest my back against the stone wall and gaze into the darkness. "Sorin. Samaria. Jarek. Galen. Loxley." I repeat the names aloud over and over again until the voices in my head settle to a low roar. Still there. But dulled nonetheless. "Sorin. Samaria. Jarek. Galen." I let out a shaky breath, bringing my knees to my chest.

If this is my test, my payment to get the others through safely, then by any means necessary, I will not fail.

CHAPTER 34
ELORA

WOULDN'T IT BE NICE TO SEE THEM AGAIN.

To feel them.

Let us take you to them, Elora.

The voices slam into me repeatedly as I force myself up from the ground. Echoing louder and louder with each breath I struggle to take. Shaking my head, I steady myself against the wall as another voice drips into my ears.

Use your daggers, Elora.

End this now.

My hands are no longer mine as my fingers brush against the hilts of my daggers in response. Using all my strength, I pull my hands from the blades, the unseen resistance yanks them back in a tug of war of will. I gasp as I take back control of my hands, planting them firmly on the wall.

"I will not break for you." I'm not sure who I'm talking to. No one. Everyone. I grit my teeth as the voices explode in a violent rage. My mother's voice. Cade's voice. The guard's voice. Grawgeth's. All mixed into one.

Weak.

Broken.

Useless.

You killed them.

Killed them.

Killed them.

Killed US.

My throat becomes hoarse from screaming as I push my hands against my ears. "Stop, stop, STOP!" I scream.

Then, in an instant, they do.

Terrifying, deafening, silence hangs around me. For minutes, I stay completely still. Hands pressed firmly against my ears. Slowly, I peel my hands away, letting them hang loosely at my sides. The taste of salt hits my tongue as I lick my dry, cracked lips. Tears I didn't realize had fallen. The darkness and tightness of the stone cage disorients any concept of time. Have I been here minutes? Hours? My terror from the voices subsides momentarily as anger quickly takes over, swift and smooth.

"Is that all you've got!" I scream into nothing, balling my fists and slamming them against the stone wall. Whatever is next, I'll be ready.

At least, I thought I would be.

"*Susi.*" The word bounces between the small walls of the cage, long and drawn on like a whisper in the wind. My mother. I suck in a sharp breath, her voice like needles against my skin.

"*Suuuusi.*" My mother's melodic voice wraps around me. "Come now, Elora. We've missed you."

The eerie darkness of the cage begins to lift, a soft glow from the ground illuminates my surroundings. There, in the dim light, stands my mother. Her onyx and silver hair braided into a crown as it was the night she died. Her deep emerald gown pooled at the floor, the sleeves cropped neatly at her wrist. And her eyes. Her beautiful, silver eyes watch me with such sorrow.

Such longing.

My gaze shifts to her throat. No scar. No blood. Not the image that replays in my mind every night, but the mother I always knew before. Before Roman. Before...

It's my mother the way I always wanted to remember her. Her ivory skin glows as she holds her hand out toward me. A beacon of light. My heart tugs forward. How I've missed her. Her touch. Her laugh. Her voice.

"Come, Elora." She waves her hand again, gesturing me forward. Her lyrical voice is sweet in my ears. A sound so beautiful it shatters my heart in two. How simple a sound can be and yet so complex. It has the power to hold many memories. Memories of pain and joy and fear and heartbreak. And this sound, the sound of her voice, somehow houses them all.

"There once was an Enchantress who loved a little girl very much..."

Hanging my head, I slam my eyes shut. "This isn't real. This isn't real." I repeat the words aloud through choked sobs. Then, the press of a warm hand on my shoulder. Warm, not cold. Shooting my eyes open. I don't dare look up from the ground. I fight the urge to lean into her touch.

"Isn't it, though?" she asks, her skin soft and smooth. Her fingers run delicately over my jaw, landing under my chin, tipping it upward so I'm forced to meet her gaze. "My poor, *susi*," she says, shaking her head, glancing at the scar along my neck. The scar I received the night of the mountain, a moment of weakness so blurred and dark, I couldn't even locate the proper artery. "I'm just as real as you are," she whispers. "Just as real as this cage. Come with me now and all of this will go away. You can save your friends, no one else will have to get hurt."

So wrapped up in the sound of her voice, in the feel of her touch, I don't realize how her fingers slip into mine. How she delicately brings my hand to the hilt of the dagger tucked neatly at my side. I watch my fingers trace the hilt of the blade, but I don't feel it. Don't feel anything.

Isn't this what everybody wants? One last moment with the person they've lost. One chance to tell them all the things you did not say. Could not say. That I love her with my whole heart.

That I should have done more to protect her. Save her. That, above all else, I am sorry.

Maybe after all this time, this is my moment of retribution. To right my wrongs as Agnes said I would. I am lost in her eyes, mesmerized by the feeling of home I find within them.

"You can do this, Elora." The blade slips out from its sheath. She grips the hilt in her glowing hands. But I don't care. I can't tear my eyes away from hers as she speaks to me. Hypnotized by her voice, I don't notice when she places the blade into my hand, until it's already there.

"You can make this right," she whispers. Immediately, I know what she means. I'm the reason she is gone. Her hands cup my face, distracting me from the weight of the blade in my hand. Her smile is warm and familiar. Like coming home after a trip that lasted far too long and oh, how I so badly wish to go home. My body shudders. I don't question her words as I tighten my grip on the blade's hilt. Isn't this what I pictured so many times before? Isn't this what I planned to do on the mountain, but failed? Had planned to do in the woods the night before I met Sorin?

My mother. My beautiful, warm, mother who wanted everything for me. Who put me before anything else. Who withheld parts of who I am, who *she* was, to keep me safe. Who died to ensure I would live. Her hand grazes mine as she encourages the blade up until its sharp point pricks at the soft skin under my chin. Warm blood trickles down onto my chest but I don't fight her. I don't pull away.

"Do it now, my sweet *susi*. Save your soul from damnation by making this right. Do it now and come home with me."

In the years since she's passed, it's the only thing I've ever wanted.

All those years alone in the woods, I let the voices invade every inch of my mind, settle into its depths. I let them call my mind home. Let them believe they belonged. Kept them guarded in a box, letting them out only when I could not find the strength to fight them off.

I allowed them to replace everything in me with fear until I was nothing but a shell moving amongst the forest. They could feel it, the voices. The moment I started to give in, and that night in the woods they didn't hesitate to strike.

They seeped in slowly through my pores, driving all the way down to the core of my being, their malicious chants a constant echo in my ears.

Give up.

Give up.

Give up.

AND I ALMOST HAD. The night before I met Sorin that thought was pressed to the forefront of my mind. *That's all it would take, one careless slip of the blade,* my demons whispered in my ears, encouraging the end. But the wind whispered something else that night. *"Not yet, little susi."* And so I listened to that wind and now I am here.

Here, in this cage built of stone, looking at my mother's beautiful face, the thought more tempting than ever before. Her eyes flare as I tighten my grip around the blade. The early days in the forest cloud my mind. The thought of almost giving into those demons cracks my chest open. Had I ended everything then, I wouldn't be here now. I would have never met Sorin that very next day. Or Sam. Or any of the others.

The anger in my chest lights a fire within me as I think of Ruse and of Alaric. I picture Jarek's face as he tips his head in laughter. Galen's as he studies a book. I see Sam's eyes as she worries about me, far too often. Sorin's face flashes into my mind again, and I cling to the image in the violent storm brewing inside me.

With a strangled breath, I brush my thumb across my mother's beautiful face. "I'm so sorry." I choke on my tears. "I love you," I whisper. I know it now. I know it isn't *her,* but I have to say it. One last time to her face or what looks like her face. I had to say it.

Confusion splays across the being and in a split second, I spin the blade, slamming it deeply into the wraith's chest and yanking it back with a forceful tug. Recoiling back, the face of what looked like my mother flexes. In and out, it bounces between my mother and the nymph until finally, the black eyes and graying skin of Grawgeth slumps in the corner of the cage.

Thick black tar oozes from her chest instead of what should've been blood. Her screams so high and shrill I'm close to dropping my dagger, wishing to pull my hands to my ears to soften the blow. I let out a scream of my own.

It wasn't real, it wasn't real. I tell myself. The feeling of my blade slicing against her skin. *It wasn't her. It wasn't her.* Amidst the chaos and noise, for a moment I think I hear Sorin's voice.

"Elora!"

Then, my mind snaps back to the nymph. Blade in hand I approach her. The pool of black liquid runs across the floor. Her dark eyes meet mine, those vicious lips curve into a smile.

"Tell me how to break the bargain," I spit toward the nymph, "or I will end you now." Angling my blade, I tuck it under her chin. Gripping her chest, she lets out a laugh that quickly turns to a cough. I glance to her chest, the wound slowly closing, stitching itself back together.

"It is not that simple, Dyrsjel," she says, pausing to cough again. Black tar continues to seep from the wound on her chest. "The bargain will not end with me, you are wasting your time."

"There is always a way," I grit out, pushing the blade further into her throat. She eyes me for a moment, then grips my forearm. Pointed nails dig into my skin beneath my cloak and before I can pull away, visions flood behind my eyes.

Visions of Grawgeth, but not as she is now. But Grawgeth, the woodland nymph. Hair unbound and black. Silken waves strewn down her naked back. Her skin, not gray and sallow but pale as ivory. Her cheeks, flushed with pink, her lips as red as berries. I see her cry. Hear her. Then, a man. Her lover. Tall and thick, a mess of blonde curls. But I don't see his face, for his back is turned. Walking away. Walking away to a life unbound by the woods. A life Grawgeth could never have as a woodland nymph.

She screams. Cries. Curses the woods and all who enter. She withers away, bit by bit, until there is nothing left of her. But the woods grow stronger. More sinister. The woods, the Wicked Woods, come to life but in their life, is death. Grawgeth's.

Grawgeth releases her grip, and I am snapped back to the present.

"So, you see," she says, head lolling forward. "I have nothing left in this world. End my life, and it will still not end your lover's curse. He does not belong to me, he belongs to the *woods*. Even when I am dead, he will take my place. That has always been the bargain. Kill me now and quicker he will come."

Lover.

I shake the word off, clenching my free hand at my side into a tight fist.

"Then I will burn the woods down," I hiss, ignoring how the salt of my tears stings against my cheeks.

"And it will be in vain," Grawgeth shouts. "The magick is as sentient as Teravie. The trees will regrow, and when they do, he will be summoned here. He cannot escape this."

No. I don't accept this. My blade pushes deeper, more black begins to trickle from the underside of Grawgeth's chin. "There is always another way. Tell. Me."

Rolling her head back so it rests against the wall, her breathing is short and shallow. The black tar from her chest has covered her entirely. "There is another way, little wolf." Her consciousness flickering in and out. "But, I promise," she whispers, "you will not like it."

CHAPTER 35
SORIN

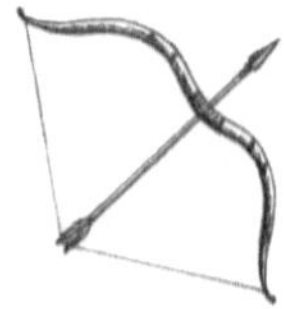

My mother knocks three times on the wooden door *before someone finally answers it. The woman's swollen belly takes up most of the doorway as she peers through the cracked oak frame. I recognized her immediately.*

"Is everything all right?" Lady Elwyn asks, pulling the door open farther. She glances from my mother down to me as I cling to my mother's gown.

"No," my mother says curtly, "everything is not *all right." She pulls me into the room, and Elwyn casts me a smile as I pass her by. I like Elwyn. She's always been nice whenever my mother visits her. Which lately, has been often. She even gave me a gift for my fourth birthday last year. A small wooden knight with a sword.*

"Why don't we...sit down," Elwyn suggests, motioning to the small settee that rests in the corner. My mother shakes her head, her dark red curls swaying and catching in the sunlight.

"Sorin," Elwyn says, keeping her eyes on my mother. "Are you hungry? I think there are a few biscuits left from this morning, would you like some?" I nod enthusiastically, my dark hair falling into my eyes.

Elwyn leads me to a small table across the room, setting a plate of iced biscuits in front of me along with a picture book filled with stencils of various plants and foliage. I dive into the sweets even though we just had breakfast. She pats my head before crossing back to my mother, rubbing a hand idly over her stomach.

"Now will you stop pacing, Celia," Elwyn says, her friendly tone turning frustrated. "What's wrong?" She pulls my mother down onto the settee. I try to keep focused on the book but my eyes drift to my mother. She hasn't been the same the last few weeks. Always muttering to herself, always pacing.

"It's Rhoda," my mother whispers, "she's pregnant."

Elwyn takes my mothers hand, giving it a tight squeeze but says nothing. I take another bite of my biscuit and wonder why she would be so upset over the queen having a baby. Isn't that what queens do?

Finishing off my biscuit, I wipe the icing on the sleeve of my shirt. Would it be rude to ask for more?

"We're leaving," my mother whispers. This grabs my attention. "Tonight."

Elwyn's brows furrow. "Leaving?" she asks, leaning forward so they're only a few inches apart. My mother stands from the settee, the nerves in my stomach swoosh and mix with the sweets I just inhaled.

"I can't stay, Elywn. I have to leave. Whatever lies beyond the Valebridge walls, I have to believe we'll find refuge. I have-"

"Celia, no." Elwyn interrupts, standing and gripping her by the elbows.

"We're leaving tonight," my mother says again in a tone that she typically only uses when I've gotten into her things. "I can't watch another woman bear his child. It's already too much to see him wed another...We'll find our way, whatever that way is."

The two of them say nothing as Elwyn pulls my mother into an embrace. My heartbeat quickens. What does she mean, leave tonight? We can't leave tonight. Tonight is the full moon and we're to have tea and then a party. She must have forgotten.

"If what your vision said is true," my mother whispers,

possibly thinking I can't hear her, "then even if I leave, they will still find each other."

Elwyn nods, a flash of understanding takes over her face as she rubs her round belly again. "The Fates have confirmed our suspicions," Elwyn says, glancing at me then to her belly. I look away quickly, pretending to be studying the plants in the book. "But we still haven't figured out why and if you leave, Celia it will be much more difficult for me to See their future. Not to mention Silas will not rest until—"

"I know," my mother says, cutting her short. "I know what he'll do to me. I know the magick he has at his disposal. But as long as he is safe"—my skin prickles as her eyes land on me, but I don't turn to look. I don't want to see the look in her eyes that is so unlike her— "as long as they find each other...that is all that matters. Whatever the Fates Saw...whatever they need them to do, they'll make sure it's done, right?" I turn just in time to see Elwyn nod, her brows pinched together. "But in the meantime, I can't sit here idle," my mother continues. "Sorin can't stay here after the baby is born. What if they see him as a threat?" She turns, her eyes finding me so I quickly look away. "And they will find each other. Won't they?"

"Yes," Elwyn whispers, her eyes flicking to me as well, "they'll find each other."

"Can you please watch him, just for a little while?" My mother's voice cracks and my stomach drops. Is she crying?

"Of course," Elwyn says, stroking my mother's hair back from her face. "He can stay as long as you need."

My mother crosses the room and crouches next to me. "Be good for Lady Elwyn," she whispers in my ear, "listen to what she says."

Nodding, I reach for her gown, grabbing a fistful, wishing she would stay a little longer. "Of course, mama," I say, but I'm still so confused. I don't want to leave. This is my home. Before I can say anything else, she kisses my head and turns to Elwyn. My stomach feels funny but I ignore the feeling, not wanting to burden my mother any further.

"Thank you," she whispers. Her eyes drag to Elwyn's belly, she places her hand there. "Do you have a name yet?" she asks, removing her hand and heading to the door.

"I think I'll name her Elora," Elwyn says, a smile splitting across her face.

"Elora," my mother repeats slowly as if committing it to memory. "The sun beam to my sun." She smiles, turning to me quickly. "I'll be back," she whispers before disappearing completely from the room. There are a few beats of silence before the large oak door creaks and I dare a glance up from my book.

"Sorin," Elwyn says, turning from the door and giving me a smile. "Have you ever heard of a game called poker?"

I'm snapped from my memory by the sound of a scream.

Elora's scream.

Jumping up to my feet, I force myself not to panic, the memory of my mother and of Elora's mother still burned into my mind. *Think, Sorin.* Like a compass directing a sailor through a storm, I close my eyes and imagine Elora's face. *Where are you?* I picture her touch. *Tell me where you are?* Her taste and smell. The freckles strewn about the bridge of her nose. *Let me help you.* The way her golden eyes flash when she's angry. The sounds she makes when I kiss her neck and the way her hair always smells of jasmine. I picture every last inch of her until *there it is.*

A tug.

A direction.

Then, I'm running.

Racing through the darkness, I don't see the stone wall before I crash into it with full force. Sucking in a breath from the sudden impact, I re-ground myself and push my ear against the stone, waiting to hear her again.

"Elora!" I shout, but can she hear me? A deep shattering sound pounds through the dark as the stone rumbles and roars beneath my hands, as if it's being ripped apart from within.

Earth rolls beneath me as deep cracks splinter down the walls of the cage.

Planting my feet firmly on the ground, I use all my weight to push against the crumbling wall, leveraging my body to widen the cracks now spiraling down. Large chunks of stone crash on the opposite side and I hear Elora yelp. Blinding pain shoots up my arm and in an instant, I'm on my knees. I brace myself on all fours, the pain comes again. Piercing and hot.

My chest heaves as I push the sleeve of my shirt up, the ink from my bargains swirling and angry. The lines of black bubble and hiss. Each breath is torturous as the pain grows more and more unbearable. Sitting back on my heels, I grip my arm, gritting through my teeth. Another scream from inside the cage and all of my pain ceases. Because getting her out is more important than whatever the hell is happening to me.

"Get on your feet, Elora!" I shout, pulling myself to my feet as well. "Put your hand through the stone." I have no idea if she can hear me, but I shout anyway, any direction I can give her, to make sure she is fighting to get out. She must get out. A crack deepens in the center of the stone cage, and through it, I can see Elora's hand. Wedging in as far as she can, I pry apart the stone, pushing my own arm through as deep as it can go. Heavy pieces of stone and earth crumble to the ground as I push my arm deeper, until finally, I have her in my grip.

The moment our hands touch through the stone, a flash of white light illuminates in the darkness. Then, a violent thrash of magick has the cage crumbling completely right as Elora's body convulses. Yanking her arm, I swiftly scoop her into my own before the tumbling rocks devour us both. Her head swings heavily as she rolls into unconsciousness.

Move, Sorin.

Darting the opposite way of the stone cage, I don't look back even when the many screams of Grawgeth sound as if they're mere inches away.

The distorted birch trees curve into a tunnel. The faint

morning light at the end and Elora's steady breaths give me the last bit of strength I need. My feet carry us feverishly through. Step by step, I will get us out of here. Alaric and Ruse's howls lead me in the correct direction, and despite the burning of my lungs, I push on. *Almost there.* As my boots pass the final threshold of the woods, an array of voices scream behind me. Different languages, most of which I can't understand.

Grawgeth.

Completely winded, I topple out of the trees, still clutching Elora to my chest as Galen, Sam, and Jarek meet us on the other side. "Is she hurt?" Sam asks, at my side in an instant. Unable to find my own voice, I nod my head, still trying to catch my breath.

"Set her down." Galen's tone is firm, but I do as he says, gently laying Elora onto the forest floor, swallowing down the fear that creeps up my throat. Galen sets to work. Checking Elora's pulse, putting his head to her chest to make sure her breathing isn't labored, visually checking for any wounds. A small speck of blood is smeared under her chin, but it's nothing compared to her foot. Peeling off her boot, the damage is evident. Dark red and swollen, I swear under my breath.

Ruse disappears to the forest while Alaric stays glued to my side, letting out the occasional whimper as we both watch Galen work. Galen sets back on his heel as the massive wolf approaches his side, nudging Elora's limp arm. Tipping his head back, he lets out a long, low howl.

"She's breathing steadily and from what I can tell the only injury is to her right foot," Galen says. His voice is assured but there's a slight tension in it that has my nerves on edge. Pushing the hair back from his eyes, I can see the wearisome look he was averting. "It could be broken, but I can't be certain. Regardless, it will take some time to heal. I have a tonic in my pack, it will help alleviate some of the pain. As for the rest," he continues, shrugging his shoulders, "she could be in shock, I'm not sure. All we can do now is monitor her until she regains consciousness and make sure she doesn't decline."

"And if she does?" Sam's voice cracks as she untucks herself from Jarek's arms. "If she declines?"

Galen's sigh is long and labored, as if he, himself, fights some other emotion he refuses to show. "Then we take it from there."

"Set up the tents, we'll camp here until she wakes," I say. Kneeling down, I brush a few strands of hair from Elora's face. Jarek's hand is heavy as it rests atop my shoulder.

"Sorin," Jarek says, "we have no idea how long she could be unconscious. If we don't keep moving—"

"It wasn't a suggestion," I snap, keeping my focus on Elora. Shrugging his hand off my shoulder, I lift her head and tuck my cloak under it. "Set up the tents."

Without another word, the sounds of scuffling starts behind me. Of course, Jarek is right. This is not the most protected spot to camp for the night. Especially since Elora used her magick, I have no doubt hunters are already on our trail. All my mind can focus on is her. Whatever comes next, we can handle it.

Alaric sits at my side, watching Elora just as intently as I do. Brushing a kiss to her forehead, it is only then I realize, I no longer bear any ink on my arm.

NIGHT FALLS in a deep shroud of purple, the crackling of the fire offers the only break in silence as the four of us sit huddled around for warmth. The elevation gain on the other side of the Wicked Wood does not go unnoticed. Summer is a distant memory as yellowing leaves litter the ground. I bundled Elora in both of our cloaks, though with how closely both wolves have kept to her, I'm not sure she needs them. Jarek wordlessly helped me lift her to my tent, tucking her in with a beast flanking either side of her.

I sit facing the tent around the hissing fire, thoughts of dread pooling in my mind when I feel Sam's hand slip into mine.

"She'll be all right, Sorin." Reluctantly, I pull my gaze from the tent to face her. "I know she will," she says. Her voice is comforting, though I'm not sure she even believes what she's saying. Squeezing her hand, I offer a quick nod and half-hearted smile before returning my eyes to the tent. I should not have brought us here.

"When we were inside...the Wicked Wood," Jarek starts, as he tosses another log into the flames. "Did any of you...hear anything?" The rippling plumes dance in the sky as the new log crackles and burns.

"I heard voices," Sam whispers, her eyes distant as she watches the flames. "I swear I could hear my father."

"I heard voices too," Jarek says, nodding. Crossing his giant arms, he leans forward for a bit more warmth. I peer to Galen who also nods, silently confirming that they had all heard the same thing. Voices of their past. I can't help but think of the memory brought forth in the Wood. My mother and Elora's mother. How they spoke of the Fates. How Elora and I would find each other.

"The voices I heard sounded just like my sisters," Jarek continues, pulling me from my memory, "but something was different about them. Like they were trying to talk under water, muffled and cloudy. But still, I'm sure it was them." He runs a hand down his face and over his beard before he leans back from the flames and glances toward Sam and I. "Why didn't you tell us of the bargain?" Jarek isn't normally one to push for the truth but after how today went, I don't blame him for being curious. Sam sucks in a breath, but I cut her off before she can begin.

"I should have, and I'm sorry I didn't," I admit, and I mean it. "I should have given you the opportunity to say no, to decline coming here." I pull my attention to Sam. "I'm sorry, Sam. I shouldn't have put you in this situation again." She leans her head against my shoulder, and I'm grateful for my sister. For her kindness and forgiving nature, even if I don't deserve it. Especially when I don't deserve it.

"What does another year sooner mean, exactly?" Galen asks, crossing his arms behind his head before settling back onto a fallen log.

"It means," I say, as Sam straightens herself from my shoulder, "I would have given Grawgeth my life one year earlier than I originally agreed."

"And when did you agree?" Galen asks again, his tone curt and icy. I don't blame him for being unhappy with me, I withheld the truth from him as well. "When were you going to give her your life? Your soul?"

Swallowing, I eye my friend through the flames. His sharp face and blue eyes show no sign of worry, only curiosity, though his voice tells a different story. "I bargained the last ten years of my life to the nymph to save Samaria. And this time, I agreed she could...have me one year sooner. Freeing her from the woods. I would have taken her place." Shame and guilt riddle my insides as I say the words aloud, but it was the only way to save Sam then, and it was the best way to save everyone this time.

"But you don't know when the last ten years of your life will be," Galen says, keeping his narrowed eyes locked on me.

"Correct," I say with a shrug. "The bargain could be called in today. Tomorrow. I wouldn't have known."

"Reckless," Jarek says, moving to slide in next to Sam.

"True," I agree.

"Why take the throne, Sorin? Why bother with any of it if that were to be your outcome?" Galen's brash words shock me, but I have no doubt it's because he is worried. Because I know he cares even when he works so hard to pretend he doesn't. He has built a hardened shell, keeping himself safe from even the most scrutinizing of people. He's had to, to protect himself. Being different in a world that expects conformity is the kind of bravery the poets write about in books, but the kind of rebellion that will land you in the gallows.

"Because if I am on the throne, even for a day, I can dictate who the next heir is," I say, leaning forward with my elbows on my knees. "It's been the law since Queen Solei and King Bastian. They made it as such—"

"I know the law," Galen says, an edge to his tone. "The first born child will have the throne, and the next in line will be the second born and so on. If an heir is not able to be produced and there is no other bloodline, the residing king and queen shall choose the next to rule as they see fit. That doesn't explain why you had to risk yourself."

"So I can leave the world a better place by ensuring Roman no longer rules," I snap. Sam flinches but she keeps her eyes trained on the fire. "Do you not think all of this is worth it? To stop him and all he's done to Enchantresses? To our country?"

Galen leans forward, cocking his head to the side. "I suppose," he says with a shrug of indifference.

"Though, something...interesting has come up," I say, ignoring a feeling I can't quite explain itching at my skin. Pushing my sleeve back, I angle my arm toward the flames, revealing my now bare skin.

"How?" Sam gasps, reaching for my arm, her eyes rake over every inch of it. "Is the bargain broken?"

"I can't be sure," I say. "But, I have a suspicion someone else will know." The four of us turn our heads to the tent to where Elora rests.

Squeezing Sam's hand before standing, I stretch my cold limbs over the fire before retreating to my tent. "You should all call it a night. The weather changes quickly this high up, and I want everyone warm and rested for tomorrow."

THE WOLVES PERK their ears as I pull back the canvas of the tent. Kneeling, I peel off my boots and leave them at the entrance before climbing inside. Holding out my hand, an offering to Ruse who sits closest to the door, she quickly declines, pushing her nose in the air and away from my touch. If it wasn't for the seriousness of the day I may have laughed at the response. Something about it reminds me so much of Elora when we first met.

Turning my attention to Alaric, the two wolves take up the entire tent. "I think I've got it from here," I whisper to the massive gray wolf. Studying me for a moment, he takes his time standing, arching his back in a deep stretch before nudging Ruse out of the tent.

I watch as the door to the tent flaps closed, the voices of my family around the fire begin to quiet, then I turn to face Elora. She's still wrapped in both of our cloaks as well as the furs we packed. Scooting closer, I brush my thumb along her forehead. Her eyelids twitch slightly at my touch and brows pinch together, the reaction gives me hope. She's still in there. Still here.

The chill of evening creeps in through the seams of our tent as the soft glow of orange from the fire dissipates into nothing. Pulling out the last of the furs, I lean down to place a kiss to Elora's forehead before finally allowing myself to lie down. Pulling the fur up to my chin, I let out a final whisper, "Please wake up, love." Then, as quickly as night arrived, so does sleep.

CHAPTER 36
ELORA

I'M DROWNING.

The water engulfs me as the light around me dims. I know I should be kicking. I should be fighting. Instead, I sink. For the first time, possibly ever, I feel at peace. The surface disappears and what's left of the sun turns to swirling black liquid. I let go. I let go of the guilt and the burdens I once bore. I let go of the responsibilities I carry like a weight on my shoulders. I let go of the last breath I've held in my lungs, not entirely sure what I've been saving it for. I push my lips forward and expel the final puff of air as it turns to tiny bubbles and close my eyes. Visions of the pooling liquid cloud my mind as my lungs begin to burn. I wait for the fight to kick in, but it never comes. So, I embrace the weightlessness of the water surrounding me. How my limbs are airy and my mind is numbingly blank. I keep my eyes closed as I wait. Wait for that final surrender. Wait for nothing at all.

My eyes snap open, and I gulp down the crisp air, immediately thankful the nightmare was nothing more than that. Whipping my head at the sound of rustling in the tent, I realize it's dark outside. Another rustling sound draws my attention and my shoulders slacken when I see it's Sorin. He's been tossing about in a restless slumber. My eyes adjust to the darkness as I watch him turn once more, this time facing me.

A deep line creases between his dark brows. His hair is messy at the crown, no doubt from the constant tossing and turning. I roll to my side to face him, the movement causing a sharp pang to pierce through my right foot. Wincing, I glance down. How could I forget about the tumbling rocks, a part of my subconscious hoping it was a dream and nothing more. But the pain is very real, which means what I did was also very real. I take a moment to examine the rest of myself. Despite escaping the rocks, I'm somewhat clean. Nails free of dirt. Skin, while prickled with tiny rips and tears, appears to have been wiped clean of everything else. I run my hand behind my neck, before Sorin's eyes slowly pull open.

"You're awake?" he gasps, his voice is a whisper but rings through an otherwise still night.

I nod and offer a breathy, "Yes." The pain in my foot is temporarily relieved as I angle myself to elevate it. The worry in Sorin's eyes washes away, his features softening as he takes me in. Sliding his hand across the furs, he grips mine.

"I can't tell you how glad I am to hear your voice," he says, kissing my hand. He holds it for a moment before placing it back down. "Galen says it's not broken," he whispers, gesturing toward my elevated foot. "He did say it'll take some time to heal, but now that you're awake he can give you a tonic for the pain."

As if reminding himself of that option, he sits up from the furs revealing his bare chest and torso. His hands are frantic in the dark as he searches for his shirt, the scene almost comical as he fails endlessly to find anything in the darkness.

"I'm fine to wait until morning," I say, "it's just a bit of bruising." I can't help the laugh that escapes me as I pull his hand closer, so he's forced to recline back. "Nothing I can't handle," I say. "Did you...clean me up?" I ask as he settles back down, scooting me closer so I'm resting my head on his chest.

"Sam and I did. Your hands and arms were so caked with blood and black, I couldn't leave you that way."

My heart beams. To be taken care of. To be cared *for*. A luxury I won't take for granted. We lay there together for several moments of silence, my head upon his warm chest listening to the steady rhythm of his heartbeat as he draws circles up and down my arm.

"Do you want to talk about what happened in there?" he asks, running his fingers through my hair.

"Not yet," I whisper, blocking the images of my mother's face from my mind.

"Okay." He plants a kiss on the top of my head. " I truly am sorry. I should have told you about who I am."

"I know," I say. And I do. He kept his identity from me just as much as I kept my past from him. While Sorin being the heir to the throne complicates whatever it is we are, it isn't fair that I remain angry at him for doing the same thing I did.

"No more secrets," he whispers, tilting my head up to meet him. "From either of us." His mouth turns upward as he bends down to kiss my lips. I press into him, savoring their full softness before nestling back onto his chest.

"Why now?" I ask. The question is vague, but I know he understands what I mean. His hands halt their dance along the sleeve of my tunic. A momentary silence sits between us.

"It wasn't always about the throne," he whispers, running his fingers through my hair again. The beating in his chest has amplified. "In fact, I didn't realize I was the heir until I was fifteen, when William died."

I tighten my grip around his torso as he continues, "I knew my mother had been wronged in Valebridge and that's why we left. But I was so young, living there is barely a memory. I close my eyes and try to remember the walls, the route we took when we left, but there's nothing but faint lines and blurry images.

"She was sick when we arrived in Loxley. Letty and Eviey tried their best to heal her. They know herbology better than the next, but Loxley is so far removed from most everything, we didn't have the resources to—" he swallows deeply, and I don't need to look to know he holds back tears. "I swore it then, even as a child. I would make whoever caused her to flee from Valebridge pay for what they'd done. The ailments they caused."

"I'm sorry you lost her," I whisper, my own chest cracking slightly for the pain I know he feels. He says nothing, his breathing heavier than before. "Isn't it exhausting?"

"What?" he asks, running his fingers down my arm.

Sighing, I press deeper into his chest. "Pretending to be okay."

Several moments of silence hang around us, and then Sorin's hands tuck under my chin.

"Yes," he admits, his eyes heavy as they meet mine. "But with you I don't feel like I have to pretend. And I hope you know with me, you don't have to pretend to be okay either." He plants a kiss to my lips, softly, and my stomach twists and swirls in response.

"Tell me more," I say, settling back onto his chest. "I want to know it all."

Taking a deep breath, Sorin continues, "As I grew older, the rumors grew with me. Whispers among the streets of Loxley of the *true heir*. I thought nothing of it until William pulled me into his room his final night. It was so hard to see him that way. He was always so strong, so brave. And here he was, frail and weak, and I hate that it's my last memory of him. That night he pulled me in and told me everything. My mother, Celia, was an Enchantress for King Silas, she was a Memoria." Sorin continues to play with my hair as he speaks, twirling and twisting the strands around his fingers. Memoria's are rare but so powerful. They have the ability to see one's memories simply by touch. I've never met one in my lifetime, it's no surprise Sorin's mother was an important Enchantress to the King.

"William told me that Silas and my mother had more of a relationship than they let on. A romantic relationship, which you and I both know at the time was against the law throughout the Kingdom." I let out a soft sigh because I know what he says to be true. There are strict rules against Enchantresses marrying or having intimate relations outside of their arrangement. "Her arrangement was never set, apparently Silas couldn't stand to see her with another man."

I remember learning of the arrangements. Made by the king and queen, simply put together to help Enchantresses bear a child. To keep magick in Valebridge, at the fingertips of the royals. It's how my mother came to meet my father, though he was long gone before I was born.

"And thus forth, from their forbidden romance, came me," Sorin continues. "My mother kept her pregnancy a secret the best she could, and somehow with the help of the other Enchantresses managed to live several years with me by her side in Valebridge. No one had a clue about her affairs with Silas, until Silas himself was forced to marry."

"Queen Rhoda," I whisper, my memories of the late queen are faint. Having passed a few years after the birth of Roman.

"I don't remember much after that," Sorin admits but his heartbeat is erratic. "Though in the Wicked Wood, a memory came to me that may explain...a few things."

"What do you mean?"

He takes a large breath, his chest rising then falling slowly as he lets it out. "The Wicked Wood revealed to me the day my mother and I fled Valebridge," he whispers. "I was nearing my fifth year, she had been frantic all morning after hearing about Rhoda being with child. We went to visit—" He stops, his breaths quicken as if he's nervous to say, "your mother."

Bolting upright, I spin so I'm facing him. "What?"

Sorin's hand runs down my back, the movement slow and reassuring. Like he knows how destructive the mere mention of her can be.

"In the memory I saw today, we visited your mother before fleeing Valebridge. And now that it's been brought forth, I do in fact remember meeting her many times." He smiles, his eyes crinkling at the edges. He's tired, but I have to know more. "She was lovely, kind."

I close my eyes as tears threaten to fall. Sorin pulls me back down so I'm laying on his chest again. Taking a few slow breaths, I focus on the warmth of his skin.

"Your mother and mine were friends," he whispers. "The memory was so clear, so familiar I'm surprised it never occurred to me before. But the mind is particular about what it decides to conceal, and mine must have decided long ago to block out the parts of my past that pain me the most. Like leaving Valebridge and watching my mother fall ill." I run my hand down his chest and press my eyes shut. "Maybe that's why you seem so familiar to me," he says, kissing the top of my head.

"I don't know why, but it makes me happy that you knew her," I admit through the lump in my throat.

"From what I remember, she was wonderful. Though a bit intense," he laughs, and I do too because she really was. "But there's something else." His hands stop on my back, so I prop myself up so I can meet his eyes.

"What is it?" I ask cautiously. His dark eyes scan my face as if he's searching for something. "What?" I ask again, a ping of something I can't place growing inside of me.

"In my memory today, your mother was still pregnant with you," he says, running his hand down my back. "She said that we were destined by the Fates to cross paths."

Chapter 37
Elora

My stomach drops, flipping and somersaulting, but I keep my eyes locked on Sorin. I open my mouth, then quickly clamp it shut.

"And what is it the Fates have planned for us?"

Sorin shrugs, his eyes tracing the lines of my face. "I haven't a clue," he admits. "But whatever it is, I'm sure glad for it." He kisses me, just once, softly on the mouth.

This feeling—this over powering, all consuming drive to be close to him makes sense. Every moment we've touched, like the first time and yet it's so familiar. So comfortable. The Fates have been quiet since the founders of Valebridge, King Bastian and Queen Solei, died centuries ago. Why the Fates have decided Sorin and I must be woven together is beyond me. The thought is too much. Too frightening to know your soul is tied with another's. Is that all this attraction is, simply the Fates?

"Say something," Sorin whispers, breaking our gaze, focusing his attention on my hand that's placed on his bare chest.

"What was it that she had?" I ask, avoiding the truth of Sorin's memory like a coward. Not willing to face that his feelings may be a force outside of our control. "Your mother?"

Sorin's smile fades as his eyes meet mine. "Letty and Eviey had never seen anything like it. I used to ask Agnes all the time, but she would always just say it was nothing more than a broken heart. The older I get, the more inclined I am to believe her. Though, more realistically, I'm certain Silas sent a Plague after her when she left."

My blood boils at the thought. Plagues have the ability to cause sickness through thought alone. All they would need is a piece of the recipient. An item of recently worn clothing, a piece of hair.

"He spared you," I say quietly.

"It would appear so," he says. "That, or my mother made sure there was nothing left of me in Valebridge for the Plagues to track."

I remain sitting with my hand on his chest, scouring his face. Trying desperately to absorb the slew of information.

"Once I knew the truth about who my father was, I couldn't get it out of my mind," Sorin continues. "Vengeance was always my goal, getting back at those who wronged my mother. Then, when Silas died so suddenly, I pushed the thought away. I was content with my life in Loxley knowing the man who hurt my mother was buried beneath the dirt. And with William gone, I wanted to be there for Agnes and Sam. I didn't care about the throne, the titles. I didn't care about anyone but my family. Until the uprising happened, or what Roman calls the uprising.

"Rumors of Enchantresses being beaten and magick ripped from them. Or hunted by anyone who fled. Women just like my mother and Agnes being abused. I couldn't sit back and do nothing anymore. And then, the blight started and I could see the affects along the coast. Within the Trinity Forest. And then, I met you." His lips brush the top of my head, and I slide my hand over his smooth chest in return.

"I met you, and you reminded me that the goal all along wasn't revenge. It's justice. And not only for her, but for all the

Enchantresses Roman has wronged. If I can get before the council, or better yet, the Guilds, I can prove I'm the true heir. We can put a stop to all of this once and for all. Galen, Jarek, Sam, and I have had a plan in place for a long time, but it was never complete," he pauses, a hitch in his breath. "It's as if a piece of myself has always been missing and I've gone my entire life searching for it."

My stomach turns again, because I have felt the exact same way. Aimlessly wandering, wondering if I'll ever feel whole again.

"Then, there you were. Scowling at me by the river," he laughs, so I pinch his side. "Honestly though," he says through another laugh, "I knew you were someone special the moment we met. And truthfully, no one wears a scowl better than you."

I lean up again, so we're face to face. I run my fingers through his hair and pull him forward until our foreheads are touching.

"If it's too much for you...the kingdom. The title. Whatever this is with the Fates," Sorin whispers, letting the words hang in the air. "All you have to do is say. I won't force you to do anything you don't want."

Fear is what I've sensed growing in my chest.

Blooming.

Spreading across my insides like a forest fire.

Fear that our plan will work. Fear that it will not.

"A deal is a deal, after all," I say as playfully as I can muster, the light tug on my hair from Sorin an indication the joke was received. "And besides, who are we to defy the Fates?" I offer a tired smile as I lean back, giving him some space. If Sorin's memory serves him, and my mother Saw our souls connected by the Fates, it's all the proof I need.

"I want you to know everything, Elora. The good and the bad. I'll tell you all of it. If it's what you want." His fingers run up and down my arm, tickling my skin. "Just promise me you'll tell me everything too. A clean slate going forward." His arms tighten around my middle. "So, promise me, from here on out, if this is what you want too, we're a team. We do everything *together.*"

Together.

It is fast becoming my favorite word.

"Do you promise?" he asks again, bringing my hand up and brushing a kiss to the backside. Fighting off a blush, I push myself up, letting my forehead rest against his again.

"Promise."

Liar.

"What would you have done?" I ask, running my hand across his abdomen. "If you had gotten the throne, the bargain would have brought you back to the woods eventually, right?"

"Yes," he says, dragging his fingers through my hair. "But to be king would have given me the power to name anyone I'd like as an heir. Blood or not."

"And who would you have named?"

His fingers curl around the back of my neck. "Samaria, of course," he says. "Who better to wear a crown than she?"

To that, I can't argue.

"But now," he says, "that the bargain is broken, all thanks to you, maybe I could stay king a little longer. Now that I don't have this...debt hanging over me, I feel even more ready to give myself completely. To you." My stomach tightens, dipping and falling in a tumble of guilt.

Leaning forward, I claim his mouth with my own before he has a chance to speak any further. To say whatever it is he wants to say.

"Must you always speak, thief?" I ask, breaking our kiss apart and echoing my words to him from the cavern.

Sorin cuts me that ear to ear grin, and I completely lose myself in it. I sink into his touch, kissing him again, the moan that is muffled behind our kiss sends a thrill down my spine. My stomach is a frenzy of flurrying motions as Sorin's kiss intensifies. A mix of tongue and his soft lips, we kiss each other deeply, like he is oxygen and I am a woman deprived.

My hands drag down his torso, taking in the warmth of his body, the curves of his muscles. His hands are in my hair, fisting around the locks at the nape of my neck. I attempt, and fail, to swing myself around to his lap. Forgetting, momentarily, the injury to my foot, I wince as it hits the ground. I land halfway in his lap and halfway off the furs. A broken giggle escapes my lips and Sorin soon chimes in with his own laughter.

"Easy, Enchantress." His voice is low and raspy as he scoops me up. "I'm going to need you to save your energy." In one swift movement I find myself flat on my back with Sorin positioned over me. The rising light outside reveals the shape of his body against mine. Tracing his fingers along the seam of my tunic, he slowly pulls it over my head. The shock of the cooler air over my exposed skin combined with the trace of Sorin's fingers along my torso leaves me gasping. Lowering himself over me, he runs his fingers through my hair, tugging gently at the scalp.

His lips part as if to say something, then quickly snap shut. I can see the contemplation in his dark brown eyes and I know what he wants to say. Because I want to say it too, but I don't give either of us the chance. That even if we weren't destined by the Fates, even if our lives were not stitched together by a higher power, we *would* still choose each other. I don't know how, but I am certain.

Gripping his hair, I tug him forward until his mouth again meets mine. A clash of tongues leaves me moaning as Sorin kisses me deeply, running his hands over my bare chest and through my hair. I writhe my body underneath him, liquid heat courses through me at the memory of the caverns. I think of all the places his mouth touched. All the places I want it to touch now.

His hands catch on my breeches.

"Lift your hips for me, Elora," he whispers, and so I do.

Carefully, he pulls my breeches over my injured foot, leaving a trail of soft kisses from my ankle up to my inner thigh before unlacing and removing his own pants and tossing them to the side.

Then, he takes his time to learn every part of me with his hands, every curve, every dip, before bending down to my abdomen. Slowly, he makes his way lower, dragging a finger through my middle. My head falls back as I struggle to pace my breathing. His movements are slow, steady, just that one finger will be my undoing. I lift my hips forward, encouraging him, but he doesn't move.

Dragging his finger again through my center, he traces his thumb over the sensitive bundle of nerves at the apex of my thighs. I drape my arm over my mouth and bite down to stifle the moan that I'm certain will wake the others. As if sensing my hesitation, Sorin stops his movements as he pulls my arm from my mouth. He kisses it all the way down until he reaches my hand.

Then, he kisses my mouth, my neck, my collarbones before nudging my legs open gently with his own. "I don't care who hears you," he says, dropping his hand from mine to grip himself. Wrapping my legs around his waist, I push my hips forward.

"Don't hold back," he whispers, dipping his head down so our foreheads meet, mimicking his words from the cavern. Gripping the back of my thighs, his fingers dig deeply into my skin. My words fail me as my eyes close with anticipation, his skin against mine lighting a fire within me.

My body aches for him but before I can beg, his words are low and dominant. "Eyes on me, love. I want to see you when you come undone." His demand has me snapping my eyes open. The thought is too intimate. To allow someone to see you at your most vulnerable. But when I meet his eyes, I'm reminded of how far we've come. That even without the Fates, I wouldn't want anyone else to see me this way.

Only him.

As if reading my mind, he guides himself in. Fighting the urge to close my eyes, I instead keep them locked on his. Gasping, I arch my back as he begins to move. I wrap my legs tighter, pulling him further into me.

His thrusts are rhythmic and slow, but I'm too impatient. His grip around my thigh tightens as he traces up my body with his free hand, over the peaks of my breasts, up to the sensitive skin of my throat before wrapping around my back, hoisting me up so I am in his lap, our chests flush with one another. I run my fingers through his hair, tugging him closer still.

Gripping his back, my nails dig slightly into the muscled planes of his shoulder blades. His pace quickens as our hips begin to roll in unison, pleasure swirls deep within me. Sorin grips my hair with one hand, using the other to hold me in place on top of him. I bite down on his shoulder to stifle another moan as his teeth scrape along the side of my neck, my name leaving his mouth in a breathless gasp.

My body ignites under his touch, ready to explode any minute as the hot friction between us grows. Sweat slicks between our bodies despite the cold air. His mouth finds mine, and I bite his bottom lip as he breaks away from another needy kiss. Tension coils low in my abdomen, but I fight it, I can't be done yet. I need this moment. I'll always need more of it. Furrowing my brow, I slow my pace only slightly.

Sorin grips my hair, the pull of it just hard enough to form the perfect mix of pain and pleasure. Rolling my hips over and over again, pleasure explodes within me, my vision blurs but I don't need it to know Sorin's watching me, which only heightens my senses.

The Fates were determined for us to find each other, for whatever reason I don't know. But I don't care. Because he is everything.

Our bodies move in sync with each other, slowing as I hold onto Sorin. Wrapping my arms around his neck, I bury my face into the crook between his neck and shoulder. Breathing heavily, Sorin slowly removes himself and the sudden lack of him is jarring.

I drop my arms, frowning in protest, but Sorin is quicker than my words. Spinning me around so I'm face down, body flush with the furs beneath me.

"Elora..." he whispers, running his hand delicately down my spine.

"Yes?" My voice comes out breathy, my body on edge in the best way as he lowers the weight of himself behind me to whisper in my ear.

"On your knees, love."

I do as he says, bringing my knees up so my face remains buried in the furs beneath me. My body aches as he runs his hands up the backs of my legs. He resumes his grip on my hips before thrusting himself back in. Finding our rhythm, waves of pleasure ripple over me as I near another release. Leaving my hips, Sorin's hand dips between my legs, finding that sensitive bundle of nerves, lighting me on fire.

I breathe out his name as waves of pleasure crash through me over and over again. Sorin replaces his hands on my hips as his pace quickens and breathing becomes ragged. He finds his own release with a deep moan as I lay breathless underneath him. His movements begin to slow, our breaths begin to steady, the ache between my legs finally satiated.

For now.

His hands trace lines along my back and through my hair as he lowers himself next to me, his chest and forehead slicked with sweat. Rolling to my side to face him, I run my hands through his damp hair before pulling him in for another kiss. Pulling himself away, he buries his face into the crook of my neck and takes a deep inhale. "You are incredible," he whispers against my skin, and my body lights up as if we hadn't just been together moments ago. My chest warms but my eyes become heavy, the weight of his arms and words drape around me like a thick blanket. I open my mouth to say anything back but instead find myself kissing the top of his head before resting my chin there.

I am undoubtedly yours, Sorin once said to me. And now I know without a sliver of doubt, that I am his too.

It takes several moments for Sorin to fall asleep. The deep rise and fall of his chest against mine has become my own personal lullabye. I wait a few moments longer, making sure he truly is asleep before I reach up and run my fingers over the back of my neck.

I trace the raised flesh, recognizing the circular pattern. A match, I'm sure, to the mark Sorin wore before I broke his bargain. Truly surprised the mask held while unconscious, I'm grateful I have more time before I must tell another secret.

Just one more secret. I try to convince myself.

Despite the brightness of the morning light trickling through the tent, I close my eyes and succumb to sleep.

CHAPTER 38

ELORA

MY EYES PRICKLE WITH TEARS AS I WATCH THE remaining plumes of smoke rise to the sky from our morning fire, my mind torn on the relief of being out of the Wicked Woods and the reality that soon enough, I'll be bound to them. Sorin and I spent most of yesterday in our tent, sleeping and also, not sleeping. The rumble of our stomachs reminding us we need to leave the comfort of the canvas sooner than later. I've perched myself against a fallen tree, watching where the Wicked Woods meets the moss-ridden ground where we've camped. The memory of the horrors held inside flash behind my eyes. The darkness of the cage. My mother's face. The thick black tar that spilled from Grawgeth's chest as I sliced it open. The bargain I made.

Swallowing deeply, I grieve the loss of the souls trapped in the birch trees I can't save. Once I am there, I vow to myself to release them somehow. The crunch of leaves under boots draws my attention backward. Galen approaches with his black pack slung neatly over his shoulder. He says nothing as he takes a seat. The silence is comfortable as we both stare at the smoke rising to the sky. The clinking of glass rattles in my ears. Peering over my shoulder, he holds out a small vial.

"I need you to take this," Galen says, gesturing to the vial. Clear liquid sloshes around as he passes it over to me. Uncorking the top with my teeth, I toss it back without a question of what it is. Galen's eyes roam over me as I wipe my mouth clean of the foul-tasting liquid, handing back the empty vial. "That should help the pain in your foot," he says, "another day or two and you should be back to walking normally." I nod before returning my focus to the woods.

"Thank you," I manage to say, grimacing at the aftertaste still dancing on my tongue.

Another clinking noise. Turning my head, he holds out a second vial, this one smaller than the last. The liquid inside a deep red, tiny gold flecks catches against the late morning light.

"And what's that for?" I ask, gesturing to the vial as he rolls it between his fingers before tossing it to me.

"That"—he points to the glass as I catch it—"is so we don't have a bunch of little Sorin's running around." Heat blooms over my cheeks as my mouth drops open. Of all the people to talk about this with, Galen is certainly last on my list. He lets out a huff of air that could *almost* pass as a laugh.

"Take it once a month. Until you know...until you decide not to, if you decide not to. Samaria's on the same tonic." I snap my mouth shut but before I can thank him again, he turns away and saunters back toward the camp. I run the vial through my fingers before removing the top and tossing it back in one gulp.

We've decided we can only spare one more night before we must move, and while I agree my foot does not. So I spend the rest of our last day around the fire, forcing myself to rest.

"How many others were there?" I ask Galen as he and I sit around the fire alone while the others are off hunting or bathing in the nearby stream. He glances at me over the edge of his book.

"Not many Dyrsjel are on record, it's difficult to say," he says, setting his book into his lap. "But there were at least two bloodlines, two families known. Queen Solei was rumored but there was no factual proof, and the only other on paper is yours. The Leigh's." He strums his fingers on top of the book, his eyes finding mine. "Your magick is rare," he continues, "invaluable. Not many Dyrsjel choose to make their gift known to others, so if there are more, there's a good chance we wouldn't know."

I straighten at his words, eyeing him over the flames. The orange light flickers against his icy hair, casting a yellow glow to his skin. "It could be dangerous if it were in the wrong hands," he whispers.

Roman.

The thought makes my stomach curl. I think of Queen Solei, the original Queen of Valebridge. How she had no heirs, therefore it wouldn't be possible for a Dyrsjel to come of her bloodline. Why would the Mother choose my family? Why would she choose...me?

"And this other magick...this Elemental magick I apparently have, is it common?" I ask, flexing my fingers, ignoring the frustration lining in my gut that I have so many unresolved questions. Galen's teeth are perfectly straight and glisten in the firelight as he casts a rare smile.

"No," he says, leaning forward so his elbows are placed on either knee. "It would appear you are an enigma. Dyrsjel magick and an Elemental, you've got your work cut out for you." He laughs.

Laughs.

Smiling, I reach down and rub my foot, the ache becoming increasingly worse since the tonic wore off from earlier. "I still don't understand how the Elemental magick works," I admit. "It's as though it has a mind of its own."

"That's because it does," Galen says casually. I glance at him again. "Magick is like a living being. It breathes, hides, unleashes its fury just as we do from time to time." I study his face as he speaks. The sharp lines of his jaw and nose. His high cheekbones and glacial eyes. This is possibly the most alone time we've had together and as I take him in, he looks relaxed. Comfortable. "But it's why you have the wolves," Galen continues. "They're here to guide you into your magick. You are very powerful, Elora," he whispers, glancing at the flames.

Glancing at my foot, I smirk. "I don't feel very powerful at the moment."

Galen nods, then bends down and reaches for something. "Take this rock," he says before hurling it at me through the fire. The abruptness catches me off guard, and I clumsily catch the rock before it hits me in the face. I shoot a narrowed gaze that he returns with a smile. "In my hands, it's nothing more than a bit of stone. But in yours...turn it to water," he says flatly, as if he's asking me to sew a button or stir a pot of soup.

Gripping the rock in my hands, I turn it over and under a few times before calling for my magick. The wolves appear from the woods a moment later, making Galen jump slightly. I smile. "It isn't safe," I whisper. "The hunters—"

"They're likely already on our trail, practicing one more time won't hurt. We'll be gone from here long before they catch up. Now turn it to water," he says a little more firmly. Sighing, I turn my attention back to the rock. Alaric plants himself at my side, his energy bringing me the calm I need to focus.

Listen to him, Alaric says.

I glare at the giant wolf for not taking my side, then close my eyes just as I had the other day with the moose. The stone sits heavily in my hand. It's cold, smooth. Gripping it into my palm, I reach for my magick, slowly waking it up after a few days rest. My skin prickles as I focus on the rock, envisioning it turning to a pool of water.

Nothing happens.

Snapping my eyes open, I drop the rock onto the dirt.

"Keep trying," Galen says, moving to seat himself closer to me. "You can do this, Elora. I've seen how powerful you are, now you just need to believe it yourself. Lean into the wolves, let them help you."

His tone is soft, so different from when we first met. He smiles at me again and my heart warms. It's only now I realize how grateful I am for Galen. Of course, I'm grateful for Sam and Sorin and Jarek, but in a different way. I'm grateful for Sorin's passion, his ability to see me for who I am. I'm grateful for Sam's jubilant outlook on life, even when it hasn't treated her fairly. For Jarek's softness, his patience. I could easily afford to borrow any one of their best traits.

But it's Galen's firm, quiet presence that has kept me centered. He's encouraged me, in his own way. Pushed me. Believed in me but not coddled me.

I find strength in his blunt words. Comfort in the way he doesn't try to be anything but himself. Even if that means being cold and distant at times. We're not that different, he and I and it's only now that I see it. He nods in my direction, gesturing to the rock with his hands.

I find myself grounded in his confidence, his belief in me. Taking a large breath, I try again.

"You can do this," I whisper to myself, picking the rock back up.

Focusing again on the physical form of the rock, I close my eyes and envision it turning to water just as I had envisioned the branch turning to ice. Alaric's presence in my mind is like a warm blanket, or a soft pillow. Ready to catch me if I fall. So, I drop my guard completely and let him push me forward.

A few moments later, the hard stone in my hand dissipates. Snapping my eyes open, they widen in disbelief. The rock is completely gone; my hand is soaked from a puddle of water that has taken its place. Alaric licks my cheek before he settles onto the ground beside me.

I whip my head to Galen, a smile tugging at his lips before he says, "Very good."

EXCITEMENT LACES with dread as we fold up our tents the next morning, rolling them neatly and storing them into our various packs. Part of me wishes we could stay in this moment forever. With Sorin and our friends and the wolves surrounded by the trees and the songbirds. Splitting up the day-to-day tasks and ending every evening in the warmth of Sorin's arms. A beam of hope shoots through me as I envision a similar life together in Loxley. How easy it would be to slip into the same routine. How much I would love nothing more. Then, as it always does, reality crashes back into me.

Sorin's goal is not a quiet life in the woods. He will be King of Valebridge. I don't allow myself to wonder how I fit into his future, because while his goals are mountainous, so are mine. With the Stones back in Enchantress hands, there will be so much work to do before I'm bound to the Wicked Woods. I believe Sorin when he says he'll end the Enchantress oppression, but what will that mean for them? How does life after being kept in a cage for years look? How will they start again?

I haven't been sure of my place here, among the four friends, but I'm certain my destiny is grander than hiding in my cabin. My eyes fall to Sorin as he secures his bow across his back. My stomach swirls, his dark eyes narrowing as he laughs at something Jarek's said. The promises he spoke in the quiet of night now are so loud and unobtainable in the bright light of day. My skin itches as I hold the mask in place where the ink swirls up the back of my neck. Sorin catches my gaze from across the camp, his smile leaving a weakness in my knees, making me forget instantly about the annoying itch. I smile back. If this time together is all we're allotted in this life, I'll be grateful for it.

"WE'VE GOT about a day's walk to the base of Kirsgard Mountain from here," Sorin says, pausing to take a deep drink from his canteen before tightening the cap back in place. "We'll camp overnight. Then, we follow Elora's lead up the mountain." My heart drops. All these weeks this has been the plan and yet to be this close to where I lost everything, nagging doubt claws at the back of my mind.

Not good enough.

Keeping my face as neutral as possible I offer a quick nod in understanding. "There's a small path, at the base of the mountain," I say. "It's rarely used because of how dense the foliage grows there." I shut my eyes momentarily. Remembering the last time I used the trail, how the snow crunched under my boots, how the screams echoed in my ears. How it was the last time I saw my family. Sorin's hand slips into mine, anchoring me to the present.

"It's a steep trek, we'll likely be better off leaving most of our supplies hidden at the bottom. Bring only the weapons you carry on your back." I eye my friends, each of them watching me speak with such trepidation, fueling the confidence I need to do this. " Once we get to the top, I'll lead the way to where I believe the Stones remain." I take a deep breath to collect myself. I never dreamt of going back to Kirsgard, its unyielding nightmares in the years past have daunted me enough.

"If my memory serves me, the Stones are located at Nevek Peak. That's where we performed my Ceremony. That's where my mother placed them before—" I stop myself and wait for the darkness to encroach my vision. Only, it doesn't come. Rolling my shoulders, I crouch down to draw a rough map into the dirt. "This is where they'll be." My voice shakes as I point to my poorly drawn map.

"And how exactly do we remove these Stones?" Jarek asks, crouching beside me on the ground, scanning his eyes over the map.

"Dyrsjel's are the only ones who can wield the Stones," Galen chimes in before I get the chance. "Elora," he says, turning his body to face me, "will be the one to pull them out."

I nod slowly. "That's where it gets...complicated," I say, glancing up at Jarek, avoiding Galen's gaze. "I have never pulled them before. Never done a Ceremony on my own."

"You'll know what to do," Galen says with such surety I almost believe him.

"But if I don't—"

"You will," he says again, cutting me a glance. "Trust yourself." His smile reminds me of how far we've come as friends. How much we've all grown these last few weeks.

Sorin's hand finds its way to my back as I stand. "We get the Stones, perform Sam's Ceremony, then head for Valebridge." Sorin goes over the plan again, as if he's waiting for it to change.

"We haven't discussed the potential for hunters," Sam says with a sigh. "I mean, rumor is they have been looking on Kirsgard for some time, the moment we use the Stones to wield my magick, surely they'll come running. And who is to say the Stones haven't been retrieved by another Dyrsjel?"

"They haven't," I blurt out, everyone's eyes landing on me in an instant. "I think I'm the only one of us left, there isn't any other Dyrsjel to pull them." Sam nods, but says nothing. Grawgeth believed me to be the last Dyrsjel. Even though Galen says there's a second bloodline, something deep inside of me confirms I'm the last.

"Better to plan for the hunters' presence than be surprised by it," Jarek says, tossing Sam a determined look. "If they're there, we'll be ready. Besides, this close to the rainy season deters most from traveling to the mountains anyway."

Sam sighs, slinging an arm around my shoulder. "That's true, I suppose," she says. "Our powerful Dyrsjel." She smiles, the jubilant tone of her voice returning. "Our fate is in your hands."

MY FOOT ACHES and swells tightly against my boot as we set up camp at the base of the Kirsgard Mountains. The chill from the elevation change settles deep in my bones as I drop and peel off my boots. A groan escapes me as I rub absently at my foot. Reading my mind, Galen passes me a familiar glass vial.

"I only have one more after this," he says, giving my shoulder a squeeze as he bends down. The liquid settles in my stomach as I swallow it down, creating a haze over my body.

WE REACHED the base of the mountain late in the day, and after agreeing it was best to wait until dawn to venture to Nevek Peak, we settled in for the night.

Inside our tent the wind hisses and slaps against the canvas. Low-hanging branches scrape against the thick fabric as Sorin and I lie awake.

"I can hear you thinking." Sorin presses his mouth to my ear before kissing it. A smile tugs at my lips as I roll to face him. Pulling my hands through his hair, I trace the outline of his face with my finger. Down his sharp jaw, over his smooth, full lips. Over the small lines that form around his eyes when he smiles.

"I'm worried I'll fail," I finally say, the admittance sounding weak and uncomfortable leaving my lips. But it's the truth. And we've sworn to be truthful, and I am trying with every breath to be that. "If I can't wield the Stones or perform the Ceremony for Sam, then this has all been for nothing."

"I don't think it's been for *nothing*." Sorin doesn't miss a beat as he grabs my hand, his lips kissing a trail up my arm, sending shivers over my skin.

"You know what I mean." I laugh even though nothing in me feels funny. Pulling my arm away, I shove him slightly, trying to ignore the lingering feeling of his lips on my skin. Would I ever tire of that?

"You'll find them, love. I know you will. And we have to try either way, don't we?" Nodding, I don't believe him but I want to. "Now," he continues, running his hands over my hips, tugging me closer to his side. "Seeing as how this could be our last night together for a while, let's make the most of it, shall we?" His smirk accentuates the dimple in his cheek and it drives me mad in all the right ways. Climbing on top of him, I pin his shoulders down with my hands until he's flat on his back. His hands drape lightly over my hips. His eyebrows raise as he laughs.

"Yes, I believe we shall," I say, lowering myself to his mouth. I hover over his lips, our breaths intertwining but not kissing him before whispering, "Arms up, thief."

He lets out a low laugh before obliging and lifting his arms above his head. I plant a soft kiss on his lips before moving my mouth to his neck, intentionally going slow. Ensuring he gets the same torturous treatment he gave me in the cavern. Kissing, licking, and nipping my way over his neck, to his broad shoulders, across his chest. Sorin's breathing is heavy as he meets my eyes, something dark flashing in them before I work my way lower. His hands reach for my hair but my narrowed glance has him laughing, putting his hands back where I told him to, above his head.

Dragging my tongue down the toned lines of his stomach, he moans as I slip my hands beneath his trousers, pulling them down and off. My tongue trails down the length of him. I dare a glance up. His eyes are on me, hungry and desperate.

So I do it again, slowly, until he's moaning my name this time.

"*Fuck*, Elora," he whispers. Casting him a glance to make sure his hands are in place, I smirk as I see him clench his fists above his head. Lowering my mouth on him again, I'm interrupted by Sorin's hands gripping my hair. I spring my head up to snap at him, but before I get the chance he hauls me up toward him, crashing his mouth into mine before peeling off my breeches, then my top.

"You have a very wicked little mouth," he says, gripping my hair.

It doesn't take long to find our rhythm. To find our pleasure. He knows exactly how to move, where to touch, what to say.

Sliding myself off of him, we both lie breathlessly for a few moments. My head swirls and my stomach dips knowing that he is mine.

And I am his.

Sorin's rough hands grip my chin, turning my face toward him. His dimple greets me as does his deviant smile. "See," he says, brushing my wild hair back from my face. "Not all for nothing."

THE NIGHTMARES HAVE LESSENED over the past few days, and I find myself slipping more and more easily into sleep. Until tonight.

Shooting upright at the same time, Sorin and I catch each other's gaze through the darkness of our tent. A silent exchange of understanding as another deep howl sounds from outside.

"It's Alaric." I'm up and pulling my clothes and boots on

before Sorin has time to respond.

Rushing out into the violence of the wind, I quickly remember I'm not wearing my cloak. The bite of the cold is a momentary distraction before I'm soon surrounded by Galen, Jarek, and Sam. Another howl, but this time it's not just Alaric. Ruse's higher pitched howl joins him and my heart races as I squint through the darkness trying to decipher where it's coming from. I don't hear Sorin approach, but his presence is heavy and warm as he stands by my side.

"Where are they?" Sam asks, as she appears beside us. Jarek wastes no time grabbing both his axes.

"I don't know," I stammer. "With...with the wind it's impossible to tell which direction they're coming from." Panic floods my veins as the darkness begins to set in around my eyes. Squeezing them shut, I count silently to three. *Now is not the time*! I hiss at the voices dancing in my ears. Cold hands cup my chin, forcing my eyes to open.

Galen.

He stands before me, his striking blue eyes hold no sign of fear. No worry. "You do not need to *hear* them, Elora. You just need to *feel* them," he says. His tone is soft in a way that makes me actually believe in myself. "The same way you've been practicing." I try to shake my head but his grip remains tight.

"I can't do it," I plead, darkness pulling at my vision. "I have no idea where they are."

"Take a deep breath," he continues. "Take a deep breath and then close your eyes and *reach out* for them." My eyes dart to Sorin, his brows furrow but he nods his head. Fear chokes me as I try to speak, so I opt not to. Another howl. Another shriek. Shaking my head, Galen grips my chin again.

"Listen to me," he hisses. "Nothing in this world is promised, least of all life. You can either sit here and wallow in your self-proclaimed misfortune or do something about this. Your wolves are out there, and they need you. Use your magick and the bond to find them."

Swallowing deeply, I attempt to nod my head but his grip is too firm. Easing up slightly, his fingers relax before sliding back into his pockets.

"Now," he says calmly. "Try again."

Closing my eyes, I take a deep breath, the cold air fills my lungs. The sound of the howls encompass my mind. I allow them to carry me through the angry gust of wind that sweeps past our camp. I picture Alaric and Ruse. Their coats, the way they move. The angles of their teeth and the shape of their paws. Pressing my eyes shut tighter, so tight stars begin to dance behind them, I keep them closed and picture my wolves until I'm there. Not physically, but somehow, I am *there*.

The branches moan under the weight of the wind. Alaric paces restlessly before tipping his head up, letting out another deep howl.

Distress. It's his call of distress.

My eyes, but they're not my eyes, scan the base of the trees. Nothing but Alaric and darkness. But then, a faint glow rises in the sky. A dim purple flash, and then it's gone. My attention shifts.

Ruse.

Where is Ruse?

My heart thumps loudly against my chest as I reach out and feel for her.

Her howl pierces my ears. So close, yet I cannot see her. Alaric paces frantically, each step of his paw creates a deep divot into the dirt. I watch him helplessly as he continues his repetitive path. Back and forth. Back and forth. It's now I realize, he isn't just pacing. His head dips down with each step. He's looking at something.

Ruse.

I suck in a sharp breath as my eyes flick open. Losing my balance, Sorin's there to catch me before I fall.

"Something's happened to Ruse." I struggle to get the words out. "I could see Alaric, he's upset. And Ruse... I could hear her but..." Once I am stable enough on my feet, Sorin ducks behind me back into our tent.

"Where are they? Could you tell?" Jarek steps closer, his axes glistening under the silver moon. I shake my head, searching for something. Any indication of where they are.

But there *was* something. "A light," I whisper. "I saw a flashing light in the sky."

"The Elsk star." Galen says, slinging his pack on his shoulders. "That's it, there." Pointing behind us, I spin and sure enough, a faint flash of purple light appears in the night sky. "We'll head north." Turning toward me, he squeezes my shoulder. "I told you, you could do it," he whispers with a wink.

"Let's go," Samaria says, her ivory bow glowing under the moonlight.

"Wait, you're all coming?" I face the three of them as Sorin emerges from our tent behind me. Handing me my cloak I sling it around my shoulders, thankful he thought to keep me warm amidst the chaos. With each of Alaric's howls, my hands twitch. Ready to move. "Surely, Sorin and I can go," I say, impatience gnawing at me. "Whatever it is with the wolves, we—"

Jarek steps in front of me, his massive frame blocking my view of the star and the mountain behind it. Placing his hand on my shoulder, I tip my head up to meet his gaze.

"We're coming with you, little susi," he says. The word sounds so beautiful coming from his mouth. Sam joins him, facing me with her bow slung neatly across her back. Her smile is radiant even in the darkness. She traces the silver arrow stitched onto my cloak above my heart. The one Jarek told me about before we left Loxley.

"Together," she says. "Remember?" I scan both of their faces. Both of their cloaks. The same silver arrow etched above their hearts, like a guide through the darkness. I peer around them to Galen and then to Sorin. He says nothing but the hint of a smile plays along his lips as he nods, just once.

Together.

Another frantic howl cuts through the trees.

"We need to go now then," I say. But as I step forward, I gasp. Wincing, I glance down at my foot. Still bruised.

"Here," Galen says, bending down, he rustles in his pack before pulling out the small glass vial. "But it's the last one so if anyone else gets hurt..." he says, and everyone nods in understanding. If anyone else gets hurt, we're on our own up here. "Take it and let's go find Ruse."

Snatching the vial, I contemplate his words before deciding Ruse's life is far too important not to drink it. The effects are nearly instant, the throbbing in my foot ceases. Relief washes over me and adrenaline soon takes its place as I take off in a sprint.

My instincts guide me through the darkened trees. Running on intuition versus sight. My pace quickens as Alaric's howls grow nearer, panic crawling over my skin as the sense of something *wrong* fills the forest air. Glancing up briefly toward the sky, I locate the Elsk star. Its faint purple flashes again, the only beacon of hope I can cling to.

Alaric's gray coat glistens against the moonlight. His heavy panting leaves puffs of white in the cold air. The restlessness of his paws digs a line in the dirt. Another deep howl rumbles from his chest as I make the final stride toward him. The clearing is large, several miles of open area caged between the forest and the mountain on the opposite side. The moon is almost full again, offering her light against the darkness.

Ruse. I ask Alaric between our silent bond. *Where is she?*

But he doesn't answer me.

Breathless, the others emerge from the forest behind us as Alaric heads to where he's been pacing. Slowing my steps, I brace myself for what I might see. Alaric leads me to the edge of a steep drop off. Sucking in a sharp breath, my heart sinks when I see Ruse's body lying at the bottom of the trench.

"Ruse!" I scream, my eyes frantically assessing the quickest way to get to her.

"What the hell?" Jarek asks as he and Sorin step to either side of me. A deep trench cracks apart the earth, lined with jagged rock at the bottom and deep, dark dirt. Spanning several feet long, a few feet wide, and several more deep. There's no way she could have missed this. Unless...

"Someone did this." My words are venom as they spill from my mouth. "She wouldn't have missed this. Someone..." A lump forms in my throat as Alaric wedges himself between Sorin and I. "Someone lured her here, it's a trap. We have to get her out," I continue, Alaric's presence giving me the guidance I need. I feel for my magick, ready to turn the earth to water if I must, but nothing greets me back.

Breathe, Elora. I remind myself as if it's so easy to stay calm in a moment like this.

"We will," Sam's reassurance brings me back to the present. "We'll get her out."

A ripple of hooves sounds in the distance. We aren't alone. My eyes widen as I turn to Sorin, who I'm sure heard the same thing.

"Hunters. Or guards," Sorin says, grabbing a rope from Jarek's pack. "We need to focus on getting Ruse out before whoever is tracking us gets any closer." Wrapping the rope around a nearby tree he secures it with a knot before dragging the loose end back toward the ditch. A low growl of approval comes from Alaric.

"I'll go," I insist, taking the rope from Sorin. He hesitates. His hand flexes as I pull the rope from him.

"Be careful," he warns, quickly kissing me on the lips.

Lowering the rope into the trench, I take a last look down to Ruse. The movements of her chest are slow and irregular, but movements nontheless.

But why can't I feel her?

Chapter 39

Sorin

Reluctantly, I turn from the ditch as Elora traverses into the darkness. "How much more rope do you have?" I ask as Jarek digs through his pack.

"Not much," he says, setting a shorter spool on the ground. "Once she assesses Ruse, she'll need to wrap this around her middle and we'll hoist them up." My eyes trace back toward Alaric. His anxious pacing has halted and his eyes are now fixated on the forest from which we just came. Cocking my head to the side, I make my way toward him. As he lowers himself, the thick patch of fur on the back of his neck raises as his lips curl up revealing his lethally sharp canines. Snapping my head back to Galen, I move on instinct.

"They're getting closer," I whisper as I pull an arrow and nock it. Sam follows suit, her slender fingers tracing the body of her arrow as she watches the woods. Jarek unsheathes his axes from his back and joins her side, twirling them effortlessly in his palms.

A snap of a branch causes a chain reaction as my arm raises an arrow pointed to the woods. Alaric's growl deepens in his chest as I meet his side. Then through the darkness, I hear it again.

A deep pounding of hooves against earth rumbles beneath my feet, and before I can think any further, I launch an arrow blindly, hoping by some miracle I'll hit whatever moves toward us.

But it isn't enough.

Swarms of navy and gold encircle us, the king's crest blares brightly across the chests of the guards. *They shouldn't be here,* I think to myself but I don't have much time to ponder it. I shoot another arrow, this time successfully hitting a guard under his chin, the spray of blood coating his uniform. The clang of metal rattles my senses as Jarek disarms a guard, pulling him from his horse and finishing him off with both axes across the man's throat.

Alaric's teeth sink deeply as another guard lets out a high shrill scream. The blood gurgles from his throat, coating the wolf's fur a deep crimson. Caught up in the bloodied image, I'm thrown off as an arrow whizzes past my face and lands in the heart of an oncoming guard inches from where I stand.

Sam.

"You're welcome!" she yells through the frenzy as she readies another arrow, aiming for another guard headed her way. I nock my arrow, but she's quicker. As she's always has been.

"Awfully violent for a delicate little thing," the guard sneers. Clearly, he has no idea what he's up against. I take a step forward, launching my arrow and landing in another guard's throat a few paces behind Jarek. As the guard in front of Sam lifts his blade, she spins, dropping to one knee. Her arrow lodges in his chest before he has the time to lower his blade. He falls, the look of shock permanently locked on his face as she stands, hovering over him.

"I've been described as many things in this life," she snarls, yanking her arrow free from the man's chest as he takes his last breaths, "but delicate has never been one of them."

Steel clashing against steel draws my attention, Jarek is

locked in place with another guard. I shoot another arrow, hitting the guard right in the throat. Blood sprays across Jarek's face, but it doesn't stop him from charging the next man.

But there are so many.

Too many.

I can't pull my arrows quick enough, and even as every arrow hits its target, we're deeply outnumbered. The horses filter in leagues, and my heart sinks as I watch Samaria frantically pull arrow after arrow. As Jarek swings heavily with his ax, landing each blow but tiring by the minute. Alaric pants heavily, his coat now a muddied red.

Frantic, my eyes scan the crowd for Galen. I ready another arrow and plow through the carnage just in time to see a wash of blonde hair on the ground.

"Galen!" I shout, letting loose my arrow and cursing as it misses the guard that hauls Galen onto the back of his horse. His body lies limply across the front and I can't see his face. Panic has my feet moving and darting around the guards. "Galen!" I shout again, and this time, I hear him call my name.

But I'm too late.

I'm a gambling man by nature, but I know the odds of a successful outcome are not great. We need to flee. My breathing is ragged as I spin from the guard that has taken Galen and take off in a sprint toward the trench. It's been minutes since the ambush, minutes that feel like hours and I hope to the Mother she and Ruse are okay in there.

"Elora!" I shout, nocking my final arrow and lining it up with the guard at the entrance of the ditch. Ready to make my last kill when the hilt of a sword collides with the back of my head and suddenly, I'm on the ground. Stars dance behind my eyes as I roll to my back. The crunch of boots lands against my ear as my vision frantically tries to steady itself. I'm hauled to my feet by a guard.

"Contain the others," the guard snaps. Several men flank me, holding my arms on either side. I can tell by the demand in his voice he's a high-ranking officer. I kick my legs out and land a blow to his lower abdomen, but the grip of the guards who hold me is too tight to do much else. The officer before me stumbles backward but as he steadies himself and finds his breath, I catch his eyes.

Familiar.

My eyes drag to a mass of bloodied fur behind the officer. Alaric. I want to shout his name, but he is fighting his own battle. Bloodied and raw, he rips apart another guard as three more move in. Five more. Ten more guards flank the wolf until he disappears behind them completely out of my view.

"Can't fight your own battles, mate?" I draw my attention back to the smug officer before me. Not a single hair out of place, not a drop of blood or dirt on his pristine boots.

Tugging against the grasp of the guards, I fail to free my grip. A smile spreads over the officer's face, boiling my blood. He leaves his eyes on me as he speaks to the men holding both my arms. "Load him up." He steps closer, angling his face so it's inches away from mine. "Lucky for you, you're to remain untouched. For now."

How lucky, indeed.

CHAPTER 40
ELORA

THE DIRT IS DAMP AND COLD UNDER MY PALMS AS I make my way to the bottom. As I glance down toward Ruse, I spot a small clearing of rock to land. Using my body as a counterweight I push off the wall and swing toward the clearing. Toppling over, I catch myself on the opposite wall which stops me from landing face first on the sharp rocks. Carefully, I push myself off the wall of dirt. I will myself to be strong as I assess the damage of Ruse's fall. Gliding my hand over her back, her lungs struggle for air, but I keep moving until my hand rests under her head. Sticky warmth greets me there and I grimace as I pull back. Deep crimson coats my hand.

Swallowing deeply, I bend so my mouth is close to her ear. "I'll get you out of here," I whisper, not sure if I'm convincing the wolf or myself. Before I can shout up to the others, a familiar noise catches me off guard, lodging my voice in my throat. A whiz of an arrow is followed by a clang of steel. The hunters have caught up to us.

Voices are muffled this low in the trench, but I can distinctly make out Sorin in the mangled web of screams. Terror fills my chest as I glance between Ruse and the opening of the trench. As if sensing my debate, Ruse's eyes flick open. My lungs fill with relief as I suck in a silent breath. Bending back down to her side, I run my hand over her thick coat. She lets out a soft whimper as I scratch the spot between her ears. A high-pitched scream echoes down the trench drawing my attention upward.

Sam.

Glancing back to Ruse, I wipe the tears from my cheeks as she nudges her face into my palm that's tucked under her chin.

Go.

Her voice in my head is faint, almost as if our bond has been weakened.

"I won't leave you, Ruse." Another scream from above. My heart and mind are racing as I weigh my options. My friends need me. Ruse needs me. I cannot leave her here. I cannot leave them there.

Go.

Her voice, again. That sweet, angelic voice that matches not her disposition, but her soul. It was Ruse who told me to follow Alaric that day. Ruse who I heard when the guards attacked me. All along I thought Ruse followed Alaric's lead. The beta to his alpha. But it's been her. Our fearless leader.

A stampede of hooves thunders loudly overhead but I can't peel my eyes from her.

"She's down 'ere!" An unfamiliar voice booms through the trenches and I know it's too late.

Dipping my head, I meet Ruse's and press it firmly to mine. "I'm so sorry, Ruse." A lap of a tongue meets my salt-stained cheeks. "I'll come back for you, I promise."

Another voice echoes through the chamber of the trench but this time I can't make out what they say. All I can focus on is Ruse. With a final nudge to my hand, I watch as she releases another strangled breath. Time is frozen. I can hear my heart thud loudly through my ears. My blood rushes through my body, but it's as cold as ice. Every inch of hair on my arms and neck rises as I watch Ruse's injured body. It's as if I can feel everything and nothing all at once. I flex my palms, but my magick doesn't come. Ruse's voice fades from my mind and I am frozen.

The men above rappel down the trench. I reach for my daggers, ready to slice them open but the men's movements are too quick. There are three of them and only one of me.

Their hands grip too firmly around my arms, heavy shackles bite against my wrists as they're clasped behind my back. Kicking my feet, I land a blow to one of the men's chest, but he recovers quickly. Their laughs of victory fade as we are hauled up the trench.

I'm drowning.

The nightmare I had after the Wicked Woods wasn't a nightmare. It was a premonition. It was this. Only it isn't me who is falling into the bottomless ocean. It's Ruse. Ruse and a piece of my own heart. My vision fades, the corners of my sight turn black as the image of Ruse's injured body disappears and I'm pulled from the trench.

The slap of cold air shocks me back to the present as I'm hauled up and tossed to the ground, landing roughly on my side. Images of navy and gold flash in my peripherals, and my worry for Ruse turns to rage as the distinct depiction of a snarling grizzly kneels before me. The king's crest. Pushing myself off the ground, my hands remaining locked behind me. Ignoring the ache in my chest, my vengeance knows no bounds for whoever is responsible for this. For Ruse. For my family.

Family.

The word stings. My ears crane for their voices but all I'm met with is the incessant chattering of the guards.

Alaric! I shout, but I may as well be shouting down an empty hallway. Only the sound of my own voice echoes back.

So many guards and hunters mingle together. Laughing as if there's cause for celebration.

Then, a voice.

In the midst of the chatter and sickening laughter is a voice I know all too well.

"I finally found you," he says and my stomach churns.

Lifting my head, I brace myself for who I know I am about to see. His blonde hair has grown significantly, knotted at the base of his neck. His pale skin is covered by the king's uniform but his eyes... His eyes are the same and I would know them anywhere. Hazel, with specks of green framed beneath full brows. My heart sinks as I take him in.

"Cade?"

Chapter 41

Elora

My mind and heart are in a battle with themselves as my eyes rake over Cade's face. The same eyes that used to bring me so much comfort and warmth now stare back at me, empty and cold.

"How can this be?" I choke out, wanting to cry. To release everything that swarms within me, but coming up short. The voices in my head scream over one another, impossible to make out any distinction of what they're saying.

"I watched them drag you away, I watched them..." I lose my voice as Cade steps closer, his fingers sweeping across my cheek until they land under my chin. My breathing stutters at his touch but it's for all the wrong reasons. His hands are cold and dry. They are not the hands I remember. They are not the hands I want touching me.

I try to step back, but am held by a guard. I want to run. No, I want to rip his hand away from me and sink my dagger through the softness of his throat. But, with my hands shackled, I am rendered useless. So, instead I stand helpless, looking at the face of a man I once loved. Or at least, I thought I had loved.

"They did drag me off, that part you're remembering

correctly." Cade's hand slides from my chin as he straightens his posture, placing both hands behind his back. His militant stance looks unnatural and stiff as he watches me. I shift under my feet, my magick begins to resurface against my palms but with them bound together by iron, there's not much I can do.

"I couldn't very well let you think I was the one who led the hunters to us, now could I?"

"What. Do. You. Mean?" I hiss, narrowing my eyes in his direction, hoping he can taste the poison dripping from my words. His catlike grin makes my stomach churn, this is not the Cade I remember. This isn't real. Can this be real? The sudden loss of Ruse's voice inside my head makes my knees weak. Desperately searching for Alaric, I reach out mentally but am met with silence. Whatever is happening with the bond has my stomach in knots.

"Sweet, Elora. Always so naïve. So set on gaining your magick, you ceased to pay attention to anything else happening around you." Now it's Cade that narrows his eyes, his grin quickly turning down. "Did you really think I wanted a life on that Mother-forsaken mountain?"

"And so you led Roman directly to us?" I ask, my mind still in disbelief as to what I'm seeing. As to what he's saying. "Why Cade? What was in it for you?" All this time I've grieved the man I loved, have held myself back from how I truly feel because of the guilt. And now... That feline smile returns as Cade steps forward, his hand grips my face again. Recoiling back, he holds my chin firmly. Too firmly.

"You know, I really did care for you once," he whispers, inclining his head so our breaths intermix. The unease in my stomach threatens to spill out onto the forest floor. I attempt to shake my chin free but his grip only tightens. "I've spent a long time searching for you, Elora," he continues. Stepping back, finally dropping my chin. "That night on the mountain, I'll admit, was a bit bloodier than anticipated. But I gave you distinct directions to stay put, didn't I? Why did you run from me? I was your fiancé after all."

"Intuition, I guess. Maybe I should have listened to it all along. You betrayed us. You betrayed *me*."

"I did what I had to do to get out." It's brief, but for a moment something resembling hurt flashes over his features. As quickly as it comes, it vanishes. "I never wanted to be there in the first place. How many nights did we dream of escape? Of something grander?" Craning his neck around me, he gestures with his hands as bootsteps sound behind me. "It was my mother who dragged me there or do you not remember? You were so wrapped up in your own life and your own desires, you never once considered mine. When rumors that Roman was searching for the Awakening Stones arised, I saw a chance. An opportunity to get out, and I took it."

"And this is what you desire? Is becoming an officer for the corrupt king worth betraying us?" I struggle against the men at my sides but it's no use.

"Getting away from that mountain was worth doing *anything*. How very typical of you," Cade says through a laugh, the noise sending a shiver down my spine, "to feign ignorance rather than admit you're at the helm of the chaos. As if you weren't desperate for your own future. Your own magick. Even now, look at you. You knew what risks coming back *here* posed and yet, here you are. You have your magick, was it worth coming? How much has it served you, Elora? This magick you risked everything to gain."

My stomach drops, because as much as it sickens me, he's right, and he knows it. Snapping his fingers at the guards, they pull me towards a row of horses. I drag my feet and flail my body against the men. "Make sure she stays apart from the others," Cade shouts.

Others.

"Where are they?" I shout to Cade over my shoulder but all I'm met with is a laugh and a shake of his head.

"And no fucking around with this one," he says to the larger guard to my right. "We need her in one piece. Keep her shackles on her. Without them, you're a dead man." He steps closer again, so close the warmth of his breath tickles my skin, the smell of tobacco thick in the air between us. "Time to put that magick of yours to good use, Elora."

CHAPTER 42

ELORA

ATOP THE MOUNTAIN THE WIND IS RELENTLESS AS I drag my feet up to Nevek Peak where the Stones are embedded. Four guards follow me, and to my surprise, Cade isn't one of them. Rage engulfs me, and despite the freezing temperatures outside, my body is scorching. My mind wanders as I think of all the ways I could end Cade's life. My daggers, once a gift from him, would be a perfect way to off him. Alaric's teeth to the throat may be even better, though.

"Pick up the pace! We ain't got all night!" one of the guards shouts before his boot lands in the center of my back. I fall to the ground as I have nothing to break my fall with my hands bound behind my back. My cheekbone takes the brunt of it and a menacing crack splits between my ears. I lie there with my eyes closed, reaching out mentally for Alaric, for my magick, until the guards force me to my feet, dragging me forward by my elbows. I reach and reach for my magick and yet I'm left unanswered. The iron burns around my wrists, nulling my magick. I whimper as a guard pulls me to my feet.

Please, Alaric.

Please, hear me.

"I'm not sayin' it again, Enchantress. Pick. Up. The. Pace." The guard's words are clipped as he spits them into my face.

The rock is jagged and the air is freezing as we make the final ascent to Nevek Peak. My breathing is labored not only from the hike up, but from the heaviness that surrounds this place. Once warded by my mother's magick, she's here in every sense except the literal. In the breeze as it brushes my long strands away from my face. In the scent of oncoming snow. Fresh and crisp. In the light of the moon, silver, just like her eyes.

As I'm lost in a pocket of grief, my breath catches when my eyes land on the Stones. There, embedded in the slate gray of the mountain peak, are four brightly shining crystals. The first, an iridescent green; *Earth*. The second, a shimmering pale blue; *Water*. My fingers itch to reach out and touch them. Like they've been waiting just for me. I guess in some way, they have.

Tears stream freely from my eyes as I glance to the final two Stones. The third, sparkling crystalized white; *Air*. And lastly, the fourth. A vibrant ruby set deeply into the stone; *Fire*.

"Get on with it!" a guard snaps behind me. I swallow down my sobs as I draw myself upward. Closing my eyes, I try to remember all the steps in retrieving them.

"I need my hands," I tell the guards, shaking the shackles still placed around my wrists.

"I don't think so, lass," one of them says, spitting brown sticky tobacco onto the ground.

"Then you will not get the Stones," I snap, meeting each of their eyes.

Reluctantly, one of the guards steps forward. "You so much as look the wrong way, these will be back on before you know what's happened." Nodding my head, I let him unlock the shackles. I flex my fingers, roll my wrists, and call upon my magick.

Nothing.

Then, a whisper beneath my hands, so quiet I can't make

out what's been said. Taking a step closer to the peak, the Stone's flicker in the darkness and the whisper grows louder. But it isn't the same call as the magick I've become used to. My body trembles as I make the final step to the peak. That whisper again, hushes over my skin, freezing my breath in my chest.

The ambient glow of the Stones radiates under the moon. I am lost in the essence. In their being. Because that is what they are. Each Stone its own being. Breathing. Living. Waiting to be called upon.

I reach for my magick again, but am interrupted by a sound I once despised. No longer is the sound an annoyance. Now, it's lovely and familiar. My eyes shoot to the sky as a caw fills the elevated mountain air. Dozens and dozens of crows circle the sky above us, their sounds both menacing and somehow hopeful. The guards and I watch in confusion as the flurry of birds, so thick, it's as if they're one solid mass, circles above us. Then without warning, their caws cease and they're nothing more than a swirling of feathers in the night sky.

"What is that?" one of the guards whispers to another.

"Probably something to do with the oncoming storm," another guard answers. But he's wrong. I know he's wrong. Because while the sky indicates a storm is coming, the birds should be flying south. And yet here they are, silently circling above us. My eyes begin to dizzy as I watch the black birds continue their circling, enraptured by their movements. I'm lost in the haze.

Then, like a bolt of obsidian lightening, a single crow breaks free from the circle and spirals downward. I watch with widened eyes as another departs from the group. Then another. And another. Until finally, they form a thick line and shoot straight at us. I scream as their beating wings and caws shoot out around me. But they continue their course, flying right past me to the guards. I keep my hands pressed tightly over my ears as I watch the birds attack with lethal precision. Every caw from the birds is met with equally unsettling yells from the guards as they try to flee.

Bloodied body parts and gouged eyes litter the rocky floor beneath us, and I'm left paralyzed by the carnage and lingering screams. My chest heaves as I watch the birds peck and rip the flesh from the men. Their attempt to fight the birds off is quickly dismissed as more and more birds land from the sky. A scrape of talons against rock catches my attention, and when I turn my head, I'm met with a single crow, perched atop Nevek Peak.

With a quick inhale, I drop my hands from my ears and watch the crow as it stands before me. Its beak is clean of blood, its feathers radiant under the moonlight. My breath catches when I finally meet the bird's eyes.

Silver eyes.

It stares at me, unmoving, as I struggle to fight back tears. All feelings of being lost vanish. Now, only hope fills me. I know it cannot be her, but somehow it is. Somehow my mother stands before me in the shape of a crow, and my heart lurches as Galen's words ring in my ears.

"Either your mother was also a Dyrsjel or your maternal grandmother."

Why didn't you tell me! I want to scream. *I could have saved us!* But the words don't come. Because they don't matter. She did what she had to do to save me. To protect me and *herself* from a fate worse than death. And now I will do what I have to do to save the rest of the Enchantresses. To ensure the Mother is appeased and the Kingdom is no longer at risk.

Without warning, the crow before me tilts its head toward the sky and lets out a deep caw. I can't explain how I know it, but she's telling me to hurry. To get the Stones and run. I want to speak. I want to thank her. Tell her I love her but I don't have the time.

Before I can open my mouth, my head is filled with her voice. The Enchantress prayer, the one used for every Ceremony. It repeats over and over in the melodic way my mother always spoke. With a final glance at the crow, she darts to the sky before I can thank her, a murder of black birds following swiftly in her wake.

I steady my breathing as I watch the last of the birds disappear over the mountains. The sudden quiet surrounding me makes my stomach coil with nerves, and I try my best not to glance behind me to where I know the lifeless bodies of the guards lay. *Focus, Elora.*

Placing my hands atop the first Stone embedded in the rock, *Earth*, I close my eyes and remember the words of the prayer.

"To our Mother Gaia, who has given us all. Provided life and magick and healing. To our ever fruitful country of Teravie. We thank you and we honor you. May our gifts be a reflection of your power. May our kindness be an ode to your heart. May our lives be a dedication for your sacrifice."

My hands begin to shake, and I know it's not only from the cold. I press my hand firmer against the Stone and repeat the prayer until, at last, it wiggles free. Opening my eyes one at a time, I glance down into my hand. The iridescent jade stone hovers just above my palm, flickering gold stardust encircles it as it floats freely. Fatigue begins to settle over me, but I push past it and close my palm, encompassing the stone. Once it touches my skin, a sting of heat rushes through my system, jolting me momentarily.

Keep moving, I tell myself and so I do. Carefully placing the Stone in the pocket of my breeches, I move onto the next. I repeat the processes, each time my energy fading, and each time a spark of heat stings across skin. As I gently place the last stone, *Fire,* into my pocket it takes every bit of strength I have left not to collapse onto the ground.

Keep moving.

Keep moving.

My feet carry me carefully as I step past the wreckage that's left of the guards. Holding the back of my hand against my mouth, I try my best not to look, not to touch, the bloodied bodies that scatter the ground. Adrenaline kicks in as I begin my descent.

Running downhill I reach out to Alaric again, hoping by some miracle I'll get a response. Get any indication as to where he or the others might be. My boots pound against the rocky ground, and I will myself past the pain in my right foot starting to come forth. The movements all too familiar of the night I fled. *There's no time to stop, no time to rest.* I need to find the others.

So focused on the line of trees at the bottom of the mountain, I don't notice the jagged rock beneath my foot. My boot snags on the top of it and I'm sent tumbling down. The fabric of my breeches where it tore in the Wicked Wood rips further, reopening the wound there. Hot blood soon fills the gash that is sliced through my flesh.

I tip my head back and yell out a curse at the pain. At Cade. At how dreadfully tired I am.

Sitting myself up, I stretch out my leg to assess the damage. My pants are ripped at the knees and it appears my left leg took the brunt of the fall. I push my hand against the gash and curse again at the amount of blood spilling from it.

Give up.

I struggle to catch my breath as tears fall rapidly, stinging against my cheeks. I know I need to get up. To keep moving, but I don't. I sit with my palms pressed to my knee and I sob. My body is worn to threads, but it is nothing compared to how shattered my mind feels.

"I can't do this!" I'm not sure who I'm shouting at, but I scream it again and again until finally my voice is hoarse and I have no energy left to speak.

Wiping my arm across my eyes, I pull myself to my feet. Wincing at the sharp pain in my knee, I continue to work my way down the mountain. My pace is slow but I'm moving. At *least* I'm moving.

As I reach the familiar dirt and mossy floor of the forest, I allow myself to sit. *Only for a moment,* I tell myself. *Only for a moment.* But as my head rests against the trunk of the tree, my eyes drift shut. My body is fading.

I'm drowning.

But it doesn't last long before a warm wet tongue laps against my hands. I jolt upright and let out a yelp of joy.

"Alaric!" The giant wolf is covered in blood, but there's no time to get hung up on whose blood and what has happened. "Are they all right?"

No response.

I wrap my arms around his thick neck in relief but he doesn't linger. His familiar low growl rumbles in his throat, telling me we aren't safe. I pull myself up, but the gash from my knee and the residual pain from my foot coming back has me toppling back to the ground. The tonic from earlier surely starting to wear. Alaric whimpers and bends his head to lick my knee again. A snap from the woods draws our attention. Resting my head back against the tree, I know what I have to do. I reach into my pocket, pulling out the black ribbon from Sorin's gift in Loxley. The memory feels as if it's from a different lifetime. Biting my bottom lip to stifle a sob, I carefully wrap each Stone inside before gently placing it between Alaric's teeth.

"You need to go. Find Samaria and the others," I whisper, stroking the top of his head.

Not without you.

His voice returns in my mind, hazy and muddled but it's there. Excitedly, I call upon my magick. Still nothing. My magick is trapped, I don't know how, but it's trapped. Locked in a cage, just as I was in the Wicked Wood.

I'll be fine. You're hurt. I tell him through our bond, but even then it's as if there's a wall between us. I'm not even certain he can hear me. I notice the weight he refuses to carry on his paw, the blood coated between his paws. *You need to find them and get to Ruse.*

The guards won't stop searching until they have me captive, and I can't risk the others being taken as well. Alaric doesn't want to leave me, but he doesn't have a choice.

Another snap behind me.

"You need to go, *now*," I grit through my teeth at the stubborn wolf. I can't risk him getting any more hurt. I can't lose him like I almost lost Ruse. I won't allow anymore bloodshed tonight. I narrow my eyes at him until he finally bows in submission. With a final kiss to his head, I whisper, "Go, find Sam." His whimper is long and drawn out but reluctantly he turns and limps into the darkness, taking the Stones with him.

Tears streak my cheeks as I watch the flash of gray and white in an otherwise dark forest disappear. Using both my hands, I wipe my eyes of tears and clear my throat.

"Get on your feet," Cade sneers, pressing a blade between my shoulder blades.

Laughing, I struggle to stand, but eventually do. Turning, I face Cade. His face is cold, distant, but in his eyes I see the boy I loved and my heart sinks. What has he gotten himself into?

"And what now, Cade?" My voice is hoarse from the events of the night. My body is limp as I lean against the tree, but my heart settles into a regular rhythm as relief replaces fear. The Stones will be safe. Sorin and the others will be safe. They have to have gotten away.

"Now, I deliver you to King Roman and my indenture is complete," he whispers.

Laughing through another sob, I don't fight as he slings me onto his horse, tightening shackles around my wrists like a coward. "And what will you do with your new found freedom?" I ask as he settles behind me on the horse. He doesn't answer me as we take off through the woods. The horse picks up its pace as we dart in the opposite direction Alaric ran. My head hangs limply as I fight to keep my eyes open. *They're safe. They must be safe.*

"Go ahead and sleep." Cade's whispers are like daggers against my skin. "You're going to want to be well rested for what's to come."

CHAPTER 43

SORIN

THE INSIDE OF THE CARAVAN IS DARK AND SMELLS OF piss. I can make out the shape of two figures next to me, and my heart races as I distinguish one of them is Sam and the other, Jarek. Attempting to move, I'm quickly reminded that I'm bound to my seat. The rope around my waist is heavy and pushes against me as I try to lean forward.

"Sam, wake up," I whisper through gritted teeth. My boot reaches her leg to nudge it but I'm left without a response. Jarek groans as his eyes peel open.

"What the bloody hell happened?" Jarek croaks as he struggles against the ropes as I did moments before.

"Roman is what happened." Resting my head back against the wall of the caravan, I note the pace in which it's moving. Not fast enough to where I'm pulled side to side, but not slow enough to miss being jolted by each bump. "We were led straight into a trap," I say, closing my eyes. "Hunters, no doubt. But someone took it upon themselves to lure the wolves." I wince thinking of Elora and Ruse trapped in the belly of the ditch. *Maybe they got out. Maybe they're okay.*

My emotions dance together as I shift from worry to confusion to rage.

The officer. There was something about him...

The rope around Jarek groans as he attempts again to wiggle and shimmy out of its hold. "But how could they know about the wolves?" he asks. Quite honestly, I haven't the faintest idea.

I let the thought simmer as my fingers begin to work on the rope behind me. Whoever tied us made a fatal mistake leaving my hands unbound, and determination outweighs every other emotion flooding through me. The caravan hits another bump and takes a slight decline, which leads me to believe we're headed off out of the woods, possibly toward Davenport.

"Likely we were followed, probably since Elora used her magick on that moose." My fingers stretch and work the knot tied around the middle of my back. "Someone knew the wolves would be the perfect lure. Maybe they thought they could get Elora alone." The rope loosens slightly as I begin on the next knot. I glance at Jarek who has fallen silent. His eyes are glued to Sam who's tied across from him, her head tilts downward, swaying lightly with every bump and turn of the caravan.

"She'll be okay," I say, returning my focus to the rope. "Probably took a hit to the head. You know damn well she didn't go down without a fight."

Jarek huffs a laugh before starting again on his own ropes. The man is massive in the tight caravan, his knees would certainly reach the side that Sam and I are positioned on if he wasn't so balled up. My mind starts turning as I think of a way to escape. Once I'm free of the ropes, I'll get Sam and Jarek out of theirs, that's easy enough. I scan our surroundings, looking for any weapons or anything that *could* be a weapon and fall short. *Hand to hand combat it is, then.* Just as I work the final knot free from my back, I unwind the rope as Jarek's voice cuts through the caravan.

"Where the fuck is Galen?" Jarek asks, panic lacing each word.

Sighing, I rest my head on the wooden siding of the caravan for a moment. "Taken," I whisper, meeting Jarek's eyes. "I tried to get to him, but I was too late." Guilt riddles my insides. Galen and Elora needed me, and I failed them. Just as I failed Sam when we ventured to the Wicked Wood. Just as I've failed every Enchantress in Teravie for not stopping Roman sooner.

I'm left with no time to weigh the possibilities of how hurt he could be, before the caravan comes to a swift halt, sending me flying forward from the now lack of restraints. Regaining my balance, I quickly untie Jarek, who then begins on Samaria's ropes. The muffled voices of the guards whirl around us, and I close my eyes to better focus on what I'm hearing.

Their words are indistinct, but I catch three voices. Three guards. I'm almost offended by how easy Roman has made this for me. Does my little brother really doubt my abilities?

"Wake up, Sam," Jarek whispers to her as he unties the final knot behind her back. She rolls forward into Jarek's arms, her unconscious body limp, but from what I can see, her breathing is steady.

"She's not waking up, Sorin." Jarek's panic pulses through the small space, but now is not the time. I'm just as worried about my sister, but we have minutes, if we're lucky, and being one body down is going to make things that much more difficult.

"Lay her on the floor," I say in a hushed tone. Jarek does as I say. He cradles Sam's head onto the floor and places her there gently. As he pulls his hand back, it's blood soaked. Leaning down, I lift her head to get a better look. The contusion is small but still bleeding.

"I'll kill them all, brother. Let me the fuck out of here and I swear to your gods I'll kill them all."

"Lower your voice," I hiss through my teeth, sitting back in my place, draping the rope loosely around my middle. The guards outside have moved to the back of the caravan. Their laughter is a momentary distraction leaving me a few extra minutes to put a plan in place.

"What the hell is going on 'ere! What's she doing on the

floor!" the guard yells as he opens the door and steps inside, hand placed lightly on the hilt of the sword.

"She fell." I roll my head to face him. "Apparently tying a simple knot isn't among the skillsets of the royal guard."

"Shut your mouth." The guard steps towards Sam, and Jarek's face reddens, his rage about to boil over and ruin any attempt at freedom. I cut him a glance. *Not yet.* He steadies his breathing as the guard lifts Samaria up, propping her against the back of the caravan.

"Hurry up in there!" a guard shouts from outside. His steps are heavy against rock as he paces back to the front of the caravan where the other stayed put.

Evidently happy with his work, the guard fastens Sam's ropes and steps toward the exit. Stopping to face me, he leans low. His breath hot in my face. "Try anything," he says, "and I won't hesitate to gut you. Boss' orders or not." The boss. I fight to roll my eyes, thinking of that ridiculous officer as *the boss*. I know I shouldn't but I can't help myself, so I laugh. A low and drawn out laugh as the guard's fury dances across his face. Before he can open his mouth, I'm on my feet and have him pinned against the caravan wall.

"*You* try anything, and I'll have this sword embedded in your belly before your two mindless companions out there have the slightest inkling as to what's happening." Keeping my voice low, I pull the sword from its sheath at his side, as well as the dagger he wears on his opposite hip. Jarek's already untying Sam as I hold the guard by his throat, my nails digging into the flesh. "Do you understand?" I ask him as my fingers tighten even further. With wide eyes he does his best to nod. "Good."

With Sam untied and tucked into Jarek's arms, I quietly push the guard out the back of the door, keeping the dagger pinned against his back.

"About time," one of the guards shouts as the door of the caravan slams shut. With slow steps I weave the guard in my captivity toward the front. With Samaria placed gently under a nearby tree, Jarek's footsteps follow closely. The sword I swiped from the guard now looks comically small in his large hands. He silently moves to the opposite side of the caravan while I make my way to the front. Night is deep and with how sporadic the trees grow, I can tell we were headed east, likely to Davenport as I suspected. Luckily, as I round the corner, the moon gives just enough of her light to see the shock that spills over the guards faces as I come into view.

"Lower your weapons, or your pal here will cease to breathe another breath." The guards swap glances at each other before they break into laughter.

"You think we give two shits about 'im? Go on then, make right on your word. Won't stop the boss from slitting you across the middle when we haul your sorry asses to 'im." Before their boots can land in the dirt, Jarek's growl pierces the air as the swing of the sword blows through the first guard, leaving his innards displayed grotesquely across the caravan.

The second guard jumps down and immediately bolts through the woods. *Coward.* The guard I'm holding uses my momentary distraction to his advantage, wriggling free before spinning on me.

"You should be ashamed, mingling with that filthy Enchantress," he says, pulling a hidden dagger from his boot. His words ignite a rage within me I didn't know I possessed. It takes two strides before I'm on him. My fist collides with his jaw, a loud crack sounds through the forest as he stumbles backwards, pinning himself between me and the caravan.

The shock of my punch has caused him to drop his dagger, and I kick it away, reuniting my hand with his throat.

"What did you say," I whisper, leaning down so I'm inches away from his face.

"No—nothing," he stammers, blood trickling from the split in his lip.

"Tell me where she is," I whisper, inching my face closer, wrapping my palm tighter around his throat.

"I don't know." His words are forced between shallow breaths, his airway constricting with each second.

"If you're a praying man," I whisper again, "now is the time to start." He opens his mouth again, but before he gets the chance to speak, I squeeze tighter around his neck. And tighter. Until finally, his eyes are bulging and his arms flail around me. Hitting my sides, my shoulders.

I loosen my grip and relief temporarily washes over his features, until he sees the dagger. *His* dagger I'd taken in the caravan. It takes a second to slice it across his throat. He sinks to the ground, blood coating my boots.

Wiping my hands clean on his doublet, I yell at Jarek. "Follow that guard." Before Jarek can take a step toward the woods, a gurgled yelp sounds. The gnashing of teeth and clawing of nails is all I need to know what happened.

Alaric.

Hobbling out of the woods, his white and gray fur is mangled, stained various shades of red and brown. The limp in his leg is profound. I swallow deeply, my stomach churns at the bits of flesh still hanging from his teeth. A paradox to his aggressively wagging tail.

"Well done, mate." I stretch my hand up to scratch the beast under his chin. He lets out a huff of air in protest as I pull my hand away. "What have you got there?" His amber eyes turn down as he drops something from his mouth onto the ground.

A ribbon, I realize. Black satin, just as the one I'd wrapped Elora's new clothes in.

"She's awake!" Jarek hollers, drawing my attention. Scooping up the bundled ribbon, it's heavier than I expected, turning I jog to meet Jarek and Sam.

"Can you please not yell?" Sam rubs her temples, body still slumped against the tree. "My head is throbbing."

"I'm sorry, my queen," Jarek says, kissing her forehead. "You had me scared to death." He pulls her hand from her lap and kisses it. Sam's face softens at this before her eyes shift to me, then to the wolf.

"Elora and Galen?" she asks, her brows drawing together.

Shaking my head, I shift the bundled ribbon to my opposite hand.

"Shite," Sam whispers, tears filling her eyes. "What the hell are we going to do?"

"WE CANNOT GO BACK WITHOUT THEM," I say again. Sam and I have been in the same argument for hours, getting absolutely nowhere.

"Sorin, it's been almost two days out here in the woods, and we're no closer to Valebridge than we were when we started. We're exhausted, our supplies are minimal, there are guards around every corner. We can't stay hidden forever. I'm not saying we're going back for good I'm just saying—"

"You're saying we give up." I cross my arms, staring her down. Jarek inches closer to my peripheral. The bags under Sam's eyes are a mirror to my own. We're exhausted. Our resources are depleted, and I know she's right. Of course, she's right. But my mind is not my own right now. I can feel myself spiraling out of control. Galen is gone. Elora is gone, and whatever Fate has decided for us has only made her absence more painful. Like a physical hole in my chest. Sam squeezes my arm, anchoring me back to the present momentarily.

"Of course not, Sorin." Her voice is soft, a wave of comfort in the chaos I'm currently residing in. "All I'm saying is we need to gain some distance between these guards. We *need* to gather supplies, recharge, and restabilize before we head into a place where we have no idea just what's waiting for us."

The thought of Elora and Galen with Roman rips me apart.

"And Ruse." She gestures to the black wolf lying at my side. "She needs proper stitching. Proper rest."

Relief plagues me as I eye the wolf. Her usual cold and stoic demeanor dampened since we pulled her from the trench. I thank the Mother we got to her before the guards realized she survived.

"She is *everything*, Sam," I whisper the words because they don't feel real. Elora cannot be gone. "And Galen can't fight. If they hurt him—" I pause, shifting my eyes to the ground. The guilt swallowing me whole. I've let them down. They will be hurt and it's because of my selfishness. My stupidity. Clearing my throat, I face my sister again. "I can't leave them."

"I'm not asking you to." Sam wraps her arms around me, resting her head on my shoulder as we're almost the same height. "I'm just asking you to use that big head of yours." She reaches up to ruffle my hair, the same she has done since we were children, and sure enough it brings a smile to my face.

"Let's head back to Wickersham," she continues, "get the horses, *rest*. Heal Ruse. We'll send word for Agnes to meet us, and together we'll form a plan." She takes a step backward, her eyes scanning my face. "Others will help us fight this battle, Sorin. We don't have to do this alone. There are plenty who want to see you on the throne, and you know it." She smiles, and my shoulders relax a bit. "And then we'll come back for them. I promise you."

I hate the plan, but Mother above I know it's the only way to successfully get Elora and Galen back. Reluctantly, I nod my head. Jarek's hand lands on my shoulder and offers a light squeeze.

"Let's get on then, nightfall is nearing," he says, hoisting his pack over his shoulder. I place the black ribbon inside of my bag, the Awakening Stones heavy despite how small they are.

"Alaric won't follow us," I say, and I have no idea what brings me to say it.

Jarek pulls Ruse in a make-shift gurney but stops to look at me. Nodding, he knows it too. Alaric will stay in the woods. Just as I wish to. We haven't seen him since he dropped the Stones with us, and if my gut tells me anything, it's that he will not stop looking for Elora.

Taking the long route around the Wicked Woods, a faint and familiar howl fills the trees. The three of us stop to scan for where he is, but Alaric is nowhere to be seen. Ruse lets out a howl of her own, defeated and whimpering she makes no attempt to stand. Smart as she is, she knows she would not last long on her own in her condition.

Another broken cry cuts through the vibrant orange and pink sky, disrupting a flock of birds from a nearby tree, sending them scattering through the air.

"He's calling for her. Looking for Elora," Jarek says as Alaric lets out another howl. "The susi aren't meant to be alone." The three of us form a line, shoulder to shoulder, as we listen to the broken heart of a lone wolf cry out into the setting sun.

CHAPTER 44

ELORA

THE GUARDS ON EITHER SIDE OF ME GRIP MY ELBOWS as they drag me down a darkened stairway. The shackles on my wrists clink together as I reach the last step. The several days' ride to Valebridge with Cade was mostly silent, aside from his occasional chatter and prod of questions. When he realized I no longer possessed the Stones, his questions turned to anger. And that anger turned physical. But I gave him nothing, of course. As I never would again.

My eyes roam through the dark room, the push of magick against my skin has come back in full force over the last few days, but with the iron shackles Cade has placed on me since we left the mountain, I'm useless. My magick whips in a storm-like fury waiting to break through the threshold. Frustrated, it hasn't been unleashed. Hasn't been used.

One of the guards lights an oil lantern on the wall. The flame flickers orange in the darkness and the shape of several other cells come into view. All of them empty. Marble walls encompass a small area blocked by a thick iron door. Inside the cell in front of me is a small cot on an iron frame. An empty bucket sits in the far corner. I swallow a lump in my throat and square my shoulders. *Be strong, Elora.*

The guards shove me in a cell so hard I lose my balance and topple to the ground. With my wrists bound, I'm unable to break my fall. "You should be ashamed of yourselves!" I shout, righting myself, turning to face the men.

"You're lucky we've been given clear instructions to leave you unharmed," one of the guards says, turning the lantern low so the flame extinguishes. "Enjoy the darkness." He laughs as he makes his way up the stairs with his companion. Sitting myself down, I scoot backward until my back rests upon the cool marble wall behind me. Closing my eyes, I wait for the voices to come.

Magick thrums and pushes against my palms, the ache becoming more and more prominent, but still, the voices aren't there. In the darkness of my cell, for the first time since my mother died, I sit in total silence. I've lived with my demons for so long, I've forgotten what life could be like without them. The voices have become a regular part of my daily life that I find myself uncomfortable in the silence that follows their absence. I think of Sorin. To his memory of our mothers. How confident they were that the Fates would bring Sorin and I together.

Then I think of Samaria and Jarek, and then Galen and Alaric. To the ink stinging and swirling up the back of my neck. Let them have my body, for in a short time, I'll belong to the woods. As long as the Stones are safe, Sorin and Sam will work the rest out. I know it.

Finally, my mind settles on Ruse. How the shape of her too-still body laid on the ground. How her emerald eyes flickered with fear. The struggled breaths she took as I was pulled from the trench and away from her.

Snapping my eyes open, they adjust to the dark rather quickly. And then I picture Cade. And all the things I will do to him. The many ways I'll rip him apart slowly for what he's done. A kernel of anger sparks within me. Anger I've let fester far longer than tonight. An anger I fought so hard to swallow down and avoid. Never once giving the option of letting it grow.

How long had I stamped those voices out? Pushed them down until their words were smothered and broken? What if instead of fighting the voices in my head, I accepted that they are a part of who I am? Because what is more fearsome? The monster that stands before you? Or the one that lives within you? Tonight, I won't fight that monster anymore. I'll become it.

Eyes closed, I take a deep inhale of the stagnant air, then a long exhale before reaching out to the voices.

Where are you? My own internal voice echoes down into the depths of my soul. Trying desperately for the demons that have haunted and festered there.

Silence.

I know you're still there. Help me.

I try again, furrowing my brow in concentration, coaxing those demons out like flint to a fire. Over and over I ask until I feel a shift within me. It's subtle but it's there. Like a beast rousing awake after a restful winter. My skin prickles, the hairs on my arms and neck raise and the moment I hear them, I let my shoulders loosen only slightly.

Hello, Enchantress.

Opening my eyes, I dart them around the cell to make sure the voices I hear are that of which reside in me. Nothing but inky black stares back and a smile curves across my lips. For so long I've feared the voices I hear in my head, but no more. If they are destined to be a part of me, so be it. I'll let them speak, let them have their turn. Let them guide me the way the wolves have. I refuse to break for these people who see me as nothing more than a pawn in their games. As a means to their most ruthless desires. I deserve justice. My *people* deserve justice. And I will fight like hell to get it.

MY HEAD GROWS heavy and as much as I fight it, I can't help the fatigue that plagues my bones. I'm lost in a feverish nightmare as the echoey creak of a door opens at the top of the stairs. Two sets of heavy boots make their descent down the stairs.

"Wake up, Enchantress. You've got yourself a meeting." An unfamiliar voice sounds. The crackle of a fire fills the space as a lantern on the wall illuminates again. My eyes widen, adjusting to the light, then narrow in the guard's direction. I can only make out their silhouettes in the dim candle light but there are definitely two men.

The kernel of anger I felt before erupts in a fury as I brace myself to meet the one responsible for all the loss. I twist my hands inside my shackles, but it's no use. The iron burns cold against my skin.

"Hello, Elora."

Pulling myself upright, I do my best not to put too much weight on my knee. Pressing myself up against the bars of the cell, I suck in a sharp breath as reality hits me square in the chest. I take a long look at the person before me and the voices within me growl in response. Only this time, they're finally on my side.

Traitor.

Traitor.

Traitor.

A flood of nausea makes me waiver on my feet as Galen steps forward and into the light.

Chapter 45

Elora

"What are you doing?" My mind won't accept what I believe to be true. Galen's expression doesn't falter. Doesn't flinch. Doesn't show a single sign of remorse. Surely, he's here to help me. Surely... As he says nothing, reality settles into my stomach. He is not here to help me.

Crossing his arms over his chest my eyes lock onto the silver arrow stitched on his cloak he has the nerve to still wear. Grinding my teeth, the voices inside my head roar loudly. Good. Let them be angry.

Taking a step forward he presses himself up against the iron bars of my cell. "King Silas was a coward," he says, his eyes trailing past me momentarily. "He let Enchantresses walk all over him. Use their magick freely without thinking twice about the dangers it might cause for the rest of us. The dangers it had *already* caused. The uprising alone yielded many human casualties." His eyes snap back to me. Swallowing down my anger, I take a step back from the bars.

"You and I both know, there was *no* uprising," I whisper, my head dizzying again as I brace my hand against a wall. When was the last time I ate? Drank water? I need to lie down or I fear I'll be sick. But I can't move.

Galen smirks, unblinking, his icy stares bores into me. "Of course not, Enchantress. But you and your people played the part so well before, it was easy to convince the rest of the world that you rebelled first. So locking you up was seen as the *justified* thing to do. You Enchantresses have always been so entitled. So enamored with yourselves you could care less about the fate of the rest of us."

"All we do is care for you!" I shout, my knee throbbing from the pain. Galen smirks, running a hand through his perfectly combed hair. "We heal you, work for you, work for your kings. It's all we've ever done, and yet it isn't enough?" It's never enough though, is it? We break ourselves for the comfort of men, and are immediately seen as a threat when we collectively say "we've had enough".

"It wasn't enough," Galen says quietly. His narrowed eyes shift, his brows softening for a moment before the hardened exterior snaps back into place. "Enchantresses have had their free rein since Silas' rule, I'm simply restoring the order as it was before his time. As it always should have been."

I suck in a sharp breath as I remember the book Galen gave me in the woods. How he knew right away that I was a Dyrsjel. How he *helped* me take control of my power with the wolves. "Why help me understand what I am if you only wanted to bring me to Roman anyway?"

His serpentine laugh curls up my spine. Stepping back, he leans against the wall opposite the cell. The stance, so casual and relaxed, as if he didn't just betray all his friends. His *family*.

"If I must spell it out for you..." he draws the words out in annoyance. "Without control of your magick, it's basically useless to whomever harvests it. You had to know of your history, of who you are, how to control the wolves and the elements, otherwise it would be much more difficult for Roman and I to take what we need from you. And the wolves would have been *much* more difficult to control."

"You and Roman…" My voice trails off. This isn't happening. This can't be happening.

Galen shrugs, his lips turning upward. "It looks as though we share an affinity for the Rudhek brothers," he says with a laugh. He and Roman are together. And all this time Sorin trusted him. *I* trusted him.

"Though, to be fair," Galen continues, "when I went looking for the last Dyrsjel, I never expected you to show up on my best friend's doorstep. A complicated addition to my plan involving Sorin. You can blame yourself for that." He smirks and my heart sinks while my head spins. I really need to lie down.

"And so what?" I ask, taking a step forward, fighting off the drowsiness that threatens to throw me to the ground. "What is in this for you Galen? Power? Control?" That slithering laughter curls around me again and I all but shudder to get it out of my ears.

"You know," he says, gripping his hands around the bars, leaning close. "Sorin was fine to let his vendetta go. He was happy in Loxley before he met you."

"I trusted you," I grit through my teeth, tears running down either side of my face. Choosing to not focus on the fact that Galen is right. Sorin is likely in this mess because of me. "I thought you were my friend, Galen."

"Wrong bet."

"You are a *coward*," I whisper, bracing myself against the bars, wishing so deeply I could reach right through and wrap my hand around his throat.

"And you, Elora Leigh, are the last known Dyrsjel. The last Enchantress of your kind that can wield the Stones."

Ignoring him, I stand on my toes, pushing past the pain in my knee to meet him at eye level. "Let the Stones remain hidden. Use me as you wish. Take my Elemental magick and leave the Stones. Let the other Enchantresses go. What need could you still have for them?"

"Wrong bet, again." He bends down, pushing his face against the bars so all that separates us is the thick iron. "With your magick, we will achieve greatness, but with the Stones, we will achieve *everything*. We'll take back control of Teravie, just as King Bastian and Queen Solei intended. Mother Gaia gave you magick to aid us, not to control us."

Baffled, I stumble back a step. Hardly registering what the original king and queen have to do with this. "Mother Gaia?" I whisper, stretching my hands again against the iron shackles. "It isn't possible. No one has harnessed magick through the Mother without an Enchantress before."

Galen's grin reveals the sharp points of his teeth. "No one, until now. I've been mocked as a scholar, made fun of for always having my nose in a book. And when my sister was killed because of your supposed Healers, it was the moment I knew there had to be a change. It's all led me here. To unlocking the very root of all magick."

My heart stumbles, thinking of a sister Galen's lost. One I didn't know he had. But I reground myself.

"Sorin is your *family*, Galen," I say again. "What about him?"

"I've lived a long time chasing Sorin's dream," he says quickly, covering the wince I swear I see flash across his features. Placing his hands in his pockets, he glances at the stairs as if he has somewhere better to be. "Avenge his mother, take the throne. But when I met Roman in Valebridge all those years ago, I decided right then that I wouldn't be a shadow in someone else's story. I would pave my own way. Seek my own revenge."

A strangled laugh creeps up my throat, the exhaustion of the last few days making my mind delusional.

"Some history you're making. Using the magick of others because you possess none of your own. Whatever happened with your sister, I'm sorry for it. But this isn't the way." He frowns, his mouth tight as he watches me struggle to find my balance. "And Sorin isn't perfect, none of us are. He may have visions of revenge and justice, but at least he isn't hurting anybody to do so."

He shakes his head, his eyes scanning my face. "Maybe what I'm doing isn't dignified," he whispers, a shadow of the man I called my friend passes over his face. Like he's still in there, somewhere, but this need for control has consumed him. "But maybe it's not. Maybe I'm doing what should have been done long ago. Enchantresses have been held to such a high standard for centuries, it's time for change." His voice slithers through the cell. His eyes fill with hunger. Rage. Power. Though, there's a desperation lining them that only someone who is tired of being seen as weak could possibly possess. I recognize it, because I too have felt that desperation.

"Now," he says, straightening himself, "make this easy on yourself, Elora, and no one else has to get hurt." The guard behind him steps forward, passing him a familiar vial.

The same vial he has been giving me for my injured foot.

"You...poisoned me?" I take a step back, distancing myself from the door of the cell. Galen laughs again but nothing about it is humorous. Cold and vicious, he uncorks the vial.

"You're far too important to be poisoned. This"—he swirls the small glass tube—"is meant to treat injuries *and* dampen magick. You were all too eager to take it, just as your mother was when I instructed that guard to slip it to her all those years ago." With a wave of his hand, he dismisses the statement like it's unordinary.

Cade.

Cade gave my mother a magick dampening potion. He was the reason she didn't sense the hunters. The reason she is dead. The voices ignite within me. Their shouts fill my ears and fuel my rage. *This will not end well for them,* the voices in my head scream.

No, it will not.

"Lucky for me, it renders your magick useless to you,

making it much easier to access," Galen says. The guard unlocks the cell as Galen passes him the vial. Scurrying back, I don't make it far before I'm grabbed by my hair. Wrists shackled, knee bleeding, I am powerless. "Another benefit to my years spent learning instead of fighting."

I wince as the man grips my chin, prying my mouth open before forcing the liquid down my throat. Dropping to my knees, the effects leave me dizzy. My magick is nulled to silence, tears fall freely as the guard relocks the iron bars on the other side of the cell. My mind snags on our conversation back in Wickersham, about the hunter's using a potion of their own to hunt magick.

"You...you made something similar for the hunters," I whisper, my chest cracks as more tears fall. "Something to sense our magick when it's used."

"See, it's all coming together," Galen says as he crouches down on the opposite side of my cell, his head tilted to the side as he watches me struggle to catch my breath through the sobs that won't stop. "Now tell me where you hid the Stones, or watch as Loxley burns."

Epilogue
Roman

"Have you heard?" I ask the guard stationed outside the door. I can't remember his name and quite honestly, I don't care.

"No, Your Majesty, no word yet." He shakes his head, keeping it hung low to avoid my eyes.

"The moment you hear from him, send word," I say, taking a step closer. I tilt his chin with my index finger, forcing his gaze. "The *moment*," I say again, and he nods. He's young, inexperienced, not my usual guard, Cade, who I've grown to trust. Though, I suppose now he's an officer he won't be stationed outside my door as much. Pity.

"Yes, Your Majesty." The guard's voice shakes, so I remove my hand from his chin. The new ones always fear me. Perhaps that's for the best.

Stepping back through the oak doors of the study, I slam them shut before pacing the room. I should be in my quarters, but the study brings me peace. Or, should I say, *it usually* brings me peace. I often find comfort among the bookshelves that line the walls, the spines cracked with age and good use.

But tonight, I'm nothing but nerves. Galen was to be back by now, and with him, Sorin and the others.

Sorin.

His name turns my gut upside down. A half-brother Galen insisted I have.

As far as I've known, I'm an only child, until a few weeks ago when Galen wrote to me about a half-brother that has been living in the forest. My stomach sours at the thought. A brother. A threat to my throne.

My focus shifts to the first time Galen and I met. We were eighteen. Young and in love. He was so different from the other scholars that often toured Valebridge and our libraries. He was the only one that didn't bow when my father and I entered a room. Silas hated it, I was smitten.

I POUR MYSELF A DRINK, three fingers deep and toss it back in a single pull, attempting to numb the sting of what we've done.

What *I've* done.

A quick knock at the door has me gritting my teeth.

"Come in," I say, pouring myself another drink.

"Your Majesty," the guard says, his voice wavering slightly in the presence of the *Corrupt* King. I know it's what they call me. Not everyone agrees with the vision Galen and I have for the future of Valebridge, of Teravie.

Sometimes I'm not sure I even agree with it. Regret is like a poison that kills slowly, quietly, until one day you wake up and all you're left with is skin and bone.

"He's here, Your Majesty," the guard says. I toss the drink back, grimacing at the bitter after taste.

"The prisoner?" I ask, setting the crystal glass down on the bar top before turning to face him. Careful not to address Sorin as my brother.

Shaking his head, he avoids my gaze again. "No, sire. Just your—" he stops himself, shifting on his feet. "Just Sir Galen, Your Majesty."

Running a hand down my face, exhaustion seeps deep into my bones. When was the last time I slept properly? I suppose it was the last time he was here, I never sleep well when he's gone and this time it's been weeks.

"And the others?" I ask.

The guard dares to glance at me now, fear emanating in his eyes.

The Corrupt King.

"The others?" I ask again, stepping forward, so close our boot tips nearly touch.

"There was an issue in the transport," he says, shifting his eyes to either side of my face. My heart sinks and despite the several drinks I've had, panic begins its deep crescendo in my chest.

"Go on," I say, "tell me where they are."

"We...they...no one knows, sire," the guard stutters. "The guards who were to bring them have all been killed and," he pauses to glance down momentarily, shifting in his boots, "the prisoners have escaped."

Biting down on my tongue, I press my eyes shut. Only for a moment. But that moment is all I need to snap into the role of the king they deem so corrupt. A mask I've learned to wear well these last five years, fitting the mold of merciless ruler.

"Then why"—lunging forward I grasp the man's chin in my hand, squeezing tighter until his face is contorted with pain— "are you still standing here?" I grit through my teeth. "Find. Them."

"Y-yes, sire," he stammers. Releasing his chin, I snap my fingers and without hesitation he's out the door and I'm alone.

I sink down into one of the chairs by the fireplace, staring at the dark void where the embers should glow. My father loved the study. I've never thought much about it, but maybe that's why I often come here, to try and remove his memory and make it my own.

A few moments later, another rap at the door.

"I thought I told you—"

"It's me," Galen says, slinking into the room silently.

My heart slams in my chest, all feelings of panic slowly replaced by relief as he stalks toward me. He is here and he is safe. An entire kingdom at my disposal, and yet the only thing I truly feel is mine has just walked through the door.

Corrupt.

Let them think it, I tell myself.

It was all worth it for this, wasn't it? For him.

"You're back," I say with a long sigh, tension unclenching between my shoulders at the sight of him.

"I am," he says, sliding into the chair next to me, his hands grazing my shoulders ever so slightly as he does. "Though, I'm sure as you've heard there was an issue with the transport of Sorin and the others."

Nodding, I glance at him in my peripherals. Drinking in the sight of his sharp features, his icy, blonde hair and even cooler gaze. He looks tired, but with a face like his, it doesn't change the beauty of it. My nerves settle and the need for sleep intensifies knowing he's here.

To all others, I am the king.

Tainted.

Damaged.

Too weak to fill the shoes of his late father.

But to Galen, I'm simply Roman. He saw me when no one else did. He saw all the things my father *wanted* me to be and he saved me from them.

"I received your message a few weeks ago," I say. "The one about the Dyrsjel and...Sorin. Did you at least obtain her?" I ask, clearing my throat, ignoring the way my stomach flips when his eyes meet mine.

"She's here." He nods, rolling his shoulders and pinching the bridge of his nose. "I've spoken with her already." His tone is so calm. Smooth. As if nothing about what we're doing is wrong. I lean into his assurance, pretending it's my own. "The plan is still in place," he continues. "Despite Sorin acting the hero as usual. Elora will bring us the Awakening Stones, all I have to do is break her first."

Break her.

So often I forget what Galen is capable of. So often I forget the things he does that I don't see. Rather, the things he doesn't *let* me see.

I swallow down the words stuck on my tongue.

Stop this.

Stop this and let us just be you and me.

If I were a strong man, I *would* stop him.

If I were a strong man, I wouldn't have let it get this far in the first place.

Another threat of bile rises in my throat.

If I were a strong man, I would have stopped Galen from killing my father all those years ago despite how desperately he deserved it.

But as Galen leans forward to grasp my hand, fire ignites in my veins. My breath hitches as he brings my knuckles to his lips and kisses them. And I know with absolute certainty, I am not a strong man.

Through A Somber Sky

Enchantress Awakens Book Two

See how it all ends, Fall 2024

Acknowledgments

First and foremost... I wrote a book and if you've made it this far, it means that you've read it! So, thank you. Even if this book wasn't your favorite, you took the time to read my work and that means everything to me.

To my husband, Matt, for believing in me every step of the way. For cheering me on every late night and early morning. For listening to me ramble. For loving me. Thank you. I love you.

To my son, for being my shining light and biggest motivator.

To my mom, sister, and brother. Your support and encouragement has meant the world to me. I love you three little weirdos so much and wouldn't be who I am today without you. I'm so lucky to have you in my corner. A special shout out to my brother for walking me through the inaccuracies of my poker scenes and helping correct them.

To my alpha AND proofreader, Katie. You've seen this book at every stage (even the very, very rough ones) and you never lost faith in this story.

To my brilliant beta readers: Ash, Jaclyn, Karin, Krystal, and Leah. This book truly would not be what it is without your guidance and love for the characters and the story. I owe you so much and I'm so lucky to have each of you in my life.

To, Brit. My beautiful, smart, talented, and very punny editor. You've been my rock the last year. Thank you for seeing my vision and doing the absolute most to enhance it.

To my bookstagram girls and ARC readers. You know who you are. Every comment, DM, like, share has powered me through this process. Through the Wicked Wood exists because of *you*. Let this be a reminder that, together, we can accomplish anything.

Lastly, for Nan and my dad, John. Who I know would be so proud. I miss you and love you both to pieces.

About Kristen

Kristen is a lifelong native to the Pacific Northwest, which is where most of her inspiration for writing comes from. She's been a lover of fantasy worlds for as long as she can remember. She and her husband live with their son and dog in Washington State. When she's not working, writing or chasing her toddler, you'll find her sipping coffee and exploring the woods or the nearby rivers. Through the Wicked Wood is her debut novel with many more to come.

More from Kristen

Enchantress Awakens

Through the Wicked Wood

As the Moon Falls

Through A Somber Sky (Fall 2024)